continued . . .

Also by S. M. Peters

Whitechapel Gods

GHOST
OCEAN

S. M. Peters

A ROC BOOK

ROC
Published by New American Library, a division of
Penguin Group (USA) Inc., 375 Hudson Street,
New York, New York 10014, USA
Penguin Group (Canada), 90 Eglinton Avenue East, Suite 700, Toronto,
Ontario M4P 2Y3, Canada (a division of Pearson Penguin Canada Inc.)
Penguin Books Ltd., 80 Strand, London WC2R 0RL, England
Penguin Ireland, 25 St. Stephen's Green, Dublin 2,
Ireland (a division of Penguin Books Ltd.)
Penguin Group (Australia), 250 Camberwell Road, Camberwell, Victoria 3124,
Australia (a division of Pearson Australia Group Pty. Ltd.)
Penguin Books India Pvt. Ltd., 11 Community Centre, Panchsheel Park,
New Delhi - 110 017, India
Penguin Group (NZ), 67 Apollo Drive, Rosedale, North Shore 0632,
New Zealand (a division of Pearson New Zealand Ltd.)
Penguin Books (South Africa) (Pty.) Ltd., 24 Sturdee Avenue,
Rosebank, Johannesburg 2196, South Africa

Penguin Books Ltd., Registered Offices:
80 Strand, London WC2R 0RL, England

First published by Roc, an imprint of New American Library,
a division of Penguin Group (USA) Inc.

First printing, May 2009
10 9 8 7 6 5 4 3 2 1

For my brother

Acknowledgments

To Alan Moore (again) for inspiring me with his prodigious beard, and to all the other artists who fed my ravenous brain, and to the great Mystery. To my brother for his depth of imagination and his friendship. To Whitmore for showing me that it can be done. To Jessica for working miracles with word count (I believe!). To Don for his faith and understanding. To Cam, Greg, Andrew, Jen, Leah, Erin, and everyone else (you know who you are)—good luck, chums! And to my muse, with a kiss and a soft touch.

Chapter 1

The Comical Girl

This is a sham, Te thought.

Te shut the car door behind her and pulled her jacket collar close around her neck. *Always raining in this damn town.* They'd pulled up beside a country house walled in by a giant hedge. It sure didn't *look* haunted.

Her boss, Babu Cherian, crashed things around in the trunk of the Cadillac and at last handed her a canvas backpack.

"Full gear today," he grumbled, which was the first thing the big African man had said since he'd pulled up in front of Te's place and barked at her to get her shit together because they had a job.

Te sighed. "Full gear" meant three flashlights, candles and matches, two cameras, two notebooks, extra EMF detectors, barometers, a dozen other electronics, and extra batteries for everything. The backpack must have weighed sixty pounds.

"I appreciate this, Babu," Te said, "but I don't need to be distracted. I'm really okay."

Babu didn't even glare at her as he busied himself jamming things into another backpack.

Te knew this investigation was just to get her out of her apartment and keep her busy. Te's dad had died when she was seventeen, five years ago, on this day—she checked her watch—and pretty close to this time, and every year there was someone who didn't trust her to be alone.

Te watched Babu's broad shoulders bang against the sides of the trunk as he packed. She hated him for babying her and she was glad he cared enough.

"You said this was just a sighting," Te said. Tired of clawing her uncombed black hair out of her face, she bunched it into a rough ponytail and secured it with a tie. She glanced at her hands—the midmorning light made her skin look paler than usual.

"I lied," said Babu.

"Then are you going to tell me why we're here?"

"No. Just stay close to me." His hand shot out as Te finished buckling the chest and waist straps of her pack around her thin frame.

"What's that?" She took the object he was holding out, a small animal-skin sack of some sort on a long string. She tried to place it. African? Native American?

"Put it around your neck," he said.

"I thought you didn't believe in this stuff."

Babu chewed at the cigarette between his teeth. "I don't," he said, "but it was your dad who taught me the power of psychology. Just put it on, okay?"

Te grumbled a bit, but slung the rough string over her neck. The little sack rested on her chest, just below her collarbone. It was dry and stiff, and gave her a shiver when it touched her skin.

Babu had finished suiting up. He straightened and

slammed the trunk. His own backpack looked even heavier than hers, and he had a utility belt to boot.

Te found herself listening to that little twitter in her gut.

"What's going on?" she asked.

Then he did something that made her heart seize up.

He offered her a gun.

She could only stare at it—and at him. His jaw was tight beneath the close beard, his eyes hard. "What's that for?" Te stared down at the gun—a pistol, black and gleaming like a shark.

"I once told your dad I would protect you," he said. "It's only in case I can't do that."

Gingerly, she took the cold metal from his palm. It was heavier than it should have been for its size.

"Nine millimeter," he said. "Safety's here." He pointed to the little switch and moved it back and forth. "On—means it can't fire. Off—means it can. Sight along the top through these metal tabs here. Make sure to use both hands, and don't lock your elbows."

Te could only stare at it for some long seconds. First she thought, *The job isn't a sham.* And then, *He said this was a paranormal job. What does a ghost hunter need a gun for?*

Babu had one, too, hanging from his utility belt. He passed her a holster. "Loop it onto your belt."

She did so mechanically, watching him closely now. During the long ride here, to this country estate upriver from the city, Babu had been silent, his heavy brows down, shoulders hunched inside his blazer. Te hadn't thought it was anything more than the date's significance. She hadn't noticed the taut muscles in his jaw, the slight shake of his fingers as he fiddled with clips and straps.

"Babu, what's going on?" she asked.

"Maybe nothing," he said. "Just let me go first, okay?"

"Always do," she murmured. The gun bit into her hip. She noticed Babu had removed the safety clasp on his. Babu threw his cigarette into a puddle and went first. Te pushed after him through the gate, beneath an arch of hedge leading into the yard. The gate swung silently closed, shaking free drops of rain.

The hedge seemed taller from the inside, muffling sound from the outside world and hiding everything but the overcast sky and the tops of the hills on either side of the St. Ives valley. Blank-eyed garden statues of Indian gods stared at her from their domains around little ponds, flower beds, and the roots of trees. The garden was dominated by a cast-iron Shiva, trident aimed at the chest of any intruders who dared trespass under the arch.

Te nearly jumped out of her shoes when Babu started yelling. "Sanjay?" he called out. "Sanjay!"

He walked cautiously up the footpath, his EMF meter out in front. She thumbed hers on, to find the needle jumping erratically. It didn't necessarily mean ghosts. Maybe the guy was doing levitation experiments in his basement or something.

Or something.

She was ten feet back from Babu when he took to the front steps. The house leaned over them, two stories of old-timey, canary yellow charm—white shutters, green eaves troughs—which was about as far from leering statues of Hindu deities as you could get. Just moved in, maybe? Set up the statues but hadn't had time to repaint?

A sudden rustling from the right caught her attention. She spun toward it, swinging her EMF reflexively. A little black nose poked out of the hedge, followed by a white and pale yellow snout.

A fox. We're way out in the country, so of course there'll be foxes.

But there weren't any birds—at least not inside the hedges—and, when she paid attention, no insect sounds, either.

She was three feet back from Babu when he got to the front door. He rang the doorbell. *Protocol over peril,* she guessed. It was Babu's personal motto.

When that got no answer, he knocked loudly, yelling Sanjay's name a few more times.

From his tool belt, he took a police lock breaker and jammed it into the lock. Weren't those illegal? Where was Babu getting his gear?

He twisted the knob and nudged the door open with his foot. It opened onto a small front hall, leading down to a bigger room that was too dark to make out.

"Lay out a coin," he said, suddenly quiet. He pointed to a little stool next to the door.

Protocol over peril. She fished an envelope out of her pocket and dropped a penny into it. She placed the envelope flat on the stool, and drew an outline of the coin to mark its location in the envelope. Any movement of the coin would be evidence of paranormal activity.

That was routine enough. It calmed her nerves a bit.

"Lay a line of salt across the door," said Babu, already down past the kitchen entrance on the left, and another open arch on the right. Te did as she was told, pouring some of Babu's own special blend of salts and minerals across the doorjamb, making sure the line went straight to the wall on either side, as she'd been taught.

When she looked up, her boss was gone.

"Babu?"

The hall faded into darkness. She checked both of the close arches—a kitchen and what looked like a prayer room of some kind, decked out in Hindu tapestries and statues and incense burners, none of which were lit.

Light. Forgot.

She retrieved her big flashlight from where it hung on her pack and flicked the switch. For an instant, a burst of silver light illuminated the room beyond: a curving wooden staircase on the left, a living room on the right. Then the flashlight and its fresh battery flickered and went dead.

Evidence of paranormal activity?

With unsteady hands, Te clipped the light back onto the pack, and drew a candle and matches from the pocket of her leather jacket. She told herself it wasn't the first time a light had failed on a job. She struck a match and lit the candle.

Navigating by the scant light, she entered the room, trying to figure where her sometime employer would have gone.

She craned her neck to look up the curving stairs, seeing nothing. Out of the dark came a repeating wet sound. Out of habit, she thumbed on the tape recorder hanging off her pack's other strap.

Just poltergeist stuff, she said to herself. *Like rapping, or plates moving. Creepy, but I've heard it before.*

She chose the stairs. Up she went, silently. On the top floor, she heard voices, faint and indistinct. She rubbed her solar plexus, as if to calm the anxiety there.

Voices weren't so strange, really. She'd heard that before, too.

Except this one was Babu's voice, reciting the address of the house, and quavering.

She had to take three deep breaths before opening the closest door.

"Oh, God."

Babu crouched, head bowed. A phone lay on the carpet beside him, cord trailing up to the desk of what looked like a study.

"They're coming, Sanjay," Babu was saying. "Just hold on."

Wax dribbled onto her hand but Te did not feel it. Her whole mind was filled with the blood, the gasping breaths, the wide, unseeing eyes.

Babu knelt, fiercely clutching the hand of a dying man.

"Free," the man hissed, bubbling the spit and blood on his lips. "He's free. Kitsune."

"Don't worry about it now," Babu said. "We'll catch him. We'll—"

The other man grasped aimlessly for Babu's face, his eyes wildly tracking the ceiling. "Rob knew," he said. "It's why he went to fight . . . The Man, he . . . he . . ."

Te saw it then, the man's head tilting back, his eyes rolling upward. Her private fears and horrors welled up, concentrated in her gut, and came rushing, angrily, inexorably upward. She turned away and keeled over. Hot, acrid vomit splattered on the carpet.

Her own gagging was not enough; she still heard the last gasp, the hesitation, the long, slow exhalation of the escaping final breath.

The silence that followed was worse, and perhaps to fill it, her guts betrayed her again.

"Oh, Jesus," she muttered. The smell drove her up; the sight of the now-empty body drove her away down the hall.

She collapsed at the bottom of the stairs, landing hard on the last one before the ground floor. "Steady," she muttered. "Steady, girl."

You didn't know him. He was just some guy. But she knew his name—Sanjay—and she knew that he was Babu's friend. *But it wasn't as bad as when Dad went. And you got through that.*

She took a deliberate, slow breath, then set about licking the horrid taste out of her mouth.

She heard someone else licking, too, and glanced right, down the hall, to where she had left the door open. In the half-light of the doorway, she saw the little yellow fox, licking up the line of salt. It had licked clear a full patch about two inches wide.

It perked up at her attention. She could have sworn it smiled at her. Then it was gone, off into the grass and the rain.

She heard Babu thumping heavily down the steps behind her.

"Babu . . . what . . . wh . . ."

"He was a friend of mine," Babu said. Her boss walked past, shoulders drooping. He looked into space.

Te licked her teeth and swallowed. "He said 'Rob.' He was talking about my dad, wasn't he?"

Babu turned farther away, so that Te couldn't see his face, and said nothing.

"What did he mean about Dad going off to fight someone?"

"I'll call a cab for you," he said. "Please don't talk to the police."

Te pushed herself to her feet. "Damn it, Babu. You *know* what he was talking about." Te hugged herself, hesitating. "Did ... This fight. Is that why Dad ... why he ..."

Babu made a sound that Te realized after a moment was him grinding his teeth together.

"I have to go," he said. "There are people I have to talk to."

"Babu, what happened?"

In the scant light from the doorway, Te saw moisture on his cheeks.

"A bad thing" was all he said.

The ambulance arrived first; the cab shortly after. The paramedics ran into the house, as if there were still something to do. Babu led them upstairs, leaving Te alone on the front lawn.

On the way down to the cab, she stole Babu's casebook from the car. It was a bulging binder four inches thick and was damn well going to tell her what Babu knew.

Babu had insisted she keep the gun. Te had jammed it into her coat pocket, which was not quite big enough for it. It made an embarrassing bulge in the front and she had to constantly keep her hand in her pocket to hide the butt end of it with her sleeve.

The cabbie didn't seem to notice it, except that when he dropped her off at the curb in front of the big house where she lived, he drove away without asking for money.

The morning's rain had turned the scraggly lawn to mud, and the worn stones of the front walk were still slick. Te shrugged deeper into her coat against the chill of the overcast day and navigated her way up the walk, around cracks and puddles and strangely placed concrete planters. Babu's casebook fit awkwardly in the crook of her arm.

She found Jack Jr. sitting on the front step. Te had been living in the big house for only three years, but in that time she'd watched Jack fill out from a skinny teenager to a wiry young man. He'd met her the day she moved in—he hadn't offered to help; he'd just stood there and watched her with a kind of awe. After that, it seemed he was always looking over her shoulder whenever she was doing anything—testing her ghost-hunting gear or fiddling with her charcoals or just sitting bored. He never said a word. Eventually, she'd just taken the initiative and spoken to him.

He'd come to her in a panic when he got his first pimple. It was stupid, but that meant a lot to her.

Jack jumped to his feet as she approached, as if he'd been waiting for her the whole time. Te stopped him with an upraised hand.

"Whatever it is, I don't want to know."

"But . . ." Jack stopped. His face creased in confusion and he blinked at her with eyes magnified through thick prescription glasses. "Well . . . they need you around back."

Te sighed.

"All right. What is it?"

Jack pointed broadly around the right side of the house. "The world is ending again."

Crap. Hadn't she gone through enough this morning? Wouldn't she go through enough tonight?

The grassy mud that had been the lawn sucked her

shoes down with every step as she made her way around the house. Jack slunk after her like a lost dog.

Te heard the shouting before she turned the corner.

"You come down off there! Don't make me call the police again." A too-familiar scene greeted her as she stepped through the broken gate into the backyard. Jack's parents, the landlords who lived on the bottom floor, were out in their bathrobes, staring up at the roof.

"Oh!" Mrs. Sprat cried when she caught sight of Te. "Talk him down. Oh, please talk him down."

Jack's dad, Jack Sprat Sr., stretched his jaw and jowels and turned away in disgust. "Ah, just let him jump. Then we can go back in before it rains again."

"Oh, grow some decency," his wife snapped.

"Damn communist, anyway," Mr. Sprat spat back.

"Kent . . . ," Te said, to herself, or to the man sitting on the roof. *Today of all days . . .*

She shuffled the casebook a bit to try to free a hand, failed, and just yelled upward. "Kent!"

Two stories up, on one of the house's many interlocking roofs, Kent Allard raised his head from his hands.

"Te?" Kent cast around as if he didn't realize where he was. His eyes were wide and bulging from sunken sockets. Even from two stories down, Te could see that his perpetual dark circles and pale skin were worse than usual.

"I'm down here."

Wringing his skeletal hands, Kent finally locked eyes with her.

"Te!" he cried. "I'm so sorry. I held him for . . . I tried! You have to believe me! Seventy years, Te, I couldn't do it. It's a mortal sin." He broke down into tears.

"Kent, please come down," Te said.

"Just jump!" yelled Mr. Sprat. "Think of the rest of us standing here in this damn cold."

Te shushed him. "Kent," she said, "is your door open?"

Kent looked startled, as if woken out of a sleep.

"What?"

"Is your door open?"

"No, no," he said, fingernails creeping between his teeth, "of course it isn't."

"Unlock it for me. I'm coming up." Without another word, Te started marching toward the rickety back stairs. When Jack Jr. fell into an interested march behind her, Te used him to block his parents' view of her pocket.

Kent had riveted a plate of steel over his door, quite to Mr. Sprat's distress, though once it was installed, there was nothing anyone could do about it. Te stood in the center of the little landing that served as his doorstep, where she could be clearly seen through the fish-eye camera.

Bolts, both manual and electrically controlled, slid back. A few chains jangled as they were removed. Three keys turned in three locks. Kent Allard's veined eyes peeked out from the small crack that opened. They shot all around, looking at Te and back at Jack behind her, at the trees and rooftops and windows within line-of-sight. Through the open door came the growl of white noise, static blasting from a dozen radios, and the flicker of snow from a dozen TVs.

"Hi, Mr. Allard," said Jack.

"Te?" Kent said finally.

"Yes, it's me," Te said. "You want to tell me what's wrong?"

He licked a swollen tongue over dried lips. His jaw trembled as he spoke and Te found herself wondering again how old the man was.

"The frequencies have changed," he said.

Te's gut sank. *Not again, Kent.*

"What frequencies?" she asked.

"The aberrations in the white noise," he said. "The shapes in the static. It's *you*—I should have seen it. It was in the shapes."

"Oh?"

"The white noise should break down into an even spectrum of frequencies. Of course, there are random spikes—there are always random spikes—but now there are *random spikes*! *Very* random. *Too* random."

"What?"

"Randomness is unpredictable," Kent said, opening his door another inch so that Te could see his flaring nostrils as he spoke. "But it's also natural. But ... it's still unpredictable, but it's not random. It's not random like the universe is random. And yesterday"—he lowered his voice confidentially—"I saw a line."

Te couldn't believe it. Hadn't she had a bad enough day? Didn't she have a bad enough evening ahead of her? Why couldn't they just leave her alone for ten minutes? But she said, "What do you mean, a line?"

"A line! A line on a screen of static. It was there only a moment, but even a child could have picked it out."

"Kent ..."

"That *does not* happen," Kent went on. "The odds against it are astronomical."

"But you just said that it's random."

"Yes, but not random like that!" he cried. "Natural randomness is the inability of the human mind to see the source variables—but this was randomness *without* source variables. Without any cause at all!"

Te felt her patience slipping, the day's trials overwhelming her diminishing sense of pity for this man. "That's what's bothering you?"

Kent was almost screaming now. "But without cause, there can only be one cause! There can only be an unnatural cause! The factors all …" His eyes bulged. His jaw worked even as his words died out. "The factors … they point …" He was staring at Te's stomach. The suspicious lump in her right pocket had caught his attention.

She looked back up to see his eyes wide with terror.

"The black man gave that to you," he said—almost an accusation.

"Kent," Te began, "this isn't—"

"I knew it!" he cried. "I'm too late. I'm sorry. I'm so sorry!"

The door slammed shut. Bolts and chains slid back into place. Locks clicked shut. Te stared at the dull metal in front of her and sighed. A couple of drops bounced off her hair as the rain started again.

"Guess he's not gonna jump, then," said Jack.

"Yeah." Te turned and started back down. Jack followed her lead.

"My dad doesn't like him," he said. "But I think he's okay. Y'know. For being crazy."

Jack's folks were long gone, safe indoors from the drizzle. He stayed a silent step or two behind Te all the way down.

A raindrop hit Te in the forehead. "Aren't you cold?" she asked.

"Nope," he said. "What's in your pocket?"

Jesus. It's that obvious?

"Nothing, Jack." Te planted her feet back in the muddy lawn and started tromping around the building again, to the left side where the stairs up to her own apartment were nailed into the siding.

"Oh." Jack fell silent, but kept pace with her all the way to the foot of her own stairway.

"Jack, look," Te began, turning to look at him. Not that Jack had much expression at the best of times, but his magnified eyes made him even more impossible to read. "I've had a rough day, all right? I just think I need a few minutes to myself."

"All right. Should I wait here?"

"A *long* few minutes."

"Oh." Jack looked down and shuffled his feet a bit in the mud. "Bye." He slouched off, the cuffs of his pants dragging through the wet grass.

Te's feet weighed a thousand pounds on the long climb up to her doorway.

Hers was a little one-room apartment, with a token kitchenette, on the top floor. Judging by its size, it should by all rights simply have been another room added to Kent's suite, but the landlord, in his self-serving wisdom, had decided to make it an apartment all its own. It was cramped and it was cold, and it had only one single-paned window, but it was home.

And right now, it was protection from her thoughts.

Lukewarm air and the soft drone of Kent's white noise coming through the wall greeted her. Dozens of her charcoal drawings hanging on the walls stared down, the products of half-remembered nightmares and unconscious scribblings. But of course, the first thing her eyes rested on was a picture of her father.

She shut the door and kicked off her muddy shoes.

Then she took the gun from her pocket and the photograph from the wall, and sat down heavily on her bed.

Her dad smiled out of the frame, his thin face and high forehead the picture of her own. Her mother was there, too, arm around Dad's waist, round and fat like always, with her button nose and huge smile. And between them was a shaggy-haired, gap-toothed little girl holding a kite and beaming. It was the only picture she had of him, of them as a family, before everything had started going wrong.

Interlude

Te is seventeen years old and she's watching her father die.

She's standing at a window in the short hall of the emergency ward, looking through into a separate room. Some orderly has forgotten to draw the curtain.

I don't think Te can see him—he is obscured by doctors and staff racing around the room. There are machines that she doesn't recognize. There are needles. There are the wide eyes of nurses who shake visibly even while working with speed and skill.

It's not like TV. She'll remember thinking that when the shock goes away, days from now.

I can't see her face from where I'm sitting. I see her hugging herself, wrapping her skinny arms over her abdomen. Her knees are weak, but not yet shaking.

It is then that the motion of the doctors carries them aside for a moment, just for a moment, and Te can see her father's face. She can see the foam coming from his lips, the muscles so tight that his skin stretches taut over his skull. She sees the wild, crazed eyes, so thoroughly consumed with fear that they cannot see the world around them, cannot see the loved ones so close by.

Her mother, Sonore, stands beside her, looking through the same window, watching the same scene. Her face I can see: she is smiling.

Te's arms leave her torso and fall upon the thin sill of the window. Still she stands, though her knees are fading, bending, so slowly as almost to deny perception. Her mouth is agape now, her eyes open and twitching. She does not blink.

She watches her father's mute cry of terror as the pain reaches its height. She watches as his eyes drift upward, and for an instant, he seizes up. It is a moment frozen in time. She watches as he at last sees mortality. She watches as her father turns to meat.

The pain leaves his body as he does, and he slumps back onto the table. Machines that neither Te nor I can hear flare to life in alarm. The medical staff grab for paddles and respirators, even knowing it's too late.

Te's knees fail. I watch and smile as the bottom falls out of her world, and she crashes to the linoleum in an awkward heap. She doesn't cry. She won't for some hours.

Her mother watches through the window with a lazy smile. She says two words, words only I hear because I am the only one listening.

"Good-bye, Robert."

She turns away, turns her back on her daughter, turns her back on the meat beyond the window. She hikes up the fur collar of her coat, surrounding her face in softness.

As she walks away, she looks at me, looks right at me—hits me with a wide, immaculate grin, red around white—and I get the unsettling feeling that she knows exactly who I am, and why I'm here.

But she is gone an instant later, clicking down the hall on her high heels.

Te is on the floor—frozen, lost. She can't move. No one sees her.

In the operating room, the doctor pulls a sheet over Rob Evangeline's face and my emotions stir. I will not cry. I have cried enough over him already.

My witness here is over, and so I turn to leave.

I can't say what makes me do it. I should leave Te to rot, leave the skinny girl to the devouring emotions within her. It might break her, I know, and that might save me a lot of trouble later on.

But I don't. Instead, I get a nurse and tell her that Te needs help. Maybe I'm too young. Maybe I know that Robert would want me to.

The reason doesn't matter and I dismiss it from my mind.

I walk out of the hospital and into the snow. I let a snowflake fall on my cheek, its touch as soft as his, and I realize at last that I've done a terrible thing.

Chapter 2

The Boy Who Sat in the Corner and Ate Dry Noodles

Babu hated this place. He never came here when he could be somewhere else, and when he did come here, he chain-smoked as if it were going out of style and usually had to stop to buy a few more packs. A sure sign of stress, Rob had told him. He didn't need Rob to tell him what was stressful.

His piece-of-crap Cadillac chugged to a stop in front of the house. It looked for all the world like any ordinary suburban house from the late fifties, repainted and refurbished a half dozen times and never looking less old for it. The steps from the front door ended right at the sidewalk, and another set of stairs led down to the basement suite door, where, even through the rain, Babu could see the sign with the eye and triangle.

Babu let the engine choke a few times before turning it off. He sucked back a few whole cigarettes to steady himself. The damn things would give him cancer, he knew. They might already have. Not that a long, healthy life was a possibility in his line of work, anyway.

What the hell. He let his mind roll while he finished the pack.

The paramedics had looked at Sanjay and said stroke. Fine. Less paperwork and no giving awkward statements. These were small-town police, anyway. They wouldn't go looking for more trouble if they could close their files and go back to catching speeding high school kids. When they'd questioned him about the line of salt and all the gear, he'd just told them the truth—*it's ghost-hunting gear*—and they'd had their private laugh and left him alone. Didn't even check his pack, where he'd hidden the gun.

Jesus Christ, Sanjay. Babu had stayed until they'd taken his friend off in a body bag. It was the same type that had carried off O'Shae and Julia, and King and Rob. And Nyawela . . . Christ, they'd taken his wife away in a damn bag, years and years ago.

He shook the thought out and took a tally: Sanjay dead. Kitsune free. Possible involvement of the Man. Anything else was an unknown, and Babu hated un-knowns. No, more accurately, they caused him a sting-ing, aching pain—the pain of wishing he'd known, back when something still could have been done for Rob.

He stubbed out his last cigarette and decided to stop being so morbid. He reached into the backseat for his casebook, and found it wasn't there.

"What the hell?"

He leaned awkwardly over the console into the backseat, straining the lower back, which his doctor always nagged him to take better care of. He rooted for it under mounds of files and papers and random pieces of gear. It wasn't there. Could he have left it? When Sanjay'd called him, he'd got out of the house in a damn hurry, so maybe . . .

Whatever. He snagged a blank piece of paper and made some notes.

Nov. 3, 1996—Call from Sanjay, 10:15 a.m. Said his barriers were breaking. Said something about temptation. Means someone's come to him with the key for Kitsune's cell. Geared up, drove over. Picked up Te on the way.

Why the hell had he stopped to pick up Te? He could have just buzzed over on his own and maybe he'd have got there in time to—*No. It was already too late when I got the phone call. Can't think like that.*

Found Sanjay dying. Hemorrhaging from eyes, ears, nose. Final words: "He's free. Kitsune. Rob knew. It's why he went to fight the Man." Kitsune escaped. The Man may be responsible. Makes no sense, since it was on his orders that we put Kitsune away in the first place (cross-reference: Kitsune Case, 1986). Further investigation needed.

He laid aside his gear, including his firearm, and, with one final intake of breath, threw the door open.

The rain pounded him all the way around the car and up to the house. At the bottom of the staircase, he squeezed the worn brass handle and let himself in.

Door chimes in whole-tone harmony greeted his entrance. His nose sucked up incense thicker than smoke and he coughed reflexively.

A figure moved behind a bead curtain across the room. Blunt-nailed fingers weighted with multiple rings parted the strings and Babu saw a hint of the smile that always made his skin crawl.

"Babu Cherian," said Angrel. "What does our resident hypocrite want from the spirit world today, I wonder?"

Babu wiped raindrops off his bald head and the shoulders of his blazer.

"Sanjay's dead," he said, refusing to fence words with the woman. He started to navigate his way across the room, around statues and incense burners, stacks of little round pillows, various crystal mobiles, and pots with sprigs of sage and lavender.

She let the curtain drop and vanished from view.

"I know," she said from the next room. "A bad way to go, too."

Babu pushed through the curtain into the back room while Angrel lit candles with a plastic cigarette lighter. She sat down at the room's tiny table and laid a purple cloth over it with a practiced flourish. "I suppose I'd pity Sanjay if it weren't his own mental lapse that did it."

She offered Babu a seat. In the candlelight, her bleach white skin looked like carved stone, and her white dreadlocks like Medusa's hair.

Babu shook his head and reminded himself that this was part of her persona. She was an albino, and expertly worked it for the "mystique." Babu waved her quiet.

"Just hold on." There were three chairs at the table. Babu took one and hefted it into the other room, where he tilted it forward and laid it down on its face.

Angrel was watching him with a raised eyebrow when he returned.

"It's a little unfriendly not to even invite him."

Babu took his seat. "Maybe I don't want him here."

From somewhere in her flowing gray dress, Angrel produced a pack of well-worn tarot cards and began to shuffle. "Then I guess you've got something interesting to tell me."

"Put the cards away," Babu said.

"If the shuffling is bothering you," she said, placing the deck on the table between them, "I can stop."

The deck of cards stared up at him. *There's no power in there*, he said to himself. *It's all intuition and archetypes.*

"Sanjay's dead," he repeated.

"I know. Should that worry me? The man betrayed his own beliefs—an ascetic with a two-bedroom house in the country? Of *course* he came to a bad end."

Babu tried not to look into those eyes that glittered like the candle flames. "He didn't just give up."

"Of course he did," said Angrel. Did the woman ever blink? "He knew what would happen if he let his guard down. He said as much to us when he took on the responsibility—'attachment means death.' "

Babu crossed his arms and tried to find certainty in his words. "Sanjay didn't let us down. He was broken from the outside."

Angrel's smile was patient, like a teacher with a young child. "The Kitsune had ten years to plan an escape. I'd be interested to know how he finally managed it."

"So you don't already?" said Babu.

Angrel eyed him with amusement, recognizing the question for what it was. "And why would I know?" she asked.

Babu pointed to her tarot deck. Angrel lifted the deck with her white fingers and shook her head.

"No, you didn't mean this," she said. "You meant, did *the Man* know this was going to happen?"

Babu licked the inside of his teeth and wished he had another cigarette.

"Did he?"

Angrel leaned back and smiled coyly. "That's not for me to know. He doesn't tell me everything."

"What do you tell him?"

"Usually," she said, "nothing he doesn't already know."

Babu drummed his fingers on the table, choking back his frustration at the woman's answers. They sat a moment in silence as she shuffled her cards. There was something far too young about the woman, and also far too old.

"I'm calling a moot."

Angrel raised an eyebrow at that. "Only the Man can call a moot."

"Not tonight," said Babu. "We need to get on this fast, find Yun Kitsune another cage and another keeper."

"Anyone in mind?"

"We'll talk tonight." Babu pushed his chair back and got up, not letting his eyes leave her. Angrel drew a card and Babu jabbed a finger at it.

"Put that damn thing away."

Angrel smirked and slipped the card back into the deck. "Babu, tell me," she said. "You asked if the Man knew Kitsune was going to escape. Didn't you really want to ask whether the Man *arranged* it?"

Babu stared down at the woman, so tiny and yet taking up so much of the space in the room. Angrel stared at him without blinking.

"I see."

Babu ground his teeth. "I'm going to warn Lester," he said.

"Good luck finding him."

"Any suggestions on precautions?"

She spread her cards out on the table in front of her. "Nothing works, Babu. Not against the Kitsune. I've already done everything I can."

I'm sure you have.

"I'm going now."

"There's the door."

Babu was back out into the rain before she started drawing cards.

Babu made a phone call and then a quick stop at the graveyard. It was two o'clock and pitch black by the time he got to Darktown.

The rain lessened when he crossed the line of shadow at the border of the neighborhood. Darktown was sunk down into what might have once been a lakebed, surrounded on all sides by the walls of clay plateaus that lined the St. Ives valley on both banks.

The old car shuddered as it hit the potholed streets. Babu cursed the suspension and gripped tight to the wheel.

He passed the first intersection, where the stoplight flashed a continual red signal. A quick check told him that the local youth had once again made off with all the street signs. They did it in order to confuse and discourage visitors, as the streets became so tangled down in the bottom of the bowl, it was tough to find one's way out. But Babu had been here often enough, and knew the way by memory.

He encountered not another soul on the street, nor any other cars. The sidewalk gutters overflowed with the rain, and the crooked decks on the second and third stories of the tenements leaked as though they were crying.

Babu shook himself. It was Te's obsession with scary movies that put this stuff in his imagination. It was raining; the buildings were old; the bowl walls blocked out the sun. That was all.

His route took him right down to the back wall of the bowl, where he pulled his car up in front of a dilapidated little house not unlike his own. Squashed between two apartment buildings on either side, the place looked like a forgotten toolshed.

But that was how any self-respecting bohemian kept his place, and he was here to see the worst of them.

Once again, Babu braved the rain, this time with his full tool belt weighing him down. Around his neck he hung the African charm that he'd used that morning.

And once again, he took the gun.

The door shuddered as he knocked on it. He slipped his EMF detector into his palm and switched it on, watching the needle jump back and forth.

"There are places man was not meant to go," called a voice from inside. "Beware the dark that imperils the soul. Be you man or nightmare, know that this house is a house of death and of transfiguration . . ."

The voice went on for some time, finally ending with, "Then enter, if you dare."

Babu stuffed his EMF detector away and retrieved a white dishcloth, using that to open the door. His gun he slipped into an inside pocket on his blazer.

The rot stench almost made him wretch, even though he was expecting it. As it was, he managed to strangle his cough.

"Inside," said the voice. "We brook not the foul light of day."

Babu obediently stepped inside and shut the door. The hall was pitch-black, the only light the faint haze of the overcast sky slipping through holes in the walls. Babu breathed carefully in the rank, damp air, looking down the hall in both directions.

"I'm here to see Lester," he said to the darkness, or to whoever had answered.

"Of course," said the shadows in the hall. "He is the Master. Everyone comes to see the Master. They come to swear loyalty to his undying grace."

As his eyes adjusted, Babu made out the two teenagers, standing against the outer walls on either side of him, maybe three paces away. Strutters. Should have known.

"Just let me see Lester," Babu insisted. "We know each other."

"Everyone knows the Master," said the first boy. "Sooner or later."

"Hey, man, look," said the second. "He's marked." Babu saw the boy pointing to the fetish around his neck. "You recognize it?"

The first boy leaned forward, less concerned with hiding now, and examined Babu's charm. Babu made no move to block it, staying as still as possible.

"I don't know. You a voodoo priest or something?" said the first boy. "Maybe we *will* take you to the Master."

The second boy nodded. "He'll know what to do."

"Thank you," said Babu.

The second boy poked him in the arm with a long, pointed nail. It was sharp enough that Babu could feel it through the blazer's heavy tweed. "Now go! March into the long, dark night of your soul."

Babu complied, knowing better than to aggravate kids who filed their teeth and ate raw meat and lived entirely in the dark.

They took him through a series of turns, all darkened halls that Babu had a hard time mentally reconciling with the size of the house, and then down a set of stairs that swayed with age and rot.

The dark was impenetrable. Babu stumbled forward, the one boy in front, the other behind. He'd seen no other Strutters on their cyclic journey, but had no doubt they had been there, invisible in the shadows.

The boys led him to a door.

"Keep him, man," said the first. "I'll see."

"Cool."

The first boy went through the door, shutting it behind him. Babu saw a flash of dull light and smelled the unmistakable odor of marijuana. Around him, in the dark, he heard the breath of more than just the boy who kept those nails at his back.

Nothing was said, by Babu or his captor, for several minutes. The first boy returned.

"In," he said. "The Master waits for no one, living or dead."

"Thank you." Babu pushed past the boy into the room.

At least there was light. Two ornate table lamps glowed and flickered from the corners of the room. To the left and right, long lines of used and weather-beaten couches flanked a coffee table in the center. Young people filled the room, lounging on the couches and one another, lying on the floor under moth-bitten blankets.

They were dressed in gothic designer clothes intentionally torn and soiled, and many scratched at him with their sharpened nails and licked their filed teeth as he walked between them. Lester himself was sprawled out on a cracked armchair of red leather, at the room's far end. A prodigious assortment of bongs, foil, lighters, and cigarette paper was laid out on the table in front of him, along with ominous bottles of dark fluid and a broad bowl filled with raw hamburger.

Lester looked up as he pinched some tobacco out of a plastic bag and started rolling. The bones pushed out around his eyes and his skin was yogurt yellow from fifteen years without seeing the sun.

"Babu Cherian," he said with a chuckle. " 'What brings you down to the Kingdom of Darkness? To this abode of the Lost and the Damned? What price has bought your soul that you walk these halls in search of forbidden truths, and knowing or unknowing, find your end?' "

A few of the Strutters nodded in sage understanding.

Lester grinned. "Like that? It's from a poem Jill wrote."

He pointed to a young, skinny girl who could not have been older than thirteen. The girl sucked on a cigarette and smiled.

"Nice suit," Lester said. "Gone respectable?" He offered Babu the newly rolled cigarette. Babu took it and fired it up. Unfiltered—like a campfire in his chest.

"No."

"Sure you have," Lester said. "Take it this isn't a friendly call." He lit a joint from the table and took a pull.

Saying it again made Babu more tired than he would have thought. "Sanjay's dead, Les. Yun's free."

Lester finished a long, almost thoughtful drag and slowly exhaled before speaking.

"My children," he said, with a grand gesture toward the door, "leave us."

Some of the older ones jumped to obey. Those who were younger or just looked more out of it took their time rolling off the couches. Evidently it was too long.

Lester leapt to his feet and slashed the air with his long nails.

"Get out!" he cried. His voice shook the loose boards in the floor. "Get the fuck out, everybody!"

The kids ran and in seconds the room was clear. One of them had overturned the hamburger, and it now lay on the floor in a spreading pool of blood.

Lester settled down into his armchair again, taking another long pull, another long exhalation.

" 'My children,' " he said with a dry chuckle. "They eat that shit up. All this grand Dracula stuff. I even dressed up in, like, this old suit for them once."

Babu stared down the length of the table at this pale, shriveled man who had once been alive and whole.

"Did you hear what I said, Les?"

"You said we're all gonna die," Lester said, eyes still down on the table, wandering aimlessly.

That was all either of them said for a while. Lester puffed into the rank, damp air. When the joint was finished, he spoke again, through a cloud of curling smoke.

"We shouldn't take this to the Man."

"I think he knows already," Babu said.

"Course he knows. S'not what I meant." Les took a sudden, desperate pull from one of the dark bottles. "We don't mention this. We don't get involved again. The

Man can find someone else to do his dirty work. I got my own shit to take care of—the kids, you know. They look up to me."

Lester, suddenly alert, fixed Babu with a tight stare, as if the drugs meant nothing to him. Babu shied back, unconsciously fleeing the man's sudden suspicion.

"Is that why you're here, Babu?" Lester hissed. "You come recruiting?"

"Yeah."

Lester jabbed Babu in the chest with one of his nails, thankfully, blunted.

"I'm retired, man. I don't work for that fucker anymore."

Babu shoved Lester's arm away. "I'm not working for him on this one, either."

"Bullshit, man. You're a believer." But Les retreated, fondling the bottle in one hand. "Sometimes I think you're more fucked up than me, working for a shadow and teaching Rob's kid that ghosts don't exist."

To that, Babu just shrugged. "It's the job."

"Working in a mill's a job, man," Lester said, settling back. "Packing trucks is a job."

Babu hunched forward, elbows on knees, and exhaled, not liking Lester's sudden stoned insight. He looked at his sometime friend, reflecting that the man never seemed to age—he just grew more tired.

"I'm calling a moot tonight," Babu said.

"Good for you."

"Les, we need a tracker if we're going to survive this."

"We're not gonna survive it," Lester said, nursing the bottle close to his lips. "Funny, though, you not going straight to the Man with this."

Babu stood and straightened his blazer, then smoothed down the lapels. "Like I said, he already knows." He slipped a business card out of his pocket and laid it on the table. "If you need me."

"Don't wait by the phone," Les said. He took a swig and sat a moment, licking the red from his teeth.

Babu walked over to the door, suddenly wondering if he'd have to find his way back upstairs to the street, when he heard Lester choke on his drink.

"Wait a minute!"

Babu turned as Les came running up.

"You think *he* did it. You think the Man let him out."

Babu looked into Lester's dilated, bloodshot eyes. "I think he turned on us all when Rob Evangeline went after him."

"No," Les said. "No way would he do that."

"Who's died, Les? Who's left of the original team?" Babu counted on his fingers. "Rob's gone, King's gone, Martin's gone, O'Shae's gone, Julia's gone. And now Sanjay. That doesn't leave a whole lot. The Man certainly isn't looking out for us anymore."

Lester's look was the fright of sudden realization. Instead of feeling sorry for the man, Babu guiltily found himself lamenting his own position, in that his only confidant was a drug-addicted vampire who hung around with teenagers.

Lester stood stunned, as if unable to answer. Babu shook his head and turned away.

"Tonight," he said, and, drawing his flashlight, reentered the maze of the house.

Chapter 3

Forks Dissolving in Black Tea

Te would rather have stayed home. She'd rather have done anything else. But it was a special day, after all, her mother had said. It was a day the family should be together, and her mother didn't take no for an answer.

"I might have to make you sing," the answering machine message had said. "And no one wants that, do they, m'dear?"

Te got off the bus at the base of Lamont Heights, a hilly subdivision of green lawns and people with golf memberships—she'd spent most of her childhood pretending she didn't live there. The roads were steep, but familiar, with pavement that never seemed to crack, sidewalks that never seemed to grow weeds, fire hydrants whose paint never seemed to chip off.

She trudged up to her mother's house through cold rain and a light wind that cut right through her leather jacket into her skin. The house sat imperially on the uphill side of a road, looking down over the rooftops of the houses below, fixed high above the St. Ives' sprawl that coated the valley floor. Funny how she always thought of this as her mother's house. Her dad had lived here. So had she. Still, with one look at the rainbow-checked curtains in the windows and the mock Buddhist prayer flags fluttering above the doorway in lime green and pastel pink, there was no doubt whose house this was.

She took to the front steps, used to the way each step never quite seemed to match the height or proportion of the one before it. The doorbell rang like a drunken songbird.

"Come in, Te, m'dear," came her mother's wide, warm voice. "Imagine, ringing the doorbell at your own home."

Te took a deep breath and turned the doorknob.

The house smelled like a greenhouse. Te stepped in and kicked her shoes off, hung her dripping coat on the ornate coat hanger that had been her dad's, and dodged the potted plants hanging everywhere.

"In here, dear."

Te found them in the living room. Her mother, Sonore Evangeline, swirled to her feet to greet her, a tornado of tie-dye and beads, the smile on her round face so matronly as to border on caricature.

"My little girl," she said, touching Te's cheek and squinting into her eyes. After a few seconds of examination, her expression fell into a scowl. "No smile for your poor mother?"

Te pushed the hand away. "Mom, don't, all right?" She walked past her into the room. "Hi, Aunt Syd, Aunt Babs."

Her two aunts were seated on a wicker couch. Aunt Sydney was like a supermodel in old age, her features still well shaped, her limbs still long and slim, but all cov-

ered by fine wrinkles and age spots. Her hair had gone
white and wiry but still fell more or less consistently to
her shoulders. It was only her eyes, and the little twitchy
movements of her hands she never seemed to stop making, that reminded Te how much her mind was going.
Sydney turned a sleepy set of eyes on her niece and
seemed to jump to life.

"Little pollywog!" she cried. "Will you sit and drink
with us?"

Aunt Babs glared at Te and, by way of a greeting,
sniffed in her general direction. She was fat, frumpy,
wrinkly, had thin, shaggy hair, bone-skinny legs, and a
long, pointed nose with big nostrils. She was only missing a wart on her nose.

There was a third guest in the house, a slim, pale man
reclining in the leopard-print armchair on the far side
of the room. He had long, delicate limbs, golden blond
hair, and a smooth face. He wore a white turtleneck with
sport coat and slacks perfectly coordinated with his hair
color.

He was already staring at Te by the time she noticed
him. His gaze was calm and clear-eyed and made her
very nervous.

She sat gingerly in the other armchair, an uncomfortable thing made of driftwood, across from the couch.

"Drink something," her mother offered/ordered, gesturing to an already full cup of impenetrable black liquid.

Te caught a glimpse of Aunt Babs sucking some of
the syrupy stuff into her mouth and cringed.

"No, thanks."

Her mother shrugged and was instantly congenial
again. "Te, this is a friend of ours from the Old Country,"

she said, bustling back to the couch to squish in beside her sisters. "Yun, this is my daughter, Te."

Yun's smile was simple and disarming as he extended his hand.

" 'O, the moon shone bright on Mrs. Porter and on her daughter,' " he said. "Yun Kitsune, at your service." Te watched him for a second, insides squirming, then shot out her fingers and quickly shook his soft, manicured hand.

Kitsune?

She realized she was staring and added a hasty "Nice to meet you." He returned the courtesy with something equally empty. She watched him out of the corner of her eye as her mother gathered their attention with a flick of her rainbow bracelets. The "Kitsune" from that morning had escaped from somewhere, according to the man Sanjay. This Kitsune looked too well groomed and put together to have escaped from somewhere so recently, and to have killed someone. Coincidence? *Maybe.*

Sydney swayed and bent like a windblown blade of grass. "Pollywog, pollywog. Does she breathe the air?" Everyone ignored her. Babs put down her tea and meticulously counted the teaspoons on the table. Sonore waited for her to finish before speaking.

"Now that everyone's here," her mother said, raising her cup of tea, "a toast to my poor Robert, gone these past five years."

Te watched her mother set her tea down and look sullen. But it was a beautiful kind of sullen, a movie starlet's melodrama, with cheeks and lips animated, a vocal sigh, and visible deflation.

"Good riddance," Babs snorted. "Bad temper."

"Oh, yes, I know," her mother said, then sighed heavily. "I did used to love the arguments."

Te's nails dug into the arms of her chair. Her mother's annual sympathy play brought bile up to the back of her throat every time. It made Te furious, and maybe that was why her mother did it.

She shouldn't have come. She said it to herself every year, and every year she went—because they were family, maybe, or maybe because even a mock remembrance was better than nothing at all.

"I remember once," Sonore was lamenting, "I switched out our bed for the prettiest pile of tatami mats. Oh, was he *angry*."

"He was always angry," Barbara said. She slurped some liquid and smacked her lips. "Can't believe you married him."

"Ah, now *that* was a lovely day . . ."

Te tuned them out. She'd heard it before: commiserating, remembering, false tears, and sometimes even false stories—and always, always insulting and slandering the one person who had told Te he loved her and actually meant it.

Why on earth did she stay in this town? Why not buy some beater car and run down to California? Get lost on some back road and never have to listen to this kind of crap again.

Because it was her family.

Because they were all she had.

She sank deeper into her chair, tiny tears twitching in the corners of her eyes—she'd never let them fall, though. Sonore would take the tears as tears of sympathy, and Te was not about to give her anything.

Yun Kitsune was still staring at her. Te looked over.

He clearly wanted to start a conversation and that was a perfect opening to probe him, see if he was the one from the morning. It did occur to her as she gave him her attention that there could be a murderer sitting in the armchair beside her, but Babu had taught her to follow her hunches.

"Protocol over peril," right?

"You've grown up marvelously," Yun said, a gentle smile playing on his face.

"I don't think I've met you before," Te said.

"No, of course not," said Yun. "I worked with your dad awhile, about ten or so years ago. I saw you a few times, though you wouldn't have seen me."

"What did you do?"

"I grant wishes," he said, as if Te was supposed to read some deeper meaning from that. "I granted one for your father."

"Oh, yes, that," her mother cut in. "Wondrous times, those were."

Yun's quiet smile twisted down. "It's not how I would describe them, truth be told."

"What do you mean, 'a wish'?" Te asked.

"That really isn't for me to say," Yun said. "What do you think, dear Sonore?"

Te's mother hid her expression behind a cup of tea held too high. "Oh, what's the harm now that my *dear* husband is laid to rest?"

Te passed up the opportunity to make a face at her mother's comment, eyes on Yun.

The fair-haired man contemplated his tea a moment. "It's a simple story, really. I was a criminal. Your father was a policeman."

Escaped . . .

"Dad was a psychologist," Te said, shooting her eyes sideways, interested in her mother's reaction, but there was nothing to be seen beneath that placid smile.

"Metaphor, my dear," her mother said. "Mr. Kitsune and your father were adversaries, of a type. Mr. Kitsune was quite the little rebel back then, weren't you?"

"I like to think of myself as a naturalist," Yun said. "A free spirit."

"Hippie," Babs scoffed, and stoppered her thin lips with another gulp of tea.

Te ignored her and turned back to Yun, who had resumed his posture of quiet repose. "What kind of adversaries?" she asked.

"Ideological adversaries, Miss Evangeline. The very worst kind."

"What do you mean?"

"Now, now, Yun," her mother said, starting to her feet. "We shouldn't dump all my late husband's secrets out all at once, should we? I *did* want Te to sing for us today."

Te felt her solar plexus tighten up. "Mom?"

Sonore stood and moved behind her, placing her hands on Te's shoulders—comforting, very motherly. Her smile spread wide.

"A song, my dear. One of those nursery rhymes you so used to like."

Te swallowed hard. God, no. Not this time. It had been more than a year, but the black, cold wounds of last time came right back to the surface.

"I'm not a kid anymore, Mom," Te said, trying to keep the tremble out of her voice. Maybe her mother would bow to the rebuke in the face of guests.

"Oh, yes, your voice is getting so lovely and mature,"

her mother said. Her fingers dug into Te's shoulders, as if in a hint of a massage. "But you still have no passion behind it, m'dear. There's no *life* in those words when they come from you. You need practice."

Te shrugged her mother's hands away. "Mom, I'm not singing."

"Bunch of troublemakers, people today," Babs said. "No appreciation for ritual."

"I'm not going to do it this time, Mom," Te said. She started to rise from the chair, when something soft and cold slipped over her left hand.

She turned to see Mr. Kitsune's long, delicate fingers on her skin. Their touch stung like ice, but warmed her blood beneath the skin. They felt smooth, rubbery, almost like plastic. The lilac scent of the man wafted into her nose, and she found her eyes pulled up to meet his, slate gray and placidly calm.

"I would very much like to hear you sing, Miss Evangeline," Yun said, articulating each word with precise motions of his lips. "I've been a long time without hearing anything at all."

Te felt her breath quicken, felt her jaw start to quiver. The fingers of her right hand started to twitch against the arm of the chair.

"We want to hear you sing, pollywog," said Sydney. "We want to hear you speaking sunshine."

Sonore was at her side, ushering her through nudges to full standing position. Yun's hand never left hers, trailing faintly over her skin as their relative positions changed.

"You've done this a thousand times, darling," her mother said, close to her ear. "Sing us that little rhyme your father taught you. That little one that goes all the way back to when you were just mewling about in your crib."

Te's breath now came in shudders, in shallow gasps as all her muscles seemed to tremble, her bones to vibrate. She could not break from Yun's gaze.

"No," she whispered, but she felt her posture changing, her lungs expanding with a preparatory breath. It was never like this before. She had always thought she had a choice, that she had always been just a weak-willed girl caving in to a mother's pleading. Now it was as if she couldn't resist it.

Sydney started giggling.

"Give us the lullaby, Te," said her mother. "Give us the deep one."

Te shivered all over, cold and hot and sick flooding her in waves.

"Sing for me." It was Yun's voice. He was very far away.

Te opened her mouth and notes fell out:

> H-h-hush little baby, don't say a word.
> Papa's gonna buy you a mockingbird

She heard, somewhere, Sydney inhaling in a deep whoop of exaggerated pleasure.

> And if that mockingbird don't sing,
> Papa's gonna buy you a diamond ring

Her mother's fingers, still lingering on her back, shivered as she drew her own ecstatic breath. White spots began to appear in Te's vision. She felt her heart jump and skip, and sudden pulses of blood into her head shook her balance.

> And if that diamond ring turns brass,
> Papa's gonna buy you a looking glass

Barbara rumbled deep in her chest. Te's vision began to swim, images swirling about like paint in water. Yun's eyes held her, captured her perception, until they were a single constant in a shifting, unstable world.

> And if that l-l-looking g-glass gets broke,
> Papa's gonna b-buy y-y—a b-b-billy g—

Yun smiled broadly, then raised his head to face directly into hers. There was a sudden, sharp stabbing in the middle of her forehead. The words died. Drool slipped from her mouth and her limp body crashed to the living room floor.

She was first aware of her cheek resting on something hard. After a minute, she recognized it as the tiled floor in her mother's kitchen.

She wished she could cry right then. As a little girl, she would cry into her dad's shoulder afterward, and ask him why, and he would hug her and whisper to her that it was all right, and that he and her mother loved her very much, and he would never answer her question.

But that was a long time ago. She was a big girl now. The tears didn't come so easily.

The first thing she did when she regained movement in her arms and legs was to curl up into a fetal ball. But that gave no comfort, either. She was empty, drained, tired as if she hadn't slept a night in her twenty-two years.

She sighed heavily and opened her eyes.

"The coffee is fresh, Miss Evangeline," she heard a voice say. "Sugar and cream and a dash of nutmeg is how dear Sonore tells me you like it."

"Black," Te grumbled. Her head knocked about like an old car engine when she tried to move. "Aah."

"You're ambitious to be trying to get up so soon after." It was Yun, at the counter, his pale gold slacks ticking and smearing together in her vision. "Incredible that you survived, really. And I gather this is not the first time Sonore and her bitch-sisters have listened to you, eh?"

Te cut off a reply, fearing what her stomach would send up if she opened her mouth again. A sudden flush raced into her cheeks. It had just been those three women her entire life, but now Mom had . . . done it in front of a stranger.

For an instant she felt the tears budding in her eyes, but even they fell away into the emptiness. She felt dead. She was dead. She should be dead.

She made it to a sitting position with another shove. Her body collapsed back like a stuffed doll and her head clattered against the cupboards. For an instant, her world was the noise of that strike, echoing deep into her skull, and then it was the cracked skin around her lips and nostrils and the strands of black hair, gummy with dried sweat, sticking to her forehead and face.

She wanted to run and hide—under the bushes out front, in the garden shed behind the lawn-mower bag, back to her decrepit apartment, away to another whole continent. It was the same impulse that always came up.

Wishing never made a difference. She forced her eyes to focus.

Yun was sitting at the little birch-lined kitchen table, reclining slightly in one of the chairs, sipping daintily from a white mug. Another mug sat across the table from him, steaming.

"I understand that chairs are more comfortable," he said.

It slowly occurred to Te that Yun's face was not flushed, that he was not breathing heavily, and his eyes were not drooping in a dreamy, opiumlike glaze. Maybe he didn't . . . didn't *partake*.

He waited silently, nursing his coffee, while she lurched to her feet and thumped into the chair opposite. All the while, she kept glancing at him, finding those cool eyes patient, not looking away in embarrassment. She clawed some of her hair away from her face. Her fingers creaked like rusty hinges; her hair crinkled like dry grass.

"Where's Mom?" she finally asked, through thin, short breaths.

"Sonore and her sisters are in the living room," he said, "prattling on like old women just back from a Chippendale show. Your mother professed her disappointment in your performance—I gather, not for the first time."

Te's hands shook violently as she closed them around the coffee cup. Voices in her emptiness chided that you couldn't fill a hole with a cup of coffee. She felt hollow behind her ribs, right down to the base of her pelvis— nothing could fill that. But another voice in her knew she was dehydrated, and she drank anyway.

Sugar and cream, with nutmeg on top.

Yun took a sip of his own coffee. "I have a feeling you actually like it better that way."

Te looked down again. "Yeah." She sipped her coffee.

Yun passed her a silk handkerchief out of his breast pocket. It shimmered as it moved and was embroidered in the corner with the letter K. Te took it with a skeptical expression. The man was a living anachronism.

"You should wipe up," he said, gesturing with his coffee cup.

Te lazily wiped the dried drool from her chin and the corners of her mouth; her appearance, like so much else, didn't seem to matter right then.

"Did you?" she asked. She might have wanted to sound accusative, but there was nothing behind the words. It didn't matter, beyond idle curiosity.

"Oh, yes," said Yun. "I could not help myself from tasting, as it were. One learns a lot about another through their flavor."

Te couldn't reply. The movement, the few words, had utterly exhausted her. Her head fell, as if in very low gravity, down onto her chest, and then her body was drawn down onto the table. The fingers around the coffee cup twitched and released, too weak to hold on. The cool of polished oak met her cheek, and again the world faded.

She did not sleep, not as normal people sleep. Her next few hours were a jumble of images, sounds, impressions of heat and motion. She felt her heels skidding on the floor. Rough hands struggled her into a coat. There was cold air, night air, sounds of traffic, sounds of bushes rustling.

She opened her eyes to dark scenery, blurring with speed. A seat belt bit tight into her neck and her head bounced with the contours of the road. It was a road she knew—the twisting one switching down the steep hills of grass and sagebrush below Lamont Heights. She smelled leather. Her mouth tasted like dust.

She knew what was coming, and hid from it as long as she could, pressing her forehead against the cold glass of the window. But when she saw the ghostly reflection of her own eyes in the sparse light of the city below, she knew she couldn't hold it in.

She cried. It began as a whimper, a quivering of the lip, a twitching under the eyelids that she could not quiet. In minutes, tears flooded down her cheeks and she was sobbing and choking, smearing her face into the glass, hugging herself with a death grip around her rib cage. She cried until the corners of her mouth hurt from the sobbing, until her skin was bruised where she clutched at herself. She struck her head against the window, hard, and slapped herself over and over on the cheek. There was no sympathetic hand from the driver to stop her, and she didn't want one. Nothing could make it go away.

It was the feeling, the wrongness of being dead inside but still alive, the wrongness that they should do this to her over and over and that no one should care.

She screamed because the emptiness wouldn't go away. She shrieked until her throat burned and her ears stung from reflected sound. Maybe her voice would be ruined and she would never have to sing again. Even then, she knew it wouldn't matter. Not to her mother, not to her aunts.

It would never end. She would never feel right ever again.

She cried and screamed herself into exhaustion. At length, she pulled her face from the window. Her breath came hoarse and shallow. She scrubbed her sopping cheeks with the back of one hand, then the unladylike dribbling under her nose. She wiped it off on her jeans.

The car was her mother's car, and it was deep into downtown by then. Traffic and streetlights, illuminated signs and neon, played outside the window. The night crowds were out: the Freak People in their neo-Victorian dresses and tailcoats, the Strutters in their designer rags, body piercings, and faux-medieval weaponry.

Te sighed, knowing sooner or later she would have to look over and see who was driving, ask where they were going—mundane, everyday things. It was with a certain reluctance that she let her fit pass.

It happened, she said to herself. *There's nothing you can do.*

In the corner of her vision, she saw a pale hand reach for the shifter as the car started up again.

She closed her eyes and sighed, trying to purge the cold shame she felt in her gut. She wasn't ashamed of what had happened at her mother's house. It was the crying she was ashamed of, and the fact that a stranger had witnessed it; she told herself that kind of thinking was stupid and didn't help.

"Where are we going?" she asked.

She could feel Yun smiling beside her.

"Your mother asked me to take you home," he said.

"Did she tell you where?"

"I know the way."

Te ground her teeth a moment. "She usually leaves me in the kitchen, or in the basement."

"Neither very obliging to the needs of the human

back," said Yun. "My preference has always been for some long grass, or loam in the right places, or a down comforter at least. But one must make do, I suppose."

" 'Ours is not to question why,' " Te said, staring out the side at the dark waters of the Sacradown River, as the car rumbled over the bridge.

"Why ask questions?" said Yun. "One only asks questions when one doubts one's own certainty."

"What does that mean?"

"All the answers are around you, Miss Evangeline," said Yun. "If you want to know the future, look in a mirror, or ask a Magic 8 Ball. You, for example, have never asked the question of just what it is that your mother is doing to you when you sing."

The city fled past, as if nervous of staying too long close to the car.

"I asked it all the time," Te said. "No one ever answered me."

"You never asked it of yourself," said Yun. "Sonore has been answering you for a decade or more."

The car clattered onto the potholed streets of Brightontown, bouncing on its suspension.

"So?" said Te finally. "What is she doing?"

"What indeed?" said Yun, with a twitch of an eyebrow.

Te sighed and tried to think past the dark spots in her head. "I've always thought they were ... eating part of me or taking something out of me. I thought it was just a normal thing that people do, until I was twelve or so."

"And what do you think now?"

"It doesn't matter," Te said. "She'll never explain it to me. Dad never did. You won't, will you?"

Yun shook his head.

"Then what's the point of asking the question?"

Yun stopped the car at the end of the little path leading to Te's building. He hadn't even had to look for address numbers.

"You seem to have an affinity for such questions, Miss Evangeline."

Te placed her hand on the door handle. "Here's one, then: where were you this morning around ten?"

"Chewing on a field mouse in someone's garden, upriver," he said. It was Te's turn to raise an eyebrow.

"Suit yourself."

Te pulled the handle.

"I find it curious," Yun said, "that despite your obvious interest in the subject of your relatives' sound fetish, you have yet to ask the most interesting question of all."

Te already had the door open. She turned and looked back into Yun's gray eyes.

"Why is it," he continued, "that your mother may feast of you, but you may not do the same to her?"

Te placed one foot out on the slick, cracked sidewalk, making sure her leg would hold her before committing.

"Just one of those things," she said. "She can do it and I can't."

"Or she knows how to do it and you don't."

"Sure, whatever." Te was up, steady on her feet, and shutting the door before she really heard the words. She stopped. "Wait. What do you mean?"

Yun smiled at her. "That all things change, Miss Evangeline, given an opportunity and a little effort. Opportunities are my purview. Effort is yours. Good night."

And he was off. As Te watched the car go, she felt faint again. Her entire life all she had told herself was that there was nothing she could do. It's what her dad had said; it's what her mom had said. It was how she got through it. There was nothing she could do.

Had Yun just said there was?

She stood, paralyzed and wondering, on the curb, minute after long minute, until the wet snow settling on her hair reminded her to head inside.

The bottle shattered in Lester's spasming fingers. He watched his hand shake until all the sharp pieces of glass had dropped out onto the floor.

That was his last bottle. There was no more unless he sent someone to get some, and the butcher's was probably closed. God, what time was it? No clocks, no daylight. Where were his Strutters? Where were his little slaves? Why weren't they here?

He cried out, but his words were a drunken slur. How much had he had? The table was littered with empty bottles and spilled blood, along with coke, needles, grass. He couldn't remember. There was only one thing in the whole of his mind.

Yun was free. Yun was free and he was going to die.

His legs failed him when he tried to get up, and he found himself sprawled on the floor, bottles spilled on the floor beside him. The room spun. The light from the lamp splashed across the ceiling like fluorescent water.

I'm going to die, he thought.

His little slaves told him that he couldn't die, told him that he was immortal and that only sunlight or a stake through the heart could kill him.

He laughed out loud at that. "Couldn't die." They were just a bunch of stupid kids. They didn't know.

They didn't know Yun. They didn't know the things he could let loose.

It was too much to think about. Lester rolled over onto his stomach, fighting nausea. Out of habit he snorted some of the powder on the floor. His nose, raw inside, stung for a second before the rush started. It was just a little chill, nowhere near what it used to be when he was human.

It brought his vision back a little, and there were his Strutters, the teenage devotees who rotated in and out of his life, slumped on the couches and the chairs, unmoving.

"Fuck! You guys," he said, shouted, spat as drool slid down his chin, "gemme some blood. Gemme some more."

He broke a corner off the table getting to his knees. He grabbed the leg of the nearest kid and shook it.

"Get up!" he screamed. Why was no one moving? Why was no one groveling or serving him?

Then he laughed because it was so stupid to be worrying about that when he was about to die.

He crawled to the nearest kid and pulled her by the shoulder until she flopped forward. She had no face—no eyes, no nose, no mouth, just a featureless stretch of skin.

He laughed at that, too, because he was terrified.

"Ah, the merriment of the forty-year-old teenager."

Lester turned to the door and laughed harder, and cried tears of blood.

Yun shut the door softly behind him.

"You can't kill me," Lester shouted. "I can't die. They said so." He pointed to all his Strutters, his little slaves, all slumped on their couches or patches of floor, faceless and still.

"Much to your surprise and mine, Lester, I did not come here to kill you," Yun said.

"Bullsh-shit-t-t-t . . . ," Lester stammered. He staggered up, grabbing a little battle-ax from the table. "Bullshit!"

Yun stood with his hands folded in front of him, placid and smiling. In the scant light of the room, his gold and white clothes seemed to glow. He took two steps forward, polished shoes clicking on the floorboards.

"I have ever only one motivation, Lester," he said. "I come to grant your wish."

Lester took a swing at him, lightning fast with all the power of his inhuman muscles. He missed. The ax's head tore off with the momentum, and for a second he just stared at the broken haft.

"It is a fake, remember," said Yun. "Like so many things in this room."

Yun was close, now, in front of him, beside him, behind him. Yun's voice came from everywhere; Yun's eyes looked into him from every direction.

"You cannot kill me with it and you do not wish to, Lester. Your wish is only for yourself, as it has always been, from the time you were a living man. I know your wish."

Lester felt the soothing, pleasuring touch of Yun against his mind. It was a rush like no other, a field of white opening in his consciousness, washing him, purifying him, making him forget.

"You've waited for this, haven't you?" Yun said, the words of a summer's wind. "You've tried to fill it with your drugs and with these little people that worship you. But adoration is not what you wish for, Lester. Even sensation is not what you wish for. Even pleasure."

The white was in him, the bliss, and Yun's voice was a tremor in perfection.

"You wish yourself obliterated."

Lester cried out and sank to his knees. Yes, *God*, yes, it was what he wanted. When that feeling touched him, pains old and deep vanished.

"No!" he screamed, and lashed out with his claws. The white pleasure blotted his vision, but he felt his nails shred fabric and then something meaty and wet.

The pleasure didn't stop, and he was so happy that he cried for joy. The white was in him now, a well of light stretching deep inside, from his flittering conscious mind to his core. The pleasure filled the whole depth of him.

With some inner eye, he saw Yun standing in that light, nine white-tipped, golden tails waving behind him.

"It was the rapture of your bite that made these little people your slaves, Lester," Yun said. "Are you my slave now? Are you slave to my rapture?"

"Yes," Lester muttered between quivering lips. "Yes."

He felt Yun's real hand on his real jaw. He felt Yun's claws in his brain.

"I have much to do and much arranging of things. There are certain wishes I am here for, Lester, and certain things for which I need your obedience. Do I have it, Lester?"

Yun's fingers twisted, and the white became everything, obliterating all self, all thought and sound. There was no room, no Yun, no Lester.

"You will go to the moot tonight."

"Yes," Lester breathed.

"And when the Maskim comes, you will open the door for it."

"Yes."

"And then you will do nothing but listen."

"Yes!"

"Ah, that's good."

Lester's skin prickled as Yun pulled his claws out, and then Lester was on the floor, on his back, blood running down his face. His skin tingled. His bones vibrated. His breath came deep and pure. It was like sunshine again, sunshine on his face after a decade in the dark.

Yun's voice floated in from miles away. "You know me, Lester, for I am a granter of wishes. You will have what you most desire."

Lester washed away in sensation.

When he awoke, his Strutters were all around him, swarming up and down, talking to him. He opened his eyes and he saw some of them crying for him, crying tears of salty water, for they were only human.

"I'm alive," Lester said to them. "I'm alive again."

And he grabbed the nearest and sank his fangs into her neck. The rest cheered as fresh blood splattered on the floor.

Chapter 4

The Man in the Empty Chair

It's a cold night and I'm shivering in the wind. Only Babu is here with me. His face is lined with worry and he fiddles with his hands. He's wondering whether the others will show up.

We're on the hill, on the one hill around this valley that has no name. We are in the bowl-shaped gully halfway up its height, beneath the sacred tree, a dead and lightning-split pine. The ground is bare clay—against all logic, still dry and cracked despite the heavy rains. Tonight, the sky is clear, as it always is on the night of a moot. The moon is still hidden.

I'm shuffling my deck when King arrives. Dead two years, of heart disease—no one saw it coming and only the rest of our group were at his funeral. He walks into the bowl on his artificial feet that look like cloven hooves, sweeping low with each step. Babu and I both see him, for though he's dead and would normally go unseen, there are no secrets in the Sacred Grove.

King rarely speaks, and he does not speak now. He simply takes his place at the edge of the dry ground, folds his arms over, and stares at us.

I draw a card for him and look at it, hidden, in my palm. It is The Hermit, a card showing a tall, bent, and lonely man with a lantern, alone in the dark.

The next to appear is Munin, our mechanical expert. Munin comes with goggles rimmed in tinfoil and a net of wires woven into his hair to keep the aliens from reading his thoughts, and at his side is his trusty weapon, a ray gun made of plastic that lights up and makes sound when the trigger is pulled. It is the only thing he trusts to protect him.

Munin and Babu exchange pleasantries. The philosophical gulf between them yawns wide in their empty smiles and tight handshake.

I draw a card for Munin, and am not surprised to draw the ten of wands, showing a young man struggling to hold together a brace of ten sticks.

We wait in silence a time. The wind tears into me, through the thin fabric of my dress, and scrapes over my skin. I wish for a moment that I'd brought a coat, the thick black and pink ski jacket that I've passed over and over again in the mall, and have never bought. I can't buy those kinds of things. They're not who I am, no matter how much I might want them.

I draw a card for myself and shuffle it back into the deck without looking at it.

No one else will show. The cards have told me this much, so when Lester lurches over the rise, I am more surprised than anyone. Babu smiles with some relief and our resident vampire smiles back, displaying a small facial tick. He takes his place at the edge of the circle.

And that's all. Five of us, left from eleven, and one of those already dead. The rest, gone to one end or another—mundane as Babu's brother, locked in the asylum, horrific as Sanjay's bloody end—or Robert's. At the memory of Rob, I feel sickness in my gut, and not for the first time.

I forget to draw a card for Lester.

Babu is speaking.

"Thanks for coming, everybody."

Munin cuts in right away, his shrill voice echoing across the bowl.

"Where is the Man, Babu?" he said. "Why did he get you to call the moot and not the girl?"

The girl is me. I am the one the Man always comes to.

"The Man didn't call the moot," Babu says. "I did."

King's eyes narrow. Munin starts as if he's been electrified.

"We do not work for you, Babu," he says. "Are we to expect him tonight?"

"No," says Babu, and waits. He has anticipated this.

"Are you claiming the position, then?" Munin asks. "Has the Man moved on to become Warden and appointed you in his place?"

"No," Babu says again.

Munin's eyes narrow behind his dark lenses.

"Then you had better have a very good reason for calling us," Munin says, crossing his arms. "The hour is not favorable for this thing."

Babu hisses a breath of smoke out between closed teeth. "Some of you already know this. Yun is free again. He escaped this morning."

King lowers his head and broods. Munin starts fiddling with his fingers.

"And Sanjay?" Munin asks.

"Dead." Babu waits a moment before speaking again,

letting the cigarette's smoke curl up around his nose and brows. "I believe the Man is responsible."

"Unlikely," Munin says. King spits onto the sacred soil, where the liquid evaporates, never having been real in the first place. Even Lester, in my experience rarely sober enough to follow basic conversation, looks shaken and paler than usual.

King speaks, his spectral voice resonating all across the bowl, and shimmering like the overtones of a gong. "No," he says.

"I agree," says Munin. "We have worked for him for years—decades, even. It defies logic and all of my predictions that he would betray us so. You have been with him longer than any of us. How can you say this thing?"

Babu stands unfazed, a dark shadow against a darker sky. This is the Babu I remember, from before Robert died.

"Sanjay tried to tell me," Babu says. "I think he knew it."

"What, *exactly*, did he say?" Munin asks. Babu tells him. The ground rumbles under King's hooves, resonating with his indignation.

I am shuffling my cards again. I cut the deck and peek at one to see how this will play out: the eight of cups, showing a man walking away from a mound of golden goblets. Does it mean the moot is going to fail?

"That?" Munin says. "It may have been his dying brain. It may have been several sentences started but not finished, and unrelated. If I knew the timing of the words, I could calculate it with certainty. Why must you interpret that alone to mean that the Man has turned on us?"

Babu holds up a finger. "O'Shae," he says. He holds

up another. "Martin." Then he holds up one more for each comrade lost. "Julia. Robert. King."

King shifts on his hooves, and his threadbare feathered headdress waves in a breeze that the living cannot feel.

"Why do you think you had that heart attack, King?" Babu says. "Why couldn't your magic save you?"

King's eyes are granite. Babu grinds his cigarette down between thumb and forefinger.

"I know you tried it," Babu says, and there's silence for a moment.

Surprisingly, Lester is the next to speak. "It . . . um . . . It doesn't make sense, Babu," he says, long-nailed fingers clutching at nothing. "Why would the Man want to turn Yun loose? After what it took to put him away . . ."

"I don't know yet," Babu answers.

The rest shuffle. Munin looks fit to explode, Lester to curl up into a ball and vanish.

I speak quietly into the still air. "Does that matter so much? It doesn't change the fact that the Kitsune is out. It doesn't change the fact that he's probably going to start opening cages."

I look up at each of them, matching gazes, and seeing the thoughts behind them. I think Babu is surprised that I am advocating this, assuming me to be on the side of the Man. Well, I have my orders. "We don't even know why he came here in the first place, but it was enough to worry the Man, and that takes a lot."

"Fine," says Munin. "Conceded. But we should bring the Man into it. We need more resources. We need a vessel. We need a suppressor. Most of all, we need a binder, yes?"

"Don't look at me, man," says Lester. No one had looked at him. Munin and King are eyeing me.

I just shake my head.

"Not me," I say, and I mean it. "The Old Powers are dead in me. I'm just a medium."

"Robert," King says, and the fading in the posture of all these men shows they know it, too.

Robert had been our binder. It was Rob who had the power that all of us lacked. He had a spark, a well of pure creative genius that no one could match. I remember seeing it in his eyes, in that little catch of breath when inspiration hit him. Why does that memory keep coming back—his smile, his little smile on our first morning together—no, I *refuse* to remember it. It was duty. I am Iron. I am a thousand years without a heart. The tears cease before they begin, but my hands are shaking.

"I can find us a vessel," Munin says. "I shall calculate probabilities from the community here. We will need your brother as suppressor."

Babu nods. I can see the deep scars when he thinks of his kin. "I know."

"A binder, I cannot find. I ran the numbers when Robert died, and they do not stack for any of us, not against the Kitsune."

"Well, we don't have Rob," Babu snaps. He has another cigarette out—his third of the moot. He lights it with a match. "Any suggestions?"

"Could the Man do it himself?" Lester asks.

"We're not going to tell him," Babu growls.

"But . . ."

"No! Not until we know more about the situation." Lester shrinks back.

"Got a card for us?" Babu asks me.

I've already shuffled. My finger is already on the card we need. I pull it and show it faceup: the eight of swords, a woman bound and blindfolded in a field of swords thrust into the earth.

Inverted. It shouldn't be inverted. Not from what the Man told me.

"Whom does it picture?" Munin says.

I swallow my uncertainty and turn an unblinking gaze on Babu. Iron is in my expression. "You know who."

Babu stares a moment at the card, sucking and puffing.

"Fuck."

"Who is it?" Lester asks.

"The comical girl," I answer. "The happy yet estranged girl. Robert's daughter."

Munin nods sagely. "I will run her numbers. Shall you bring her in, Angrel? Girl talk and such?"

"Girl talk?" I laugh at that.

"I'll bring her," says Babu. "She's my responsibility, anyway."

"Settled, then," Munin says, and Lester and King nod in agreement. "I will round up the gear. Lester, do you want to open the old safe house?"

Lester nods meekly.

"King will be backup suppressor, yes?"

The ghost glares down at the little wild-haired man, but nods grimly a second later.

Lester speaks to Babu. "Won't we need your brother?"

Stillness falls again, as Babu's big shoulders settle back and he stares down at the cringing vampire across the bowl. "Not now."

"Oh, no," Munin says. "His suppression is superior to all of ours."

I speak quietly, sidelong.

"We'll need him eventually, Babu."

He regards the spent butt of his cigarette. "I know. But I won't be calling him out until we're ready. He's no use to us during setup, anyway."

Babu tosses the butt down onto the open clay. It will be gone when we return, though who cleans the ground here is unknown to us. "We'll meet at the safe house, then," Babu says. "Les, you can have it open by tomorrow?"

"Uh . . . yeah. Don't worry about it."

"Good. See you all then."

The moot ends. King shimmers and fades away. Munin departs with that peculiar expression on his face that means he's calculating in his head. Lester gives us all a strange look. It's one I can't read, but that is not unusual for Lester; it may be the result of his drugs or his natural dullness, and I ignore it.

Then he is gone, too, and it is just Babu and I alone on the hill, under the sacred tree.

"Munin will probably inform the Man," I say.

He smiles. "You didn't beat him to it?"

It would not surprise me if Babu knew what I had and hadn't told the Man, but I look into his face and I wonder. Maybe he's trying to draw me out. This is a new deviousness in Babu I haven't seen before.

"You asked me not to tell him," I say, "So I haven't."

"And if he already knew, you wouldn't have to," Babu replies. There is no accusation in his voice. He is looking up at the stars, lost in an inner world.

I smile because I know he's about to open to me. All men do, even those who hate me. They always have, through the thousand lifetimes I've walked this earth.

"Rob came to see me the night before he died," the

big man says. "He told me to take care of Te, and to never, ever, let her become part of what we do."

I nod, and my sympathy may be real. "He said once that all he wanted was for her to live a normal life. He must have known it wouldn't work out."

My little white fingers are on his arm, comforting, a surprise for both of us, I think.

Babu looks down at me, big dark eyes under a heavy brow. "I should have got her right out of the city."

"She can't leave, any more than any of us can."

"She doesn't work for *him*."

"The Man in the Empty Chair is a prison keeper, remember. Some of us are guards and some of us are prisoners, but all of us are inside the walls."

Babu coldly withdraws his arm from my hand. My fingers curl in on themselves, as if grasping for the warmth they felt. I get them busy shuffling my deck.

He walks off slowly, smoking his fourth cigarette of the hour.

I am alone in the Sacred Grove. I stand and wait, the only sound the pattering of my deck.

My deck is a Rider-Waite, printed in 1909 and originally owned by a stupid old woman who had dabbled just enough to bring a hex on her whole family, but not enough to know how to get rid of it. The cards are all original, all well-worn and used many, many times. Only one of them is different. I had it made myself, from my own design, when I was ten and first moved to St. Ives. My shuffling brings this card to the top of the deck, where I draw it and hold it before me, so that the shadows of the dead branches above fall across it.

Blank. No number, no image. It has ever represented only one person.

There is sound behind me, the soft splintering of dry pine needles breaking beneath leather-soled shoes, the soft swish of a long coat brushing the ground.

Emptiness fills me. I feel nothing. My thoughts fall away in a terrifying and blissful release. I turn on my sandaled feet, floating on my limbs as if in water.

I bow my head to the Man in the Empty Chair.

Chapter 5

The In-Between Day

Jul. 14, 1986 [Kitsune Case]—Fire went out. Minimal damage to safe house. Found subject Marshall Willis on the scene (see attached). History of pyromania. Must have been his wish at the time. As always, Kitsune left no trail. Set of paw prints on concrete ends after two feet. Angrel and Munin tracking. Rob looking bad. Hasn't slept, I think. Neither have I.

Te jolted awake at the first knock on the door. She'd fallen asleep reading Babu's casebook, and now loose pages of it lay scattered across the bed. Her limbs protested mightily as she tried to move them.

She rubbed her eyes. *Stupid dreams.*

Other people dreamed about sex or showing up late to work. Te dreamed of half-seen monsters, stalking through weird, moonlit landscapes. And caves—there was always a cave or a dark doorway or something, usually near the end. She'd never dreamed of anything else, as far back as she could remember. Cursing, she groped blindly over the edge of her bed for her paper and charcoal—sometimes drawing the things helped get them out of her head in the morning.

The knock again.

"What!" she snapped.

"Te?" It was Jack Jr.'s warbling baritone.

"Yeah?" said Te, trying to rub some feeling back into the arm she'd been sleeping on.

"Are you awake?"

Te rolled her eyes, though no one could see her do it. "What do you think?" She glanced quickly around the room to make sure there was no underwear lying out or anything. "Come in. It's not locked."

Jack quietly turned the handle and slid inside, moving as if he were carrying a wineglass on his head.

"Jack, it's all right; I was up," Te lied. "What time is it?"

"Six-ish."

Te stretched out a bit. Her skin felt icky; she'd slept in her clothes. "Isn't that a little early for teenagers?"

Jack shrugged and offered no answer. He walked over to the bed and slouched, his hands deep in the pockets of his cargoes. "What's that?"

Te tried to sweep the pages back into the casebook. The book was just a large ring binder that was overfull and didn't close properly. Luckily, the pages had just slid out and hadn't gotten too much out of order.

"Case histories," she said. "Babu's old cases. Files and stuff."

"Doin' homework?" He squatted down beside the bed, running his magnified eyes over the pages closest.

"Something like that," Te said. "Our case yesterday had something to do with my dad. And there's this name—Kitsune. It, uh, came up yesterday a couple of times and I'm reading up on it. You know Babu writes down everything we do? He writes bios on all our contacts and clients and witnesses. It's pretty mundane stuff—interviews and phone records, raps and lights flickering from our paranormal jobs. That kind of thing."

"That's normal?" said Jack, with a smile.

Te gave him a look, then flipped through a few more pages, to one she'd dog-eared last night. "But any of these cases where he mentions my dad, he always talks about fugitives and suspects and escapees."

"Sounds like cop lingo."

Te pointed to an entry. " 'May 9, 1985—Call at 4:15 p.m. Moot after sundown. Assignment given to Rob, O'Shae, and me. Escort. Prisoner coming in through the perimeter at dawn tomorrow (5:45 a.m.). Worked out details of hand-off. O'Shae will be suppressor. Rob, binder. Myself, backup suppression. Subject: Maskim. Term unknown. Research pending.' "

"Cool," said Jack. "What's it mean?"

"Don't know." Te scanned down the rest of the page with her finger.

" 'May 10, 1985—Little sleep. No food as per Man's instructions. Met Rob and O'Shae at perimeter (I 6 exit) 5:00 a.m. for morning prayer (Catholic). Prisoner (Maskim) sighted 5:37 a.m. Driven by external team up to the perimeter, with keeper—unknown individual, male, cloven hooves (look prosthetic), feathers in hair (see attached).' "

"Have you asked Babu about it?"

Te looked up from the page. "He doesn't tell me anything. I don't think he wants me to know."

"But he gave you the book?"

It was Te's turn to squirm a bit. "Not as such."

Jack smiled. His eyebrows went up. "Oh, yeah?"

Te felt an uncomfortable adult-type impulse. "Um ... Stealing is wrong."

Jack whistled his admiration. Te smirked at him.

She hefted the book a bit and closed it. Then she sat back and drew her knees up.

"Dad was never home," she said. "He was always off on"—she made quotation mark symbols with her fingers—" 'business trips,' for days at a time. I always thought he was cheating on Mom."

She stared down at the worn black of the casebook and all its unspoken promises.

"But maybe not."

"I wish my dad would go away for days at a time," Jack said. "He just sits on the couch and watches TV and complains. Sometimes Mom says she's gonna hit him with a rolling pin if he doesn't get a job."

"How very domestic of her." Te looked the kid over. His eyes were roaming all over the room, lingering on some of Te's more grotesque charcoal drawings, some copied from horror movies, but most the result of frantic morning scribblings. He looked totally comfortable, in his way, and comfortable with her in all her weirdness.

Huh.

"Doing anything today?" she asked.

"School."

"You going?"

Jack shrugged.

"I'm gonna do some research," said Te, tapping the casebook. "Wanna come?"

"Okay."

"All right," Te said, feeling better with that answer than she expected. "I've just gotta have a shower. Then we'll head."

"Are we taking your piece?"

Oh, yeah. Te looked over at the ugly black piece of metal. Why would Babu give it to her—why would he insist she keep it—if there wasn't something dangerous around to use it on?

That sent a whole new kind of shudder up and down Te's spine. "He's free," the dying man had said. Was this "Kitsune" dangerous enough that she had to take this gun home with her?

Jesus, what's going on?

"Maybe . . ." Her mouth went dry just saying it. "Maybe we should."

"Cool," said Jack. "Better wear a bigger coat. You know, like a trench coat or something."

She hadn't thought of that. "Yeah, I guess."

Jack stood up, waiting expectantly.

Te pointed to the door.

"I'll see you around front in a few minutes."

Jack stared at her, uncomprehending.

"Shower," she said. "Out front. Few minutes."

"Oh, yeah. Sorry." He slunk out the door.

She opened the casebook a crack and flipped through to the first dog-eared page, taking a minute to figure out where to go first.

Jul. 17, 1986 [Kitsune Case]—Eight bodies found in park (see attached, clipping). Aviary empty. Bird free. Tracked to 1616 Rosedale. Robert already on scene. Informs me Bird holed up in flower shop. Proprietor Ms. Gibbledy (Gibbley?) witness inter-

view (see attached—transcript). Effected capture.
No casualties.

* * *

They stepped off the bus on the north shore at Rose-dale Street. The casebook was starting to get enor-mously heavy. It had tired Te's arm holding it yesterday, so she'd put it in a shoulder bag before heading out, only to find the strap biting into her shoulder more painful than the strain of holding the thing in one arm. The gun was packed with it.

"Flower shop," she said to herself.

Jack trailed after her as she walked up the street, searching for the address. He was walking with a little pickup in his stride.

She halted in front of the flower shop in the middle of a little series of neighborhood stores selling candy bars and Greek food. The yellow and white awning was so dirty as to be almost gray, and there was a large display of dead flowers on shelves outside the windows.

Jack idly fingered one of the dry roses, which fell apart.

"Is this one of those art things?" he asked.

"I don't think so." Through the big front window, Te saw into a studio decked in more dry flowers and walls the most hideous shade of orange she'd ever seen.

"So, what are you gonna ask them?" Jack said.

I knew I'd forget something, Te thought.

"I'll improvise." She opened the door and went in.

A little bell dinged. To her surprise, some of the plants inside were still alive, or perhaps it was just lichen growing on the sagging leaves. Dust and fibers in the air tickled Te's nose.

"Maybe the Freak People buy them," Jack said. "They're weird like that."

"Yeah, maybe." Te dinged the bell on the counter.

"Be there in a second," came a cracking voice from the back room.

Te waited. The voice continued.

"Oh, bother."

A very little old lady tottered out of the back, pushing aside the stiff tweed curtain.

"Sorry for that—old knees, you know. What can I do for you? Want to buy some flowers?"

Te and Jack shared a look. The woman had no eyes.

Te swallowed and dove in. "I'm with Cherian Investigations, ma'am. Doing some follow-up on a case here about six years ago." Te found herself offering a business card. Of course, the blind woman didn't know this, so Te hastily put it back in her pocket. "Are you Ms. Gibbledy? Gibbley?"

"Peterborough," said the lady. "But close enough." Little muscles twitched at the back of her empty sockets. "Cherian. He was the Negro fellow, was he? Sounded like it, anyway."

"That's right," said Te. She inhaled deeply, not quite ready to hear it; not quite ready to know this dad she'd never met. But, well . . . "And there was another man, a Robert Evangeline?"

"Oh, yes," she said. "Charming fellow. Good jokes. Sounded like he would have been a catch in younger days, you know?" She made suggestive motions with her eyebrows. "Now, you want roses? Course not. Should be a handsome young man buying *you* roses."

Te swallowed hard. She wasn't ready. Her jaw moved without sound.

Jack nudged her in the ribs. She cleared her throat and spilled ahead:

"Can you tell me why they were here?" she asked. "I mean . . . you know, they do a lot of weird kinda work and I thought there might have been . . . I just wanted to get a few details about the . . ."

The lady smiled and reached out toward Te's arm. Te drew back as she saw that the woman also had no fingernails, just lumps of scar tissue. The hand fell short and probed around a bit as the old lady spoke.

"Marvelous," she said. "Best day of my whole life. I knew He heard me. Knew He'd answer my prayers."

Her hand stopped questing and went to her face to wipe away a tear that never appeared.

"I met an angel," she said. "Oh, such a beautiful angel."

Te looked again to Jack, who just shrugged and hung around a few steps back in one of the aisles.

"An angel?" Te asked.

"Wanted to eat the flowers," she said. "Wanted to eat beautiful things." She smiled broadly as her head tilted randomly back and forth. "Said I had beautiful eyes. Said I had beautiful hands." She sniffed. "It got right mad when the men showed up, even when that charming Robert man was speaking to it. Didn't like the other fellow much—said it wouldn't eat him."

By now, Te had unconsciouly backed up until she was touching the closest shelf. The little woman bobbed her head back and forth.

"Suppose it's good they got rid of it," she said. "Can't have too much happiness, can you?" She sighed contentedly and fell silent.

"Pardon me, ma'am," said Te. "How did they get rid of it?"

"The nice Robert man talked to it," said the old

woman. "What a charming voice he had. Talked it down like talking a kitty out of a tree. Don't know how they got it out of here, though. It was awful big." She rubbed her wrinkled chin. "Come to think of it, I wonder how it got in. Maybe you want something potted? Got some orchids in the back."

"No," said Te. "I'm just wanting to get some information about . . ."

"I am sorry, dear," the lady cut in. "You sound nice, but if you're not buying, then you'll have to leave. I have to be available for my customers."

Te and Jack glanced at the empty store.

Te decided to point that out, and a minute later they found themselves thrown out in the street.

"So," Jack said slowly, "your dad was an angel hunter?"

Te wiped a thin sheen of sweat from her forehead. "Or a bird catcher, maybe."

"I know a guy at school who saw a man-eating cow in Darktown once," said Jack. "Do you think that lady got her eyes pecked out?"

"I don't know," said Te. "The entry mentions the aviary. That's in the park."

"Oh." Jack licked the inside of his cheek.

"What?"

"Well"—he shuffled his feet—"you know there's usually Freak People in the park."

Te smiled in sympathy. "I don't like them, either."

Jul. 12, 1986 [Kitsune Case]—General report: see clippings (attached). Eighteen inexplicable deaths reported in paper. Checked Bird, cage still locked, though prisoner agitated. Said it would use me as bedding, rather than eat me. Pretty.

To read the editorials in the paper, one would think that Darktown was the bowels of the earth. In Te's opinion, Darktown wasn't nearly as bad as the park. True, the park had beautiful cobblestone paths along the riverbank, vast green lawns, elegant, drooping willows, and well-maintained flower beds that somehow bloomed even in the winter. As parks went, it was a gem.

But no sane person in St. Ives went to the park. Ever.

Except, today, Te and Jack.

It was never really clear to Te why the park was so shunned. It was the main hangout of the Freak People, and that was bothersome in itself, but not enough to keep the park free from the lunchtime crowds and the elderly. There was something about it being *too* cheerful, as if the whole place shouldn't be there at all, and that something unspecified but unvaryingly terrible would happen to you if you dared to go in. Standing there on the sidewalk of Second Avenue, slowly plucking up her courage, Te couldn't shake that feeling.

A well-kept hedge surrounded the park, isolating it from downtown and the rest of the civilized world. The main entrance was a wrought-iron archway grown over with flowering clematis.

They lingered a long time on the sidewalk.

"In, to the aviary," Te said, "and back out. We're just checking for a big bird that looks like an angel, and if there's a keeper or something, we talk to him."

"Right," said Jack.

"Good."

Te took a step. Jack followed.

The arch passed over their heads and they were in a Victorian Eden.

The path immediately changed from concrete to cobblestones and was flanked by lamps resembling gas-lights. Every flower bed and setting had its own little cu-pid. The sun seemed to dull, the light to get more gray than yellow. The air was heavier in Te's lungs—textured, gritty.

The aviary was down at the river and hung out over the water. Te had seen it before from the north shore. She'd never been there.

Just through the arch, they came to a broad lawn hedged in on all sides. Scattered about the open space stood a dozen or so of the youth gang called the Freak People—teenagers dressed in the latest fashions of 1894. The boys wore top hats, coats and suits, slacks and wing-tips; the girls, flared dresses and bustles, corsets to crunch their waists, elaborate hats on their heads, and twisted lace parasols over their shoulders. The colors were gray and cream, the clothes uniformly faded and full of moth holes. The people strolled about amiably, talking in light, formal conversation, with the men puffing their chests and the women giggling at any stupid thing.

"Fine day," said a teenaged boy as Te and Jack slipped by. "Reminds me of my time along the Rhine. Beautiful country, that, but lacking charm, what with the dearth of English country girls to be found, eh?"

"Oh, do go on," giggled his teenage companion.

The papers seemed to think the Freak People were just a social club of some kind. They didn't call them Freak People, of course. It had started years ago—teenagers occasionally walking off in a daze from work or school and coming down here to parade around in costume. Te remembered it happening when she was in middle school—and not to the weird outcast kids, but the pretty, popular girls and the fit jocks who shouldn't even know what "Victorian" meant. Parents and teachers seemed to think it was charming, or at least a good way to keep the youth out of trouble. Kids just didn't talk about it because it frightened them too much. It was like a disease that could strike anyone, at any time.

Middle school. That would have been around 1986 wouldn't it?

The path wound quickly out of the common area and into a series of small gardens blocked off by tall hedges, where the flowers were just coming into bloom . . . at the beginning of November.

"That was Jason," Jack said, thumbing back at the couple. "He used to be in my math class. No one's really noticed he's missing."

Jack brooded for a moment.

"Actually," he continued, "I only have, like, fifteen people left in my math class."

Te had an annoying impulse to say something adult and reassuring.

"Maybe they're all playing hookey," she said, with an attempt at a smile. "I hear kids do that sometimes."

Jack blinked at her and said nothing.

Each garden led to another, each with a slightly different color palette and high hedges blocking out the surrounding area. Even the sun seemed to come from different directions whenever they moved to the next garden. They passed more Freak People as they went, ignoring them, avoiding eye contact, not answering when addressed with a "How'd you do?" or "Fine day, don't you agree?" When they had traveled what Te figured was at least five times the actual length of the park without coming back to some place they recognized, Te stopped them for a rest.

They were lost—lost in a stretch of land two hundred yards wide with a river on one side and a concrete street on the other.

"I told you I didn't want to come here," said Jack, going up on his toes to try to look over the hedge.

Te hauled the casebook out of her shoulder bag and flipped through it. She found a loose sheet of paper with scribbled notes on the park.

> *Profile Entry: Park. Area of circular logic (Munin's term). Disorientation Manifest (Rob's term). "Cursed hole of madness" (King's term). Bird's influence suspected—environmental shaping documented by external teams. Attempted mapping Apr 15, 1993, without success (see map attempt, attached). Eight hours lost in gardens. Heard horses' hooves much of the time. Followed sound out.*

The map attempt showed the entrance, the river, and the closest street. Apparently Babu's route had taken him into the little maze gardens as well. He had them mapped as overlapping the street and going far into downtown, with a little "screw it" penciled in where the map petered out.

"There we go, then," said Te. She lifted her head and heard horses' hooves clattering at a slow walk.

Jack looked up, hearing them, too. "They're just over here," he said.

They left the little garden through one of the archways cut into the hedges. On the other side, the gardens ended, replaced by a stretch of shaded lawn and a walking path that paralleled the riverbank. The trees swayed in a warm, gentle breeze, and the water sparkled in the sunlight.

"Guess we just gave up one garden too early," said Jack.

Te said nothing, trying to ignore the vague, queasy feeling that had been building up since they'd walked in here. She glanced up the path, to where a horse came lazily clomping beneath the leaves, pulling an old-fashioned hansom cab.

"Oooookay," she said. Jack nodded in sympathetic bewilderment.

"Driver!" came a gruff voice from the cab. "I say, ol' bean, rein that creature in, will you?"

The driver, a lanky adolescent, sank into a black tailcoat four sizes too large, pulled smartly back on the reins and guided the horse to a stop. The animal had large worn patches all over its back, and shone with perspiration. The cab had once been black, she guessed, but now the paint was flaking and faded.

"Don't talk to anyone," Te said. Jack nodded.

The cab's door opened. A fat, middle-aged man in a bowler hat, vest, and tailcoat leaned out. The man's mustache overpowered all his other facial features.

"Ho, there," he said, jolly and red cheeked with skin the color of dry cement and black, black circles under his eyes. "I say, my dear, what the devil is such a lovely young lady doing walking about on a day like this? Why, the weather is perfectly dreadful!"

Jack squinted questioningly up at the sun. Te squirmed inwardly for a few seconds. She couldn't just not answer the man. He was looking right at her. He was getting out of the cab, stepping over, taking her hand in a gentlemanly fashion. It was all so proper.

"My word—at the risk of being brazen—you are *stunning*, madam," he said. He kissed the back of her hand. His lips were like rocks scraping on her skin, and his mustache was like a wire brush. Only at that touch did she finally snap out of it and yank her hand away.

"Stop it!" she said reflexively. He seemed completely unperturbed and rocked back on his heels, grinning, thumbs stuck into his vest pockets.

"Martin's the name," he said, "Corwinder Martin, Esquire. I don't believe I've had the pleasure." He gestured for her to give her own name.

She almost did. It just seemed the thing to do, the right response. Te swallowed hard. *Goddamn Freak People. Don't get involved. In and out, remember?*

"Look, we're just trying to get to the aviary," she said, hand up between them like a shield.

He gave her a knowing wink.

"Following in Father's footsteps, are we?" he said. "Not to worry. Old Bird is still in her coop. I'd have let her out ages ago, of course, if I'd been trusted with the key. Hard spot between me and him, that always was."

Te blinked in shock.

"How do you know who I am?"

"I knew your father briefly, all too briefly," he said, removing his hat and placing it over his heart. His head was bald, and spotted with worn, dead patches like the horse. "I've never met his equal in all my days and I daresay I don't expect to." The man replaced his hat. "And you . . . well. Your father never failed to show me your latest school photograph when it came in. You've grown into a fine young lady."

She felt Jack tugging at her sleeve.

"Don't talk to them, remember?" he whispered.

Jack was right to be cautious—in, take a look, get out—but this man, if he knew even a little . . .

"How did you know him?" Te asked the man.

He frowned at her question, then brightened into an absurdly cheerful grin. "Why, Miss Evangeline, this is no manner of day to have our chat on the street, eh? Come, I'll have my driver take us where you need to go."

He turned back to his carriage and held the door for her.

"Plenty of room for all, you and your friend, there. What's your name, son?"

And there *was* room. Instead of a two-seater hansom cab, the horse was now hauling a four-wheeled, white, open-topped carriage. A lady sat in one of the seats, dressed in a gray dress with dirty lace trim.

Te sucked in a breath. Jack was dragging hard at her sleeve now.

"Let's go. Now."

She shook him off.

"One moment, if you please," she said. *If you please?*

She turned to Jack. There was plain, stark terror in his magnified eyes.

"Let's go!" he hissed.

"Jack, look," Te said. "We got this far. We'll be fine."

"It's doing stuff to my head," Jack said.

Te settled a hand on his shoulder. "Jack, this is what I do for a living. I'm an investigator. Sometimes I have to take risks. We'll be okay." She took a deep breath, looked into the teenager's wide eyes, and realized she didn't believe herself, either. Her adult tone faltered.

"Jack, I need to know this," she said, pleading now. "I need to."

Jack chewed his lower lip. After a moment, he swallowed, nodded, dropped his eyes.

"All right. Fine."

Te turned back to Corwinder Martin, Esquire.

"You're most gracious, sir." The words slipped out of her, complete with faux-British accent. She accepted his hand, and he conveyed her up into the cab.

"Oh, *won*derful to see you again, darling," the woman said, brushing Te's forearm with her hand. Te was certain she'd never met this woman. "It pleases me *so* that you'll be having a drive with us. The Lord and I want for company some days."

Te seated herself straight-backed and prim, knees together. After only a few seconds, she realized how uncomfortable the position was and shook her shoulders out. She slumped down in defiance of the other woman's poise.

"Oh, isn't the sun just beastly today," she said. "Take up a parasol, dear. You may have one of mine."

And there was a parasol beside Te on the seat. She knew she didn't remember it being there a moment before. She picked it up and idly turned it over, thinking somehow that she should have had more of a problem with its sudden appearance than she did. But it *was* hot, wasn't it? And the sun *was* beastly.

Beastly?

She opened the thing and held it awkwardly over herself as Jack thumped down dejectedly on the next seat and Martin settled his wide butt on the one opposite.

"On, driver!" he cried, as if the kid weren't five feet away from him. "Down to the Aviary. Pick us a pleasant route, would you?"

The kid cracked his whip and the horse lurched ahead at a reluctant plod.

The lady leaned against Martin and smiled warmly.

"He's such a romantic, aren't you, Corry?"

"I know what makes you happy, my lovely," he replied, caressing her chin with one yellow-nailed finger. She made a deeply satisfied, purrlike sound.

Te felt ill.

The lady was in as bad shape as her man: gray, mottled skin, fraying white hair, dark circles under her eyes. She was so thin, Te could clearly trace the bones in her face, neck, and wrists. They were a pair of corpse lovers. She had a sudden, involuntary flash in her imagination of them doing the deed, and shivered.

She jammed the parasol down between two seat cushions and shoved herself up.

"You said you knew my dad," she said, using an investigator's tone—or what she imagined one should sound like.

"Yes, indeed, my dear," said Martin, fending off an affectionate peck by his lady. "Why, we put the ol' Bird away here together. Goodness, so long ago, where to start?"

"Oh, tell the story, ducky," begged the woman. "I *so* like it when you tell the story."

Te wanted to slap her, but she also wanted to hear the story.

"You flatter me, lady," said Martin, inclining his head.

"It is only because I love you, my duck."

"And I you, my little tigress."

The two were hypnotic, somehow. Te bit her cheek and interrupted them. "Tell the story," she snapped. "Please."

"Ah, very well. A good day for reminiscences in any case, eh?" Martin settled back against the seat. "Where to begin? Ah, yes.

"I used to work in the British Museum, in London," he said. "My, that was a long time ago. Yes, I was a purchaser, a collector for the museum. Huge expense account, traveled all over the world. Very important man I was."

"And my dad?"

"Getting there, Miss Evangeline, getting there." He stopped to fill a pipe, light it, take a few puffs. Te resisted the urge to strangle him. "Let's see. I'd bought out a private collection. Few old paintings, silverware, that sort. The order came with a seal shipping crate, stamped 1864, and unopened since that date. The chap seemed quite happy to be rid of it, but weaseled out of revealing its contents. Suppose that should have been my first tip-off, eh? Ah, well. Hindsight is twenty-twenty and all that.

"Anyway, the lads and I let it linger a few months. Was a slow Friday when we got around to opening it up. James, poor lad—just his second job, you know—cracked it with a crowbar, and Bird came out of it all radiant and beautiful and shining like a morning sunrise and ate the poor lad down to his boots."

"What?"

"Of course, I was quite shocked at the time, seeing as he was a likable lad and I certainly hadn't given permission for him to be eaten."

"Corry's such a generous man, isn't he?" piped the lady.

"We eventually forgave Bird and sat to have a talk with her. No harm in a little civilized discourse, I always say." Martin sucked on his pipe and blew a few rings. Te eyed him up and down, trying to reconcile her trained open-mindedness with the fact that this man was totally off his rocker.

"Anyway," said Martin, "we set to talking, Bird and I, and she kept repeating how she loved beautiful things and I kept telling her I hadn't given her permission to eat my lad, and she was saying my lad was the most beautiful boy she'd seen in a long while and she was hungry besides. We came to a kind of compromise. 'Plenty of beautiful things in the museum besides lads,' I said to her, and oh, wasn't she happy."

Te stopped him with the obvious question. "The bird can talk?"

Martin started, as if he hadn't realized anyone was listening. "Hard to have a conversation with her otherwise," he said.

"So, we decided on a few things. She'd have to take a bit at a time—no more of this gobbling people up whole—and she was amenable to it. The lads were all falling all over themselves to see her, for she's the most beautiful sight. Got some girls down there for her, too. She'd fluff her feathers, Bird would, and the rest'd fall into a kind of swoon. Rapture, you know. Pheromones." He puffed his pipe. "Always wanting to take more of them—eyes, hearts, faces, a couple of less wholesome parts—but I soon put a stop to that, I tell you! Never got any of me, though. Your father explained it to me later. I'm naturally resistant to their charms, you see."

"Oh, Corry has a will like iron, I do say," said the lady.

Te stopped him again with an upraised hand. "Whose charms?"

Martin nodded knowingly, as if Te already knew what he was talking about and they shared some private understanding.

"*Theirs*," he said, then went on. "So we had our compromise, and she didn't get to eat any of me, and I made sure she didn't eat too much of anyone else. Then one day, it was . . . oh, dear what was it?"

"July 1980, dear."

"Ah, yes, July. Fierce hot one it was, too. Anyway, these men showed up at the museum. Had all the official papers—government papers, you know, IDs and so forth. They came on down to the basement to see Bird. My, did she throw a fit."

Te's mind was reeling from trying to picture all this and she spat her question automatically: "What men?"

Martin frowned. "An external team, my lass. Agents of the Warden, as it turned out, though I didn't know anything about it at the time. They came to take Bird away, lock her up with the rest of the unusual beasties they go about removing from the world. It's their job, you know."

"No, I…"

"Anyway, as it came out, I ended up being designated Bird's keeper on account of my seeming immunity to her. The external team passed her off to your dear father and that Mr. Cherian, and I came along into St. Ives to be a watcher like them."

"A watcher?" Te said. Finally, something fit and her mind started racing. "Wait a minute." She slipped Babu's casebook out of her shoulder bag and flipped to the page detailing the delivery of the "Maskim" creature. The entry also mentioned an "external team."

"So," she said, "it was my dad's job to take care of things like this Bird?"

Martin nodded. "It was our job, my lass, to make sure our charges stayed in their cells and to put them back there if they got out."

"Like a bobby," Jack said, the first interest he'd shown. Te started at his use of the English term.

Martin smiled at him. "Aye, there's a sharp lad. Yes, indeed, we were."

"Wild animal hunter," he whispered. "Didn't I say it?" Then Jack seemed to realize the air he'd just been using, and shrank into his shoulders in horror.

For the moment, Te's mind was bouncing too fast to worry. She flipped in the casebook to July 1980, and there it was.

Jul. 21, 1980—Call at 3:45 p.m. Moot after sundown. Assignment given to me and Rob. Escort. Prisoner being delivered through perimeter on or around noon tomorrow. External team classifies it as "Bird" (see attached—also research paper, Haley, Gertrude; Brown University; "Hypnosis without Transmission" 1975). Suppressor/keeper also en route, Corwinder Martin (see personnel file). Rob will be binder. Myself, backup suppression.

"You worked with him." Te stared up into Martin's satisfied, round face. She had so many questions, now, all ramming together in her head. She had pieces of a puzzle that had been torturing her all her life. She had hope. She stammered a few times before she could get anything out, and Martin waited for her.

"He wasn't a psychologist?" she said.

"Oh, but he was," said Martin. "UCLA, if I recall. Just not practicing in his field beyond what he needed to pay the bills. Brilliant binder, though. None of the rest of us had half his gift for it."

"What do you mean, 'binder'?" she said.

Martin gave her a quizzical look. "Am I to take by your question that he didn't tell you anything about his employment?"

Te felt her face flush. No, he hadn't told her anything. Her whole life, he'd been coming in and out of the house at all times of the day, vanishing without any word for weeks, sometimes coming back so exhausted, he'd slept for days. At ten years old, she'd given up asking him where he went. And it seemed so quickly after that he was gone, gone forever, and he'd never trusted her enough to tell her.

"Terrible of him," said Martin's lady. "Just terrible."

"Excuse me," Te said. She took a deep breath and let her gaze drift out to the scenery.

Hot, bright sun spiked into her eyes. The lawn and the path were littered with fallen orange and brown leaves, and the park's long lines of trees reached with bony fingers into the sky. The river ran clear and cold, not ten feet away down a rocky, grassy embankment. A hundred yards downstream, she saw their destination— a white, octagonal building with pleasant wood screens all around it, picnic tables, and water fountains. It had "municipal beautification project" written all over it. There wasn't a bird to be seen.

Teeth grinding, fingers clawing into the casebook,

ashamed of herself and her dad, Te turned back to them
and spoke evenly, in a controlled manner.

"Show me Bird."

The carriage rolled to a stop at Martin's command
and he assisted his lady down. Jack tried to do the same
for Te, a stupid, eager, boyish smile on his face. Te slapped
his hand, hard.

"Snap out of it!" she whispered.

Jack cringed back, then paused, drooped, nodded.
He fell into step behind the group in his usual slouch-
ing gait.

"As I said," Martin was saying, "I haven't the key
to her cage, so you'll have to talk to her through the
wire. Your father always kept the keys himself, and a
good thing it was, too, him being the most unflappable
of us."

He led the way, his lady trailing on his arm, through
the ornate wooden arch that led into the aviary. Te
shoved the casebook away and followed, alert and wary
as they passed into the peaked roof of the building. The
place stank of bird shit and dust.

Martin was still talking. "If I'd had them, I'd have let
our Bird out long ago. It's murder on her to keep her
locked up, one so free and wonderful as she."

They approached a huge chicken wire cage in the
center of the building. Otherwise, the whole place was a
cavernous, empty space.

"As it turns out, I was not entirely immune," he said.
"Eventually, I was hers, just like the lads and lasses of
our quaint park here."

Martin and his lady stepped aside. Inside the cage,
feathers shifted, claws flexed and opened, raptor eyes
blinked, lifted, saw.

Martin's next words were a whisper. "She said I had a beautiful heart."

Te felt any confidence left to her shrivel away.

"Oh, God."

One human hand, black and rough, tipped in claws and backed in feathers, snaked up and grasped the wire mesh. Then came another, curving with yellow talons on the fingertips. Two silver wings unfolded to fill the whole space of the cage with feathers. An androgynous, human face rose from the shadows: a great crown of plumes above; a thick ruff of down beneath. It stared at her with an eagle's unblinking gaze.

"What have you brought me?" Its voice was deep and resonant, delicate like a girl's and powerful like a man's, breathy like wind over long grass.

But Corwinder Martin didn't answer. He and his lady stood still as statues, their rapture written on their features.

Te's whole body started to quake. She couldn't take it in. She could only stare as the thing reared to its full height and fluffed itself, a flashing pattern of silver and black spots. She'd heard raps and she'd seen objects move by themselves and she'd read a thousand tales of visitations, but this overwhelmed her.

A *monster*. An inhuman creature, in the flesh.

The thing fluttered its wings and a strong, warm wind pressed against Te's face, wafting a tickling, lilac scent. Te's head spun. Her vision swam. The smell went into her nose, her lungs, her joints and muscles and brain, and she nearly fainted.

"So beautiful," said Bird. "A pretty face, and strong. Fit and tall." It reached its fingers through the mesh, grasping for them. "And the other. Yearning and innocent."

Te fell. She struck the hard concrete hip-first, losing her shoulder bag, and for a second was blinded with pain. An instant later she collapsed in a fit of coughing. She gasped and hacked until her lungs burned, until she tasted copper in her mouth.

"Come here," said that alien, hypnotic voice. "Child, come here. Take those things from your face."

Still gagging, Te forced herself to look. Jack had walked up to the cage. He was standing not a foot from the mesh, his face bright with happiness.

"You're beautiful," he said.

"Jack!" Te cried, then the coughing took her again. She tried to crawl, but the ground seemed to pull her back. "Get away from it!"

Bird hunched and swung around, placing its face level with Jack's. It smiled and Te saw the points of fanged teeth.

"You poor boy," it said. "Did people tell you that your eyes were ugly? Let me see them."

Jack reached up and slipped his glasses off. Bird's claws reached through the mesh.

"Jack!" Te shoved with her feet, sliding inch by inch through dried bird shit. She reached out and snagged the cuff of his pant leg. He didn't react.

"Oh, your eyes are beautiful," said Bird. "May I have them?"

Jack shuffled forward, breaking out of Te's tenuous grip. He pressed himself up to the mesh. The claws snaked through and sank into his face.

"Jack!"

Te shoved one more time. She threw her arms up around his thigh and yanked back. He came down on top of her, landing on her head and shoulders. Her forehead knocked against the concrete and her vision went spotty. She almost let go.

Jack started to struggle, reaching out for the cage.

"That's it, child," said Bird. "Come to me."

Te wrapped herself around Jack's leg and held him down with her weight. She gagged as his free foot kicked her in the abdomen.

"Jack! Stop it!"

His response was a deep, wordless scream of fright and pain.

Her grip shifted as he turned and wrenched. In two spasms he'd broken free and squirmed out of her reach. Instead of snatching for him, Te dove her hand into the nearby shoulder bag and came away with Babu's gun.

She pointed it at Bird and pulled the trigger. Nothing happened.

The safety!

She drew the gun back and struggled to find and flip that tiny switch. Jack crashed against the mesh with wide arms and Bird drove claws through the mesh into his eyes.

Te's first shot went into the ceiling. She wasn't prepared for the kick. The weapon slipped out of her fingers and cracked her in the sternum. She gasped for air and grabbed for the gun. At the sound of the shot, Bird had stood erect and Jack had dropped to the ground with his hands over his head.

Te's hand shook as she took aim on the creature in the cage. Still gasping, she struggled to her feet. Bird crouched down, wings folded up, and eyed her with a patient, predator gaze from within a nest of feathers.

"My word!" It was Martin, freed from the rapture.

"What the devil do you think you're doing, young lady?"

"Shut up," Te wheezed, not letting her eyes leave the monster in the cage. "Jack?"

Jack, still curled up and shuddering, lifted his bloody face and squinted her way. "Te?"

"Get up. Get your glasses."

He swallowed hard and obeyed. When he was up and at her side, Te backed away slowly.

"Now, see here," said Martin, taking a step forward.

"Put that filthy thing down," the lady scolded. "It is completely unladylike."

"Shut up," Te said. Her breath was back and her whole body quivered from adrenaline.

Te and Jack backed up. They were almost at the door.

Martin took his lady by the hand. "Don't worry yourself now, my dear," he said. "They'll come back. The lad particularly. He was quite taken with her." He looked directly at Te. "They won't be able to stay away."

"Get outside, Jack," Te said. She had both hands on the gun, now, trying to look down the sight with her hands jerking back and forth.

She heard Jack suck in a breath.

"Te!"

Suddenly, a sharp pain stabbed her ankle. She cried out and the gun went off.

Bird reeled. A scream went up like a multiphonic owl's cry. Feathers flew in the cage.

Te looked down. A yellow fox fled from her vision, racing up to Bird's cage and leaping at the latch on the door. Blood welled up where it had bit her.

With a crash, Bird threw itself against the cage. It beat

on the frail mesh with its claws and bit at it with its teeth. The fox leapt again, snapping at the lock.

Te turned and ran. She grabbed Jack by the shoulder and hauled him after her.

The sunlight stabbed into her eyes the instant she passed out of the aviary. Blurred patches of orange and gray wobbled in front of her. She blinked and blinked, but her vision wouldn't clear. Jack began to struggle against her.

"Te, I need to go back."

"No way."

She dug her nails into his arm and yanked him along.

Bird's shrieks still blasted out from the aviary, echoing everywhere, seeming to get louder with every step Te and Jack took away from it. The wind caught the wet leaves on the trees and whipped them into a cyclone all over the park. The rustling filled her ears. The leaves slapped against her face and body.

"Te, she's upset," Jack said. "Let's go back. She'll calm down. You'll see."

Te heard the words but didn't understand them. From some distant vantage point, she realized something had gone in her mind. There was nothing rational in her anymore, just the cold horror of a world suddenly larger and more frightening for containing the creature she had just seen. There was only fear.

Te knew she was slowing, knew her strength was ebbing away. She knew that the leaves and trees and the park itself were angry at her and that the anger was Bird's. She knew that this place belonged to the thing in the cage, and that all inside its borders were prey under her raptor's eye.

The path had turned from cobblestones to pavement, slick with rain though the sky was clear. She stumbled blindly forward, holding on to Jack with a death grip as he squirmed and whined and wriggled. Suddenly, a torrent of rain hit her, driven almost horizontal by the wind. Iron-hard drops hammered her face.

A few more yards and the rain was so thick she could barely take a breath without it slipping into her mouth and nose. It quickly soaked through her jacket and pants, through her shirt and her hair, until she was drenched to the skin, and the rain's chill started to eat away at her. It was no good. Another yard, two. Then her hand slipped and she went down, face-first into the stones. She was cold, burning cold, and the rain pounded into her, pressing her inexorably into the ground.

Footsteps sounded in the din. Te craned her neck around, panting, water gushing over her face and mouth. A shadow loomed over her, and reached for her with monstrous hands.

"Goddamn stupid . . ."

One big hand was around her arm, the other around Jack's, just below where her fingers still held tight. Raw strength pulled her to her feet.

Babu was yelling in her face. "Why the *hell* did you come in here?"

Leaves battered her face and she couldn't answer.

Babu grunted. "Let's get you out."

He released her and she swayed in place. He jammed something up under her nose and suddenly there was a smell to wake the dead.

"Jesus Christ!" Both hands flew to her nose. The scent had almost burned her nostrils, but suddenly her vision was clear. Suddenly the swarm of leaves was a mere half dozen dancing on the wind. Suddenly the torrent of rain was a drizzle.

Babu pushed down the hand that still held the gun, then stuck a little open bottle up under Jack's nose. Jack went stiff as a board for a second, then started to cough like an aging smoker.

"Let's go," said her boss.

But she wasn't in any mood to take orders. He'd *known* about all this. He'd known about the park and that ... thing ... and her father. She grabbed his blazer by the lapels.

"What the fuck is going on?" she screamed. "Babu, what the *fuck*!"

"Calm down!" His voice thundered like a bass drum at close range. "First we get out. *Then* you ask your questions."

He hauled them around with brute strength and pushed them ahead. To their left, a hedge stood some seven feet high, and Te spotted the arch they'd come through not twenty feet away.

"There!" she said, pointing.

"I know," Babu growled.

A cry like an eagle's cut the air, and they all froze. Instinctually, every muscle in Te's body shriveled and hid from that cry, and her pulse pounded in her temples.

Another cry. Babu's voice hissed from just over her shoulder.

"Run for the arch," he said.

Then he shoved them. His powerful hands sent Te and Jack sprawling forward. Once again, Te snagged Jack's arm, and in ten steps they were through the arch and into the first of the small gardens. An instant later they heard a sound tearing the air, heard something huge crash into the dirt, and Babu toppled through the arch, rolling to a stop, spread-eagled on a bed of violets.

There was no rain here. Only the soft light of the setting sun, and the whisper of a cool autumn breeze. For a second, they were still, breathing.

No cry followed. Shaking violently, Te forced herself to look up at the sky.

Clouds. Nothing else.

And she finally exhaled.

Jack dropped straight to the ground and sat on his haunches. A second later, Te joined him. Unconsciously, they pressed together, quivering from fright and exhaustion. Te wrapped her arm around him and rubbed his frigid shoulders.

"We're all right now," she said, then looked at Babu. "Right?"

The big man nodded. He groaned and sat up. Moving as if his every joint ached, he shrugged out of his jacket.

"Did *you* let her out?" he said.

"Babu, I really don't know what the hell you're talking about," Te answered. She finally pried her fingers off the gun and dropped it on the ground as if it were a poisonous snake. "You okay?" she said to Jack.

"My eyes hurt," he said. He hadn't put his glasses back on yet. Te pushed his soaked hair off his forehead. Little puncture marks bled all around both eyes, just inside the bone ring of the eye socket.

"Let me see," she said. He blinked and stared toward her. His eyelids and cheeks were smeared with blood, but the eyes themselves were intact. Te breathed a sigh of relief. "You're all right."

Jack nodded and didn't reply.

"On your feet," said Babu, who was rising to his. "We

still have to get out of the park. And I *don't* want anything more out of you until we're back in downtown, got it?"

Te bit her tongue and nodded.

"Good." Babu held up his blazer and examined the three long, jagged slashes down the back of it. He grunted and threw it away. He already had a cigarette between two fingers.

"Now run," he said. "We don't want to be stuck in here after dark."

Chapter 6

Over the Rainbow

"Feast your eyes, my children," Lester said, sweeping one arm to encompass the whole of the lot across the street: rusting link fence, heaps of scrap metal, and garbage and all. "Behold the magical safe house, from which we launched our assault against the shape-shifter Kitsune. This is where we held the Red God for three days and three nights before he bowed his knee to us. This is where we put down the Cult of the Dragon Star and stopped them from opening the Door to the Outside. Behold!"

He looked around a second at his awestruck Strutters.

"Behold, behold, behold," he said.

His little poet, Jill, gave him a funny look. He grinned back.

"All right, enough beholding. Let's get to work."

He slipped on some sunglasses and led the way out across the street. Yes, it was nighttime, but he was out on the town and had to look good—and sunglasses looked good any time of day.

He walked directly into traffic. His Strutters fanned around him in a loose crowd, running interference in front of the screeching, swerving cars and their enraged motorists.

He reached the gate to the fence surrounding the little property and tore the padlock off it with a quick squeeze of his fingers—one of the upsides of being supernatural.

"In we go," he said as one of his Strutters pushed the gate open and made a path for him. "Don't touch anything."

His Strutters fanned out into the little scrap yard inside the fence, fiercely brandishing their replica knives and axes (one had a crossbow). Lester hunched down and sprinted between the mounds of rusting metal as quickly as he could. Father O'Shae had blessed a lot of this stuff in the name of Christ and that made him uncomfortable. Lester wasn't sure what crosses and holy water and blessed things would do to him, having had no other vampire to ask, but he wasn't about to tempt fate.

At the back of the scrap yard was a little repair shop, with one carport sealed over with a padlocked aluminum door attached to a small office area with boarded-up windows and cracks in the stucco.

He slipped over to the office door and pulled out a big, jangling ring of identical keys. He picked the one that *wouldn't* lead to certain death and stuck it in the keyhole. It was a moment before he brought himself to turn it. It entered into his brain that old wards and booby traps might not recognize him. His imagination fed him images of explosions, lights, pain—and those crippling hypnotic tricks Rob and Angrel could do, not to mention whatever might be left over from the crews of previous generations.

Too many drugs, he thought to himself. *Getting paranoid.*

Then again, why would they send him to do this, other than that he was the most indestructible?

Did they know? Did they know that Yun had visited him? Would Angrel and her cards . . . ? Or the Man himself, who seemed to be able to be anywhere . . . ?

The old adage came back to him: "It's not paranoia if they're really out to get you."

The lock clicked and he didn't die. Something sank heavy in his stomach, a sour tang like disappointment.

The door protested as he dragged it open. It was an effort for even him to break the crusts on those grinding hinges. The place hadn't been used in almost two years.

"Inside, people," he said, then stepped aside. They hustled in, a troupe of tromping combat boots and swishing skirts of black lace.

"Home base," he said, mostly to himself. He looked around at the worn couches, salvaged off street corners, and the little wobbling card table with three pipe-metal chairs probably stolen from a school classroom.

"That's it?" It was one of his Strutters, a teenager who, Lester suspected, was a perfectly respectable football player, when he wasn't wearing monochromatic hell-clown makeup and calling himself Ravndark.

Lester laid a benevolent hand on the young man's shoulder.

"Not much to look at, I know," he said. "But there's power in these walls, layers and layers of it. Each time a new crew comes in, they paint over the old wards and make their new ones."

Lester strode over to an expanse of wall beside the boarded window.

"Look here, my children," he said. "Look and learn."

His fingers traced the ridges where numbers had been scratched into the walls. "Numerology," he said. "A friend of mine does number magic, although he calls it something else. And here"—he moved to the adjacent wall, where bundles of feathers and the skulls and skins of animals hung, dulled and decaying—"these are African charms. And these are Wicca, I think." He moved along to where a large pentagram had been painted, surrounded in rings and circles all labeled in an indecipherable language. He pointed to a few others, wishing he knew enough about them to impress the slaves.

"Cool, huh?" he finished lamely. His Strutters thought so. All of them oohed at the room, in awe of the secrets they imagined each charm and symbol held. Even little Jill, who, Lester thought, knew all about this stuff, was wide-eyed and amazed.

No. He'd seen that look before—she was . . . *inspired*.

And Lester felt good. He was still riding the high Yun had infused into him. He was still charged, confident, invincible. He had banished all thoughts of the future, all thoughts of what Yun wanted of him, beneath a mountain of denial and the remembrance of bliss.

"We gonna be fightin' anyone?" Ravndark asked.

Lester experienced a moment of doubt, in which his happiness almost broke apart. *No*, his mind said. *You'll be dying, and I'll be watching, and it'll be all my fault.* And all that Yun had asked of him came rushing back: deceit, betrayal, death. But Yun had promised oblivion forever, and the man would deliver, because that's what Yun did.

Because it was Lester's wish.

Lester buried the thoughts with a choked cough and answered, "Dunno. Depends on what's out there."

The rest of their comments faded in and out of his consciousness, his Strutters talking about the obvious coolness of a secret base manned by a secret commando squad out to rid the world of evil, and the *extra* coolness of them being part of it. Lester knew that kind of talk was his fault—always playing up the war stories, glamorizing them, leaving out the bits where he was pissing himself scared, and the bits where people died.

The bliss was gone, ebbed away in a single moment of self-doubt and remembrance.

"Make yourselves at home," he said, forcing his voice back into high spirits. "Jill, go out and get us some munchies, all right?"

His little poet snorted at him and continued to scribble lines onto the notepad she always carried. The others shoved and cajoled for the best seats on the couches, calling each other lewd names in the best traditions of teenagers.

And Lester thought, *Jesus, they're just kids.*

Yun had told him to wait for the Maskim, which meant Yun was going to free it, if he hadn't already.

Yun had told him to open the door, which meant Lester was going to let the Maskim into the safe house.

Yun had told him to listen, which meant that he wasn't supposed to interfere once the Maskim was inside. The Maskim would be hungry after its long slumber under the graveyard, and it never ate quickly. Lester could guess what he'd be listening to.

Lester watched his Strutters huddling together on the couch, pouring over the new lines Jill had just written, while his little poet scribbled and scribbled on a new sheet of paper, deep in the grip of her art. He saw in them such vitality, such life.

And again, he thought, *They're just kids.*

And then, *Once it's done, you won't remember.*

And they were calling him over to look at Jill's poetry. And he went, forcing a smile.

"You know how some people feel that the world is a prison?"

The streetlights flashed over Babu's face as he drove. He was shadow, then bone, then shadow. His teeth were clenched around a bent cigarette and the smoke was making Te nauseated. "You know. Depressed people," he went on, "social scientists, anarchists, whatever."

Te had both hands tight around the strap of her seat belt. The vision kept coming back. She saw it everywhere: in the shapes of the neon signs, in the shifting of the rain outside, in her own reflection in the window.

Bird's face. Her inhuman face.

"Well, it actually is," Babu said, as if she'd made a response. "It's run by a guy called the Warden. No one's seen him. No one knows who he really is. Secret ruler of the world, right? Remember that stuff?"

"Esotericism," Te mumbled. "Theosophy. Tibetan masters." The rain shifted and she might have seen a winged shape in the sky.

"Right," Babu said. "So, this new guy took over as Warden in the Renaissance, started rewriting the rules of the old world. Actually it had been going on a lot longer, but he really put the nail in the coffin." Babu jammed his cigarette out in the ashtray, half finished, and drew another one, one hand on the wheel. "The new guy is into rules: sciences, bureaucracies, regulated sports. Except we've got all these things still running around from the old days, right? Ghosts and spirits and demons and all that kind of stuff."·

A shadow over the still-lit windows of an office building. Bird? No—a leaf stuck on the outside of the window. Hands tight on the seat belt strap, Te, still shaking, closed her eyes and willed herself calm, but the face of Bird, the colors of its feathers, the smell of it—she couldn't blot them out.

"They claim to come from a place called the Old Country," Babu said. "No one knows where it is, but they say they left it millions of years ago and have been kind of hanging around on Earth since then."

He stopped talking. It was half a block before Te realized he was looking at her. She pried her eyes open and looked back. Her lids felt heavy as lead.

"The drowsiness'll pass," Babu said. "You should probably take a shower as soon as you can, to get the stuff off your skin. And wash your clothes. Same with him."

He jammed his thumb at the backseat where Jack drooped, asleep, exhaustion or Bird's scent having taken its toll.

"All right," said Te. She blinked, shook her head a bit, unraveled her fingers from the seat belt, which was like bending rebar. "Old Country?"

"Good, now listen," Babu said, returning his eyes to the road. "The Warden couldn't have the myth-creatures from the old world wandering around and breaking all of his rules, so he made *prisons* for them. Cities and caves and deserts and stretches of ocean—most of them inhospitable chunks of the planet no one in their right mind would go to."

"Except you, I bet." Te still felt like a thousand pounds. The whole car stank of smoke and unhealthy sweat. Her hands fell in her lap, unable to stay up under their own power.

Babu ground his cigarette between his teeth until the filter was a mess, then stubbed it out, again half finished, and reached for another.

"Yeah, I've been to a few," he said. "The point is, St. Ives is one of those places."

"An inhospitable chunk of the planet no one in their right mind would go to?"

Babu grunted something.

Te leaned her head back and stared at the car's roof, where the padded lining had started to peel off near the windshield. "Sorry. Go on."

"We've got things from all over the world pinned down in this town," Babu said. "That's why the town was founded in 1881. That's why they put it in this valley with only the one road out. Are you listening to me?"

Te dug the heel of her hand into her stomach. The nausea was worsening. "Yeah. Could you put that cigarette out?"

Babu looked at it a minute, rolled through a stop sign while he was distracted, then stubbed the just-barely-lit thing out, muttering, "Damn things'll give me cancer anyway." Te desperately wanted to open the windows, but she was afraid of the sky.

Babu went to draw another cigarette, then stopped himself. "I work for a man," he said. "We just call him the Man in the Empty Chair. He's in charge of St. Ives."

Te glanced up from her pain to give him a look.

"Yeah, I know," Babu grumbled. "I don't know if he has a real name. Anyway, I'm part of a team that keeps the monsters in their cells. Our job was to catch them when they got out. They can't get out of the valley because there's a second barrier at the city limit, but that mostly just pisses them off." He choked off. Te's eyes hovered on him, on his stiff jaw and flaring nostrils, on hunched shoulders and a forehead wrinkled from long worry. "Your dad was one of us."

"I know," said Te.

Babu looked over in surprise. The car swerved and he diverted some of his attention back to the road. "I thought he never told you."

"He didn't," said Te. The words still tasted bitter. "He didn't tell me anything. We met a man named Corwinder Martin."

"Martin!" Babu exclaimed. "In the park? Jesus Christ. I wish I'd been there."

The rattle in Babu's tone told Te it would not have been pleasant if he had.

"Martin was one of us," Babu explained. "Then Bird got to him." He ground his teeth as if he were chewing on a cigarette. "Ate his heart right out of his chest."

Te remembered the flower shop woman's empty eye sockets. "So Bird and these other things are what? Monsters?"

Babu shrugged. "Sure."

"You think someone would have mentioned them," Te said. A panic started up in her. "Jesus Christ, Babu. You think we would have known about this!"

" 'We,' who?" Babu growled. " 'We' everybody? The whole damn world?"

Te crossed her arms. "Yeah! Why—*how*—could you keep this kind of stuff secret?"

"Secret?" Babu glared over at her. "I know Rob

read you fairy tales when you were a kid, same as everybody."

"But those were stories," Te said. "No one said they were real."

"I bet your dad did. And I bet you believed him until you were six or seven." Babu slowed and started to pull the car over. "And then you stopped."

The car bounced on and off the sidewalk as Babu maneuvered the ungainly vehicle into a parking spot barely larger than the thing's bumpers. He threw it into park.

"Same as everybody," he said. He inhaled and straightened his shoulders as if he were going to say something serious. Te was not in a mood to be lectured to, so she cut him off:

"So even the people who've seen these things—like those people in Martin's museum, and that old lady at the flower shop . . . Why don't they tell anybody?"

"They do," Babu snapped. "No one believes them. You didn't."

Te exhaled. "I guess not." Then something occurred to her and she squinted at him. "How do you know that?"

The big man looked uncomfortable. He squirmed around a bit before answering. "I've been tailing you."

"No way," said Te, jamming a finger at him. "Absolutely not. You can see this land boat of yours a mile away, Babu. And you're what, six foot three? And the *one* black guy in this whole town? Hard to miss."

Babu's big lips turned up in a smirk. "Damned if you weren't actually listening to me. Aware of your environment."

Te returned the smirk, though hers had no mirth behind it. " 'Sharp eyes and good ears,' sure. So?"

Babu drummed his hands on the wheel. "I wasn't using the car."

"What, then?"

"Tarot cards."

Te was aghast. *"Tarot cards?"*

Babu nodded.

"That stuff you told me was all unconscious psychological clues or cold reading, right?" Te said, arms wrapped tight on her abdomen now. Her stomach surged with anxiety and her heart was pounding. "That stuff you said you'd personally debunked a dozen times when you lived in Boston, right?"

"Te, look . . ."

"Have you been lying to me all this time, then? There really isn't a scientific explanation for any of it?" Te tightened her arms until her ribs hurt. She spoke through clenched teeth. "You've been training me on all these methods and processes that you don't even believe in?"

Babu stared hard out the windshield as the first drops of rain spattered across it. "It isn't like that."

Te felt herself start to vibrate. "Oh, yes it is!"

Babu snorted out through his nose and deflated. "Yeah, I guess."

Te was frozen a minute, staring at this huge man, resigned and worn, older than she was by decades and showing every minute of it. This man had been her dad's friend, and she'd thought he was her friend, too, but he'd lied to her and had made her believe that parapsychology was a respectable discipline, and then it turned out there were monsters in the world.

It was too much. She opened the door and got out.

Babu snatched at her arm. "Te!"

"It's all right," she mumbled back to him. The pavement slammed up under her feet and she leaned on the car for support. Rain tickled her hair, cooled her forehead and arms. Her skin was flushed, her blood pumping fiercely. She was like a furnace, burning up from inside, bursting into ash and rust, flaking away. Then the air bit at her, the chill of November prickling her exposed skin, the damp in the air pressing through her clothing, licking the heat of her anger away.

Babu opened his own door and got out. Te saw him out of the corner of her eye, staring at her across the car's roof. He said nothing, getting soaked by the same rains as she.

Te took a deep breath and turned her face up to the sky. The drops fell heavier, deflecting from her cheeks and forehead, running down her neck, soothing the tight tendons there. Somewhere up in those clouds was an avian nightmare that some blind woman believed was an angel.

"Why'd you do it?" Te asked. "Why'd you hire me?"

Te heard Babu drumming his fingers on the car's roof.

"Because your dad asked me to," he said. "He didn't want you to have any part in what he did. He wanted me to show you that the supernatural didn't exist."

"He didn't trust me."

"He wasn't allowed to trust you."

"Did Mom know?"

"I don't know."

Te took a deep, long breath. The rain and dark were already obscuring the street. Here and there, yellow streetlights struggled to be seen. The buildings were thin, old houses without yards, their front steps descending directly onto the sidewalk. Their windows glittered here and there with the blue flicker of televisions.

"Where are we?" she asked.

Babu closed his door. "Cranstontown, the old half on the south shore." He walked around the car's huge front end and mounted the sidewalk.

Te reached into the car and got her coat. She shrugged into it, suddenly cold. "What's in Cranstontown?"

Babu pointed down a near set of stairs that led to the lower floor of one of the houses, to a door pasted over with posters of eyes in pyramids and yin and yang symbols. The sign above the door read ANGREL BLUMENTHAL, MEDIUM. TAROT READINGS. PALMISTRY. SÉANCES.

"I asked her to keep an eye on you with her cards," Babu said. "I wasn't going to come after you until she told me you were in the park."

Te rubbed her forehead, a flush of embarrassment rising on her face.

"Thanks," she said, "for helping us in the park. I didn't mean to snip at you just now."

Babu grunted. "Don't worry about it. I promised your dad I'd keep you safe."

"I hope you didn't promise you'd keep me out of trouble."

Babu barked a laugh. "He knew better than to ask."

He headed for the stairs. *He cares enough, remember. Maybe you should tell him about Mom's dinner guest.*

But he was waiting for her, and from his manner, the edge in that laugh, she knew he was really nervous about something. Questions could wait, couldn't they? The anger that had trickled away flashed back. She knew it was childish, but *he'd* kept things from *her*. He wouldn't have told her anything, except that she found it out herself. She decided to take a page from his book—sit back and observe.

Te followed him down. By now the rain had become a steady downpour, and the roof of the house above provided some shelter.

"Are you going to tell me why we're here?" she asked.

"To meet someone," Babu said, resting his hand on the doorknob. He turned and looked down at her in earnest.

"This isn't going to be easy on you," he said. "But time's short, so we need to do this the hard way. You can only trust Angrel to a point. Do what I taught you. Keep your eyes and ears open. Take in everything. Don't jump to any conclusions. You can figure things out afterward. Go in there as an investigator." His big hand was on her shoulder, protective, worried.

Te laid her fingers over his. She fixed him in the eyes and spoke with excruciating clarity.

"What's. Going. On?"

Babu turned away, dropped his hand. His sigh was long and hard, and mingled with the swishing of the rain. He shook his head.

"You know what else I promised your dad?" he said. "I promised him I'd never bring you into our world. I promised him you'd have a boring, normal little life and grow up to be a hairdresser or something."

He fumbled a cigarette out, and a lighter. Te watched his fingers shaking and saw in him a wealth of emotional exhaustion, saw a man worn away by stress and the heavy weight of responsibility. He sucked on the cigarette like a drowning man reaching for the shore.

"But I also promised to keep you safe. And when I

came to visit after your graduation, you had this look, and I thought you might . . . you know . . . do something drastic."

Te shrank away. Sure, she'd thought about it—graduation had been unbearable without her dad to watch her. She'd thought about it a lot. Actually, if she was being totally honest with herself, she'd stolen a bottle of sleeping pills out of a friend's medicine cabinet. It had all seemed so logical then, the only thing to do, the only way out. And then Babu had showed up at the door of her mother's house, and asked her if she wanted a job.

"That's why you hired me?" Te asked, to push the conversation on.

Babu shrug-nodded noncommittally. "I thought I could give you a bit of a distraction. You know, get you going on some project to get your mind off it all—you sitting in your room with nothing to do but think. I never thought you'd be any good at it." This sentiment seemed to upset him further. "Shoulda known, I guess."

"Known what?"

"You're good with the supernatural. Like your dad."

He sighed, exhaling a cloud of gray smoke into the air.

"I'm about to break both those promises, kid," he said, to himself or something else, but not really to her. "But it's the only thing to do now."

He threw the cigarette down into a little puddle at the base of the stairs. He looked at her once more with that earnest look, his expression shaded with sadness, with regret.

"We got a lot of trouble coming and we need your help," he said. "Your dad was a binder, the best we've ever seen. The rest of us are rusty at best, or can't do it at all."

"But I can?"

"Angrel and Munin seem to think so." One hand worked the wheel on his lighter a moment. "So do I."

Te was cold inside and out now, shivering. She hugged herself. "I don't know anything about it."

"You'll learn," Babu said. "You'll remember."

Te thought of her father, pictured him talking to Bird, inside that little flower shop. She saw him standing calmly between the rows of dead plants, his face serene, his voice wordless and melodious and hypnotic. She saw Bird raging helplessly before him, thrashing and shrieking, its wings toppling shelves and its claws tearing at the floor and walls. It was furious, but impotent, rendered helpless by her father simply because he spoke to it and was not afraid.

Te looked up. "All right. I'm game."

Babu nodded. "Angrel will get you initiated."

Though the fresh night air had quelled her stomach a bit, Te felt it rising up again, at the sound and implication of that word.

"Initiated into what?"

Babu pushed the door open. A chime sounded an ethereal chord.

"The Old Powers," he said. "You're gonna join the team."

Lester hated the rain. He had hated it since he was a little kid, staying inside when his three sisters went out to play in puddles and splash around. It was cold and clammy, and it made his skin feel rubbery and uncomfortable. Even now, he still hated the rain. And yet it was where he went when the despair came over him. When the drugs had been exhausted, when his Strutters had used every last drop of their youthful energy and passed out on couches and floor, and he had nothing else to distract him, he always went to the rain.

It was the one constant in St. Ives. It rained all the time; from drizzles to showers to storms, there was always water falling from the sky. Maybe that was why he sought it out: it was predictable, a comfort that could be relied upon, even if it was an uncomfortable comfort.

His Strutters had gone out and fetched him what he needed. The skinny kid who called himself Black-Rimmed Pathos always went to the trouble of putting the blood in beer bottles. And he did it reverently, formally, as if it were the most important thing, fit for a king. Lester took another swig of the bottle he held. Pig's blood, tasting powerfully porcine. It was nothing, animal blood. There was no pleasure in it. He drank it like he used to drink the shitty beer of his youth, that suspiciously piss yellow no-name brand stuff that was good only for getting drunk and inspiring complaints about how much it tasted like piss. What Lester preferred was human blood, straight from the neck or the wrist. His Strutters were always offering themselves to him—some even claimed to wash their necks with all sorts of weird hippie soaps and oils, just for him. But no matter how exhilarating the taste of it, Lester almost never had any. He so rarely "embraced" anyone—that was Jill's word. He was too afraid that he might overdo it and kill someone.

The lights from around the city skittered up onto the falling sheets of rain, reflected in sparkles by the drops. A selfish voice in Lester's head told him he had better go inside and start sucking, because all that beautiful human blood was about to go to waste.

No. The Maskim needed them alive. There was no going back now. None of it would matter once Yun followed through.

But that didn't stop the doubts, and Lester quelled them with another mouthful of blood that made him think he was licking raw pork. This was the last bottle for tonight. Funny. Why did he always seem to be down to his last bottle?

Out across the little scrap yard, the fence rattled. Lester straightened, peering out through the dark. Here and there, a piece of scrap shivered as it was touched by the passage of something low to the ground.

Lester placed his hand on the doorknob to the little shop where his Strutters slept, insensible and unaware. For a moment, he imagined the Maskim entering and the wards and glyphs, layer by layer, ripping it apart with old power. He didn't know much about that stuff, but a lead certainty in his stomach told him that the wards would lie still, and that they would do so because it was Lester who would open the door, and he was a friend.

He could see it in the dark, now, a long shadow, glistening, slithering between the piles of junk, skirting the ones blessed by Father O'Shae, unhurried in its undulations.

It had been trapped under the ground almost ten years. It would be hungry. And if Lester didn't open the door, it would still need to eat.

He toyed with the idea of fighting it, of dying heroically in a battle with this creature of earth and the dead. He choked this thought, too, with the blood. No one could face St. Ives' inmates alone, these gods and beasts out of legend. Lester was not a god or a beast out of legend. He was a poor kid, now a poor man, who liked hanging out with teenagers and getting high and who had been turned into a vampire for no reason at all.

The Maskim made no sound as it emerged from a stack of old tires ten feet from the door. Its body glimmered in the rain, massive and serpentine. Hints of its true red color, red like fire, like pale wine, flashed over its scales in the changing light from the streetlamps, distorted by distance and rain. It raised its eyeless head, turning it toward him—like a crocodile, like a snake. The black spines down its crest waved slowly like grass in the wind, and it emitted a dry smell like the dust of old tombs.

Lester's breath burned icy cold passing his lips. He thought of the last time he had seen this creature in its aspect, after Yun had set it loose. Ten years ago he had watched it bite off Julia Kinnen's arm, then tear out Father O'Shae's ribs, and plunge its teeth into what was revealed. It had been hungry then, too.

The sightless muzzle stared into him, penetrating him with a fiery cold. Lester shuddered under its nongaze, beset with a sensation of emptiness, of ancient eyes, and the spirits of the vast deserts that were this thing's home. Impressions followed—flashes of imagery from its consciousness, distorted and alien in form, but conveying what needed to be said: it had also made a bargain with Yun. It had not eaten since gaining its freedom, and it was very, very hungry.

The bottle shook in Lester's hand. His mouth opened to speak to it, perhaps to beg. Here, at the moment, he found he couldn't just go through with the agreement. He ached that this evil he was about to do should be lessened, should be mitigated somehow, and that in some tiny, absurd way, he should know in his own mind that he was a good man.

"Please," he said, "don't take Jill."

The Maskim did not alter its featureless face, and Lester did not know if it agreed, or even understood, or cared to.

His hand turned on the knob. A beam of light split the darkened yard as the door cracked open. Lester turned away, facing the darkness and the soothing, aggravating rain.

The sound of the Maskim entering the safe house was one of silence within the constant noise of the rain.

Lester wished there was another way, something deep in him recognizing his cowardice at this moment, and at so many, many others.

He did nothing and listened, as the screams began.

The reek of incense was overpowering. It seemed to cascade up from every corner of the dark shop, twirling in curls of smoke, flickering and alive in the candlelight. The candles were all well used, some only puddles of wax, still flickering on the shelves and tables, between books and display cases holding crystals and jewelry. Little plastic figurines of Asian gods and demons winked out from the gloom.

Across the room, a curtain of beads was drawn aside by a hand white as porcelain.

"So," said a demure, feminine voice, "the comical girl."

The words gave her a chill. Te squinted into the dark, unable to see any of the other's features in the scant candlelight before and behind her. Other than the occasional gutter of bubbling wax, there was complete silence for a few moments.

"My dad used to call me that," Te said.

"He got it from a nursery rhyme," said the other. "One you laughed at when you were a tiny baby, when he would read to you before bed."

Te squinted at the figure. Something held her from going closer, an intense aura of the sacred permeating the shop with all its shadows and scents.

"How did you know?" she asked.

"He told me." The figure shifted, holding the curtain aside. "Shall we?"

Walking through the shop was like walking through a dream, with that same tickling feeling that it wasn't real, that the landscape could shift at any moment. Te ducked under the curtain and into a small back room, where she found a round table covered in a felt cloth, and candles burning all around. The woman smelled of lavender and smoke when Te got close.

"Have a seat," said her hostess, indicating one of three chairs with a simple gesture of her hand. The hand sported nails the color of pale ice, short but sharp. Te sat and crossed her arms.

The woman—Angrel—took the chair opposite. The third stood empty. The candlelight flowed and flickered on Angrel's face, pale and smooth like untouched snow, topped and flanked by white hair in misshapen dreadlocks. She wore a loose white dress of some natural weave, and jewelry of brass and various woods. Her eyes flickered red-pink.

"I'm an oculocutaneous albino," Angrel said, with an amused little smile—Te smarted that she'd let her expression tell. "It's my karma to always be born into an

imperfect body. Could have been worse, though. Club
foot or malformed hands."

The woman pulled out a deck of oversized cards and
started shuffling. "I know Babu wants me to initiate you
right away, but let's do a reading anyway, shall we?"

"Sure," Te said, not knowing what else to do. *Keep
your eyes and ears open*, Babu had said. Fine.

Tarot was not easily provable as charlatanry, Te knew.
There was nothing physical to give away the fraud—
unless raps or apparitions manifested themselves, in
which case you could trace the source to lights or the use
of remote control, or an accomplice, to create the effects.
Tarot was essentially a psychological effect: the reader,
consciously or unconsciously, picking up on unconscious
signals given off by the subject, interpreting them, consciously or unconsciously, and feeding them back. A reading was essentially telling the subject what she wants to
hear. Te had been to more than one tarot reading in the
last few years—Babu had insisted, to sharpen her awareness of her own prejudices and beliefs when confronting
something "mysterious."

Angrel laid down the eight of swords in the center of
the table.

" 'A woman, bound and hoodwinked, with the swords
of the card about her,' " she said. " 'Yet it is rather a
card of temporary durance than of irretrievable bondage. *Divinatory Meanings*: Bad news, violent chagrin,
crisis, censure, power in trammels, conflict, calumny; also
sickness. *Reversed*: Disquiet, difficulty, opposition, accident, treachery; what is unforeseen; fatality.' "

"That's Waite," Te said. *"Pictorial Key to the Tarot."*

Angrel nodded her approval. "How about this:

'The first requisite for causing any change is through qualitative and quantitative understanding of the conditions.' "

"Crowley," Te said. *"Magic in Theory and Practice."*

"You're remarkably well-informed for someone Robert wanted to keep out of the business," Angrel said, drawing her second card. "Babu gave you a bit of an education, I suppose?"

Te watched the back of that second card, which seemed to float in Angrel's fingers without touching them. "He taught me a bit about tarot readers, too."

"Oooh, a skeptic," Angrel said with a smile on her colorless lips. She laid the second card down, crossing the first: the five of cups.

" 'A dark, cloaked figure, looking sideways at three prone cups; two others stand upright behind him,' " Angrel quoted. " 'A bridge is in the background, leading to a small keep or holding. It is a card of loss, but something remains over; three have been taken, but two are left; it is a card of inheritance, patrimony, transmission, but not corresponding to expectations.' "

Staring at the dark-haired, cloaked figure on the card, tall and proud, but with his head drooping in resigned sadness, Te felt her arms tighten against her sides. She'd seen this pose before.

The week before he'd died, her father had come to see her. By then he was living somewhere else, in some apartment downtown, Te had thought, and rarely came home. He called once a month for a minute or two. There'd been a knock at the door. She'd been upstairs and had let her mother answer it. She'd heard voices, and then her mother calling her down. She'd gone down and there he was, standing at the door, silhouetted by a streetlight. He was rail-thin, his cheeks sunken into his face, and his hands knobbly like an old man's.

Angrel was watching her with glistening pink eyes.

"You suspect that he and Sonore have just had a serious conversation," said Angrel. "He looks exhausted, and in an instant you know something is terribly wrong with him, that something is happening to him, and you take a few hurried steps forward down that little plant-choked hall as if to throw yourself into his arms."

Te started, looking hard at Angrel, whose eyes wandered away, closing slowly as she continued to speak.

"And your eyes fall to his feet, and there are just his shoes on the front step. You wanted to see a suitcase. You wanted to see evidence that he was coming home, that he was moving back in—and when you don't see it, a crushing weight falls on your shoulders and all these little hopes you had about the family being whole again, about the comfort of your father's arms after your mother had made you sing—are all dashed and broken. You feel them break like sticks. You stop, cross your arms"—her eyes opened and she grinned slyly—"like now"—the eyes closed again—"and glare out at him all the fresh pain just reopened by his return."

Te felt herself shrink away from this strange albino woman. Te knew she should be looking for a trick, here, looking for ways to debunk this performance. Only once every possibility of fraud had been eliminated could one assume the supernatural was at work. But Babu hadn't really believed any of that, had he?

"You look at Sonore's face," Angrel said, eyes still closed, fingers now caressing the card's edges, "and you see the same wicked smile you've endured in the three years since your father moved out. You know she's once again driven him away, and you find all your anger directed, not at your mother, but at *him*. You're angry because he's given you false hope, coming home when he's just going to run out on you again. And you say something to him . . . Do you remember what?"

Te's face and neck were like concrete. "I said, 'I've got nothing to say to you.' "

Angrel's eyes were open again, boring into her with reflected flames. "Those were your last words to him. And then . . . then he took this pose." Her finger drifted on the card. "And he said good-bye to your mother, and he left."

Te clutched herself against the hot shame, and wetness leaked from her eyes, but she wasn't so much feeling guilty as furious at the woman for knowing these things. She breathed hard through her teeth and choked back her emotions.

Angrel was staring down at the cloaked figure on the card. Te watched her as her head tilted to the side, and her gaze softened, almost to tears, and she whispered, "This is Rob."

And the change was immediate after that. The woman became suddenly tense in the face and eyes. Her fingers jerked away from the card and she brought her stare back to Te's.

Te returned it with fierce defiance.

"He told you what happened," Te said. "You just reasoned out the rest."

Angrel laughed: a girlish, bouncing laugh. "Yes, he did tell me," she said. "I asked him how it went, and he told me." She pointed to the card. "This card crosses you, blocks you, suffocates you."

"When are you going to show me something interesting?" Te said.

"Oh, yes," said Angrel. She laid down another card, above the first two: The Wheel of Fortune, showing the wheel itself, etched with ancient symbols, hanging in the sky and surrounded by the four beasts of the apocalypse.

"Do you know what Babu wants me to teach you?" she asked, adjusting the card into place.

"Binding," Te said.

"Do you know what that is?"

Again, a vision of her father crossed her imagination, an image of him standing calm and firm, tall, unafraid, a little smile on his lips and shadowy monsters all around him.

"No," said Te.

"Then how am I supposed to teach you in one night? I wonder," Angrel said.

It wasn't really a question. It wasn't exactly a rhetorical lament, either. Te waited.

Angrel's eyes drifted away, lingering on candlelight. She held one white finger on the Wheel of Fortune. "The world has been turning a long time. It's had its share of masters—gods and despots and the occasional humanitarian. Babu told you something about this?"

"The Warden."

"The Master of the world," Angrel said, eyes still floating. "But not a master in the normal sense. He doesn't govern; he's simply a source of ideas. Our current Warden was an oily man of limited stature and limited vision. He was an architect, one who took great joy in making little boxes and poles fit together exactly right. He never drank. He never smoked. He was completely chaste and rarely spoke to another human being, except to conduct his business."

The albino woman began to tap her fingers on The Wheel of Fortune.

"How does a man like that get to rule the world?" she asked, rhetorical this time. Te kept still and aware. Angrel continued. "I don't know. The theory goes that, during periods of great social upheaval, when the world as everyone knows it alters beyond return, the people unconsciously look for someone who can make the world make sense. Maybe he was just the right man for the job.

"In any case, it's his world, now. It's a world of machines and measurements and laws, where every existing thing has a designated place, where everything is categorized and named and deconstructed. When he's done, all will be in stasis and there won't be an original thought left in any human being.

"And the wheel—this wheel—will stop."

Angrel's eyes flared to life again, fire blazing in them, disproportionate to the candlelight. Te jolted back as she felt that heat on her cheeks.

"What do you see?" The woman's voice was deep and ancient, loud and echoing.

Te felt herself falling, pulled backward by an invisible hand. The candles became stars, whirling in blurred motion. Angrel's white face became a streak across the heavens, a line linking across time. In bursts of imagery, Te witnessed the undulating rise and fall of civilization. She was a slave in the desert of Egypt, a pig farmer in the dry plains of Mesopotamia, a cook's boy in the kitchens of Rome, a sailor lost at sea—always the lowest of the low, and the weight of short lives lived in bondage crushed her down until she gasped. She saw fire: the fires of Pompeii and Alexandria, of London and Chicago, of Mount St. Helens and the bomb over Hiroshima. She trembled in the grip of earthquakes, bled puss in the plagues, died on the spear tips of her fellow men, or with a ball of iron eating at her guts and screaming, screaming. Faces flashed between the visions, laughing, the same laugh, the same face, age after age.

It was Angrel's face, sitting across a dying campfire, her whiteness now a death mask of dried clay on black skin, her face changed, neck and limbs thin, flattened breasts hanging down a bare chest half hidden by chains of bones and teeth and feathers. Around Te and the fortune-teller, the impossible emptiness of the primeval savanna shrieked its power into Te's mind, the vast silent presence of the ages now marred by the thinking mind of man.

Then her head hit the floor and she was back. She'd fallen over in her chair.

Cursing, she rolled over and struggled to her feet. She righted her chair, gave her head a final rub, and sat. Angrel watched her the whole time with impassive, unblinking eyes.

"There are Old Powers," Angrel said, as if nothing had happened. "Powers of vision and will that were common in the humans of prehistory. They're all but forgotten now, crushed out of existence by the last several Wardens, who put more emphasis on dogma, doubt, and reason than on mystery. Everyone has them, though only a few of us remember how to use them."

She drew another card.

"Sight across time was one of those powers. Suppression as well. Binding is another. You don't need to *learn* how to use them, so much as remember."

Te stared at the back of that next card. How had Angrel given her that vision? Drugs? Hypnotism?

The card came down and whatever she'd wanted to say fled her mind.

Strength, showing a girl taming a lion with a chain of flowers.

Te caught a momentary hesitation in the woman across from her, the momentary hardening of the amused smile, when she saw the card. Then Angrel fell smoothly into her fortune-teller's mystique.

"Binding," Angrel said, "is the art of kindness. It is the art of compassion. Bind the beast with chains or beat him with clubs and he grows fiercer inside, and one day he'll break out. Bind him with roses, and he will lick your hand and purr as you lock him in his cage."

She tapped the girl on the card, near where the twisted loop of infinity hovered over her head.

"This was your father," she said, and again came that slight softening of the eyes. Te watched the woman intently while she drifted with whatever emotion was eking its way to the surface. "He was born for binding. He had such an understanding of the forces of the psyche."

Then the fire again.

"What do you see?"

A pulse of sensation ripped across the table from the fortune-teller. In the instant before it overcame her, Te swore she saw the tablecloth ripple, the cards shift, and the shadows turn to look at her with conscious intention.

And then she was falling again. She fiercely willed herself forward, upright, even as the awareness of her own body evaporated, and she was once more wheeling in the galaxy of candle stars.

The heavens spun above with terrifying speed, sun and moon blazing by in streaks of fire and luminescence. She sat cross-legged beneath a tree, leaves fluttering down above her, growing back, fluttering down. Before her, on the plain, a legion of devils screamed and hollered and tore at one another. They slashed at her clothing, pulled out her hair, dug their claws into her skin and flesh, and she did not move. They howled in rage and burned the world and fell upon one another in fury, for it was their lifeblood that they be hated, and Te felt only love for them.

She lied to herself and said it wasn't real.

The desert winds bit her, the red dust of Eden billowing down from the sky, carving through the mesas and scouring the land of living things. The earth rumbled and shifted beneath her, changing shape as the continents shifted—eons passing in moments. Around her danced the supple bodies of young women and boys, behind them a legion of servants carrying all the wonders of the earth, and behind them an army that stretched to the horizon, an army that came to her on bended knee and worshipped her. She turned to the one face in all of that vast parade that did not worship her, and forgave it these temptations it had conjured, and it cursed her name forever and ever.

It was real, she knew. Once, it had all been real.

She stood beneath a dead evergreen on a bed of dry orange needles that crunched under her shoes as she walked. On the hills around her, the dry grasses whispered names and secret words, and in the distance the city belched its litany of cars passing on the highways. She looked upon a yellow fox that sat at the base of the tree, waving nine golden tails behind it, staring calmly with simple animal eyes. She spoke to it, using her father's voice.

"You want me to make a wish, don't you? That's all you ever want."

The fox stared at her without expression, but she found an answer in that silence, and spoke:

"Then I'll make one."

Then Angrel's reading room spilled back into existence around her. For the barest instant, she saw the fortune-teller as an ancient woman, impossibly old and impossibly ugly, marred by pockmarks and twisted by arthritis, and bent low under the strain of a long, cruel life. To her right, she thought she saw, for the barest instant, the flicker of someone sitting in the third chair—the empty chair.

Te had a white-knuckled grip on the table when she came back, and she was panting. Angrel already had another card ready, upheld, back side facing Te. The albino woman was smiling.

Te took a deep breath, making a performance out of steadying herself to win time to think.

What the hell was going on? This wasn't hypnosis and it wasn't just Te's imagination. Under the pretense of wiping the sweat from her forehead, Te glanced quickly around the room. *It could be some hallucinogen*, she reasoned, *except that Angrel doesn't seem affected, and I don't feel anything weird until she looks at me like that. Be open, girl. Why does this feel familiar?*

"Binding is a talent," Angrel was saying. "It's not really a teachable skill. It's hereditary. Some would say it's genetic. Others would say it's like an heirloom passed on to a worthy heir when the binder dies."

Angrel's smile was somewhere between wicked and

compassionate. She laid down the fifth card, to the left of the first two: Death.

"And the binder always dies," she said, distant and quiet. "It's one of those stupid requirements of fate, like those trade-offs you read about in the old stories."

Angrel's face was marble, and Te felt a chill wander down her spine.

"If you're going to be a binder, you're going to be a martyr," Angrel spat. "You can't get out of it. You can't avoid it. When you become one, you join a long line of proud, venerated dead people. Accept that and you can do the job. Don't, and you can't."

Te watched Angrel take a deep, shaky breath, and knew the look was coming. This time, Te braced herself for it. Her instincts told her to look deeper, to look for something Angrel was trying to hide from her. As Angrel's eyes opened, fiery, into hers, she remembered what this felt like—like her mother's stare when she made Te sing. Were these things the "Old Powers" she was talking about?

She remembered Yun. "Why is it that you may not do the same to them?"

Old Powers. Everyone has them. All right, then.

"What do you see?"

As the wheel of stars started its spin, Te stared back. She felt a giddying rush of energy up from her gut, a bolt of enthusiasm. The candle stars spun and blurred, but this time, Angrel did not fade, to be replaced by visions. Across that psychedelic abyss, the two made eye contact, and held it, and for an instant, that was all that existed in the world. Then Angrel gasped and drew away, and Te suddenly cringed as a headache hit her like a railroad spike through the eye.

She saw Angrel in a thousand poses of death, ages and ages of dying and suffering, dying from asthma, from heart attacks, from diseases, at the hands of angry mobs, tied to burning poles, and over and over as a malformed infant left to a death by the elements on a lonely hillside.

Across the table, Te could hear Angrel gasp. The visions layered on top of a blurred view of the room and the table. Te pressed the sides of her skull inward and groaned. The pain blazed higher, now like a split down the length of her brain. Somewhere inside she knew she could stop this, but the pain was so much, she couldn't think, couldn't concentrate.

There was more death. This time it was the deaths of others. Angrel cackled or chanted or murmured her spells and made these deaths real. Te watched her burn effigies and photographs, wave fetishes over clippings of hair and toenails, gaze at a lone man through the web of her own fingers and, with a twitch, make him fall under the hooves of his horse.

Through the relentless flood of images, Te saw something that stood out, distinct in detail and dark against the bright sensation of the pain: a hand, shadowed but clear, clasped in a glove, reached out into the space between Te and the fortune-teller, into the space that was the table and was a thousand, thousand years of dying women. The hand seemed to grab hold of something in a tight fist, then turned over and opened, as if releasing a bird and allowing it to fly away.

The visions stopped. The headache evaporated. Te rocked back in her chair and blinked and blinked, rubbing her scalp through a matt of sweaty, sticky hair. Angrel was recovering herself across the table, but Te's

eyes followed the retreating hand as it drew back to the
empty chair, where a figure sat, draped in a heavy coat
and a broad hat, only a small band exposed between the
collar and the hat's brim, and even this in shadow. She
blinked and the chair was empty.

The Man in the Empty Chair . . .

Flames flickered in their wax homes. Barely visible
candle smoke curled against the ceiling. The air was
heavy with the tang of sweat and the too-sweet smell of
burning wax.

Angrel was murmuring "thank you" to someone, and
again Te flicked her glance to the empty chair. "Who's
the chair for?"

Angrel gave a little cough. "It's for séances," she said.
"Channeling. Sometimes the departed like to come sit
at the table. They find it inviting."

"So am I a binder now?"

"As much as you ever were," Angrel said. "Babu
didn't send you here so that I could teach you."

"It was so you could help me remember, right?"

"Exactly," Angrel spoke through clenched teeth.
"Normally I wouldn't have any part in it. Your dad would
have taught you. He'd have taken you out to practice on
some little creature until you were good enough."

Te felt a pang in her chest and fought against curling
up. She focused on Angrel, who had just quickly wiped
at her eyes.

"But he's dead and we don't have any time for you to
practice," she said, "so Babu asked me to take you back.
Some of the Old Powers live on in me, and I have . . . a
history of enlightening people."

"As a fortune-teller?"

Angrel barked a laugh and seemed to recover herself.

"As witch and wisewoman and oracle and goddess. You saw it, didn't you?"

Te's eyes flicked to Death, then back to Angrel. "Something like that."

Angrel cleared her throat and tapped Death again with a professional air. "Death is your past. Both as Te Evangeline and as a binder. This"—she drew another card—"is your future."

She laid it down: The Hanged Man. Despite herself, Te sucked in a breath.

"It isn't what you think," Angrel said quickly. "It's not about martyrdom or persecution or any of that. This card has no set meaning. Not even Waite had one for it."

Te scoffed. "So it's a wild card, and you can make it mean whatever you like."

"Oh, no," Angrel said. "Its meaning is very specific, just not clear. This card represents the mystery."

"What mystery?"

"The only mystery. The *divine* mystery. The unknowable law of concurrences. Direct knowledge of reality."

Te bit her tongue and tried to be open to it. "Right."

"Remarkably closed-minded for an investigator," Angrel said. "Or did Babu tell you not to trust me?"

Te said nothing.

"I see," said Angrel. "It's just as well. I have a tainted soul, and in better times you'd be burning me at the stake. People have forgotten the reasons they used to do that." The albino woman rested a single fingernail on The Hanged Man. "Do you want to do it, or shall I?"

Te stared down at the card. It showed a man dangling from a living tree by one foot. There was no fear, no pain in his face. He wore a look of mute contemplation, of perfect ease, and a nimbus of light encircled his head. Te reached out and touched it. Looking up, she saw deep into Angrel's red eyes. One of them said it, or maybe both:

"What do you see?"

The room fell away. The candle flames cut streaks across the abyss.

Te saw Angrel at ten years old, a white-skinned little girl, getting off the bus in St. Ives—a girl looking at the buildings as if looking at prison walls. She looked up and saw a man there, swathed in a long coat and hat, all features hidden from view—a man whom the bus station crowds passed by as if he were not present. The girl took this man's hand, and they left together.

It was two years later and Angrel's fingers were shaking as she laid down card after card and each was something no one had seen before: The Abyss, The Emptiness, The Snake, The Fallen Angel, The Goat with a Thousand Young. Around the table, people bent over the cards and fretted and muttered and took notes. Babu was there, and Corwinder Martin, both much younger, and her dad, though his eyes drifted not over the cards, but over the little girl laying them with skill and confidence despite her fear.

It was four years later and Angrel was a young woman, with hips and breasts filling out, arms and fingers long and slender. She was on a couch, kneeling astride a much older man. She reached out two pale hands and caressed his cheeks, lowered her face, and kissed him, long and passionately, her soft lips sliding over his rough ones, her flawless porcelain face pressing against his weathered and stubbly chin. His hands came up and enveloped her in an embrace of eager passion. The girl was sixteen years old. The man was Robert Evangeline.

Te yanked away and the vision shattered in an instant. This time, when she looked across the table, she saw Angrel exactly as she was.

Angrel lifted her fingers slowly away from The Hanged Man. She'd become, if possible, even paler.

Neither of them said anything for a long time. The candles guttered and smoked. One popped and went out.

"Maybe you should go," Angrel said.

"Yeah."

Te carefully and deliberately rose from her chair. She swept through the bead curtain and out into the rain without another word. The jangle of the door chimes followed her into the night. Babu was waiting for her. He opened the car door, but she shook her head.

"Take Jack home," she said. "I . . . need to walk this off." Babu nodded, as if he actually understood how she felt—as if that were possible.

She walked home in the constant drizzle and the cold sting of the November winds, the visions replaying in her head over and over, stinging her each time with the final image. When she reached her apartment, she knocked down the picture of her family at the park and smashed it under her heel.

Faces. Eyes. Looking at him. Not one of them breathing. Not one of them blinking.

"Master," they said, whispering with a last escaping breath.

"Oh, God, oh, God, oh, God."

Lester's fingers clattered and shook against the doorknob. The lifeless shapes of his Strutters—*his* Strutters— rose up from the couches and the floor and held out their hands to him.

"Master," they said.

They moved. They spoke. They still knew him, but they were not the same. Lester's vampire body, so aware of things like pulse and body warmth, found nothing in them resembling life.

"Master!"

Little Jill, in the corner, curled up, mascara and eyeliner a dark wash down her face. Reaching for him, crying, sobbing, still alive—impossibly, cruelly alive.

Lester had one foot across the threshold and couldn't take that second step. The Maskim had hidden, having feasted. He could not see it, but it was as if he could sense it inside the safe house, waiting in perfect contentment for fresh life to wander into its snare. It was a creature that did not know urgency; it would wait forever.

"Master!" Jill screamed.

"Master," the others whispered.

"Oh, God," Lester whispered. "Oh, God, I'm sorry. I'm so sorry."

He closed the door and locked it. Then he ran, out into the drizzle, into the night that would hide him, into the streets that would give him shelter from the horror crushing him from the inside.

Jill's screams followed him for six blocks before distance finally silenced them.

Chapter 7

Suppositions

Babu pounded on Munin's door at eleven o'clock. The handle turned after the second knock.

"The numbers expected you."

Babu looked down at the hunch-shouldered pseudo-scientist. He was wearing a bathrobe over dirty pajamas and a tinfoil hat, and looked like a child of ten in the body of a man of seventy; Babu didn't know his real age. The pocket of the robe bulged with the distinct shape of Munin's toy ray gun, which he always carried. Munin moved aside and politely gestured him in past a half dozen monitoring devices mounted in holes carved in the walls and doorjamb.

"Bird's out," Babu said, not bothering to remove his shoes. "We'll need some more antidote. Nose plugs. Enough for the troop, except King, of course."

Munin was already making calculations on an abacus he'd produced from somewhere inside his bathrobe. "You, me, Angrel, Lester, Ahmadou, and then King and the Man, who need nothing. Seven. Auspicious number, good."

"Seven," Babu said. "But not the Man. Te Evangeline."

Munin frowned in ticks like a clockwork mannequin. "Her numbers are confusing, Babu. The equations give two answers. And with her, it makes eight. Eight is not a good number. Too easily divided."

"Then it's seven," Babu snarled. He ached for a cigarette.

Babu strode into Munin's living room, a place of quiet lighting, modern pastel couches, and a working model of the difference engine in place of a coffee table. Art made of sheet metal hung from the walls, and every inch of floor was covered by bit pieces: screws, fasteners, wires, plates, batteries, and the flayed remains of radios and toy cars. Babu kicked a path. Munin followed him in with scuttling steps, like a secretary, or a butler.

"You still do not trust the Man?" Munin asked.

"Kitsune's been out for more than thirty-six hours; Bird's been out for four or five, and we haven't heard one peep from the Man." Babu jerked up a finger with each accusation: "No calls. No orders. No moots. He has to know, because Angrel would have told him by now. He's either not interested or he's behind it. He's not coming."

Munin brushed an armload of small PVC pipe joints from a couch cushion and settled down onto it, wrapping his robe around him, effeminate in movement but with sharp eyes.

"I have been doing some calculations," he said, absently flicking at the abacus. "And I wonder now if you are right in your suspicions."

At that, Babu raised an eyebrow. "You seemed pretty skeptical."

"That is the proper state of all good scientists," Munin said. He paused. Babu didn't consider what Munin did a

science, and Munin knew it. "How would you character-
ize the Man?"

Babu studied a geometric piece of art on the wall
that might have been a flower. "We don't know anything
about him."

"Exactly!" Munin began flicking rapidly through
calculations. "He lives and breathes obscurity. By
means unknown to anyone, he can go about invisible
and unheard, and even when present, he is a shadow
perceived more with the intuition than the senses.
I can count on one hand the number of times I have
seen him in person, can remember the exact number
of words I have ever heard him speak. He is a mystery.
He *is* mystery."

Babu studied Munin as he might a witness, looking
up and down the man's face and hands, now animated
with a childlike energy, the excitement of discovery. No,
it was the excitement of the *expression* of a discovery.

"Not the first time you've thought about this," Babu
said.

"Of course not," said Munin, sniffing. "I have made the
Man a subject of study for many years. He is a project of
unimaginable complexity. He is *zero*. Always present yet
invisible, infinitely added to any equation without notice
or alteration. Calculations using him come to null or to
various errors and remain unsolved. He is obscured not
only from sight and sound, but from prediction, from de-
termination. I find that irresistible."

Babu leaned back against the wall, listening atten-
tively now.

"How rare it is that he gives orders himself, eh?" said
Munin. "He always issues them through Angrel, or Julia
before her. You know Julia claimed he could read minds

and be in many places at once? It might all be nonsense, of course, for she did not know him any better than the rest of us. But still . . ."

Munin tipped the abacus sideways and all the beads clacked into neat rows.

"What does that sound like, to you?"

Babu felt a chill, not of surprise but of an ancient nagging doubt finally given voice.

"Like maybe he's not human."

Munin's eyes sparkled.

"There is no rule saying St. Ives' keepers cannot also be its inmates, eh?"

Babu rubbed his forehead, massaging muscles well adapted to frowning.

"All right. We'll meet at the safe house tomorrow with Te. We're going hunting. King'll be suppressor."

Munin's eyes rolled around a bit—he was doing math in his head. "King cannot suppress the Kitsune."

"We'll go after Bird first," Babu said. It felt good to have a plan. "Bring all your bird-hunting gear. Let Angrel know. Les should already be at the house. I'll bring Te." The good feeling slithered away. "Christ, Te . . ."

"Not an easy case," Munin mused. He made a sucking sound with his teeth. "She may die."

Now cold uncertainty was all over his body. Babu drove his fingers into his forehead. "She's just a kid."

"It is always a possibility," Munin said, his face etched with wrinkles of concentration. "In many permutations of her numbers, she becomes a variable canceled out. In others, there are multiple answers, opposed."

Babu felt a rumble of anger in his chest and bit it down. "No offense, man, but I trust your predictions less than Angrel's."

Munin snorted. "The white woman will brag, but her predictions will come to little, just as mine did."

"What do you mean?"

"Yun is deeply involved in the girl's future," said Munin. "And where the Kitsune is involved, two plus two could be five, or three, depending on one's state of mind. He makes prediction impossible. All that is certain to me is that his attention is on her. Maybe it was from the beginning. You remember?"

Jul. 18, 1986 [Kitsune Case]—Munin confirms penetration of Evangeline household last night. Suspects direct transgression by Kitsune, purpose unknown. Wife and daughter alive, in good health. Robert deeply disturbed. Will not tell me why. Knows more than he lets on. Troubled.

That was how Babu had recorded the incident in his casebook ten years ago. Where was that damn casebook? After he'd dropped off Te's friend, he'd torn the whole car apart looking for it and come up empty.

"Yeah, I remember it," Babu said. He crossed his arms and leaned against the wall. "We hunted Kitsune for months the first time. Lester tracked him all over the damn city."

"I remember," said Munin. "We were always behind because we could not predict where he would be. If the Man is zero, Kitsune is X, an unknown."

"It never occurred to any of us to try to figure out why the Kitsune even came here in the first place. What he was after."

Munin blinked behind the tinfoil. "The Man did not think it was important."

Babu ground his teeth. "Well, I do. Have all that
stuff ready tomorrow. I'll call you with a location." He
strode toward the front door. Munin did not rise from
his armchair.

"Surely you are not going after the Kitsune yourself,"
he said. "I can give you odds on success if it would dis-
suade you."

Babu pulled the door open and recoiled at the blast
of chill air.

"I'm just gonna talk to him," he said.

"When one talks to the Kitsune," said Munin, "strange
things happen in the brain."

Babu didn't answer.

Thirty minutes later, Babu stood on a lonely hillside soaked by the rain. He'd had to leave the car on
the muddy dirt road, three or four hundred yards back,
and trudge up the hill on foot. He was high above the
city now, and, looking back through the rain, saw it as a
bright smear across the valley floor.

Couldn't have the Sacred Grove in the middle of town.
Maybe an awning over it. Maybe a coffee shop across the
street. Nope. Gotta be way up here in the damn hills.

Bird had ruined his blazer, and it was no good in the
rain anyway, so he'd put on an army surplus jacket that
he kept in the trunk. The thing smelled like canvas and
old paint and barely kept the rain out. He pulled the collar up and trudged on.

The last stretch was the worst. The hill up to the grove
was steep and round, and though the carpet of dry grass
kept the ground from turning to mud, it became as slip-
pery as Teflon when wet. After his third backslide, Babu
resorted to grabbing fistfuls of grass and hauling himself

up hand over hand. He crested the rise and stopped to catch his breath.

The Sacred Grove: a single dead pine in a circular patch of infertile earth. Babu hated this place. Each step toward it felt like a step away from safety, like a step back from the comforts and protections of civilization. This place, the Man had said, was a place of truth. Inside the circle there could be no lies, no illusions, no false masks or pretenses. As Babu stepped carefully over the slick ground and the rough sagebrush, he felt the presence of something ancient and primal and utterly without consideration for him or any of the accomplishments of human history.

He always expected something to happen when he crossed the perimeter, something magical or even a purely psychological shift in sensation or perception. But there was nothing, except that he felt more alone than usual.

Rain didn't fall in the Sacred Grove. Babu slipped out of his jacket and shook the rain off it. It was cold when he put it back on.

Babu lit a cigarette and waited.

He didn't wait long.

"'And at the corner of the street, a lonely cab horse steams and stamps, and then the lighting of the lamps.'" The Kitsune appeared at the edge of the circle of dry earth, in his human form as Yun Kitsune. He wore a gold suit jacket and trousers with a white turtleneck. The rain weighed his blond hair in straight lines down his face. He folded his hands in front of him and smiled.

"What is your wish, Mr. Cherian?" he asked.

"I want answers," Babu said.

Yun smiled demurely. "That is what you want, true, but not what you wish for."

Straight. Blunt. Don't talk to him. Interview him. Question him. No conversation. "Why are you here?" Babu asked.

"Certainly the little white-faced girl has explained a few things about me," Yun said. "I grant wishes."

"So does the Variety Club."

"They grant requests." Yun began a slow stroll around the perimeter of the Sacred Grove, hands clasped behind his back, face upturned into the rain. "Human beings are in the habit of granting all the wrong things. If they paid a little more attention to themselves and to each other, things could go so much more smoothly."

"Why here?" Babu said, watching the loose, animal movements of the man. "People are always making wishes somewhere else."

"You make it sound as if I'm unwelcome," Yun said.

Babu seized on this comment. "So you're here with permission, is that it?"

Yun shook his head. "Asking for permission is a very strange practice. If I always asked permission to grant my wishes, I would have nothing to do. No, Mr. Cherian, I am here because of a wish made without any doubts."

Yun stopped and swiveled to face him. Babu's hand snuck into the pocket of his coat, around the handle of his pistol.

"Example," Yun said. "What do you wish for?"

"You out of town," Babu said.

Yun clapped his hands once. "You want that, yes. What else?"

Babu sensed the meeting turning into a conversation and decided to cut himself off. "You to answer my questions."

"That too," said Yun. "You also want a new car, and though you can certainly afford one, you never buy. You want to stop smoking, but don't. You kept wanting Robert Evangeline to be your friend, even though he already was. You want someone to tell you your wife's death was not just an accident. You desperately want Robert's little girl to like you."

That stopped him dead for a second. Yun's gray eyes penetrated down somewhere inside him that trespassers weren't welcome.

Yun clapped again. "The granting of wishes is a foolish thing unless one knows what those wishes are, and which is most important. Because you people so often don't, it falls to me to know all of your wants and desires, and to sort the true from the false. I *must* know the answers to all your questions, and so I do."

Babu tossed his cigarette out into the rain and stepped forward, fear and anger propelling him closer to striking distance. "Why are you here?"

"The prisoners of this place wish for freedom with a voice like a thousand angels in a choir," Yun said. "I heard it all the way from my former home in Bangladesh. How could I stay away?"

"Did the Man bring you here?"

"I come only at the call of wishes made."

Not exactly a denial. Babu sucked back the last of his cigarette, right down to the filter. The aching, burning heat down in him gave him strength. He pressed on.

"Whose wishes?"

Yun smiled. "All these wishes may be answered through the wish of one. That is what made it attractive."

Babu lost his cool. "Dammit. Give me a straight answer! Was it the Man in the Empty Chair?"

"Was it his wish that brought me here?" Yun said. "No. Will his wish be answered through the work I am to do? Oh, yes."

Babu pulled the gun and let it dangle by his side. Yun looked down at it with amusement.

"What wish is that?" said Babu.

Yun's thin lips pursed in a very feminine coquetry. He waved his slender fingers before his eyes. "Your will to know this is a strong one," Yun said, "but your will to figure it out on your own is stronger."

Babu felt his heat rise, break, subside. The bastard was right. He hadn't come here seeking answers. He came to get a clue, a trail, a new direction on an otherwise cold investigation. This was another problem with coming to the Sacred Grove—one couldn't hide anything, even from oneself. Babu sighed, and slipped his gun back into his pocket. He lit another cigarette, tossing the match away into the dry needles beneath the dead tree, where it did not catch flame. The ashen grit of the smoke made him cough, but he welcomed it.

Babu saw Yun watching him out of the corner of his eye.

"Do you want to know if you have cancer?" Yun asked.

"No," Babu said.

"If you had it, would you wish me to cure you?" Yun asked.

"No."

"Then what would you wish for?"

"Just that—that Te's safe." The statement was less than true and Babu felt a sting as he spoke. He was sure he showed nothing outward, but Yun reacted with a grin, his thin white teeth popping out of the rain-soaked dark.

"It hurts, doesn't it," Yun said, "to speak false within a Sacred Grove? That's their purpose, you know. That's what their makers, people more ancient than you or I, wanted to give to the world." He pointed to the tree, then swept his hand to encompass the barren earth. "And their truth is death—that we all die, sooner or later. Even those like me."

Babu had heard enough. Munin was right. This was a stupid thing to do. Just *asking* the enemy, for all his secrets—what had he been thinking?

"*Your* truth is death, Mr. Cherian," Yun went on. "You hasten to it, with your cigarettes and your poor eating habits and your dangerous occupation. Your wish is only that you have someone to share these cold nights with, as you march day by day to your grave."

"I don't want you to bring my wife back."

"That's right, you don't," said Yun. "But there's another, isn't there? A young thing full of life: her inquisitive mind; her rare, bright smile. You watch her work, you steal glances at her figure, and marvel inwardly at the ease with which she attacks every problem you set her, and you feel like you could be young again, with her. You picture taking her home to your little hovel. You think about what it would be like to touch her, be with her, to take her pain away."

"Shut up!" Babu screamed. "You shut up! It's not like that."

Yun's eyes sparkled with their own light. "To have *her*, even for a night . . ."

The gun was up, aimed, hammer cocked, safety off.

"*That* is your wish."

Babu squeezed the trigger. He couldn't have missed; yet Yun wasn't there. The grasses whispered with the passage of some small animal, fleeing over the hill.

Babu bellowed into the night. "You stay away from her!"

He rubbed back stinging tears. It wasn't true. Not Te. She was like an adopted daughter, like a little sister maybe, or just a friend. Not like that. It was just Yun fucking with his head.

But it wasn't. As much as Babu told himself otherwise, it was all true. No one can lie in the Sacred Grove, not even to himself. *Jesus Christ. What the hell's wrong with me?*

He turned and fired at the tree and put a hole in its old, dry bark.

Chapter 8

Ray Guns and Ragnarok

Te was already up when Babu came by at six thirty the next morning. She hadn't slept.

She threw on a loose gray shirt and blue jeans, belt, hair tie, leather jacket. She left her shoulder bag with the casebook tucked into the bottom of her closet. She stowed her handgun, safety on, in her pocket.

On her way out, she peeked in the Sprats' window downstairs, spying Jack up and alive, choking down a huge bowl of soggy cereal while his mother worked away at something on the stove. Jack smiled and waved at her. She waved back. She felt like she was waving good-bye.

"Half hour till sunrise," Babu said as Te slipped into the passenger seat of his car. "Take a look."

He passed her the front page of the morning paper.

FOUR DEAD IN MYSTERIOUS ATTACK, read the headline. Te scanned the rest of it: the bodies found at the pulp mill, no signs of forced entry, claw marks and feathers found on the scene, no leads, call local police with any tips, etc.

"Bird," Te whispered. There was a chill there, somewhere, in the back of her head, at the sound of that name. There was a vision of a face with unblinking eagle eyes.

Babu threw the car into gear and muscled it away from the curb. "Already making herself busy," he said. "Bird's diurnal. She won't be waking up for another hour, so we've got time to track her down."

"And what?"

"Catch her. Cage her," Babu said. "It's our job. We hunt Bird down. We surround her, suppress her, and bind her."

"You mean *I* bind her."

Babu looked over at her. "Yeah. Problem?"

Much to her own surprise, Te said, "No."

Long after she'd left Angrel's shop, the visions had kept coming: flashes of battles, memories of conflicts settled without conflict. Men and women facing down horrors so outrageous, Te remembered them like cartoons. Men and women smiling with open arms, watching the creatures wither and submit, letting themselves be caught because the binder did not hate them. The visions had continued all night, and even when they faded, Te had replayed them in her imagination over and over, thinking on the processes she'd seen, on the expression of absolute confidence that these binders used. It was their armor, their weaponry: an unyielding belief that their enemy *would* be bound. The belief fired all their core, tingling out to fingernails and the ends of their hair. The moment of binding came when the belief was perfect and calm and still. It was simply true, unavoidably true, that the beast would be bound, and so it was.

And, mixed into these, there'd been visions of a cave—of those same men and women cringing before the dread terror of a hole or a doorway or a shadowed path in the woods. The sight of it stole their smile, their calm, their certainty. Some went in. Others retreated. These were binders, too. It seemed impossible that Te could be one of them, and yet Babu had asked her, and the answer had come out confident and strong.

"Try not to get nervous," said Babu with a smile. "You'll have backup."

"Just you?"

"And the rest of the team. I'll introduce you," Babu said. "And Angrel'll be there."

Te felt sick for reasons other than Brightontown's bumpy roads.

"Babu," she asked, "you know Dad moved out when I was fourteen."

Babu's brows grew heavy and thick. He nodded.

"Do you know where he went?"

"Stayed with me for a few weeks. Then got an apartment downtown."

Te struggled with the next question: "Alone?"

She watched the big man as he hunched forward and was suddenly very attentive to the road.

"Don't know," he said at last. "I always thought there was someone."

Te watched him carefully. "You don't know who it was?"

"I didn't want to go around investigating him," said Babu, then added, "Sorry."

Sorry for snapping or sorry for the whole situation? Sorry that it ever came to that in the first place? The word said all these things—and, Te suspected, sorry for lying to her about not knowing the name of her father's teenaged mistress. Sorry for not putting a stop to it whenever he'd found out.

Te sat in a sort of empty shock for several blocks, trying not to think of that vision of white, slender hands on her father's rough chin, white dreadlocks falling on his thinning hairline. Babu did not interrupt her.

Of course Babu had known. Probably her mother had as well, and her aunts, and everyone else. Everyone but her. It's not something you would tell a fourteen-year-old—Te couldn't argue with that—but it still felt like another knife in the back.

How could her dad have done it? Angrel had been almost Te's own age. Maybe her mother had driven him to it. Te remembered how he'd been that last year before he left. She remembered hearing him pacing the halls at night. She remembered the lawn going unmowed for weeks while he sat on the couch and didn't say anything. She remembered him barking at her and her mother for the tiniest mistakes—and the one day he packed a bag and left. That day he kissed her on the forehead and told her to be strong, and for that moment he was still himself.

And afterward, he'd gotten worse. He was thinner every time Te saw him. He let slip in conversation that he wasn't seeing his patients anymore. Te remembered him from their infrequent lunch dates, his eyes jumping at every shadow, every stray noise. She remembered him shrinking from people walking by, watching shadows as if they were going to bite him, skirting thin air as if there were something present there. He'd started being mean to her, snapping at her about clothes or hair, about schoolwork, about her desire to go to a college far away. And then had come that last day, when Te was finally fed up with it, and then just a few minutes in a hospital room, and then nothing.

"What happened to him?" Te wondered aloud. Maybe her mother had been doing it—*draining* him, *partaking* of him, making him sing. No, Te had never once heard her dad sing in her mother's presence. Maybe he was safeguarding himself.

"Who? Rob?" Babu asked.

Te blinked out of her thoughts, looked into Babu's eyes, saw the worry. So she said, "Yeah, I want to know. It's about time I knew."

Babu ground his teeth. "Seizure," he said.

"That's how he died, Babu," Te said. "I want to know what was happening to him before that."

Babu breathed heavily for the length of a stoplight before answering.

"I don't know," he said. Te must have made a face, because Babu gave her a quick glance and snorted. "I really don't. Something was eating him up. Lord knows there are enough things in this town that would do that to you. I'm sure he knew it was happening, but he didn't talk about it. He really didn't talk about anything, toward the end."

"Is that what killed him? This thing eating him up?"

The car jolted over a series of speed bumps leading into the broad parking lot of the pulp mill. The lot was larger than a sports field, and flat, ringed by a chain-link fence and watched over by tall four-light lampposts. Babu swore up and down, wrestling the car's uncooperative steering into a sharp right that landed them sprawled diagonally across two parking stalls. Babu angrily turned off the ignition, and kicked his door open without answering her.

Te slapped him on his broad back as he made to exit. "Hey!"

Babu hesitated. "We'll talk after," he said, and got out. Te tore open her door and went after him.

"No, we won't," she said, glaring at him over the car. "*You* don't believe he died of a seizure. What *happened*, Babu?"

"Not now," he snapped, rounding the trunk. "We have work to do."

"Fuck you," Te spat at him, but she fell silent. Babu was moving with purpose, with urgency, and the pre-dawn sky was brightening instant by instant. He hauled the trunk up and passed her a backpack, this one much lighter than normal. She yanked it away and looked inside.

"Nose plugs?" she asked. "Bug spray? Flight goggles? What is all this?"

"The right tools for the right job," said Babu. He shouldered a pack of his own, heavier than Te's. He undid his belt and began to loop his gun into it. "You brought yours?"

Te showed it to him, then threaded it into her own belt at his urging. She looked out across the parking lot, observing, stowing down her frustration. She was on the clock now: *protocol over personal things*.

The St. Ives pulp mill stood tall and dark against the sky, a tower of flat, uninteresting metal topped with stacks and chimneys. Normally, those stacks would be pumping out clouds of white steam, but today they were inert. Her first thought was that the police had shut the place down, but looking around the parking lot, she saw a number of cars still there. The morning air bit at her cheeks, and her breath floated in front of her eyes.

"No cops?" she asked.

Babu adjusted his bag on his shoulders. "Guy on duty

was a friend of mine. I had Angrel pay him to take a walk."

"That easy, huh?"

"No, it wasn't."

They set out marching across the parking lot. The mill grew larger as they approached, filling the sky with its shadow. The lights were on in office windows high up on the building's nearest cubicle wing. Te examined them but could see nothing moving.

"Shit. Where's Lester?" she heard Babu mutter. Te spotted two figures standing by the entry doors of the mill. One she hadn't seen before: a short, stooped man wearing what looked like tinfoil around his glasses. The other was Angrel, shuffling her cards and watching them approach. Her white face was unreadable, but her eyes followed Babu, not glancing away for an instant. She didn't blink.

"Lester?" Babu asked them, stepping up onto the curb and joining them in a three-sided circle. Te hung back, listening and observing.

The short man harrumphed, a sound like a horse clearing its nose. "The safe house was locked when we went by," he said. "Lester was nowhere around."

Babu turned to Angrel. "And did you look for him?"

Te watched the albino woman's face carefully, but could read nothing.

"I drew the five of pentacles," Angrel answered. "Reversed. He's in trouble and he's gone into hiding."

Babu pulled out a cigarette, lit it, sucked on it for a moment. "Munin, this is Te Evangeline. Te, this is Munin Hartford, engineer."

"Mechanologist. If you please, I prefer," said Munin, extending his hand to Te after a sharp look at Babu, which the big man ignored. Te shook his hand. His skin felt like a paper towel.

"Pleased to meet you," she said.

"And I you, young lady," said Munin. "And if I may say, you are very tall, like your father."

"Um . . . thanks."

"It is a goodness, to be like a father," Munin said. "Your numbers tell me you are something of an artist, are you?"

"A bit," said Te. Munin was still shaking her hand. Te gently pulled it away. "I do charcoals."

"Art is also good," said Munin. "We are all of us artists, are we not?"

This last question was addressed to Babu, who shrugged and tossed his cigarette away half finished. "Is King with you?"

Angrel gestured vaguely to her left. "He's there."

"Good," said Babu. He turned to the empty stretch of curb and started talking to the air. "King," he said, "get inside and do some looking around. Since Les isn't here, you're our tracker, too."

Te wondered why Babu was talking to empty space. It was as if he did it all the time and as if the other two found it the most ordinary thing. A sweep of hot wind, inexplicable in the prewinter chill, flittered across her cheeks, carrying unintelligible whispered words.

"Nose plugs, everyone. Goggles," Babu ordered. "We'll go in the front doors. Munin, get your gun out."

The old man obediently pulled out a red plastic ray gun. He also put on a huge set of goggles, with lenses covered in red cellophane and rims that looked like they might have been made out of the cross sections of tin cans.

"Angrel," said Babu, "do a reading: best entryway, traps, or surprises, that sort of thing."

Angrel nodded, dropped to a crouch, and began to lay out cards on the pavement. Babu put his hand on Te's shoulder and pulled her aside.

"How are you doing?" he asked, not as a friend but as the leader of a job. Was there anything he needed to know to make a proper assessment of the situation?

"I didn't sleep," Te said.

Babu squared off in front of her, looking directly into her eyes. "This isn't an easy case to cut your teeth on, Te. Listen, if you can't do it, you give the word. We'll pull out."

Te nodded.

"Don't get stupid," he went on. "If the binding fails, we retreat. Simple as that. Don't think you have to try again and again. You give it one shot and give me the thumbs-down if it doesn't work. We don't risk the team on a failed operation."

"How will I know if it works?"

Babu straightened. "I don't know," he said. "Honestly, you already know more about this stuff than I do."

Te squinted, back into her memories of the visions. "There's a moment," she said. "You kind of empty yourself out, and when there's nothing inside, you just know that it's going to work. The target tries to distract you, to keep you from reaching that point. To keep thoughts in your head."

Babu nodded. He pointed to her bag. "That's why the nose plugs and goggles," he said. "They'll keep Bird's pheromones out of your system. The aerosol is an antidote. It's what I gave you in the park. I've also got a respirator in there, in case you want to talk to her."

"Why the *hell* would I want to talk to it?"

Babu drew back a bit. "I don't know. Rob always did his binding by talking."

Te felt tears stinging her eyes and she covered them. Some of the memories had been of her father. In all of them he'd been tall and calm—casual, even—soothing his opponent through his words and his soft, pulsing tone of voice. In the visions he was strong and confident, and in every way the father she'd wanted—the father she'd missed.

Babu was shaking her shoulder. "Stay with me," he said.

Te cleared her throat, then wiped her eyes. "Right. Sorry."

Babu scrutinized her. "Are you *sure* you can handle this?"

Te swallowed hard and forced a smile. "Well, there's not much point in asking *now*. We're already here."

Babu looked embarrassed and grunted something unintelligible. Te froze her smile in place and thoroughly hid her terror. She jammed the plugs up her nose and slapped the goggles over her eyes. She looked like an idiot, and that helped. Babu wandered back to where Angrel was doing her card reading on the curb and Te trailed after him.

"There might be someone inside with her," Angrel said. "But no animation. No tricks. She hasn't woken up yet. She'll be docile and slow to react. But"—she showed Babu her last card—"I drew this."

The Hanged Man.

"I can't be sure of anything here," Angrel pronounced.

Babu turned to Munin, who was looking the building

up and down, making minute adjustments to the rims of his goggles.

"She is at the top of the main tower. Perched on some pipes. She is not moving. King is there with her. He taps his foot and waits for us."

"Good."

Two minutes later, Babu turned the latch and led them inside, his EMF detector in one hand, his gun still holstered. Munin followed after, brandishing his ray gun. And then Te. Angrel stood outside the doorway, arms crossed placidly. Te looked at her as she reached the doors.

"Not coming?" she asked.

"I'm a noncombatant," Angrel said simply. Her shrug said she didn't care whether Te or Babu or Munin lived or died.

Te turned away. Had her dad really slept with that woman?

The first room was a small reception area, with a desk across from the door, a company logo shining above it. The walls were a school-hallway turquoise, the carpet a mottled gray-green. Here and there, silver feathers lay perfect and shining. Yellow police tape fluttered from the doors where Babu had broken through it, and a thought hit her.

Where *were* the police? Had they just locked the place up and left it? What if some detective came by and caught them here? What if they left fingerprints or fibers or other evidence?

She inhaled to say something to Babu, but stopped herself. The big man stalked forward like a cat, silent on his feet, eyes following every twitch of the EMF meter.

Munin flanked him working a pocket calculator in his right hand using only his thumb, holding his plastic ray gun out in his left. If the professionals weren't talking, she guessed she shouldn't, either.

Behind them, Angrel softly closed the doors. Te heard the woman muttering something from outside. Babu and Munin leaned in together for a moment, murmuring to each other. Te slid up from behind, trying to overhear.

"Recent," said Babu. "Still getting a bit of a charge off . . ."

"Attitude and posture," Munin answered. "Relaxation of muscles at a rate of . . ."

". . . didn't get a chance to get into nineteenth-century dress. Sure Bird would have wanted . . ."

". . . inclined at eighty-five degrees, with hip twist against rib twist, angle of neck vertebrae . . ."

". . . around the eyes indicates order of . . ."

". . . subsequent reduction in mass, estimate seven kilos lost to . . ."

They both stopped, locked eyes.

Babu spoke first. "Six this morning."

Then Munin said, "Five twenty-one, nineteen seconds."

They both stood up and faced the reception desk. Te looked from the back of one head to the back of the other.

"Our quarry has been awake at least once this morning," Munin said. "It may not be as the white lady said."

"Damn shame," Babu replied, looking forward again. "She probably came in early to catch up after yesterday. Damn, damn shame."

"What is?"

Babu looked back at her, a raw emotion knitting up the corners of his eyes. Munin just looked back at his calculator, absently pushing its buttons. Te placed her hand gently on Babu's shoulder and pressed him aside. The big man dropped his eyes and stepped back as one who knows he can do nothing more.

They'd been talking about the receptionist, slumped over in her chair and until then hidden by Babu's broad shoulders. Only the top of her head and her shoulders could be seen: a cloud of curly, thinning brown hair, the shoulder pads of her blouse askew. Te sucked in a breath, held it. Her eyes traced again and again what little she could see of the woman.

Still. Like a piece of scenery. Like a mannequin. Like an abandoned doll.

Babu's hand fell on her shoulder. She removed it with gentle fingers. His hand was rough and sweaty.

"I have to see this," she said.

Babu just nodded. Te left him.

She approached, step over step, each conscious and exact, as if measuring the crawl of time in those actions. She walked across the carpet, around the desk, and squatted down.

This was the third dead person Te had ever seen. She had no eyes. She had no hands. Her skin was pale. Her face almost had an expression to it, as of extreme exhaustion. Her mouth hung open just a little. There was a hole at the top of her neck, and darkness inside it. The carpet underneath her was stained red.

Whatever was in this woman that had made her breathe and move and be alive was long gone. Te felt outside of herself, as if she were in the presence of something profound but was too small to grasp it. She felt as if she should be feeling more than she was, but when she looked at this dead woman, everything in her went blank and cold and said, "So what?"

Te stared at the woman until she stopped expecting her to move. Babu's hand fell on her shoulder again.

"Don't," he said. "It makes you old."

Te rose, turned away, and blinked for the first time in several minutes.

Munin was punching numbers on his calculator, standing at a glass door that led into a short hallway lit by fluorescent overheads. It had a card reader to its right, which Munin was examining closely through his goggles, hunched like an old librarian. Te watched the little man work, and spoke to Babu.

"She's number five, then?" she said.

Babu was watching her closely. His concern was sweet and also annoying, so she felt she had to say something to him.

"I'm okay," she said. "Really."

Babu nodded. "Well, now you see why we do this work. Why your dad had to do it."

"Yeah," she said. "So let's go."

She returned to the corpse and snatched the woman's ID badge. A quick swipe through the reader and the glass doors opened. Munin stood dumbfounded for a moment, then laughed.

"The easy solution," he said. "I often miss it."

Te didn't feel like laughing. She led the way into the next hall.

Staircases, elevators, janitor closets, a locker room. Feathers in some places. Scratches on the walls. Another glass door at the far end of the hall. Te swiped the card, and Babu and Munin charged in ahead of her.

Beyond was the factory floor. Walkways ran between iron boilers twice the height of a man. Brass pipes of all shapes and sizes rose up from the floor to the distant ceiling, wrapped by wooden staircases and walkways, studded with pressure gauges and held in place by wooden braces. Dim yellow electric lights hung from the underside of every walkway, from the pipes and the walls and the support beams. Sunlight cut the dust through windows high up on the tower, where the pipes pierced the roof into the morning sky.

Wood? Iron? Brass? Te scanned around. Everything looked *off*—rivets and gauges, signs in ornate writing, large levers instead of computers or digital panels. It all looked distinctly nineteenth century.

"I don't know how she does it, either," Babu muttered.

The Freak People. The carriage. The manicured park. All Bird's doing?

"Anything?" Babu asked, eyes jumping from place to place to place.

"I see no movement," said Munin.

Te lent her eyes to the search, scanning for movement or a change in color. Her skin felt clammy, and she ran a finger over her cheek. It came away faintly pink.

"You said she's up high," Babu said. "I see two staircases. Do you think . . . ?"

"No," Munin said. "We all go the same way. Strength is in numbers, I say." He gave Te a wink, which she didn't return.

"Let's hope King's ready. There's too much light in here to see him," Babu said. He placed one foot on the stairs. "Te, in the rear. Breathe through your nose."

Te did as she was told. The nose plugs hissed as she sucked air in and out of them. Her heart beat like a timpani. Her mind screamed at her that this was lunacy, and yet her feet found the next stair, and the next, and the next.

On the seventh flight, she saw it. Bird was crouched down on a support strut between two of the gleaming steam pipes that stretched to the roof. It slept, head down, wings curled in against its shoulders, talons that were too like human fingers curled around the beam. Its breath was a wet hiss, slipping in and out of its flat nose. The pipes and the crossbeams beneath it were spattered in red.

Babu signaled them silent, continuing his slow creep up the stairs. At the ninth landing, just one down from Bird, Babu turned, eyed Te, and offered her a thumbs-up, then a thumbs-down.

Te returned a wavering thumbs-up.

Babu nodded, turned, and faced an empty stretch of air just off the tenth landing, and waved to it as if beckoning someone forward.

Te heard drums. They were faint at first, more like a memory of a beat wandering for no reason through her consciousness. The sound pricked at her ears, and as it got louder, she felt vibrations in her chest as if the drums were very close. They were joined by a hissing, like a snake, or like a man spitting through his teeth to mimic one.

Bird jerked and started to stir. A warbling rattle like a crow escaped the creature, so loud that it rang from the steel walls and overlapped itself a dozen times. Babu drew and raised his gun. Munin raised his.

Bird opened its eyes. Then it let go a predator's screech, a piercing, haunting sound that vibrated off metal and bone.

No, no, no, no . . .

Te froze up. Her hand fused to the railing. Once again it overwhelmed her, the certainty that this was impossible. There was a monster here, a creature that wasn't supposed to exist, and yet here it was, its avian eyes falling on her, on Babu—its wings stretching out, fanning forth a faint pink mist—its teeth, long and sharp and translucent, opening in a terrible smile.

The drums beat hard and Bird winced back. Te heard a chanting, the stomping of feet, the roar and heat of a fire, the cool of the night. In her mind, she saw a man dancing in the desert, pounding the ground with cloven hooves, and with each stomp, Bird shrieked, twisted, recoiled.

"Te!" Babu shouted. Te started, seeing that he and Munin had run up to the tenth landing, seeing the urgency in his eyes.

So Te ran, and in a few steps she was beside them, staring into Bird's eyes, which glared back with a burning hatred. Bird flexed its wings for flight, but the unseen dancer's hooves struck the earth, and it flinched away.

"We've got her," Babu said, shouting over Bird's screams. "Go, go."

Te stepped forward, her feet carrying her without hesitation. She sucked a deep breath through her nose filters. She remembered the visions, remembered the calm, the confidence, the certainty that she'd seen in those other people, in those other times. She emptied herself, until Bird's shrieks and the dancing man's drums were like the murmur of a waterfall, distant and soothing and blended together.

God, it was so *easy*! It was as if she had done this her entire life, as if it were something she remembered.

Her eyes drifted closed and she let the utter calm radiate out into her fingers and toes. Every part of her came alive with sensation. Tingling flared up in her teeth and the ends of her hair. In a moment she would open her eyes and gaze with love and pity upon the poor, tortured creature before her. She would feel its pains, its frustrations, and the despair of endless, immortal years of crime after crime. She would understand it with the perfection of omniscience, and it would be bound in the emptiness of her love.

The steadiness was not just hers, she knew, but a tiny corner of a single great stillness, reaching back across century after century to Sumer and Egypt and the skin-clad shamans of the ice age. It was not something generated, some state attained through mental twisting, but an eternal existence hidden from the world, and in communing with it she felt the joy of finding something lost. She was a part of every binder who had ever walked the dirt of the world, and every binder was a part of her.

Every binder. Even her father.

The calm wavered, splitting at the edges with black veins. Doubts crowded her, tearing away the moment of perfect understanding, filling her head with all those questions long obsessed over, bringing her away from it all.

No, no, no, no . . .

It was gone.

Her eyes flew open and saw nothing but Bird's teeth.

"Down!" Babu crashed into her with his shoulder and she fell. Oak stairs struck her—head, flank, butt, ribs—as she tumbled down from the tenth landing. She slammed hard into the ninth, feeling the whole structure shudder as her elbow broke her momentum. The pain deafened all sensation for two heartbeats. Then she fought back the sparks in her vision, the jerking in her muscles, and rolled herself over.

Teeth. Claws. Everywhere, grabbing for her, slashing into her coat, into her shirt. And its voice, hammering her like thunder: "Binder! Ugly, ugly, ugly!"

Then a stomp, a gunshot, the force of great wings flapping, and Bird leapt away into the air.

Te's lungs burned. She gasped in the thick air, choking and coughing on Bird's scent. She clutched at her chest, pressing down, trying to stop breathing, but she couldn't. In, out, in, out. She was hyperventilating and her thoughts started flashing in pink. Black spots on her eyes, fire in her chest, legs and arms shaking. She slammed both palms down on the first stair, pressing hard.

Steady, girl. Breathe through the nose.

Reaching behind into her backpack, she caught sight of her jacket's right sleeve. The leather was torn through from slashes all the way up and down. She took a shot of Babu's antidote in her mouth and exhaled hard. The horrible smell and the shock hit her instantly, just like in the park. Her heartbeat faded to something manageable and she forced her head up.

Bird hovered above Munin and Babu, its wings whipping tornado winds everywhere. It lashed down with both claws as the two men fell onto their backs and out of its reach. Te saw the dancing man stomp, and Bird convulsed. It dropped down onto the landing, smothering Babu and Munin in feathers.

Before she even realized it, Te was barreling up the stairs two at a time. She plunged her fingernails into the closest stretch of feathers and yanked away. Her hands tore free, full of soft down and rigid spines.

A green flash, and Bird exploded up into the air, tumbling, shrieking, and slashing out. Munin rose to a crouch and fired again. His ray gun cut the air with an oscillating noise and a bright green laser. It struck Bird on the wing and spun it around. At the same instant, the dancing man's hoof came down, and Bird was thrown back against a pipe as if struck hard.

Babu was on his feet now, too. He glanced over his shoulder.

"I'll try again," Te cried. Babu nodded, and Te once more stepped up to the edge of the landing.

She took a deep breath, willing herself calm, willing that connection to the infinite stillness, like slipping on a well-worn shoe. She began her exhalation, ridding herself of clinging thoughts and terror.

With a powerful flap of its wings, Bird rocketed away from the pipes and cut through the empty air next to the tenth landing, slashing and tearing with its claws. In her imagination, Te saw the dancing man reel, saw him bleed and choke and fall, saw his face strike the dirt. The drums stopped.

For a moment, silence. Then, came Bird's cry like a diving hawk, Munin's ray gun singing its retort, Babu ordering retreat. Her smidgen of calm spilled through her like water through open fingers.

"Go!" Babu grabbed her arm and threw her at the stairs one more time. She caught the railing, spun, just in time to see Bird crash into Munin, knocking the old man to the ground. Bird's claws came down on the hand with the ray gun, vertically piercing the wrist. Bird yanked back and Munin's hand stretched and tore off like dough. The monster bent to strike again and Babu shot it three times.

Bird went over the railing and fell. Munin started screaming. Te knew her mouth was moving, knew her hand was reaching out. She should help, she knew, but . . .

In an instant Babu had hauled Munin up, cradling the tiny man with one huge arm.

"Retreat!"

They ran down the steps, feet pounding on grates, spinning from flight to flight, leaping the last few steps to each landing. Bird shot up into the air around them, snatching at them with its claws through the tangle of beams and pipes around the staircase. Its face was everywhere, and the beating of its wings blotted anything else from Te's ears.

They hit the bottom landing and bolted into the hallway, then ran for the glass doors. Te fumbled the receptionist's card into the card reader, and the doors began their slow parting. Babu went first, hobbling with the still-screaming Munin. Bird's cries filled the hall and Te pulled out her gun and fired blindly back.

Both hands, don't lock your elbows.

Her ears rang by the time the gun clicked empty. She turned and ran.

She crashed through the exit doors and the sun blinded her. She tripped and fell to her knees on the pavement, blinking away the spots, looking back. Was it following?

She saw Angrel unhurriedly close the doors and then place her palm across the seam between them. They buckled outward as Bird hit them from behind, but held.

Te rolled over to see Babu holding tight to Munin's shoulders as the older man buckled over himself, pressing his crippled arm into his belly and swearing and crying out in Swedish. Babu's stare was the snarl of an enraged animal, teeth bared and all. Te followed his gaze to where it rested on Angrel's placid, porcelain face.

"The Man did this!" Babu roared. "You *know* he did! It's his fucking fault. *Rob* saw this coming and you killed him for it. Well, don't think I'll go down so easily, you *cunt*!"

Angrel folded her hands together in front of her and looked down and said nothing at all.

"Te," Babu growled, "get in the car."

Te did as she was told.

Munin swore all the way to the hospital.

Chapter 9

Silent Jay Singing

I fall through my door with the weight of all of my unknown ages upon this earth. The bell jingles as the door
of my shop closes behind me, merrily locking me inside
with my tears. Why am I crying? I have not cried for a
dozen lifetimes. Why am I curled up on the floor, with
my face to the carpet? Why does it feel like I am coming
apart, like my chest is caving inward without cease?

"But I've killed *before*!" I scream into the dark of my
shop. "I've killed a thousand, thousand times. I've killed
all the men I've loved. Rob was no different."

The unlit candles and inert incense burners give me
no answer. My cards are in my hand. I know they will
comfort me. They will tell me why I feel this way, why
the harsh words of a man as small as Babu Cherian
should provoke this tearing within. I do not want to
know. I cast them away into the corner, where they scatter like snow.

I am crawling now, crawling like the babe I have been
a hundred times, born with a twisted limb, a deformed
face, or a birthmark too big to ignore; left on a hillside
or in a desert—left to the mercy of the sun and the snow

and the cold, which have no mercy. I am crawling as I have done in my moments of deepest despair, when my life is wasted before it's begun.

I am sobbing now. Babu's words ring in my head, huge and thunderous, distorting, so that he accuses me of things he could not know, jabs me with words he did not say.

"Yes, Rob knew!" I scream into the carpet, into Babu's face in a memory of what I wished I could have said to him. "Rob found out. Rob tried to stop him. I might have helped him. I could have, but he didn't ask me. *He didn't ask me!* It's not my fault."

I am crawling and a trail of tears is staining the carpet in my wake. Beads brush my hair as my nails claw into the softer carpet of my reading room.

"I didn't want him to die."

I crawl around to the third chair of my sitting room, the chair that always sits empty, and there my hand slides forward, and my fingers wrap into the fabric of a heavy trench coat. A gloved hand slips beneath my chin and lifts me, gently, to my knees, and I look up into the dark between the hat's brim and the coat's high collar.

The Man in the Empty Chair. Such a thing we call him, because such a thing cannot be. He is the impossible, the man who does not exist. He is like a shadow of a living thing, without any living thing to cast it. I do not know where he came from, and I do not care. He is the one creature on this earth as lost as I, as empty and divorced from any meaningful purpose. He is my companion, my counterpart, and yet he is not real, and he cannot see this kinship I feel with him.

I want him to comfort me, but he cannot, so I wrap my arms around his legs and lean against him, rocking like a small child. The gloved hand strokes my head, but there is no warmth there. He is with me and I am alone.

He tells me that it had to be done. He reminds me that Robert Evangeline was the aggressor, that it was Robert Evangeline who met him in the Sacred Grove and tried to kill him. He tells me that Rob would never have stopped until one of them was dead.

"But it was just because of his daughter," is my answer. "If you had left her alone . . ."

He says that he had no choice. She is the only way any of us can be free.

He says Te Evangeline will break open the walls of St. Ives and that this act will change the world. He says that after she does this, all of us, all of the lost peoples, the creatures of myth and the cursed and weary wanderers—the people will want us back and the world will be ours again.

It used to be the only thing that mattered to me. Five thousand years ago I was bound into a human body, into a body doomed to be slain and reborn into ridicule, into oddity and deformity. I don't even remember who did this to me. It never mattered. All that has ever mattered was ending it. All that mattered was my freedom from the endless cycle.

But somehow that isn't enough anymore. Now something else matters. Something else tears at my heart and makes me forget the ages and ages of sorrow, in favor of a fresher loss.

"I loved him," I say.

The Man in the Empty Chair tells me it was a stupid thing to do, to fall in love. He does not scold me or reprimand me; he states only the truth, and I agree with him. I knew that the love of a wastrel like me for such a man as Robert Evangeline was a stupid thing. But, to feel safe, to feel cared for after so many lifetimes of fear and hatred ...

I have been burned at the stake thirty-five times, and thirty-five times I have visited my wrath upon my destroyers from the safety of a new face. Thousands have been murdered by my hand and the will of my magic. Thousands more have turned their hands against me, and robbed me of my lifetime again and again. And here was a man who kissed me and told me my past didn't matter, told me each life was a new start, a chance to be someone I had not been, someone who was not bitter, not twisted up by cruel things done to her.

Rob was nice to me. Just nice. I had not had that in a very, very long time.

"I could have talked to him," I say to the Man, knowing he can't understand, knowing he is not someone who can feel as I do. "I would have lied to him and he'd have believed me. He could have been saved."

The Man tells me it wouldn't have mattered. He reminds me how many will die before the new year comes, tells me how Rob would have been among the first, standing on the front lines against the hordes his daughter will unleash. I know the Man is right. Rob would have led the charge. He would never have survived.

"It's not worth it," I say to him. My cheeks are red from tears, and I press my face hard against the rough canvas of the Man's coat. "What we're doing. It's not worth feeling like this."

I leap to my feet. I stare into the gap between collar and brim and I plead with him. I knit my fingers together and I beg him. "We can still stop it. You can get the Kitsune back. I know you can. We've still got the time to ..."

He reaches into me and tears the thought away. His touch is the vacant caress of nothingness against the psychedelic burst of the confused mind. Once again I am on the floor, panting, defeated. He has done this to me many times, touched a part of me and made it as nonexistent as himself. I expect he will do more to me, and I wait for him to.

But he doesn't. He looks down on me, his pose perhaps one of pity, though I know he is incapable of pity. He tells me something he has never said before.

He says Rob was binding me. He says he bound me with love, using my emotions as chains to hold me in the tradition of his profession, and made me forget the vengeful goddess I once was. The Man says that Rob made me weak.

I can't believe it. Rob loved me. I know he did. It wasn't a manufactured love like that conjured to bind the inmates of St. Ives, but a true love, a deeper love—the love of a man for a woman.

The Man says he will not waste any more time on me. He says if I cross him, he will break me. But if I side with him, he says he will give me a place in the new world he is building; he says that he will restore me to what I was, and then all my loneliness and pain will be as a shadow of a thing that does not exist. He offers me this place though he does not need me, though he cannot love me.

All I need do now is nothing. Hunt the Kitsune in Babu's company if necessary, but do not allow him to be captured, and preserve Te Evangeline from destruction—but not from death and pain. He says that when Te comes to me, I will remember what I was before the curse, before the endless cycle of wasted lives began. My love for Robert Evangeline will be forgotten, and these torments I feel will vanish.

And I thank him, as I ever have. He promises me freedom. That is all I have ever wanted. It is all I want now.

He leaves, vanishing into the dark like he always does.

I sit awhile on the floor beside his chair. I think of Rob, of his thin but strong arms, of the dry smell of his skin when he held me close. I try to remember his face, his eyes, when he told me he loved me. Was there a lie in those eyes? I can't remember.

Could he have been binding me, and nothing more?

I breathe deeply until I settle myself and regain some of my objectivity. Whether he was or not, it no longer matters. He's gone, and what he felt or didn't feel for me went with him.

I gather my cards, hoping I have not offended them by tossing them away. I shuffle them. The sound soothes me. I light a candle and sit at my reading table, its purple felt identical to so many similar tables I have owned over my lifetimes.

The thought nags me. It floats up from an empty well deep inside and will not be pushed away:

Did he love me?

Here I sit, on the cusp of freedom from a curse five millennia old, and that is all I can think about—the affections of one man.

Did he love me?

I must know.

I whisper my question to my cards, and deal. The first

spread tells me nothing, as does a second, and a third. I wonder briefly if they are angry with me for discarding them, and then I notice their pattern. Each spread contains the eight of swords, and in each spread it lies in the one spot I need clarity, yet gives me none. It blocks my intuition, so that the truth behind the spread does not come.

But who is the eight of swords, I ask them. And I remember that I have used it recently to signify a person.

Te Evangeline.

Maybe she knows. Maybe she can tell me.

I know I can't ask her. Her hatred for me is long simmered and powerful. She has hated me since before she knew who I was, for taking her father away from her home.

"Well," I say aloud to the spirits, "there are plenty of ways to know without asking."

I lean back and breathe. The Old Powers swell up in me, and I sense the faintest hint of what I might have been before the curse: I smell dry dust, and feel the heavy heat of close flame. I feel as broad as a cloudless sky, as restless as the magma beneath the crust of the earth. My mouth splits and utters sacred words that were mine in a former life. The world falls away, and I *see* . . .

It is the present, this time. Te Evangeline is twenty-two years old and she is sitting on the bottom step of the staircase leading to her tiny apartment, dressed as she was this morning, and I recognize the shoulder bag sitting by her side. She has just come from the hospital, where the doctors have successfully bandaged the stump of Munin Hartford's arm. He will live, but he will be crippled for the rest of his brief life. Te is watching an ant clambering through the grasses, imagining that he is trying to make his way back underground before the rains begin again.

Her thoughts are difficult to penetrate, difficult to sort out. Her self-recrimination for the botched mission has come and gone. Now she is thinking about her parents. She summons memories of her childhood, some of them mixing with the new binders' memories I helped open her to. She is confused, but this confusion does not seem to frighten her.

What is it that I see in her? There are shades, there—shades of the old world. I wish I could see more clearly, but the Old Powers have dulled in me, life after life, as I get farther away from what I was before. As I forget.

My path has crossed many of my fellow outcasts from ancient times. We're drawn to each other, by fate or destiny, or sometimes just to huddle together in fear of sacred and secular law. Sometimes I would look at them with the Old Sight, and I would see in them something fundamentally different than what I see in human beings. We are different in kind than they are. Even I, trapped in this human body, bound to the human cycles of birth, death and cruelty, have the taint of the old world inside.

And here I can see it in Rob's daughter. But she's just a human girl, right? The cards have never told me any different. Rob never hinted . . .

So what am I seeing?

I try to pierce closer, but I've forgotten so much of what I was, and it's painful. There is a kind of feedback, like a needle pressed into the skin of my forehead.

The exercise of the Old Powers is not one of concentration, but of release. One does not use the power so much as become the power. I'm no expert at this anymore. I suspect that I was once a master of Sight, and perhaps of other things, but I can't remember. So I fumble around.

She is thinking of me with her father. It's an image taken right out of my own memory: Rob and I, on the couch in his apartment downtown. He thrills to the touch of my smooth young skin. I play into it, using my smile, my delicate body. I tell myself that I'm seducing him, but I'm actually falling in love with his touch. It will be a long time before I can admit that to myself.

Te is seeing this as if she were present in the room. Is she using Sight, like I am? It hardly seems conceivable.

Suddenly, there is a pulse of such ferocity that I am rocked back in my chair. My cards drop from one hand and again scatter on the floor. Te's anger blasts me like live heat. My hands go over my face to ward it off, but the heat is perceived in my mind and the hands can't help.

She glances to the side. Her eyes approach dangerously close to the point of view I have chosen. She couldn't know I'm watching, could she?

I lean forward again, my bare feet brushing through my fallen cards, and look into her. If she is aware of me, she will probably react again.

I am in her thoughts. She looks up. She sees someone walking toward her across the grass: tall, slim, blond. The vision slips and I try to focus through it. I can't. The Sight is sliding away, tilting to something else whenever I try to focus it. The needle in my forehead is like a hot brand now. It isn't her shutting me out; something else is happening. I squint harder as my mind begins to swim. I forget where I am, what I am doing. The Sight fails. The Old Powers vanish from my consciousness once again.

I'm left leaning on my table with a migraine and feeling like I've been rubbed between two blocks of concrete.

I tell myself that whoever I was before the curse—goddess or witch or saint—I'm not her anymore. I don't have the command over the Old Powers like I think I do.

I gather my cards, extinguish my one candle, and sit very still in the dark, willing the headache to go away. The buzzing of the fridge upstairs, of the electrical current in the walls, all scream in my ears.

It isn't until much later that I realize I recognize the man Te had seen, and, with a shudder, that she'd recognized him, too.

"Miss Evangeline," he said. "Fabulous to see you again."

Te didn't answer him right away. She leaned back into a casual slouch, resting her elbows on the stairs behind her.

Yun smiled at her from across the grass.

"You don't look surprised to see me."

"I'm not."

Yun approached, strolling across the wet and soggy lawn. He stopped a few feet from her and folded his arms in front of him.

"Don't you have something to ask?"

Te looked up into his slender face.

"Did you kill that man, Sanjay?"

Yun's smile broadened.

"Yes," he said.

Te nodded. She reached down into her bag and withdrew Babu's casebook.

"Why?" she asked.

"It was what he wanted," was the answer. "He had become too attached to worldly things. He obsessed over his possessions and could never achieve a proper state of meditation. He wanted a chance to start over."

Te nodded again. She opened the casebook to a page she'd marked earlier.

" 'August 3, 1986 [Kitsune Case (final entry)]—Found vessel Sanjay Sharma. Agreed to be prison for Kitsune. Did not go smoothly. Sanjay now blind in one eye, loss of feeling in index finger and thumb of right hand. Medical follow-up in afternoon confirmed nerve damage during insertion.' " She looked up at the man, who still stood calmly, gazing at her. "That was you?"

"Correct once more," Yun said.

"What does 'insertion' mean?"

"I was kept in Mr. Sharma's mind, Miss Evangeline," said Yun. "After your father and his compatriots caught me, they found me my own cell inside Mr. Sharma's head, and I, of course, did not go quietly. Supposedly, Mr. Sharma was enlightened, and wished for nothing, and thus was immune to me."

"So you're one of *them*?"

"Oh, yes."

"And you're . . . what?"

"Creatures of the Old Country, Miss Evangeline. We were here before the age of Man and will likely be here long after."

"There're a lot of you?"

"We are legion, as they say."

"Anyone else I know?"

"Several. Some, you may suspect. Others, never in your wildest imaginings."

Te let her head drift down to the casebook. She flipped pages, letting her mind run, letting her eyes be drawn to this phrase or that. Her hair drooped in strings across her vision. She was too exhausted to lift her hand and brush it back.

"May I ask a question?" Yun said. Te looked back up at him. His hair shone in the sun.

"Shoot."

"You seem less surprised at all this than I'd have suspected."

Te sighed deeply. "I've been up for thirty-some-odd hours. I've almost been killed twice. I've almost got two other people killed, too." She paused. "I've also found out that everyone I trust has been lying to me my whole life." Her eyeballs were heavy; she dropped her gaze. "Guess I'm just tired."

"And alone," Yun said. He crouched down in front of her, bringing his face level with hers. "You've always been alone." His hand rested lightly on hers, his fingers like the brush of silk, and cold like snow.

Te snorted a laugh. "Is that sympathy? From you? This whole mess is *your* fault, man. *And* you're a murderer."

Yun drew his hand back. He looked hurt. *Well, good.* Te leaned close to his face.

" 'Jul 1, 1986 [Kitsune Case],' " she recited. " 'Search party: Lester, tracker. Rob, Ahmadou, O'Shae, Julia, myself. Found six dead: homeless, from clothing and general condition. Believe Kitsune is trying to elude us. Must know Lester's sense of smell is distracted by blood. Trail leading us into Darktown. Called Angrel. She said the Man will try to intercept.' " Te ripped the page out of the book and jammed it in Yun's face. He flinched back. "A *multiple* murderer, right?"

She slammed the page back into the book and clapped it closed.

"Did you let Bird out?" she snapped.

Yun smiled again and opened his hands in a gesture of humility. "I am here only to serve those who . . ."

"Shut up. Did you let Bird out?"

Yun's smile died. "Yes."

"And you're the fox, the one with nine tails that I keep seeing my dad talking to under some dead tree?"

"Yes."

She shook the casebook at him. "And you're the one in here, the one who had everyone pissing themselves scared? Who slipped out of all the traps they set for you, who can escape from anything?"

"Yes," he said.

Te exhaled. She put the casebook back in the bag and stoked her courage. She almost choked on the words. "Then can you get me out of this town?"

She stared right at him. Lines of surprise covered his otherwise flawless skin. It was eight long breaths before he answered her.

"No," he said.

Te hung her head and bit her lip. That was it, then. She was stuck. All she'd ever wanted was a way out—a way out of this town, out of her mother's house, out of her own wasted life. Babu wouldn't help her. He just drew her in more and more and told her shit-all. Her dad was dead, but he'd had plenty of chances to help her get away and didn't, so maybe even he didn't care.

Yun's voice was barely a whisper. "What do you wish for?"

The words jumped out of her. "I want to leave all this behind. I want to be free."

Yun patted her on the knee in a friendly, even fatherly manner. She looked up to see him smiling again.

"Go talk to your aunts," he said.

"Why the hell would I do that?"

"Because they can tell you more than I can," Yun said. "But they have to be asked, you see. They've been waiting a long time for you to ask them."

Again that hope, that faint, damnable, stupid hope rose up in her. She prayed to herself that he wasn't just screwing with her. She didn't think she could take it. But, Christ, if Babu wouldn't tell her anything . . .

"About what?" she asked.

Yun stood, grinning like a man with an amusing secret. "Everything," he said.

"Everything. Right."

He immediately took two steps back, and gave a short bow. "I'll leave you to it," he said. "I'm sorry, but I have somewhat more to do today. We'll meet again."

And he became a yellow fox, without sound or ceremony, as if he had never been a man. The fox spun and dashed silently away through a hole in the fence. Te heard a gasp and looked up just in time to see Kent Allard's door click quietly shut. Then she heard the sound of many locks closing.

Te sat there for a long time, her mind flicking between the creature she'd read about in Babu's casebook and the man she'd just spoken with, who, in the two times she'd met him, hadn't once hurt her or avoided her or lied to her.

Footfalls on the grass. Jack walked up beside her, hands in his pockets, and leaned on the rail. "Who was that?" he asked.

Te gave him a sly glance. "Were you eavesdropping?"

Jack shrugged. "I was bored."

"Not going to school today?"

"I had a test," he explained.

She smiled at him, and he smiled back in his own small style, and suddenly she desperately needed the companionship of someone entirely normal. It was a completely selfish desire and all kinds of wrong, and she couldn't bring herself to care.

"Then are you up for another road trip?" she asked. Her insides shook as if she were fourteen and asking a boy to the dance. "I promise that I won't . . . almost get you killed this time."

"Sure."

"Good." She stood up and looked at him, at the scabbed puncture marks around the eyes.

"You're okay?" she asked. "Really?"

Jack shrugged. "I've seen scarier stuff in movies. Really."

To Te's surprise, she completely believed him.

"Good," she said. She picked up her bag and led the way around the house to the street. "You held up better than I did."

Jack flushed a bit, and looked away.

Babu was downtown, in the rain, looking for Lester. When Lester was scared, he took to the street. He hid in Dumpsters and fed on rats and slept in cardboard boxes. He went back to his roots, back to the anonymity of being homeless, the secrecy that came from people never looking your way.

Babu weaved his way through the lunchtime crowds, his size and his radiant foul mood enough to convince most people to get the hell out of his way. He'd blown through a dozen blocks and half a pack of smokes when a pay phone next to him started ringing. He picked it up. It was Angrel.

"Babu," she said.

"What the hell do you want?"

The voice was unfazed. "I was just eavesdropping on Te."

Babu almost snapped at her for doing it, but some note of uncertainty in her voice stopped him.

"And?" he said.

"She was talking with Kitsune," Angrel said. "They *know* each other, Babu."

"What?"

And in an instant he was sucking on a new cigarette, needing the hot, stark comfort. *Jesus Christ.*

"I couldn't hear all of it," Angrel was saying, "but it wasn't the first time they'd spoken, I'm sure of it."

Babu thought, *Hell, Munin was right. The Kitsune's here for Te.*

He thought back. He'd never seen Rob so worried as during Kitsune's first appearance. He hadn't thought anything of it because that was the worst near-disaster they'd ever faced, and all of them were pushed to their limits. But what if the Kitsune had been after Te specifically? What if Rob knew about it? That would account for his extra stress, his being tight-lipped about everything. Babu bit his cigarette filter. *You could have come to me, man. I could have helped.*

"Is he still with her?"

"He left a few minutes ago. He said he had something else to do."

"And Te?"

"She's left, too. I don't know where."

"Well, what do your cards say? Can you confirm where she's going?"

"No, Babu. I can't predict *anything* when the Kitsune's involved."

A thought hit him and Babu almost dropped the receiver.

"Ah, shit."

Angrel hesitated before replying. "What?"

"Last time," Babu said. "Ten years ago. Who did he free?"

"What's that got to . . ."

"First," Babu snapped, counting off on his fingers, "he freed the Maskim. Then, he freed Bird. And then he tried to free the things under Darktown."

"Oh." Angrel hesitated again. "Then you have to get down there. You have to find Lester and . . ."

Babu lost it. "What do you think I'm trying to do? I've been out here in the fucking rain for three fucking hours!"

"Babu, we can't . . ."

"Shut up." Babu stopped himself, took a breath. "Just . . . See if you can get anything on Lester. And find out what happened to King after Bird tore him up. Is he still around? Has he passed on—what? See if your cards can find Bird or the Maskim. See if you can find if anything else is out, or what Te's doing, or *anything*! We are *so* blind, right now."

"Babu, we need to . . ."

"Just do it!" Babu snapped.

"Fine."

Babu slammed the phone back into the receiver. His fingers lingered on the handle, water droplets sliding over his nails. He'd talked to her as if nothing had happened—as if he hadn't said anything; as if he didn't hold the suspicions he did. She was still part of his team; he still needed her.

Everything was falling apart. At least last time, they'd been working together, as one unit, with the Man taking a personal hand in fighting what they couldn't handle. And they'd had Rob, and Julia and Martin and O'Shae, and King had been alive. They'd died to put these creatures away where they belonged, and now it was all coming undone.

Cars rolled by without slowing. People dashed past him, heads down against the rain. He was alone. So goddamn alone. He'd been alone ever since he'd lost his wife, Nyawela, to a stupid accident. After that, he'd thrown himself into his work and into a friendship with Rob Evangeline and his family. Then Rob was gone, worn slowly away while Babu watched and did nothing. But then he'd had Te, and even as an assistant, sometimes as a friend—that had been just barely enough.

And now the Kitsune had her. She might even have turned traitor on him. Now there was no one left.

He squeezed his eyes shut, felt his insides quaking, felt something nameless and agonizing come up from deep in him, a pain he'd hidden for so much of his life.

He picked up the receiver, then slammed it back down, hard. He did it again. And again—over and over until the phone snapped in two. Then he kicked at the phone booth, cracked its walls, hammered the Plexiglas with his fist. And all through, a wordless, senseless scream of rage and pain ripped up out of him, bloody and terrifying. He roared at the rain and the street and the sickened spite of his own life. People gave him a good ten feet.

Eventually, he was sitting on a bus stop bench, on the sidewalk, face in his hands. No one looked at him. No one asked if he was all right. The rage came back up when he realized this, and his knuckles pounded over and over into the armrest. It was no good. Nothing helped. Nothing would ever help.

He spent himself. His body ached. He was cold. His knuckles stung.

Te isn't gone, he told himself. *Just because she knows him doesn't mean she's working with him, doesn't mean he's got to her yet. And even if he has, then . . .*

Then Babu had to rescue her. He told Rob he'd protect her. He swore to Rob he'd protect his little girl. It was the promise that brought strength back into his feet. It was that sworn word given that started the gears churning in his mind again. *Can't do anything for Te until Angrel tracks her down. In the meantime, find Lester. Lester can track these things and that's a place to start.*

His promise to Rob would keep him going. Babu thanked him profoundly, wherever he'd gone. Then, more plans came:

Need to fortify the prison in Darktown. Maybe Lester just returned to base. Might have gone back to the safe house. Have to check both places. Munin'll be conscious again by now, too. Wonder if he's up for making any predictions.

Babu moved to call the hospital, but the pay phone was broken.

It was funny. He laughed.

Hide. Have to hide.

Lester curled up inside the old refrigerator box, clutching himself. His nails punctured the sleeves of his jacket, then his own skin. There was blood, and pain, but they were nothing—nothing—next to the fear.

Stop him. Have to stop him.

Yun would be heading for Darktown. Of course, he might do other things first. He might wander around back and forth and back and forth across the city for days—but sooner or later, Yun would go into Darktown. He would head to Lester's home, that hundred-and-fifty-year-old piece-of-shit house, and he would take the stairs to the bottom floor, to the very bottom, down, down, down, and he would find the door and he would turn the handle, and let the night things loose.

No. Have to hide.

Because the things under Darktown were not the same as the rest. The Man had explained it all, when he'd first come to Lester and designated him their keeper. The things under Darktown had been trapped there since prehistoric times. St. Ives had been built on top of their prison to draw sympathetic strength from its eternally locked door. The Man said the things a hundred feet below Lester's home were alien, inhuman invaders from the Outside, from a void beyond human understanding, and that they desired nothing less than the scouring of all life from the face of the world.

It's why he has to be stopped. He has to be.

Lester buried his face in his hands and cried tears of blood.

I'm such a coward. I'm such a piece of shit.

A rustling. A swishing of short skirts.

"Who is it?" Lester squeaked. He wiped the blood from his bleary eyes.

A shadow at the other end of the box. A figure silhouetted against the dull light of the sun. Hair in pigtails. Short skirt over a leotard. Spiked bracelets on the wrists.

"Jill?"

No answer from the silhouette. But who else could it be, with those thin shoulders, that skinny neck? She knelt with feet splayed to either side, palms resting on the pavement, leaning into Lester's solitude.

"Oh, God," Lester groaned. His hands came up, shaking, trying to cover his eyes. "I'm sorry. Don't you know I'm sorry?"

No answer. His fingers would not block the vision; he stared into the eyes he could not see, feeling their judgment, their hate.

"I couldn't fight it. It would have killed me," he said, his voice growing weaker with each word. A sudden enthusiasm gripped him. "But . . . I locked it in, didn't I? It can't get out of there, not with all that stuff on the walls. I caught it again, right? It can't hurt anyone, right?"

But he'd left her there, left her alive.

"I just . . ." Lester started shaking, though his vampire body didn't feel the cold. "Oh, God, I screwed up, didn't I?"

The silhouette dropped its head, and shook it slowly, side to side.

"I didn't know what to do!" Lester screamed. He pivoted and came to his knees, reaching his hands out to her. "You don't know what it's like! All the blood, the cravings—oh, God." More tears fell on his cheeks. "I'll never eat vegetables again! I can't go out into the sun. This is *hell*. I just wanted a way out."

The silhouette lifted her head again, and under the gaze of those eyes he couldn't see, Lester shrieked and scuttled back.

"No! God, please! Please! I didn't want to, but there was no other way."

The silhouette said nothing, but Lester felt every splinter of its accusation and every needle of its hate. There had always been another way: sunlight fading bright and dim with the motion of the clouds, its merest touch acid. A few steps out the door at noon and he could have ended it at any time. A flash, a scream, and then peace. But he was too much of a coward, even for that.

The silhouette stared into him some time longer, oblivious to his misery.

"Where's your notebook?" he asked.

She didn't need it anymore. No more poems. No more lines witty or moody or plain. Not after the Maskim had its way with her.

"Jill . . ."

Lester had only asked it not to kill her.

It wouldn't matter. It would all be over, sooner or later. When the dark things came up from under the ground, when the shadows of Darktown stretched everywhere, even the Maskim would meet its end, and Lester would be nothing but food for the Goat and its thousand children.

Lester curled up in his box until the silhouette faded away into the sunlight.

His conscience persisted: *Have to do something.*

He closed his eyes and did not listen.

Chapter 10

A Working Kidney

"Are you hurt?"

Te started out of thought. "Why do you ask?"

Jack pointed to her arm. "You keep rubbing your wrist."

Te looked down. She was doing it right now. "It's sore," Te said, putting her attention for a moment on the throbbing ache flushing out of the tendons and muscles in her forearm. "I had to"—she dropped her voice—"do some shooting this morning."

Jack's eyebrows went up. "Are you okay?"

"I'm fine."

"Was it like a gunfight? Bad guys popping up out of windows with AK-47s?"

Te couldn't help but chuckle.

"Not really."

The bus rattled over a few potholes. The motion knocked their shoulders together and bumped Jack against the window. Jack gave her a kind of strained smile. It was obvious he wanted to know more about the shooting, but Te was too hesitant to recall it and he was too polite to ask.

Te looked at Jack. When she was very small, Te had once asked her mother for a little sister for Christmas. Or a brother, if that was all they could afford. Her mother had patted her on the head and said, "But you're all that I need." Well, if any of the other people on the bus were looking at them now, they would probably see an older sister and younger brother.

Or . . . you know, if you really stretched it—boyfriend and girlfriend?

Te cleared her throat so loudly, Jack turned and looked at her. "It's the next stop," she said, ineffectually fighting a flush. "Pull the cord."

Jack did. The bus stopped and they got out. They stood on the curb and watched the bus pull away.

They started up the street. The neighborhood was called Riverside Vincent after someone or other and was situated on a low, flat area right beside the river and prone to flooding in the spring. This was the kind of neighborhood where everyone had a pool and a half dozen trees to dump leaves into it in the fall, and you almost couldn't see the houses for the high fences and the ivy. The sun had finally come out, but the air had picked up a bitter prewinter chill. Te kicked a path through the last of the autumn leaves and led them on toward the river.

"So where are we going?" Jack asked.

"I didn't say?"

"Nope."

"Oh. We're going to see my aunts."

"What for?"

"To ask them things."

Jack nodded as if that made perfect sense. "Investigator stuff, then."

"Sure." She honestly hadn't considered what she was

going to say yet. Was she going to ask for help? Help what? Being free? She could start with questions about Yun, how they knew him, where he came from, that kind of thing—she could press them with it. If that went well, she could maybe see what they knew about binding, about the Old Powers Angrel had talked about—see if that was how they did what they did to her—and if *that* went well, she could move on to Angrel and Dad. She let out a shuddering breath. That was somewhere she wasn't sure she could go.

"This is it."

They came up to a wrought-iron fence ringing a small property enclosed with thick trees on all sides. The cottage inside was ancient, cracked plaster with yellowed, latticed glass in the windows. Ivy, withered from the cold, crawled all over the fence and the house, and a thick layer of soggy brown leaves coated every inch of the yard. Te led them up to the front gate, where a playful-looking iron skull was mounted in the center.

"There's no handle," Jack said, looking over the gate.

"It's hidden." Te reached into the skull's left eye and flicked the catch. The gate came unlatched and she pushed through. "Kind of morbid, isn't it?"

"You have a drawing like that on your wall," Jack said.

Te rapped a couple of times on the cottage door and heard the creaking shuffle of Aunt Babs approaching the other side.

"You little bastards!" came the growl from inside. "I swear, this time I'll cook you up and suck the marrow out of your bones!" The door flew open and there was Babs, clad in sweatpants and a faded pink T-shirt, her fat belly hanging out over her skinny legs.

"Oh," Babs said, seeing Te there, "it's you."

Much as she was expecting it, the disgust in Babs' twisted features started Te's blood boiling.

"Good to see you, too, Auntie," Te ground out between her teeth.

Babs worked her bulbous lips and swallowed what sounded like a gallon of saliva. "Well? What the hell do you want?"

"I need to ask you some questions."

Babs broke into a lip-twitching scowl of crooked, gray teeth. "Let's hope they're the right ones. I don't like people wasting my time, even if they're family."

Te glared at her. "If you don't waste mine, I won't waste yours. Deal?"

Babs grunted: a phlegmy, unhealthy sound. "That's respect of a kind."

Te nodded to Jack and they both stepped into the house, onto warped and creaking floorboards. The whole place smelled like dust and old people.

"Syd!" Babs bellowed. "Got company. Te and some boy."

"I'm Jack," Jack offered.

"You're gamey and unappetizing—that's what you are," Babs snapped. She snorted through her long nose. "So, did you come all the way down here to see us of your own free will, or did someone send you?"

"Yun Kitsune said I should stop by," Te said.

"*The* Kitsune," Babs barked. "That whole first and last name business is just silly."

Babs stomped down the hall, leading them through the tight corridors toward the back of the house. Te and Jack, both much taller than Barbara, had to duck under the crossbeams that periodically cut the low ceiling.

"Syd!" she called. "Hasn't got a bone of sense in her head."

She led them into Aunt Sydney's art studio. It was in fact a concrete back patio completely enclosed in glass, like a sunroom (of course, the layers of leaves stuck to the outside of the glass by rain and rot thoroughly blotted out the sun). A half dozen easels stood in no particular pattern around the room, some tilting so far to one side that it looked as if their canvases should slide off. Sydney was dancing around the room and humming to herself, brush in one hand and palette in the other, eyes closed.

Te didn't like much about her aunts, but one thing she had always loved was watching her aunt Sydney dance. Syd's silver hair flowed behind her like the afterimage of a moving light, floating as if buoyed in water. Her feet spun and leapt, brushing the ground, now heel, now *en pointe*, never seeming to linger more than an instant. Sydney's loose, pleated dress spilled through the air after her, as she added a splotch of color to this painting, a random line or streak to that one.

"Syd!" Barbara roared.

Sydney gave a little shake of her head.

"Wench." Babs turned away, back to Te and Jack. "She won't listen till she's done with the color. Sit down."

Not an offer. An order. Te and Jack took seats in steel chairs at a little circular garden table off to the side.

"I'll get some food or something, I guess," Babs muttered, and tottered out.

Jack and Te sat for a moment, watching Aunt Sydney dance.

"Can I look at her paintings?" Jack asked. None of the easels faced the table.

"I don't know," Te said. "They do things to your head."

Jack crossed his arms and hunched down, clearly disappointed. "What do we do then?"

"Wait," said Te. "It's just easier to let them do their thing sometimes."

They waited. Babs came back with a plate of cold drumsticks, probably straight out of the fridge, and a pitcher of something warm, thick, and red-brown. By the time she was done pouring, Sydney was putting away her brushes and sighing contentedly.

"Oh, stop it," Babs snapped. "Bad enough you have to dance and sing and all that."

Sydney floated over and sat, beginning a slow rock side to side. "Hello, pollywog," she said. "Hello, bug-eyed boy. Welcome to our home."

"You going to eat?" Babs said. "Drink?"

Jack shrugged and reached for a cold drumstick; Te held up a refusing palm.

"Then ask your whatever."

So Te did.

"Where is the Old Country?"

Te had a hard time keeping a little smirk off her lips at Babs' reaction. The old woman literally bolted up from her chair. Sydney clapped her hands.

"Oh, pollywog," she exclaimed. "You remember it! Sister Sonore sings a song, Sister Baba smiles ghastly—you didn't forget, you didn't forget."

Babs glared a moment at her sister, then turned back to Te with a wary, compressed eye. Her tone was business:

"What else did Kitsune tell you?"

"Why don't you answer my question first?"

Babs just stared into her, hinting at a grotesque smile. Te felt something quiver inside her, like the beginnings of a song, as if Te were singing and her mother were about to do that awful, awful thing to her. Te clenched her teeth to keep her jaw from shaking.

"Answer the question," she said.

Babs narrowed her squint. Her saggy cheeks began to twitch. Her breathing grew heavier, quicker.

Sydney cut in before anything could be said. "Green fields," she said, staring into her cup as if watching a floating bug. Te and Barbara broke eye contact and glanced over. "And skies of perfect color," Sydney continued. "A road of glass singing under the wind, glitter in the breath." Her hands went up to encompass the leaves lying on the glass roof and the trees above it. "And Everything! The rain kisses with lips, and everything is there and shining." With eyes suddenly completely lucid, Sydney flashed her gaze at Te. Te felt her heart jump. *"Everything!"* Syd hissed.

Then Aunt Sydney's neck went limp, and her head rolled to the side and around, and she began her slow rocking again. She took another sip of her drink.

When Babs spoke, Te snapped her head back.

"It's nowhere," her aunt said. "That's not even its name. That's only what people call it." She fingered a chicken leg. "It's a possibility," she said. "Everything that could ever be, *is*. No contradictions."

Something resonated across the table, through both aunts. Te saw it in their faces and the sudden listlessness that seized their movements.

"You've been there," she said.

Babs nodded again. Syd gave a little chuckle and licked some syrupy drink from her lip. "Once upon a time," she said, "when water was shiny."

"How do you get there?"

"You travel a long way," said Babs.

Te gestured for more. Babs just shrugged. "Any direction's fine. Walk long enough and you always wind up at the gates. 'All roads lead to Rome'—like that. No-good now, though. We can't go back."

"Why not?"

Babs shrugged. "The gates are closed. We don't know how it happened. We don't know how to open them again. We can't go back."

Te looked from one to the other, filing the information. "Is that where you met Yun?"

"Kitsune," Babs spat, though there was no bite behind the word. "No. I met him in Russia. He came around harassing my sheep, no-good pest."

"You lived in Russia?"

Babs smirked, contemplating a drumstick she now held in her gnarled fingers. "Another life. Got dragged out here about the time your mother married that skinny, balding runt you called a father."

"Don't talk about him like that."

Babs laughed, sounding like a gargling crocodile. Syd joined her a moment later. "He was a rat," Babs barked. "He treated you both like shit and he slept around."

"He *didn't* . . ." Te's anger filled and burst and withered. "Didn't treat us like shit."

"Not that our sister didn't deserve it," her aunt continued, talking askance to Sydney, who was sharing a look with her and giggling. "They had the white dress and the cake and the priest and the whole bit. I think I laughed through the whole ceremony."

Sydney stripped a sliver of meat off her drumstick with a flourish. "I got drunk," she proclaimed.

Te felt her muscles quaking. "How can you *say* that?"

Babs jammed the remains of her own drumstick in Te's face: a stripped piece of bone. "Robert was a tyrant. He kept your mother locked up in that old house the entire time he was alive. He denied her every freedom. She couldn't go out. She wasn't allowed to sing. Not even hum while she changed your diapers." Babs let the chicken bone clatter to the table and reached for another. "That's why he had you, you know. To keep your mother busy. By the end, the only thing she had was listening to *your* singing, and if that isn't small pickings, I don't know what is."

Sydney pitched over onto the table, laughing hysterically. Te could only stare at her, stunned.

"And if you didn't see that, niece," Babs finished, tearing another mouthful of cold chicken, "it's only because you weren't looking."

The words came automatically. "Dad wasn't like that."

"How do you know?" Babs snorted. "Though it all came to a good end. Now our sister has the run of the place, and she has you all to herself, and she can sing now, as often as she likes—and your dad, well, he got his comeuppance, right, Sis?"

Sydney's laugh, until then dying away, renewed itself.

Te pushed the question up a dry throat, over a dry tongue, past quivering lips: "Was it the Man in the Empty Chair?"

"Like I said," Babs said, leering across with chicken between her teeth, "got his comeuppance."

One thought rolled over and over in Te's mind: *Shouldn't have started looking into it. Should have let it rest. Should have told Babu where to shove it when he offered to train me.* She wished she could turn it all around, go back and not ask the questions, not wonder who her father was, not wonder at anything, and just be happy scribbling with charcoals to dull the ache.

"Excuse me," she managed. She ran to the bathroom while her aunts burst once more into laughter.

When Babu knocked at the door, he got no answer.

He stepped back. Lester's decrepit house loomed over him, threatening to topple off its hundred-year-old foundations at any instant. Babu did a quick circuit of the place, peeking between the boards that covered the windows: no movement, no light. He even tried his lock breaker, but the lock had been broken for some time, and Babu concluded there must be an old-fashioned bolt on the other side.

Lester could be hiding inside, down in his room in the subbasements. He would hear the knock, Babu knew, since Lester's vampire senses were much keener than a normal person's. Babu wondered, not for the first time, how the man had become a vampire—and more important, why he was a guard and not an inmate.

Creatures of the Old Country could do things to the human body—alter it or reshape it. Babu had some half dozen instances catalogued. Bird certainly did it, stripping body parts off the Freak People without otherwise damaging them. Then there was what had happened to his brother. Lester was maybe another such case, but he'd denied encountering anything monstrous before Babu had recruited him.

Babu pounded on the door again and waited, listening. "Shit," he said aloud. He couldn't even be sure the Kitsune wasn't inside right now, heading down the long stairs beneath the building. Kitsune certainly didn't need unlocked doors or open windows to get places.

He drew a cigarette, lit it, inhaled, and wondered what to do.

Call Angrel. See if she can give me a lead. That left a sour taste in his mouth. When he'd last talked to her, he'd given her orders as if she were still trustworthy. He'd been so frustrated, he'd just fallen into role and hadn't stopped to think.

God damn it, you know she's in on this.

I haven't got too many options for personnel right now.

She didn't make a mistake reading that Bird was asleep. She lied right to your face to get you killed.

No evidence of that.

Bullshit. Evidence of character.

Circumstantial. Could be she's on the level.

But you don't really believe that. This is your gut telling you not to trust her.

Well, what else have we got?

Te. Munin. Ahmadou.

At the thought of his brother, Babu felt something tense up in his chest.

Not yet.

You know he can do it. When you locate Bird, you'll need him to make the capture.

Not unless it's absolutely necessary.

Munin lost a hand today. Ahmadou could have pre-vented that.

Don't need this right now! Okay, let's think order of events. One: regroup. Two: catch Kitsune. He has to be our highest priority, higher than Bird or the Maskim. He'll make things worse until he's caught.

You'll need Lester.

I know that. So . . . Two: find Lester. Should form up a contingency in case Kitsune breaks the seal on Darktown.

If that happens, we go straight to the Man.

His cigarette finished, he tossed it into a puddle on his way back to the car.

"Hey, voodoo man," said someone. Babu turned.

Four Strutters, kids, early teens, were all dressed in goth wear. They were rain-soaked and hunched. The oldest, a freckle-faced boy with white makeup spread poorly on his face, spoke again. "You know the Master, right?"

Babu nodded.

"Uh . . ." The boy swallowed. "Do you know where he is? The door's never been locked like this before."

"I'm actually looking for him," said Babu. "Any ideas?"

They shrugged.

"Ravndark and Dracia are missing, too," the boy said. The others contributed some names. Babu slipped a notepad from his pocket and jotted them down.

"I'll let you know if I find them," Babu said, knowing he wouldn't. The kids slunk off with mournful looks at the house. *Probably better if they stay away for a while*, Babu thought.

He glanced around Darktown. As usual the streets

were deserted, and here and there he saw a flicker of movement in a window, a balcony, an alley. People living like mice hiding from owls, scurrying in the holes and tunnels built for people. He'd done enough cases in Darktown to know that the people here weren't *consciously* afraid of the long shadows outside their little apartments. They just seemed adapted to living like night creatures.

Did the shadows seem deeper than the last time he was in here? He looked up. It was still overcast, but given the angle of the sun at this hour, Darktown should have been getting at least some light. The dull gray of the streets waned to black, and the shadows, though indistinct in the rough light, seemed to blacken the roads and sidewalks like spots of ink.

Babu had been on this job too long not to recognize an omen when he saw one. He lurched up to the car and got in.

First, regroup. First, Te.

He drove back out into the waning light. The ground shook and he felt it through the car's ancient suspension.

After she'd calmed down, Te came back into her aunt's studio with her hands in her pockets and a slump in her shoulders. She wanted nothing more than to slink home and sleep for a thousand years—but there was more to ask.

She walked into a scene that wiped everything from her mind:

Jack was on his feet, out in the center of the room, staring blankly into one of Aunt Syndey's paintings. Drool fell from his lips. To the left, Babs and Sydney lounged in their chairs, eyes closed, breathing heavy, faces flushed.

"No!" Te screamed. She stormed forward and crashed the easel in front of Jack to the ground. The art landed faceup and Te caught a glimpse: swirling, maddening color, random lines that seemed to squirm and wiggle across the canvas. Te gave the thing a savage kick to get it out of the way and turned to Jack.

"Jack?" She grabbed him by the shoulders and shook him. "Jack, wake up."

Jack blinked. His face rolled, and his eyes flickered close and far away as if trying to focus.

"T . . . t . . ."

His knees gave out and he toppled forward. Te rushed under him and caught him in her arms. He was shaking and covered in sweat. Te lowered him as gently as she could against her shoulder. Her own eyes stung with tears. *Not him. Jesus, not him.*

Air escaped Jack's lips like the hissing of a last breath. Clutching him tightly, holding him up, Te spun her gaze at her aunts, still in that rapture she knew so well, in that state of contentment where they *drank*, where they *took* from the mesmerized person in front of them.

"Stop it!" she cried. "Damn it, wake up!"

Babs' smile twitched wider, twisting at the corners. Syndey's mouth drooped open and emitted a sigh of orgasmic pleasure.

"I won't let you do this."

A gasp from Jack stole her attention back. He was convulsing. His fingers clutched out at the air, and his eyes stared aimlessly forward. Froth oozed over the lips.

She'd seen it before. It was the last instant. The last

possible moment. Seconds now, and seconds only. Te laid Jack down on the concrete floor; her hands continued to tremble when she drew them off his shaking body.

Te felt a burst, a fire of rage flooding up from her solar plexus, spreading out through her to her toes and fingers—willful, a pulse of something deep and primal. It fell into her not from within, but from a place outside herself, a distant place where a great reservoir of anger sat, waiting to be tapped, and as she reached into it with a jab of her instinct, visions fell on top of her perceptions:

Te sat upon a throne of gold and ivory, two sculpted hawks arching over her and fixing with their lapis eyes the object of her ire. She plucked a grape from a platter held by a dark-skinned slave boy. Her eyes lingered on her enemy and with a blown kiss, she set him alight and he burned to ashes and oil.

Te leapt from the shadows into the path of a wild animal. Two children fled across the cobbles into a darkened arch behind her. The beast was a mound of fur and claws and it thundered at her, pushing ahead of it the stench of mange and rotting meat. She raised her hands and called the lightning down from a clear sky.

Te looked up from the roof of the house, where rising clouds of smoke seemed to slither and whirl in the shifting light of tracer rounds and bursts of flak. She heard the whine of the falling bomb above her, the bustle of the men shuffling in the bunker below. She squinted into the night and the bomb exploded at seventeen hundred feet.

Te stood in a glass-covered patio between her aunts and a defenseless young man. She was ablaze.

Barbara and Sydney had opened their eyes, and in a

kind of overlapping vision, Te saw those eyes streaming with watery light, spreading out like negative shadows of a creeping vine.

Yun's words rang through her brain like a mantra, like the voice of intention.

Why may you not do the same to them?

Her hands found themselves curled into fists. She ran at them. Each step took a second and it took a lifetime. The moment was eternal.

She felt a rush of something flooding through her, almost playful for how terrible it was. She felt in her the cruel smile of another, of a thousand others—the smile of the conqueror. This energy or emotion that she had called out of the other space split the room, catching her aunts in a wash of spectral fire, and they both cried out.

For a flash, Te saw Babs as a woman as ancient as the mountains, with skin like the bark of a dead oak, and stringy hair white as ashes. In that same instant, she saw Sydney as a young maiden, timeless skin tinged in blue, eyes of crystal, hair a rainbow stream that had no end, but trailed off to the horizon in all directions.

Then she reached them and knocked them both over with sharp fists.

Babs' head cracked on the stone with a pop. Sydney's limbs made snapping noises. Te's hands stung as if they'd been dunked in too-hot water, and for one horrible instant, she thought she'd just killed her aunts. But then they started to laugh.

"Is she a frog?" Sydney was asking between giggles.

Babs' laugh ground out of her throat like the cough of a lifetime smoker. "Oh, ye gods be good, she's waking up."

Te stood back in astonishment as both women raised themselves to their feet without any signs of their age. Babs' perpetual hunch vanished and she stood like a woman twenty years younger and fifty pounds lighter. Sydney uncurled herself to a height of well over six feet, and stood still and poised like a true dancer. They both grinned with smiles too wide for their faces, and Te saw it immediately:

"You're like Yun," she breathed.

Her aunts laughed again, the sound ringing too loudly, as if the room were ten times its actual size. Te backed away, feeling with her heels after each step for Jack, listening hard until she heard the sound of his labored breathing. She watched her aunts constantly, afraid even to blink.

"It's finally started, sister," Babs said, tracking Te with veined yellow eyes. "Years of trying. All we needed was a boy to kick things off."

"Sister Sonore sings a song," Sydney replied. "Sister Sydney dances a dance. Sister Baba sweeps the mountaintop."

Babs grunted her agreement. "Won't our sister be happy."

"Won't she."

Te's heel knocked against something. As she knelt, she held one hand up in front of her like a shield. The other probed behind her, feeling Jack's sweat-soaked shirt until it found his arm. Te fixed her aunts with a glare. Her inner fire was gone, snuffed out in the rush of its expansion, and Te's mental door to wherever it had come from was closed, but she could still bluff.

"You both stay there," she warned, surprised at the conviction in her voice. "One step and I'll fry you."

"Oh, how she plays," said Sydney, gazing into Te with steady, patient eyes.

"It is a beautiful thing," Babs agreed.

"Jack?" Te risked a glance down at him. He blinked and twitched, then burbled something unintelligible. At least he'd responded to his name. *Jesus, if that's the good news . . .*

Te stepped back over him and slipped her arm around his back. With a grunt she hauled him to his feet, straining against his weight. All through this, Te's aunts watched her, and she watched them. Jack's head lolled as Te dragged him backward out of the room, out of the house, not daring to turn around until the skull-gate clicked shut in their wake.

Every spread: The Hanged Man, the eight of swords, The Tower, Death. The eight of swords so often paired with Strength. I've been laying cards for hours now. At first, it was a halfhearted attempt to locate Lester Brown, but now I am driven by confusion and dread as the future crosses itself against all prediction. I have laid a dozen spreads. I have used Celtic, Horseshow, Dark of Moon, and Elemental spreads. It's always the same— unknowns lying in the spaces between Kitsune and Te Evangeline, with Death as a foundation and The Tower as the symbol of fate.

I run my fingers over The Tower, trying to sense something from it. The card depicts a castle tower being destroyed by a bolt of lightning, with two terrified figures falling away from it. It means collapse. It means destruction of the order of things as they now stand. This much I can get from my reading, but nothing more.

A sigh escapes me and I gather my cards for another

cast. I have one memory of a lifetime spent in Africa, when I cast a handful of little bones across a sheet of tiger skin, and the spirit of the dead animal told me all I needed to know. Those were simpler times, and the bones a simpler divinatory tool. I wish I could remember how to use them.

I mean no offense to my cards, of course.

I have also conducted three solo séances, attempting to contact King, but I sense nothing. He has perhaps moved on to the other side, or he may be resting beneath the earth, healing. It once seemed odd to me that ghosts could be injured; then a wise man told me, "All things that live can die," and ghosts have a kind of life, after a fashion.

I do not feel any great deal of apprehension that I cannot reach members of the team. It is not my place to help them. The Man wants Kitsune free, for reasons he has not shared with me. Ten years ago, when he first arrived, the Man's intention had been the same, but then Yun tried to break the seal on Darktown, and let out the horrors that slumber there. The Man had contained them, of course, wielding whatever occult disciplines it is his privilege to know. But after the Kitsune had shown himself capable of such a horrendous act, as dangerous to himself as to us, the Man had ordered Yun hunted and caught.

One thing I can be thankful for is that I have not drawn any of the cards that signal the coming of the dark things. These were not cards I kept in my deck, but when the prediction required them, they appeared and shuffled themselves to the top. A transformation of the cards meant the nearness of something outside their purview—outside of both the realm of the mythic and of the psychological. Anything outside those could only be quite alien.

With a sigh, I finish my shuffle and set my cards aside. The basement where I keep my little shop is perpetually cold in the rain. I have little in the way to heat it but my candles, so I gather a blanket from a drawer in my back office and wrap it over my shoulders.

My shop is a front. I open to customers every once in a while, but mostly it is simply a quiet place to do my work. The Man takes care of any material needs I have.

I huddle the blanket around myself back at my séance table, gathering it to conceal everything but my face and hands, and draping the unused length over my feet. My cards find my hands again and I begin to shuffle.

The Man in the Empty Chair intends to be the Warden of the world. This much I've gleaned from his talk of building a new future where he will be welcome. I am not a confidant in his plans, and, when I sometimes stop to think about it, am unsure why he thinks me necessary. It gives me hope to think that he is taking me along with him because he wants to. I know he doesn't love me. He can't even like me. But there is something there.

My cards flicker one atop the other. My fingers tap, pry, flip, and the shuffle begins again.

I wonder what will happen once the Man becomes Warden. In history it was the nature of the human world to alter to suit the Warden's peculiar tastes. What will his tastes bring, he who is invisible, who can read minds and come and go without traversing the space in between? He may not be a man at all, so how his Wardenship will affect the earth is something I can't predict. But I'm all right with that. I am comfortable with him, even as an employee. I trust him, because I know the world he builds will have a place for me.

Babu's words. Munin's hand. Rob's convulsing face on that impersonal operating table.

I do trust him, don't I?

My fingers tap, pry, flip, and something slips. My cards spill out onto the purple velvet, one half tumbling like a waterfall, the other slamming down whole and bursting like a bomb. A sigh passes out of me. There was a time I would have been terrified of an omen like this, but now it only makes me feel old.

I gather my cards together with sweeps of my fingers. Two pinch a third together and pop it out of the bunch. It lands faceup.

The Night Terrors.

My fingers freeze. I stare at this card, foreign to the Rider-Waite deck. It shows a black background, eyes and teeth staring out of it in faded dot matrix color. There is a suggestion of claws, of unhealthy motion, and at the base of the card lies a man in bed, reaching toward the ceiling, blindfolded.

I have never seen this before.

I take it up in my fingers, handling it by its edges as if it were sharp or poisonous. With a sweep of my other hand, I clear a patch of my table, and lay the card down. My hands seek in the scattered piles of my deck and come away with something. I turn it over: the queen of pentacles. This, I know, is my own card.

I lay this card crosswise over the last, in the proper position for the second card of a Celtic cross. I now cross the Night Terrors. I am in their way.

My fingers walk like spiders through the scattered cards until another card rises into them. I lay this to the left of the two. This is *their* past, and yet my intuition jumps as in an old film, and I know as I lay it that this card is also my own past:

The Devil.

Images whirl in my mind, the remnants of my seer's vision that has been waning these five millennia. I see a vista of terrible halls cut from the crust of the earth, pits of fire that send their leaping flames up before my eyes. Legions of the damned, entirely burned and thus deprived of any resemblance to their past lives, kneel before me, awaiting my pleasure. I am queen here. I know. I shield these wretches from the deepest terror, which is that of nothingness. Faced with the horror of nonbeing, these departed souls have come to me, thinking even the most meaningless existence preferable to utter extinction.

I mock them aloud. I ask them if they would like to know why extinction can be preferable to life, and as ever, they answer, "Yes, Goddess." So I raise my hand, and calling upon the Old Powers that are fully at my command, I tear open the roof, the sky, the stars themselves and tunnel into something darker. I tunnel into the void, into the Apsu, into places Outside. I bring something in, to show them what terror really is.

The vision is gone. The flicker of the old power I saw used lingers in me, chilling my blood and making it painful to pump around my body.

I reach for another card: The Hanged Man. I place it in position to the right, representing the future. The figure on the card hangs not from gallows , but from a living tree. His face is calm and his head glows with the nimbus of ascended wisdom. This represents the Kitsune. Here he is again, blocking my prediction, preventing me from tasting the future with my Sight. The face on the card seems to mock me without smiling.

I reach for another, and I cry out when I see it and drop it into its place like a hot iron. The card shows a purple sky crossed by blue clouds, and below this, a cornfield bent to the wind. Between the two, a black mass hovers, stretched to the side as if blown by a wind. The card is titled The Haunter in the Dark.

It is laid in the foundation place, holding up the Night Terrors, its younger, bolder brethren.

My hands are shaking. Against tradition, I leave the table in the middle of a reading—I run away from it—and gulp a glass of water from the sink in the back of my office. I let the icy water stream over my hands and dash it three times against my face. As I wipe my eyes, I make the mistake of looking in the mirror.

For I see there the thousand faces I have worn, overlapping, all wearing the same shaken expression. The eyes stare out at me, their confidence waning as year after year brings more suffering. But behind them, the dimmest of the overlapping reflections looks not at me but away. Her face is in her hands, her shoulders have fallen. She bears a burden, of guilt or failure, or responsibility shirked. I blink and all the faces are gone.

I rush back to the table. My hands scramble for purchase in my scattered deck, which my broad sleeves have now dragged into a sea of cards all over the tabletop. My fingers clamp on a card and slap it in place above the center.

The nine of swords. The card depicts a man sitting up in bed, in the middle of the night, crying into his hands so that his face cannot be seen. Above him, on the wall, nine swords hang horizontally. This is a card of utter lamentation, of a mistake made that cannot be undone.

And again my vision swims, and I am again in that dark cavern where endless ranks of burned men kneel to me. The air pulses as if pushed by the breath of something very large. A tunnel above me darkens; a dark and shapeless thing emerges. I lift my hands to strike it down with the ancient powers I possess. I clench my fist and astral fires swirl up to engulf it, but it does not react. It is incapable of fearing me. In that moment, it is I who am afraid.

I sit back in my chair, my perceptions once again in the present time. I am hot and sweating now under the blanket, and tear it aside. My elbows find the table. My forehead finds my palms.

What have I seen tonight . . . ? I wonder. A vision of myself, perhaps a memory of the time before the curse? What did I let into the world? Was that the reason for my eternal punishment?

There are no answers in my fractured and ancient mind. I am twenty-one years of age in this body and for this moment I feel only those few years and no more. I know so little, even about myself.

My fingers move automatically. Four cards will make the reading complete. Again, I part from tradition, and lay all four without taking the time to contemplate them individually. I draw The Tower, the three and four of swords, and the nine of cups. I sit back and my breath slips slowly out of me in a sigh of relief. I did not draw The Goat with a Thousand Young. Yun has not yet reached its prison under Darktown.

Yet he has released something. I lift The Night Terrors and The Haunter in the Dark from the deck and hold them up. I do not know these things, but they are doubtless ancient creatures like all our charges—and like them, restless and angry.

Their images memorized, I toss them back into the chaos of my scattered deck. I sweep the deck together, organize it, and sort through it until I find my special blank card.

I will inform the Man first, and request instructions. Then I will contact Babu, and let him know we may have two more escapees.

When Jack woke up, he cried. His sobs were almost inaudible, slipping up from his gut and out in tiny puffs of air. He shook, and there were tears. Te held him all the while. She held him because there had been no one to hold her. Jack should have someone.

Te's tears were pouring out almost as fast as his. When it had just happened to her, it had been hard enough. But now, seeing Jack gasping and weeping into her shoulder, she felt that pain reflected and multiplied. She held him as tight as he held her, knowing there was nothing more terrible in suffering than suffering alone.

Te had led them down to the riverbank, beneath an arching pine where the ground was dry, on what must have been the corner of an extensive private estate. The river rolled past just a few feet from them, fattened on the glut of rainfall. Raindrops pattered on the needles above. Jack's fingers dug into her sides, and he began a whispered keening, small and lost. It was a knife through Te's core to hear that wordless, hopeless sound. And there was nothing, nothing that she could do for him—except hold him tighter, and so she did.

We are legion, Yun had said. From the myths and sto-

ries of ancient history, even the few she knew, the creatures of the Old Country must have covered the globe.
Te realized she had seen them in the visions that had
come to her in the night, in dreams and nightmares as
far back as she could remember—rank upon rank of
creatures inimicable to man: beasts, sorcerors, animals
warped and twisted, things in human shape that were
not men. And her aunts? Had she seen them there? She
couldn't remember.

What were they? Why did they leave their Old Country in the first place? Why did they all seem to insist on
destroying innocent people?

And why hadn't they destroyed her?

Yun had said it was a miracle that Te had survived
what her mother and aunts did to her. Seeing Jack, seeing him come so close . . . Te saw how right Yun was. Yes,
it had hurt her, but it had never done to her what it had
done to Jack, or Dad.

It had been the same, Jack in the sunroom and her
father five years past on the hospital stretcher. The seizure, the convulsions—it had been exactly the same.
That meant there was a creature out there, somewhere
in this valley, in this town, that had killed her dad. It
meant he had died feeling that emptiness, that void of
living death, that she'd dealt with her entire life. As mad
as she'd been at him—God, for so many years—she had
always hoped he'd been too insensate to feel, at the end.
Now she knew: it had been the worst of all sensations.

She thought of tracking down whichever one had
killed her dad, of exacting revenge or, maybe, of just
asking why. But in her arms there was a weeping friend,
shuddering and alone. And he would be alone no matter
how much she was with him, because so much of him

had been lost. But she held him anyway, kissed him on his feverish forehead. She couldn't bring herself to tell him everything would be okay.

Because it had occurred to her that her aunts had a sister, and that that sister had a daughter, and that that daughter could have visions and could call up invisible fire and could survive what, from all evidence, should kill any normal human being.

Te buried herself in Jack's sorrow, and tried not to think anymore.

It rained. In St. Ives, the sky was always weeping.

Chapter 11

The Waterfall in Dreams

"It is a fountain," Yun said, "a spring leaking forth the stinking effluent of the mother world."

Lester covered his eyes and tried not to see. He could hear them, not in his ears but in a silent, mental perception: the crowd of tiny black things massing on the other side of the door, buzzing like angry bees.

"All things excrete," Yun went on, running his fingers over the edges of the door as if to caress the things beyond it. "Every agent of change in the universe produces waste. This is as true for the earth as for any parasite upon her skin. Pushed up through the various currents of magma, up through the shifting plates and strata, the rock and the soil, these poor wretches found themselves in an alien world, a world of infinite cold compared to their million-degree home."

Yun glanced back to where Lester leaned on the hallway wall. Lester was already shivering, from cold and stiffness and an ever-intensifying hunger for blood. He hadn't drunk in almost a day. *What does he want from me now?*

Lester had awoken and, half aware, rolled out of his

box, to find himself in an underground parking garage with Yun waiting for him, sitting cross-legged on the hood of a black car and smiling.

Why me? I just wanted to be left alone. Why me?

Then Yun had kidnapped him, forced him out of the box, up a grimy back stair that smelled of beer piss and old vomit. Using nothing but his voice and that terrifying smile, Yun had driven Lester down this hallway, to the door of this apartment, with peeling paint on the frame and no number on the door. The hallway had no windows at all, just worn purple carpet and flickering, bug-filled overheads.

Yun's fingers played over the doorknob. "Do you know what they did when they first felt the light on their skins?" Yun asked.

He won't grant my wish, Lester thought.

Yun's hand slipped back into his coat poket. He gave Lester the full force of his amused-Buddha stare. "Well, what did *you* do," he asked, "when you first became a creature of the night?"

Lester shut his eyes and tried not to remember, but it was as if a hand reached into his concentration and pried it back, bent it up, hauled it out of the way like so much debris. The memory came blasting into him: the sting of sunlight, not understood but obeyed; a day spent indoors, with a hunger building moment by moment, unquenchable with alcohol or food; and then, with that last gasp of the sun vanishing over the mountains, a great hunt, a great feast.

"A feast of plenty," said Yun, answering Lester's thoughts. "Five women. Four men. One child of seven. One infant."

Lester choked. The image assaulted him, that single

moment when, sated by all he'd drunk, Lester had come back to himself to find all these people dead around him, blood covering him from his cheeks down to his stomach.

"Why are you doing this to me?" he whined. "You promised. My Strutters were . . . because of me . . ."

"Oh, you can't take it back," Yun said, waving a scolding finger in front of Lester's aching eyes. "You made a wish."

Lester felt his insides seize. It wasn't his fault, was it? All this death? His Strutters? O'Shae and Julia? Those people he'd . . . eaten?

"I didn't wish for any of this!"

"Hmmm . . . Yes you did," Yun said. "You were nine years old."

"I d-don't . . . ," Lester stammered. "I don't remember . . . much."

Yun bounced his eyebrows. "This is true. You don't remember much from when you were younger. But there's one thing you remember, isn't there? The only thing from your ninth year that you can remember in every detail."

Lester swallowed, fought his contorting face to speak, failed. There was one night. Dad had been drunk. He'd come into Lester's room. Touched him. Did things to him. Then he'd left. They never talked about it. It never happened again.

"You made a wish," said Yun. "What was it?"

"I wanted to be somewhere else," Lester choked out.

Yun shook his head, took another step forward so that he filled Lester's vision. The sanitized smell of him wrinkled Lester's sensitive nose. "You wanted to be nowhere at all."

Lester rubbed his face, and his hand came away red: the tears that hadn't been just salt water for a long time. "And now I am," he said.

Again, Yun shook his head. "It was the most sincere wish you have ever made in your time on this earth, but it has yet to come true." He turned back to contemplate the door. "That's why I'm here."

He has to be stopped. It rang in his head like a siren. *He has to be stopped before he can . . .*

Yun took a purposeful stride toward the door and gripped the doorknob firmly in his fingers.

"Wait!" Lester cried.

Yun looked back, his hand still on the knob. Lester fumbled under the gaze of those dancing eyes, at a loss. Always at a loss.

"Is this"—Lester fumbled—"is this *the* door? Is it my door?"

Yun glanced around the door frame. The scurrying things on the other side had grown excited with Yun's proximity.

"No, this is not your door," Yun said. "We're in Brightontown. This is another cell, sealed in 1941 by the keepers of that time and never since opened."

A long-held breath rushed out of Lester. He collapsed back against the hallway wall. "Oh, thank God."

Relief gave way to panic.

"What's in it?" he asked.

"I've already told you," Yun said. He once again contemplated the rim of the door, as if checking an invisible lining there that kept the things inside. "They did the same thing as you did when they found themselves in a world of sunshine, and them creatures of the dark."

Yun's smile chilled him.

"They went insane," he said. "They became night-mares and crib deaths, bogeymen, and lurkers."

Lester found his fingers clutching and releasing, his long nails scraping against his palm. He struggled with it, but he had to ask.

"So, you're not going to Darktown?"

"I can't yet release the prisoners there," Yun said. "To do so would be to force the Man in the Empty Chair to intervene, for there are some things he cannot ignore, however much he might wish to. In any case, the timing of their release must be precise."

He twisted the handle slowly. Lester jumped at each click, and the after-echo sounded like crackers snapping. The things beyond shrieked with excitement.

"But our mutual friend Mr. Cherian is growing frus-trated," Yun said. "It won't be much longer before he brings his brother out of confinement to face me, and that is an encounter I would rather avoid."

One more twist. Lester heard the bolt slide away from the door.

"This," Yun said, "is to keep him distracted."

He pushed the door inward an inch, and Lester heard and felt the shattering of something thick. White flakes burst from the border of the door, tumbling into the air as if unaffected by gravity.

"Wonderful to see you again after so long," Yun said.

The answer was a chaotic keening and a tumble of scratches and growls. As Yun pushed the door open, inch by inch, living shadows flowed out into the pool of the overhead lights. Lester jumped back, slinking into a doorjamb. The cold hit him first, a wave of air like the deepest night in winter, then a stench of rich feces that made him choke. He clapped his hands over his mouth and nose, sucking air through them to try to lessen the smell.

The little shadows took form: eyes, claws, tentacles— little creatures as small as a child's shoe, or as big as a cat. They jumped and rolled, cavorted and fought with one another, devouring and being devoured, birthing and vanishing, in and out of each other in the shadows. They marched forward like a celebrating parade, swinging their spines in rhythm to their step. Some leapt, slashing at the air in their exultation, tumbling back into the press to be crushed and absorbed, absurdly like a cheerleader's baton twirling back to a practiced hand.

Lester covered his eyes and turned his face away. *There're so many. There're so many.* The sounds bit into his sensitive ears. The smell choked him. His vampire senses revolted at the presence of these lifeless things, and he felt his stomach getting sick. How did Munin and Babu fight things like this? Lester was just a tracker, and even then only because he was good at it—and even then, only when he absolutely had to. He couldn't handle this.

Why me? He stayed there, nose to the dusty wood of the other apartment's door, shivering from the cold, choking on the smell, cringing at the sounds of dark jubilation, until the creatures had fled through the gaps beneath doors and the holes in the walls.

"You can come out, now, Lester," Yun said.

Lester hid his eyes, but the tone of Yun's floating voice indicated just how he was smiling.

"What do you think of me, Lester?" Yun asked. "Do you think I'm torturing you? Do you think I'm just using you to get what I want?"

Lester felt tears of blood, so much thicker and slower than real tears, trailing down his nose.

"I don't know!" he said.

"Do you think I'm an evil man, Lester?"

What the hell . . . "Yeah, I do."

"Shall I control you with the rapture, Lester?"

A surge—*Yes! Please, yes!*—and then a death, an emptiness, a pinprick of gravity pulling him down into himself. Two days ago he would have done anything to be back in that place; he *had* done anything. But now, with his Strutters . . . and little Jill . . .

"Please don't make me do anything else."

He stood, forehead resting on the door, hands still against his face, blocking out any sight of the room. Lester heard Yun shift, waited for the rapture to hit him anyway—waited for Yun to violate his mind and bring him joy, which, though unwanted, would swallow him up just as it had before.

But instead, Yun just spoke.

"Lester, why do you think I brought you here with me tonight?"

"I don't fucking know."

"Why do I do anything?"

"I don't know, man. I don't know!"

A soft laugh.

"'You dozed, and watched the night revealing the thousand sordid images of which your soul was constituted.' I'm going to leave you now, Lester. I have many wishes to satisfy, and tonight my work begins in earnest," said Yun. "It's nearly dark out, so you can flee wherever you'd like."

Lester heard two footfalls—Yun moving away.

"Your box is just downstairs."

A pattering of something softer, lighter than man, and then nothing. The overheads buzzed, flickered, died. Power failure? The shadow creatures at work?

He was back in the comfortable dark, where he'd lived for fifteen years.

He did go to his box—down the stinking staircase, across the empty, cobwebbed garage. His box waited for him in a parking stall, backed against the wall with concrete partitions at either side of it. He knelt, crawled, slid inside, and curled up in the shadow there, in the dark that was his life. The last bare hints of sunlight bled down through the garage's entrance a hundred feet away. In that last light moved something slight, slim, with a streak of purple hair and huge white eyes surrounded in black eyeliner, its skirts moving, heavy boots clacking on the floor.

"I'm sorry," he said to her. "You must hate me."

She slid into the box with him, drew his head into her lap, and soothed him with asymetric lines of poetry to the glory of the dark and the majesty of the vampire— the power to give life, the power to take it away.

"I always liked your poetry," he whispered.

Her voice went on, small and young, line after line. Lester felt himself sinking, fading away, caught in the thrill of a twist of words, the pulse of unexpected rhyme. The lines he liked, she repeated over and over like an echo. Warm feelings came, safe ones.

It was a rapture, taking away the hostile world, the hostile self.

Lester cried into the soiled cardboard.

"I'm sorry I didn't let you die."

She stroked his cheek and whispered close into his ear. The lines flooded together: a poem he'd never heard

before. To die in the embrace, she said, to die with her
life seeping through the lips of her master—it was the
purpose of the human vessel, the highest realization
of life. It was holy, divine, and with such an end, who
needed Paradise?

And with that, she left him, her tiny fingers trailing
down over his face, the sweet scent of her blood, the
rhythm of her pulse. He felt cold without them.

Blood? Pulse? He started awake.

"Wait!" Like an old man he tumbled around to his
knees. Like a madman he scrambled out of his box and
ran to the garage's exit.

Sunlight stung his fingers and drove him back in.

It was really her. It wasn't just my imagination.

There, just outside: her shoeprint. But the sun was out
again, and he couldn't go after her.

Lester huddled down in that concrete world, knead-
ing the thick sleeves of his coat, breathing her scent as it
faded with each gust of wind.

He waited for dark.

When they reached the big house, Te took Jack, stag-
gering, leaning on her shoulder, around to the back gate
where there was no chance of his parents seeing him.
She coaxed him up the stairs with tugs and yanks and
sometimes encouraging words. She shouldered her own
door open, cleared a spot, and laid him down in her bed.
He whispered something unintelligible and was unconscious almost instantly.

Te settled back on the floor and wrapped her knees
close. What was it they did? They were clearly taking
something out of him; they "partook"—that was Yun's
word for it. Did everything from the Old Country do

that? Bird ate people, or pieces of people, which was a little more gruesome but sort of along the same lines. What else was there?

Te leaned over and grabbed Babu's casebook out of her shoulder bag. She flipped through it, looking for a description, maybe a full list, of St. Ives' prisoner creatures. Babu seemed meticulous enough to have something like that in here, but after five or so fruitless minutes, she gave up and set the heavy thing aside.

Jack's breathing had gotten steadier. She reached up and tucked her black bedcovers closer around him. The whole room stank of his sweat, with faded overtones of old dinners cooked in her kitchenette.

Questions queued up in her head, running down one side of her imagination like a shopping list:

What is the Old Country?
Why did its people come here?
Is Mom really one of them?
Am I?

Te's drawing kit—a tin box with charcoal pencils and a knife inside—lay open on the floor in front of her. She plucked out a wide-tipped pencil, found a sheet of paper, and started to sketch. Long curves, rounded edges, spines inside the curve like the sap vessels of a leaf. She tweaked, here and there, not caring what the final result looked like. She had hundreds of drawings like that— things made in moments of distraction.

What if I am? Will they lock me up with the rest?
Mom wasn't locked up.

But didn't Babs say something about Dad not letting Mom leave the house? About his holding her prisoner? Dad was a binder. Mom was a creature from the Old Country. No wonder they hated each other.

Te sketched out another set of curves and veins, a re-flection of the ones she'd just done. She smudged a few, softening edges, stretching shadows. *Babu wouldn't lock me up, would he?*

She wondered whether she could even trust Babu. Whether he knew about her mom, whether he suspected that Te might be one of these things . . .

Te squinted inwardly, her fingers working, scrib-bling, shading. On the bed, Jack stirred, in the grip of a dream. *If Babu knew, he would have taken me years ago, wouldn't he? Why wait this long?*

The answer hit her:

He hasn't had a binder until now.

Is that why her father had fought Babu's boss, this Man in the Empty Chair? To stop them from shutting her up? It would be win-win: either he beats the Man in the Empty Chair and keeps her safe, or he dies, and leaves the Man without a binder, and keeps her safe. Her hands stilled.

He really loved me, if that was the case. He died for me. He loved me, even though I might . . . not . . . be . . .

Ooooooooh, God.

She found herself looking at her hands, at her skin—maybe a bit pale, but there were the normal textured lines, there was the rough skin of the knuckles, the ten-dons and blood vessels just visible, the short, pale arm hair. She had her share of scars and some freckles and imperfections here and there. She had a heartbeat. So did her mother. So did her aunts. And aside from look-ing a bit effeminate, Yun seemed normal, too.

Jack shifted again, cried out, mumbled something. Te moved to be beside him and put a palm on his forehead. He was cold, and he was hot, and his skin was still slick with sweat and body oil. Te's fingers stuck to him, as if magnetically drawn, and in her stomach she felt an impression of hollowness that she knew only too well.

Would he recover? Te always had, but now she was thinking that he wasn't like her in ways that counted.

His mumbling faded at her touch until his breathing evened out. She knew that he wasn't a child, but with him lying there, curled in on himself, covers bunched up at his neck and armpits, she couldn't help but sing to him. In a shaking, gravelly whisper, she sang to him.

> Hush little baby, don't say a word.
> Papa's gonna buy you a mockingbird . . .

As the words slipped out, carried on her quivering breath, Te felt a warmth rising up in her. With each note, each line, the feeling grew, streaming out with the articulations of the syllables, bringing its peace into the stuffy air. Te felt that, too, like a passive breath on her skin. She could almost see it.

> And if that mockingbird don't sing,
> Papa's gonna buy you a diamond ring

The notes flickered in her vision now, like fireflies whirling in a breeze. Colors blossomed in her peripheral vision—a rainbow of flowers that never were—and echoing birdsong chirped from the room's corners, harmonizing with her grinding tone, blending a mediocre voice into a magnificent pastoral choir. She knew that they weren't real, and she knew just as certainly that it didn't matter what was real and what wasn't. What mattered was the music—no matter the tune, no matter how well or badly sung, the music was the transmission of life.

Jack was staring at her.

Ageless now and unafraid, Te placed the backs of her fingers on his face, and ran them slowly down. Her tears traced the same pattern down her own cheeks.

"You're beautiful," he said.

It stung her, with happiness or with shame, and Te drew back, covering her face with her hands—a sudden need to hide, a sudden need not to be seen.

The sparkles faded, happily twirling into nothingness as a dancer slows at the end of the music. Te bent forward over her knees, palms pressed into her eyes. The tears came in gushes, the sobs in gasps. She felt one bony hand settle on her back, and she was surrounded in male scent. He sat with her in sympathy, understanding that the pain was wordless, that with suffering one could do nothing but endure.

The warm feeling lingered. Much as she wished it away, it stayed in her and made everything magical and new.

Te Evangeline had touched the borders of the Old Country, and it had felt like coming home.

Chapter 12

The Encouraging Word

Babu rolled up in front of the big house where Te lived. She'd moved in here at nineteen, after a fight with her mother, she'd said. Babu, suddenly conscious of how little he actually paid her, had suggested she room with a friend or something to save on rent. Her expression had tightened up when he said it, and Babu had realized immediately, with a prick of embarrassment, that she didn't have any friends. He'd always wondered how that could be, but had never felt right asking.

He knew Te lived on the top floor, up one of the two staircases in the back. He worked his way around the house, soggy lawn sucking at his shoes. He glanced up and saw lights on in the upper-floor apartments. Which door was it? He stood a second in the fading afternoon light, looking from one to the other.

The one on the left let out a few mysterious clicks and clangs. It cracked open an inch.

"Hey! Black man."

Babu stood in shock for a minute. He hadn't been spoken to like *that* since he came to St. Ives. He recovered himself quickly with the help of a sudden rising indignation.

"My *name*," he said, "is *Cherian*. Anything I can do for you?"

"Cherian. Yes, that's it," the voice said. It clearly belonged to an older man and didn't carry very well down the stairs. "Babu Cherian?"

"Yeah." Babu ground his teeth. People he didn't know knowing about him never sat right.

"Brother to Ahmadou Cherian, currently incarcerated at Cloake Hill Mental Institution?"

"He's being treated," Babu growled. "Do I know you?"

"Me?" said the voice. "No. You don't know me. I don't know you, either. But there was a burst, you see. A burst of snow on the eighth set—not a random burst. Nothing lately has been random. But the burst was black, not white—the absence of the static, you see? Black, like you."

Which didn't help Babu's sizzling temper. He'd had a bad few days and this bastard was about to get the brunt of it. "And?"

"Te Evangeline," he said. "I've been tracking his movements, you see. I've been tracking them for forty years—wherever he went, whatever he did, he left a shadow of himself. A shadow of a shadow. No one else could see it but me."

Babu stepped sideways, adjusting his line of sight on the door. He caught a glimpse of a pale, withered face before it vanished backward into the apartment.

"Now he's almost ready," said the voice. "You have to shoot her."

"What?" he said.

"Te Evangeline," said the voice. "The world is ending. You have to shoot her. It won't be possible once the static dies."

"What static?"

The voice started screaming. "He'll shut down my static! She has to be killed. I can't do it. Every time I try, he stops me. *You* have to!"

Babu hammered up the first few steps. "Wait just a damn minute!"

The door pounded shut. Babu heard what sounded like multiple locks and bolts sliding closed.

What the hell.

Groaning all the while, he hauled himself up to the man's landing. For a moment, he stared at the steel door in front of him, speculating as to the strange man behind it. If the guy was a keeper, or a fellow investigator, or a prisoner himself, Babu should have known. That he didn't worried him. Just a nutcase? Lord knows, he'd seen enough of those. Still, true coincidences were rarer than they should have been in St. Ives, and he didn't like how well the man's words matched up with his own fears.

With forty years of bad habits slowing him down, Babu made the arduous journey down that flight of stairs and up the one that led to Te's apartment. He wasn't looking forward to this. Te had had a gnarled-up expression on her face when Babu had sent her home from the hospital. It was somewhere between being really pissed off at him and really angry with herself about how things turned out with Bird.

That couldn't have been helped. Well . . . maybe, but it wasn't her fault. He could reassure her of that. And it was high time he told her the rest of it—whatever she wanted to know. He'd promised Rob he wouldn't, but, damn it, she was *in* it now and she needed to know everything. And her reaction would tell him where she sat.

Yeah. He felt better having a plan. Why was he so nervous about this? Why was he prepping himself? He was her friend, and it wasn't as if he hadn't pissed her off many times before. And he was her boss, too. Couldn't he tell her she was on duty and leave it at that?

He knew it wouldn't be that simple. Maybe he didn't want it to be that simple. Yun's insinuations kept tumbling in his head.

He raised his hand to knock, and the door opened.

Te seemed paler than usual, face blanched and stained. She'd obviously been crying, and she looked drained and thin, and older than he'd ever seen her. "Come in," she said.

Babu grunted something and lurched past.

Babu had never been in Te's apartment before, and now that he was, he gaped at the state of it. Rob had been very well-off; surely Te could afford some place better than this? It was barely twelve feet across and had only one tiny, dirty window. Every available wall space was plastered with Te's charcoal drawings, and the floor was a mess of discarded magazines and clothing. The kid from the day before—Jack?—was here, too, sitting on the bed, drinking tea out of a chipped coffee mug.

Te closed the door behind him.

"Can I get you anything?" she asked: an empty courtesy. Babu felt as if he took up too much space in the room.

"No, m'all right," he replied, fumbling.

"Jack," said Te, returning to the apartment's kitchenette and picking up a mug of tea for herself, "you re-member Babu Cherian?"

The kid sort of saluted at him.

Babu managed a nod back. Then he turned to Te. "So . . . how are you doing?"

"Fine," said Te. It was the kind of "fine" women used when there was something really wrong. "You?"

"Good," he said. "Munin's okay. He's out of surgery. They want to keep him there for a few days, but, know-ing him, he'll probably check himself out by tomorrow."

Te's lips bent up in a crooked smile. "Bounces back easily, does he?"

Well, she certainly wasn't feeling guilty about it. That was good.

"Yeah," said Babu, "but really he just hates missing out on a case."

"Good for him," Te said. "Something I can do for you?"

Babu felt something was off. Something had hap-pened to her since that morning, and, as with all things he didn't know, it bothered him. His confusion prob-ably showed on his face, but Te didn't seem to notice, or maybe just didn't acknowledge it. She simply stared at him. It was eerie.

"I need to talk to you about the case," he said. He glanced over at the kid. "Maybe we should talk in private."

"No," Te said, with finality. "Jack's in on this one."

Babu was taken aback. "But he doesn't know the . . ."

"He knows everything, Babu," Te said.

"Everything?"

Te smiled. She sipped her tea.

No arguing with her, then. And the kid had already seen Bird. Naturally, Te had offered him some kind of explanation about it. And really, he hadn't told her specifically to keep it a secret.

"All right," he said. He tracked Te with his eyes while she took a spot on the floor next to the bed. He couldn't read her. Christ, he'd done years of catching cheating spouses and unscrupulous business partners back in Boston. He'd sniffed out liars and cheats and frauds, and he'd gotten to be an expert at reading emotions. Or, he thought he had.

"Look," he began, "I know this morning didn't go so well. It wasn't your fault."

Te sipped her tea and dropped her gaze. The boy kept staring at him with those magnified eyes. Who needed glasses that strong?

"But Bird's still free. And there could be more now. They're all at least as dangerous." Te didn't react. He decided to test what Angrel had told him. "But the worst one is called the Kitsune." Nothing. No reaction. "Christ, I should have told you about him sooner. He's the one that killed Sanjay Sharma. Your father and I locked him away ten years ago, but now he's out and he's letting the other ones loose. We have to catch him first to prevent any more escapes."

Silence. Te was still, her face ashen and her eyes sunken and tired. She bore all the signs of someone under monstrous strain, crushed down by stress. Babu knew it. He'd seen it. He'd felt it. But he couldn't help, so he just kind of stood there, feeling like a lump as the silence stretched. Eventually, Te took a breath and spoke.

"You told me about the Warden," Te said.

Babu started, unprepared for the change of subject. "Yeah?"

"The prisons like St. Ives—they were his idea?"

"Yes," Babu said. "Well, there were always prisons for the more dangerous ones, but he organized the large-scale operations like St. Ives. He recruited the teams, picked the locations."

"And captured all the prisoners?"

"Yeah, I suppose." Babu rubbed his chin. "He has agents that do that kind of thing. There are teams like mine that operate out in the world, tracking down the ones that got away."

"All of them?"

"I think so."

"What about the ones that aren't dangerous to people?"

He hadn't dealt with those too often. "I gather the Warden doesn't really care about the people. It's just that creatures from the Old Country don't fit into his vision of an orderly planet. Some of them can change shape, or do magic, and they can't die."

There was something infinitely sad in Te's smile just then. "Can't be killed, you mean?"

"Not like us."

"Hence the prisons."

"Yeah."

Te nodded, as if something that hadn't made sense now did.

Babu felt a bad ache for a cigarette. "Why all the questions?" he asked.

Te finally looked at him, then, a bit of the old twinkle in her eye. "Investigative method. Filling in all the gaps."

Babu didn't know whether she was making fun of him.

He cleared his throat to clear the moment. "We'll have to go out again tomorrow. Hopefully by then, Angrel will have a bearing for us on either Kistune or Lester." Babu paused, then explained. "He's another teammate, our tracker. He didn't show up this morning."

Te just nodded.

Babu shifted uncomfortably, used to at least a nominal objection.

"So," he said, "I'll be by about six."

Te shook her head.

"I'll meet you at your place."

Another surprise.

"Uh . . . all right. Whatever works."

Babu cleared his throat, wanting to say more, but there was nothing left to discuss. His eyes wandered over the walls, jumping from drawing to drawing. Most of Te's works were of vague, shadowy shapes. It was all horroresque monsters and mausoleums, that kind of thing. His eyes landed on one: a feathered, winged creature crouched on a branch, wings folded up into itself. And another, close to it: a twisted snake, eyeless, black spines leaping from its back, obscured in a blur of shadow. She'd even added a few streaks of red along its body.

Babu looked from one to the other, trying to swallow his panic. He recognized another half dozen as creatures he'd personally escorted to their cells. There were maybe another ten or twenty that he knew of by reputation. He spotted one that had to have been Lester: a man-shaped shadow slumping forward in an armchair, exhaustedly fiddling with a large, dripping bowl on the table in front of him. And there, Angrel: a woman-shaped white hole on a field of black.

His back was to Te now, but he felt her eyes boring into him. He jammed his hands into his pockets to keep them from shaking as he glanced back.

Her eyes locked to his, ancient and tired, sharp and aware.

"Good night, Babu," she said.

He showed himself out, trying not to run.

Te leaned her forehead against the door. She waited for the creaking of the staircase to stop, then for the sound of Babu's car choking to life and driving off.

"Why didn't you tell him anything?" Jack asked her.

Te sighed. It was harder than she thought, keeping secrets from Babu. "I don't know," she said. She walked back into the room and plopped down on her bed beside Jack. The steam from the tea had fogged his glasses a bit. "Guess I don't know who to trust right now."

"Oh," Jack said. "Are you really going to put Kistune in jail? He seemed okay."

"I don't know that, either."

"What's he done that's so bad?"

"You remember Bird?"

"Yeah," he said. Then his face fell. "You know, I still think she was pretty."

That chilled her a bit. "Kitsune let her out of her cage."

"Why?"

"Probably because she wished for it. That's what Yun does. He grants wishes."

"You mean like a genie? Or a leprechaun?"

"Yeah."

"Huh," he said. "Can *you* grant wishes?"

She was about to say no, but stopped.

"I don't know," she said. "I don't know how this works."

"Could you ask Cherian?"

Te returned to her place on the floor where she'd left her drawing board, shaking her head. Jack watched her.

"I'm sure he wouldn't try to arrest you," he said. "He seems like a good guy."

Her fingers found the charcoal. Her eyes and hands continued the sketch while her mind wandered. "I don't want him to know about this yet, all right?"

Jack shrugged. "Okay. But should we tell him you can make fire? And make sparkles appear when you sing?"

Te started up from her drawing. "You could see those?"

"Sure," said Jack. "And you looked different, too."

Not certain she actually wanted to hear this, Te prompted, "How?"

Jack squinted at her, as if trying to remember.

"You were glowing, like you had lights moving under your skin. Your eyes were this bright blue, and your skin was smoother."

"Smoother?"

"You looked like you didn't have a nose. Just eyes and a mouth, and all your skin was smooth like glass."

Again, Te looked down at her hands, checked the lines, checked the scars, checked the imperfections in cuticles and fingernails.

"Actually," said Jack, "you kind of looked like that."

He was pointing to her drawing. Te moved her hands aside. Half-finished, the drawing showed a woman with streaming hair, wings like those of a dragonfly sprouting from her back. Te's hands had drawn smooth, round shapes for the woman's head, neck, and shoulders. All within the outline of her body was white and unfinished.

"Minus the fairy wings," Jack finished. "What are you drawing, anyway?"

Te held the drawing up at arm's length, running her eyes over the shoulders, the subtle, casual roll of the neck. "It's my aunt," she said. "My aunt Sydney. Just before I knocked her over, she changed. She looked like this."

Jack shook his head, a grin inexorably creeping into his features. Te tried to focus on the picture, but eventually Jack's vibrating enthusiasm got annoying.

"What?" she said.

"So," said Jack slowly, "you have superpowers."

Te smirked. "Sure."

"Come *on*," he said. "You can make fire with your mind. You go around fighting monsters and saving people."

Now she was smiling in spite of herself. "I don't think that's how it works."

"Of *course* that's how it works," Jack said, gesturing forcefully with his empty mug. "You're a real, live superhero."

Te let her drawing flutter to the floor and went back to staring at her hand, this time checking it not for evidence of the inhuman but for evidence of the superhuman.

She could make invisible fire appear out of nowhere. That *was* cool.

"I knew there was some reason I kept you around," she said. Jack smiled at that and blushed. But the thought of the afternoon's encounter brought up something uncomfortable that forced its way out:

"Jack," Te began, "I'm sorry I almost got you killed again."

Jack's smile didn't twitter. "It's okay. I don't mind."

"Well ... you probably should, at least a little," Te said. "It's gotta worry your folks, at least, coming home late, half unconscious all the time."

Then Jack's face drooped. "Not really. Mostly, they don't even notice I'm gone."

Te didn't know what to say to that. Jack was silent a few more minutes, then abruptly looked up at her.

"I hate my house," he said. "My dad spends all day yelling at the TV. And they fight all the time." He stared into his empty mug. "I like it better hanging out with you. I'd like to stay here."

Te felt her solar plexus clench and inhaled a breath through her teeth. "Jack, I really don't think that's a good idea."

Te felt his disappointment fill the room. "All right," he said, "but can I come with you tomorrow?"

"It's going to be dangerous."

"So?" he said. "It's *something*."

Te felt her adult-type impulses floundering. She couldn't be the only friend he had. But why else was he always following her around?

She thought, *It isn't safe. It isn't sane.*

But she said, "All right."

A nod.

"Cool." He got up and rinsed his cup out before putting it away. "So, should I come up?"

"I'll knock on your window."

"Thanks," he said, and in his low-key way, he really meant it. Te showed him out.

She didn't sleep much. At one time, she awoke to find a little black, oily creature trying to crawl into her ear.

Its single eye spun and jiggled as she snatched it between two fingers. In her mind, she opened the fire door, letting the invisible flames flow out through her arm and surround the thing. After a second, it hung limp and docile, and she laid it in her palm. Then, she opened wide the other mental door, and bound the little creature under layers of pity and forgiveness and love.

She placed it in a shoe box. It purred and rubbed her hand.

It might have been a dream.

Static hissed from a dozen televisions. White noise filled the ears, filled the mind.

My shadow, my shadow, my shadow.

His mind settled, stretched, smoothed of rational thought. The twittering noise of the eternally panicking human brain ceased and stilled. The white noise spilled in and spoke to him.

Events produced ripples in the static. Seeing a ripple in a lake, one could track its movement, point toward its origin. Seeing its curvature, one could extrapolate the distance of the splash. Seeing its amplitude, one could deduce the size of the disturbance that caused it. Taking the ripple together with others that struck the shore by its side, one could deduce the character of the object that had breached the calm water.

The waters were never calm.

My shadow: it is gone from me.

He took up his pistol. It was an ancient thing, old cobwebs in the trigger guard, its silver gleam now dulled. It had lain on his desk for forty years, loaded and ready. He placed its tip beneath his chin, pointing up and angling back.

The invisible hand fell on his, gently, and pushed the gun aside.

"You're only proving me right," he said aloud. "You just need to keep me alive."

The invisible presence did not answer. The hand guided his gun back down to its place on the desk, where it had left an outline in the dust. The hand uncurled his fingers from the handle and set his hand back comfortably on his lap.

"Well, I think Cherian's actually going to do it. What do you think of that?"

Kent Allard turned and glared at the space next to him—glared at the empty chair, filled only by the unnatural wash of static light.

"And the other one—that white-skinned lady. Do you think she'll still be yours?"

His answer was a flicker in the static, a modulation in the white noise.

"My static has you confused," Kent said. "How *do* you like fifty years of nonstop distraction, you bastard?" He giggled, a death's-head of wrinkles and yellow teeth, skin the color of shifting electricity.

The white noise shuddered and bent, its frequency range becoming uneven, shifting and tilting in patterns only Kent Allard could have recognized as human speech.

The static spoke a prophecy: all the sticks fell across a single moment. Days now, and she would break the prison. Whatever she thought. Whatever she knew. Dead or alive.

"The white woman—she'll turn on you," Kent said. Then he began to laugh, loud and sudden, high-pitched and hysterical, because he was talking to an empty chair.

"You don't exist," he taunted it. "You don't exist, you don't exist."

The white noise sang to him.

"Heeeeeee . . ."

Chapter 13

The Turning of Vinyl; Without a Scratch

They rapped on Babu's door at six o'clock sharp.

Te had traded her torn leather jacket for a thigh-length winter coat, also black, and slim gloves. She had her hair down today as well, to keep her ears and neck warm. It had rained again last night, but the ground was frostbitten and the air stung of winter. Even Jack was wearing a coat this morning.

Te heard shuffling inside, something banging. She glanced around. Babu lived in a single-wide trailer on a barren, clay-soiled plot of land three hundred yards from the nearest paved road. He didn't even have a driveway, just a copse of scraggly evergreens, a half-collapsed aluminum toolshed, and a rotted and sagging front porch, patched over in places with unpainted particleboard.

Another crash, and the door flew open inward. Babu filled the whole frame, blinking against the daylight. His collared shirt was open to the third button and only one sleeve was rolled up to the elbow.

"Jesus Christ," he said. "Is it six already?"

Te raised an eyebrow. "Been up, have we?"

Babu wiped his eyes. "Couldn't sleep," he said. "Got a lot on my mind, I guess." He looked over Te's shoulder. "Is he coming, too?"

"I'm her sidekick," Jack said with a hint of pride.

Babu tried to share an exasperated look with Te, which she flatly refused to return. He suddenly seemed to notice that he could see his breath and waved them inside. Te and Jack trailed after him into a cramped living room with faux wood paneling on the walls and shag carpet. It smelled like old take-out pizza.

"Home sweet home," Te murmured.

"Got a call from Angrel," Babu said as he lurched into the adjoining kitchen. "She found Lester."

"That's good," Te said, not knowing if it was. According to Babu's casebook, the man named Lester Brown drank blood and hung around with fourteen-year-old girls.

"Yeah," said Babu. He poked his head in from the kitchen. "Have a seat."

Te and Jack squished into two metal-frame chairs with compacted cushioning around a circular table stacked two inches high with newspaper clippings. Babu continued his cacophonous coffee making.

"Remember that guy I told you about? Kitsune?" Babu asked.

"Sanjay mentioned him," Te said. She idly poked through the newspaper clippings as she spoke. Jack joined her, holding each one up an inch from his eyes to read the print.

"Lester can track him," Babu said. "We don't know exactly how, but Lester can sniff out where he's been. He's like a bloodhound when he's sober."

"Mmm....," Te said. The clippings were from papers from all over North America. Most were "unsolved murder baffles police"–type articles. Some of them were arguments for or against the viability of parapsychology as a science. A couple were from catalogues of ghost-hunting equipment.

"I hate to ask," Babu called, "but are you ready to go back out? I don't mean to doubt you or anything, but after yesterday . . ."

"I'm fine," Te said, scanning an article on the first sighting of the Jersey Devil since 1951. "I had a good night. I figured some things out."

Babu's voice came out of the kitchen. "Well, good," Babu said, then, asked, "Like what?"

Te heard the interrogative ring to the question, much as Babu was trying to keep it friendly. "Stuff," she said.

Te and Jack both heard the loud clang from the kitchen, felt the change in the air. When Babu came into the living room, square shouldered and hunched like a linebacker, Te was already on her feet, facing him with crossed arms.

"Listen, Te," Babu said, "I don't know if you understand how major this situation is. Yeah, I haven't been totally honest with you, but I had good reasons for it— not the least of which is that I promised your dad. And I know all this shit is new to you and I know I didn't prep you for any of it, but if we don't catch Kitsune and bottle this situation fast, people are going to die. *Lots* of people. You haven't seen this kind of shit before, but *I* have. If you know something, I need to have it."

He was breathing hard. Te looked up into his fatigue-lined face. "All right," she said, "but I get one question first."

Babu said nothing, so Te asked her question. "Why do you still work for the man who killed my dad?"

The change was profound and immediate: Babu was up to his full, towering height, filling the room with his shoulders and his suspicion.

"What do you know about it?"

Her insides shaking behind her crossed arms, Te set her jaw. "Answer the question."

Babu's breathing grew heavy and loud. His face screwed up in a scowl such as Te had never seen. For a second, he fought with himself, swaying and turning back and forth, fists clenching and unclenching.

"I don't work for him anymore," Babu growled.

"Oh yeah?" Te said. "When did that happen? I'm pretty sure it wasn't five years ago."

Babu turned, paced, stomped back and forth.

"Okay," he snapped. "*First*, *Rob* went after *him*. I don't know why. He just told me he had to kill the Man in the Empty Chair. I told him he was crazy, but who listens to me? *Second*, the Man didn't kill him. Gave him a hell of a beating, but Rob at least made it to the hospital. And the Man kills differently than that, anyway." Babu wiped his hand across his mouth. "I think it was something else. It must have been waiting for him, and Rob was just too weak to fight it off."

His posture slid downward with each word, until his shoulders looked like too much weight for one person to carry.

"I could never find out what did it," Babu said. He shot a look at Te. "No, I didn't quit working for him, because shit like that *happens* in our line of work. It was years later I got to thinking that the Man could have co-ordinated it. Could have had one of the prisoners ready and set him on Rob as soon as the fight was over. But there was no proof." He shook a warning finger at her. "No proof," he repeated, "so don't you come in here accusing me!"

The words exploded in the little space like chained thunder. Te held her ground, fighting tears, fighting anger, fighting every impulse to react. Babu stormed up to her, one huge, blunt finger aimed at her eyes.

"There's your question," he said. "Now mine. I know you know Kitsune. You've talked to him. More than once."

How did he find that out? Te felt a terror rising up. Her first instinct was to run, just to blaze out of there and never look back, but she didn't dare take her eyes off him. Even those eyes were huge—vein streaked and dark, the brows above pulled together with titan force.

"What did he say to you?" Babu growled. "What did you say to him?"

Careful, Te thought. *Remember how good he is at reading people.*

"*He* came to *me*," she said, openly defensive. "And I asked him questions. Things I'd already asked you, but we know how much you tell me." *Best defense is a good offense.* "He told me about the Old Country, and I know he let Bird out. He told me."

Babu's pointing finger drew back into a fist, which dropped at his side. "You should have told me about it. You recognized him," he said. "You'd met him before."

"I'd *seen* him before," Te said. "In my visions, I see him and Dad under some dead tree, except he's a fox with nine tails."

Babu nodded, at last moving that fierce gaze somewhere else. As he turned away, Te heard him exhale long and loud. Te took the opportunity to do the same.

"We tracked Kitsune for months," Babu said. "Finally, your dad caught him one-on-one and bound him."

"He didn't bind him," Te said. "He just made a wish."

Babu looked back at her, more puzzled than suspicious. "What wish?"

"I don't know. The vision doesn't go that far."

Babu gave her a skeptical look. Te held up one palm. "Scout's honor."

"You were never in scouts."

They stared at each other for a second. Then Te forced a smile and a little chuckle. Babu responded in kind. He clearly had other questions to ask, but after a minute he simply retreated into the kitchen to finish the coffee. Te collapsed, shaking, back into her chair.

Jack sat down beside her. He'd been up and hovering just behind her during the argument. "All good?" he whispered.

"I hope so."

Babu brought coffee out from the kitchen. He checked his watch. "We're meeting Angrel at the safe house at seven thirty," he said. "Once we start hunting Kitsune, we'll need the protection."

"Is it like an FBI safe house?" Jack asked.

"Sort of. Nothing, human or not, can get inside it without permission. Lester was supposed to open it up a couple of days ago, but"—he shrugged—"Angrel knows where he is, so we can go pick him up."

His eyes wandered over to Te and stayed there so long that Te finally gestured at him.

"What?"

"Nothing." Babu rose and pulled a bundle of thick blankets out of the hall closet. "Let's go."

They all slipped into shoes and jackets. Then Babu said casually, "By the way, have you seen my casebook?"

Te had been expecting the question for days. "Not recently. Did you lose it?"

She thought she'd sounded acceptably innocent—she was, in fact rather proud of her subtle performance— but Babu wasn't looking at her. He was watching Jack. Te didn't dare turn around far enough to see Jack's reaction.

Babu didn't answer her question.

By the time they hit the bridge cross street, Te was certain something was wrong. It was hard to put her finger on, but sitting in the passenger seat of Babu's car, watching the traffic, watching the pedestrians filing on and off buses, in and out of shops and office buildings, she knew something was off. There was a kind of dullness to every movement, a lethargy in the way people shuffled to work—dark circles under every eye, fast food uneaten on plates and plastic trays. Noises, even car engines and crosswalk beeps, were too quiet.

And . . . her spider-sense was tingling. It was the only way she could describe it. There was a sensation in her body, nonlocalized, stinging but not painful, as if she'd walked into a sauna and was getting that first blast of heat before her body adjusted. It had begun the instant she awoke and looked down at the shoe box right next to her bed. Afraid of what she'd find if she opened it, she'd carefully placed a heavy book on top and left it there.

She didn't mention any of this to the tense man beside her.

Babu drove them into the bad part of a suburb

called Schrevston, located just outside the Darktown shadows. He pulled up in front of a block-sized lot, ringed by a rusted chain-link fence and filled with piles of scrap metal. A little graffiti-covered concrete building stood in the center of the lot, windows boarded up, door closed.

"This is the safe house?" Te asked. From the case-book, she thought it would be bigger.

"Yeah." Babu started drawing a cigarette. "It doesn't look like much, but it's under a hundred years of protection, so run here if something comes after you that you can't handle."

Te glared at him. "I did my best yesterday."

Babu started, surprised. "Yeah, I know."

"And it won't happen that way next time."

"Sure, sure," Babu said. "It didn't go that badly, really. King hurt Bird pretty badly. She'll probably hole up in a bell tower to heal for a few days."

"Not that badly," Te echoed.

Babu grunted a dismissive sound and got out. Te hated not being able to read him. His face was like stone. But it hadn't been an idle boast. With what she knew now, with what she'd done recently, it *would* go differently next time.

Jack and Te followed him to the gate, or rather the gap in the fence where the gate had been, before it had broken off its hinges and dropped into the mud.

"Don't touch anything in here," Babu said. He hadn't smoked at all during the drive but had a cigarette lit in hand two steps out of the vehicle. "Father O'Shae—good friend of your father's and mine—he's blessed a lot of the stuff that's lying around."

"Why should that bother us?" Te asked.

Babu smirked askance at her. "'Only the pure of heart may pass,'" he quipped.

Te spotted Angrel before they were halfway across the yard. The fortune-teller was wearing a loose tan dress with a puffy black winter vest over it. In the morning sun she seemed to glow, a living ghost walking the daylight in reincarnated splendor.

Te thought, *Bitch*.

As they approached the little gray building, weaving through scrap, Te saw Angrel draw a card from the deck she held in her palm. Her eyes widened as she examined it, but then she slid the card back into the deck as if nothing had happened at all.

"What, you don't have a key?" Babu said.

Angrel shrugged and gave one of those secretive little smiles Te was beginning to hate.

"Rob never gave me one," she said.

"Where's Lester?" Babu asked, examining the door.

"He's back in Darktown," Angrel reported, "sitting in front of *the door*."

"The door?" Te asked. She was ignored.

"What the hell's he doing there?" Babu muttered. "I thought he was in hiding."

"He was."

"It's a funny place to hide."

Angrel smirked. "He may be taking his responsibility seriously."

Babu gave a halfhearted shrug of assent. "The safe house has been opened," he said.

Angrel raised an eyebrow. "Why do you say that?"

Te saw a hint of something smug in Babu's expression as he spoke. "Because I painted bits of it shut last time we used it. The paint's been broken. Recently."

"Hmph," said Angrel. "Well, open it."

"Just a minute," Babu murmured. His eyes wandered over the door, the step, the ground. Angrel watched his every move. Te watched Angrel.

What do you see? she asked herself. She tried to look into Angrel with that *other* sight, which she and Angrel had used together inside the fortune-teller's reading room. It didn't work exactly as she'd hoped. She got little twittering flashes, like the memories of a fading dream: hundreds of copies of the same face, all snarled in anger.

Angrel perked up, then turned those pink eyes Te's way.

"Who's your exquisite young man?" she asked.

Jack, who until then had been silent and ignored by everyone, flushed a bright red.

Te did the obligatory, "Angrel, Jack. Jack, Angrel."

"Hi," said Jack.

"*Very* pleased to meet you," Angrel said, holding her hand out in a ladylike fashion to be taken. Jack, used to regular handshakes it seemed, fumbled his way through it. Angrel slipped her eyes past Te when they left Jack. They spoke of playful, malicious intent.

But before Te's anger completely distracted her, her inner sight flashed something. The look had been a front, a distraction. She saw a vision of the card Angrel had drawn when they first pulled up: *The Snake*. Te had once sketched something very much like it, with black charcoal and a smudge of red paint.

"What are you . . . ?" she managed. Then Babu slipped a key into the door's lock and turned it, and everything started to happen very quickly. The instant the door cracked, Te was struck by a wall of images: claws, fists,

tentacles, horns and teeth, the blackened and twisted
fingernails of human hands—all those things that had
grasped and raged at the door. They hit her like a blow;
sparks exploded in her head, and she fell, crashing into a
stack of old pipes and pieces of bicycle frame.

Then the pain began in her arm, a white-hot, searing
agony that blazed through her skin, jabbing its way up
her nerves like a steel rod. Whispered words burrowed
into her skull: *"Ab omni malo, libera nos, Domine."* She
screamed through clenched teeth, wrenching her spasming hand away from a piece of pipe. Her hand scrambled against her chest like a dying spider.

Then she saw the man of fire.

For the first second, she thought it was a hallucination,
but then it shouldered its way through a pile of garden
tiles, sending them spinning and sliding all over the yard. It
was an apparition of shadow and flame and smoke, shrieking like a banshee, and with clawed hands outstretched.

Te kicked and rolled away as the thing charged past.
Flames licked at her legs. Jack was already running out
of the way, as was Angrel. Babu, head peering into the
building, was only just beginning to turn.

"Babu!" Te screamed at him too late. Babu had just
enough time to see the flames, and then the creature
struck him. They toppled into the building together in a
burst of light and heat.

Te jerked to her feet. Still clutching her quivering
hand, she raced in after them.

"You stupid shit," Babu was saying. Te ran to him, batting at the flames that clung to his coat. Babu grabbed
one lapel and, with several jerks of his huge arms, flung
it into a corner. "Lester, what the hell?"

The creature of fire had dimmed into a smoking,

smoldering man. "It's here! Get out!" he cried. He dove behind the room's couches, peering under, around. "I know it's here. It wouldn't have left. It waits." He started tearing the couch cushions apart and looking inside.

Babu angrily wiped ashes and soot off his pant legs. "Damn it. You could have gotten yourself killed."

Lester froze for a moment, staring at Babu with bloodshot, crazed eyes. His face and hands were covered in blisters and burn marks.

"Why are you still in here?" he cried, throwing his hands up. "Get out!" His eyes jumped over the walls. "Jill! Jill, where are you?" He lifted one end of a four-seater couch as if it were a lawn chair. "There's no one here," Lester whined. "They're all gone."

"God, you stink," Babu snapped. "What's supposed to be here?"

The man stared at Babu with eyes like pink golf balls, shuddering where he stood.

"The Maskim," he said. Babu's eyes widened and Lester fumbled the rest: "It was here. I saw it. I know I should have fought it. I know I should have, but my Strutters . . . my Strutters were . . ."

Te saw Babu inhale some patience. He placed a hand on Lester's shoulder and guided him down onto a couch. That turned him around and gave Te another look at his face: his skin had rapidly blistered, and in places had begun to bleed.

Babu squatted in front of him, huge hands pinning Lester into the couch so that he couldn't move. He stared Lester in the face and told him in no uncertain terms to calm down.

Babu interrogated him. Direct questions, no non-sense, no possibility of weasling around.

"When did you see it?"

"T-two days ago."

"How did it get inside?"

"I—I let it," Lester shuddered. "I had the door open."

Te watched them both—watched how Babu used his size, angling his shoulders as if always ready to spring forward, and watched how Lester's face healed right before her eyes, each blister bursting, leaking, and pulling back into the skin. Before long the front of Lester's hoody was soaked with blood and blister fluid.

According to the casebook, this was Lester Brown, the vampire. With the rate his burns were patching, and the length of his fingernails, Te didn't have any reason to doubt it. It was just, she'd sort of expected to get that spider-sense feeling off him—she'd assumed the feeling came when she got too close to things from the Old Country, but she got nothing from him.

"You locked it in?" Babu was saying.

Lester nodded.

"Then how did it get out?"

"I don't know."

"Where'd it go?"

"I don't know, man."

Babu stood up. "Angrel!"

The white woman was already at the door, leaning comfortably. "Yes?"

"Did you see anything?"

"Nothing about the Maskim."

"And Lester not being in Darktown?"

Angrel shook her head. "I can't explain that. It could be Kitsune."

"Kitsune!" Lester barked. "Kitsune. He's let something else out. Little black ... I don't know." He made a walking spider with his fingers. "And there'll be more."

Babu clapped him on the shoulder. Te was surprised when the little man didn't collapse under the weight of that hand. "I know." Then Babu slapped his hands together and rubbed them. He looked from Te to Angrel to Lester.

"Good, good," he murmured, clearly to himself. Then he started thinking out loud: "Wherever the Maskim went, it'll bed down and wait. And Bird is out of action. Perfect ... I've got your sun gear in the trunk, Les. You need to start right away."

Angrel's eyebrow went up. "You're not coming?"

Babu shook his head. "Just track him. Try not to engage until I'm back. Until then, Te's in charge."

Everyone started at that.

Angrel's words dripped venom.

"And where will you be, exactly?"

"I'm going to get my brother."

Chapter 14

No-man's Manhunt

Fear. Te smelled it all over her. She watched the albino fortune-teller constantly, wondering at every nod of the head, every flash of the eyes, every happily given piece of advice. Te had at some point come to the conclusion that this pale little harpy had seduced her father away from the family and away from her. There were nagging doubts of course—other factors such as Mom's ubiquitous subtle hostility and Dad's fading health—which she knew she should be considering, but it was just easy to assume that her family problems were all the result of some lusty, skinny porcelain girl, and Te for the time being allowed herself the luxury.

But there *was* something objectively wrong with Angrel's expressions. She'd been profoundly disappointed that the Maskim hadn't been at the safe house. She'd been nervous that Lester had suddenly shown up there. Once or twice since they'd started tracking Kitsune, she'd said they should go the opposite direction from where Lester's nose was pointing them, and only through warbling, simpering insistence from Lester and a sharp word from Te did she relent.

She was up to something.

And Te seemed to be the only one who'd noticed. Lester was perpetually up front, sniffing around like a dog, rarely speaking, sometimes stopping on a street corner and shuddering uncontrollably for a few seconds before starting back on the trail. He looked very odd in his sun gear, which consisted of a hooded plastic raincoat, far too big for him, thick black jeans and big boots, a balaclava, neck toque and sun-shaded wraparound goggles, and leather gloves that went all the way up to his elbows, just in case a sleeve slipped. With Lester in the lead, followed by white-skinned and ghostly Angrel, google-eyed Jack, and then herself, taller than the rest by a good four inches, they should have been a magnet for attention. But once they got out onto the street, Te realized she should have saved herself the worry. People passed them without so much as a glance. Everyone walked like a zombie. In the hour they'd been out tracking, Te had witnessed two fender benders, each with the occupants of both cars getting out and staring stupidly at the damage to their vehicles, saying nothing.

They had started at an apartment building in Brightontown, only six blocks from Te's house, and had wended their way through the suburbs until they were on the edge of the downtown core, where the buildings abruptly climbed to ten and fifteen stories from two. It made it harder to watch the skies for Bird, if she'd managed to recover.

With the cross over Cardona Street, the surroundings became immediately more opulent: skyscrapers, fancy restaurants, boutiques, and cafés. This was for a more wealthy, more image-conscious kind of people, worker bees in a busy commercial district that had sprung up in St. Ives with complete disregard for the fact that the little city was out in the middle of nowhere.

Still, Te couldn't help but glance at more than one pair of very nice shoes on display.

She heard Angrel snickering, and glared at her.

"What?"

Grinning, Angrel inclined her head and an image flashed into Te's brain: this very store, her father smiling as Angrel whirled, girlishly happy, in a new pair of slim suede shoes. Te shook the vision off. She came back to find Angrel gesturing subtly down. When Te followed the woman's eyes, Angrel swished her skirt just enough to show off that same pair of shoes, older and faded, but undoubtedly the same, still on her feet.

Te almost torched her right there.

Angrel tucked her hands back into her vest pockets and wandered away as if nothing had happened. Te thought, *What the hell was that?* Then, *Babu couldn't have known about her and Dad. Otherwise he'd never have let me be alone with her.*

A cynical conclusion, maybe, but it had a kind of logic. In her mind, Te forgave Babu just that little.

At the next corner, Lester stopped. Te and the rest of the group stopped with him, waiting for him to get his bearings. After a few minutes of absolute stillness, Te shared a look with Jack, who shrugged. Te walked up beside Lester. He stood now with knees bent, arms crooked, head cocked downward, his pose showing off every bump of his bony frame. He was whispering.

"I've lost her. I've lost her."

"Lost *him*?" Te prompted.

Lester almost jumped out of his boots. "What?" he said. "No, no. Him. Kitsune."

Te looked into the impenetrable goggles, wishing she could see to read him better. Lester suddenly broke into an exaggerated display of sniffing and looking around. "This way," he said, and jolted to a shuffling canter.

Three more blocks, two more alleys. In and out of the shadows of the downtown offiices, they followed Lester, pacing his bursts of enthusiasm and periods of listless silence. Te twice caught Angrel sneaking a look at a card she'd drawn, and both times tried to use her inner sight to find out what it was, without success. It was a strange feeling, trying to induce a vision. Last week, if she'd been asked, she would have insisted on a necessary relationship between visions and excessive stamp licking, yet here she was, more comfortable with ludicrous paranormal abilities than with the empty gun that she'd left at home.

Superpowers. She looked affectionately at Jack, who strolled along wordlessly, magnified eyes jumping randomly over the scenery.

"We're close," Lester suddenly said, and bolted down the sidewalk. Te and the others raced to catch up. He led them around a corner, heading for a little photography shop that looked as if it had been in business when daguerreotypes were in vogue.

In midstride, Angrel suddenly cried out. She crashed to the pavement and began tearing at her hair and scalp. Te screeched to a halt. Up ahead, Lester and Jack slowed and looked back with confusion.

"Hey!" said Te. She bent down over the twitching albino, who was muttering quietly in some strange language. "Hey," Te said again, nudging Angrel with one hand. "What are you . . ."

And then it hit her, too. An image blasted into her

mind and consciousnesss, obliterating everything in a wave of darkness and negative sensation.

She saw a living shadow stripped free of the earth like a sheet of black velvet. It glimmered and rippled, stretching outward to all horizons, flexing appendages long atrophied, tasting atmosphere so long ago denied it. It was shapeless, an inkblot on reality, the opposite of what it meant to exist, but there was awareness there; Te felt it staring into her, into everything, in all directions at once in manifest omniscience. Hanging there in the dead, senseless space of the vision, Te realized that it knew everything about her, that it knew everything that happened under its infinite wings.

Then she was back, facedown on the pavement, with her hip hurting where it had struck the sidewalk and her palms where she'd used them to try to break her fall. Someone was screaming.

Wishing her visions didn't always end with her falling down, Te groaned and lifted her head. She checked the others: Angrel and Jack were on the ground, recovering like she was. Lester was the only one standing, staring ahead and flexing his nails.

She moved her hand and was rewarded with a sting of pain. Broken glass. It was all over the sidewalk and the street. She picked the shard out of her finger. "Careful," she said to everyone.

Her eyes flicked to Angrel, who was up to her knees, gathering some cards she'd dropped. Te stood quickly and got a look at one before Angrel hid it: The Haunter in the Dark. Te immediately recognized the image on the card as the creature she'd just seen. It hadn't been a vision at all.

A crunch—glass ground under a shoe. Te turned.

The photo shop stood in ruins, exploded from the inside. No flame or smoke issued from it, but its beams and supports all bent outward, and there wasn't a shred of window glass left in its place. In front of it stood a man in a gold suit jacket and slacks, matching gold hair, leaning on a cane of gold and ebony. Yun smiled at her, and winked.

"May the best mythical creature win." He swiveled smartly on his heel, tapped his cane against the sidewalk, and strolled off, at once unhurried and faster than the eye could follow.

"Up, up!" Te ordered, hauling Lester out of his shock against a whined protest. "He was right here. Let's go, people."

As they took off at a run after Yun, the sky above grew darker and darker.

Babu hated this place.

Cloake Hill Mental Institution: a one-hundred-year-old stone and mortar box straddling a hill of poorly kept lawns and poorly shaped trees. The fence at the bottom of the hill was ten feet high and wrought iron, topped with pointed spades. Every time Babu looked at this place, he expected lightning to flash, expected the moans and screams of the deranged to echo down the hill.

But it was quiet and still, and the skies just drizzled a little. He hunched over his smoldering cigarette, tucked the bundle he carried tighter to his side, and worked his way up the path. He shouldered his way through the door and into the foyer—into stale white light and antiseptic nonsmell. He scuffed his shoes, shook off his latest jacket—a plastic rain poncho, replacing his burned army jacket—and trudged up to the receptionist's counter.

The male nurse working there spent ten seconds staring into space before he seemed to realize he was looking at someone.

"Oh," he said. "Can I help you?"

"You all right?" Babu asked him.

"Fine," said the man. "Didn't sleep very well last night."

Babu nodded in sympathy, then sucked up a breath and steeled himself. "I need to see my brother."

"Uhhh ..." The nurse seemed to take a long time thinking. "Visiting hours aren't until three."

"I'm not visiting," Babu said. The words came out hard, half a lie. "I'm taking him home."

"Oh," the nurse said. He fumbled some paperwork and a pen onto the little shelf. "Um ... Just fill these out. I'll have to get a doctor to authorize release."

Babu nodded. He waited while the nurse went and got someone, diligently scribbling on every line and ticking every box and wishing he could smoke in here and that circumstances had not forced him to come back. He hadn't seen his brother in almost a year. He couldn't stand this place—the shuffling, lurching people, the comatose and the drugged, the ones who moaned and squirmed, and the doctors who walked around talking about everything like normal people talked about yesterday's news stories. But mostly, he just couldn't stand seeing his brother. Once, Ahmadou had been a sound engineer and a musician. Once, even just walking down the street, he would have lit up at every odd sound, every strange timbre, searching it out with his ears and eyes, scribbling notes without breaking conversation. Babu missed *that* Ahmadou.

The doctor came while Babu's pen was hovering over the form's question of his brother's future care:

a. Patient will receive care at home from immediate family; b. Patient will be transferred to another medical institution. Please provide name and address of institution.

Babu hastily ticked the option for family care, knowing Ahmadou would be right back in here after their job was done. Whatever. Babu had found he could live with guilt.

"Mr. Cherian," said the doctor, who also looked like he hadn't got much sleep, "I understand you're here to take your brother home?"

Babu nodded, then fed the guy some bullshit story about having room for him, now that the kids had moved out—about the rest of the family wanting him closer, their mother worrying about him all the time, but too old herself to pay a visit. The doctor accepted everything with the ease of a person dreaming, and eventually, after a quick check of Babu's paperwork, escorted him down through the halls to his brother's room.

Babu heard it as the doctor fiddled with lock and keys: a light, hollow tap, then another, then another. They fell in no rhythm, no constance of volume or timbre. Babu almost lost it right there, almost walked right out. But . . . he had a job to do.

The doctor at last opened the thick, cell-like metal door to Ahmadou's room. Babu's chest tightened up.

Ahmadou was a skeleton. His bones protruded through stretched and sagging skin. His hair had gone almost totally gray, and he was balder now on top. His clothes, neat though they were, hung off him like rags. And the eyes—eyes that used to jump at every exciting thing—stared at the opposite wall and at a death that wouldn't come and at nothing.

For a moment, Babu couldn't speak. He could only stare as Ahmadou's bony fingers lifted slowly, up two inches in starts like a rusted hinge, and then dropped onto the skin of the djembe drum that sat on the floor in front of him. A hollow tap.

Babu had bought him that drum years ago. Ahmadou used to love drumming; he'd had a kit and a whole room full of percussion instruments. He'd told Babu how he had this dream to go back to Africa and learn drumming as it was supposed to be done. He would track down the tiny village where they'd both been born, and learn from the people there. Or, if no one drummed there anymore, he'd teach them how.

"I'll leave you two alone," the doctor said, and showed himself out.

That was the last thing Babu had wanted. But then there he was, alone in a room with the brother he loved, the brother he'd abandoned.

"Ahms," he said, quietly, his voice shaking. "Ahms?"

Ahmadou didn't answer. The fingers came up, fell. Tap. Babu sat beside him on the little bed. The frame bent and protested. "Ahms? It's time to go."

Nothing.

"We need you," Babu said. "Kitsune's free. We need you. Do you understand?"

Tap. The stare, unchanged. It tore at Babu's heart.

It had been a case in Boston, one of Babu's first paranormal investigations: reports of ghost-lights and unexplained deaths. Babu's client had been a grieving mother. She'd just wanted to know what had happened to her daughter.

Even when the trail had led him right to the creature's hiding place, Babu still hadn't wanted to believe that it was anything supernatural. When he'd seen the walking figure of blue fire, he'd thought it was some kind of illusion. He'd shot it. He'd pissed it off. Then he'd run.

Ahmadou had been visiting. He'd been sleeping upstairs when Babu raced home and slammed the door, the creature a mere hundred yards behind him, having paced his then-new car all the way back into downtown. Babu had thought, desperately, naively, that it couldn't get into the house. Maybe it needed permission or something. Maybe it just couldn't get through a locked door.

But it got through a window. It got into Ahmadou's room. Maybe it mistook Ahmadou for Babu. Maybe it was just hungry. But whatever it did before Babu drove it off had left Ahmadou like this. And Ahms had never healed.

After that, one of the Warden's hunting teams had shown up in town and caught the thing. That was the beginning of Babu's long fall away from civility and his entry into the world of the supernatural and the insane.

When the creature had hollowed out Ahmadou, it had left something behind, some force or anger that could cripple the creatures of the Old Country like no magic or prayer or device that Babu had ever seen. They'd used him on a half dozen occasions against the most dangerous creatures in St. Ives—used him, like a tool.

Protocol over family, Babu thought. All that mattered was stopping whatever happened to Ahmadou from happening to anyone else.

"I brought you some clothes," Babu said, laying his bundle on the bed and rolling it out. Shirt, pants, trench coat—much better quality than he himself would usually wear. "Come on, up you get."

Babu tried to coax his brother away from the drum, but Ahmadou was like a statue. Eventually Babu had to call in a nurse to help. The nurse lifted Ahmadou up by the armpits to a standing position, where Ahmadou stayed.

"He lets you pose him," the nurse explained. He helped Ahmadou dress while Babu tried not to see the glimpses of that sagging, emaciated body, aged so far beyond its years. When it was all done, the nurse placed Ahmadou's hand on Babu's arm. "If you pull him, he'll follow you around," he said.

The nurse stopped him as he was leading his brother out. "Hey, sir," he said, "the drum's yours, right?"

Babu looked back at that sad symbol of his brother's former life. "I'll come back for it," he said.

Yeah, he'd come back. After all the terror and pain he was about to put his brother through, Babu was going to bring him right back to this sterile cage. He wouldn't take him home. He couldn't care for him there. He could never make his brother whole again, and that was far worse a shame than abandoning him to this place. He liked to think that Ahmadou would want to be useful, that if he understood what he was being used for and why, he would appreciate the chance to do good. It was a bullshit fantasy, but Babu clung to it.

His brother followed him, step by shuffling step, without question, without awareness, into the St. Ives drizzle. The change from clinical warmth to November chill produced no reaction. When they got to the car, water, just water, was running down Ahmadou's cheeks.

*   *   *

"Which way?" the girl demanded.

Lester choked back his panic, keeping it out of his voice, but it ran into his hands and started them shaking. "Give me a second!" he snapped, ashamed at the girlish pitch of his voice.

"Tonight my work begins in earnest," Yun had said. He was going, running, right now, to free another one. Lester knew it. He felt it in his burning skin, heated to a fever even through all his sun gear. Where was Babu? Did he expect Lester to handle Yun all by himself when they finally caught him?

He has to be stopped. That was Jill's voice. It sounded so strange inside his head; she so rarely talked to him except in verse. He knew it wasn't her, that she wasn't really there, but he couldn't help but look around. *You have to save me.* She was alive. He knew it. He'd smelled her. He felt her pulse ringing in his own hungry veins.

"Lester," Rob's little girl barked at him, "which way?"

"Just a *minute*."

He felt her pulse, too, racing in her body—and racing sympathetically in his. He hadn't "partaken" for almost two days now. His vampire lust was building, and would eventually overwhelm him. He needed to stop for blood.

"Lester."

"Get back," he said. "Give me some space." Rob's girl was so bossy—nothing like Rob had been. He breathed a sigh when she grudgingly obeyed him, taking a few steps away. It cleared the air around him of the scent of her abnormally sweet blood.

All right, he thought. *Focus.* He took a sniff of the

air and caught it immediately: Yun's antiseptic, ozone smell.

"This way," he said, and began again at a run. They were now in the heart of downtown, and the sun fell almost nowhere between the buildings. Occasionally there would be a reflection from an office window, and that stung, but only for a minute.

He still couldn't believe he'd run out into the sun to the safe house. It had been panic, absolute and overwhelming. He wanted to think he'd done it to save Babu and Angrel from the Maskim—something desperate and heroic—but at the time all he'd been able to think about was the horrible picture of them finding Jill first, seeing before he did what the Maskim had done to her. They would figure it out and she would blame him for it.

But Jill wasn't there. Of course she wasn't—he didn't remember why he'd thought she would still be in the safe house. She was walking around the city. She had visited him twice. Hints of her scent were everywhere.

He led them into a driveway on one side of a building, a route behind for trucks to get to the loading docks. In his haste he stumbled for a moment to all fours, and ran that way for a few strides before remembering himself. They came down a ramp into a back lot with several large delivery trucks backed up to a loading dock. The place looked deserted, but wasn't. Lester immediately smelled the drivers, the receiving personnel. He sensed heartbeats, rapid and thin.

"There!" Te shouted from behind him. Lester caught sight of a golden tail flickering into shadow under a truck, and suddenly he wondered again what the hell they were going to do with Yun when they cornered him. He fought the panic. He fought Yun's imagined attack, an attack of confidence and smiles.

Luckily, Rob's girl took charge. "You three, block the ramp," she ordered. The slanted drive they'd come down was the only way out. Walls of concrete foundation closed off every other exit. They had him trapped.

Yun got desperate when he was trapped.

"Lester," Te was saying, "there." She pointed. Lester went, crouching down beside Angrel a few yards up the ramp. Te's tagalong kid stood a good twenty feet up the ramp behind them.

Rob's girl looked at them and nodded. "Good," she said. "Stay there. Don't let him past you."

How the hell am I supposed to stop him? Lester screamed in his head, but he nodded along with Angrel.

Rob's little girl turned away from them and started down into the loading area, step by step. Even she didn't want to do this, it seemed. That cheered him up and raised his panic at the same time.

Then he saw one of the drivers of the trucks, slumped back in his chair, head lolling. The man wasn't dead—that, Lester could have handled—no, he was alive, eyes closed, breathing deeply and with infinite satisfaction. He was in Rapture.

Lester watched Te Evangeline walk down into that concrete box with no way out, and thought over and over how Yun could make you do anything, with the Rapture.

"W-what are you going to do?" he called out.

Te Evangeline looked back over her shoulder, eyes wide as if she hadn't even thought about it.

"I'm going to talk to him," she said.

*　　*　　*

What is she up to, this unpredictable girl?

I watch Te Evangeline approach the nearest of the trucks, looking under it and behind the tires—cautious, but not smart enough to stay up here with us. Kitsune *can* be vicious. Despite his smile and his soft voice and his almost plastic face, he can be just as murderous as the rest of them.

Talk to him? Just talk to him?

I'm not sure where my anxiety is coming from. The Man had not said I needed to protect Te from death. But he had also said she was integral to his plan. If she walks down there and gets herself *damaged*, somehow . . . will the Man blame me?

No. He's not capable of that. He would see and acknowledge how things were, however they're about to be.

I know that Te Evangeline cannot catch Kitsune all on her own. She's only a binder, and binding without suppressing is next to impossible. First, the creature has to be beaten and subdued, by sound or magic or bullets or any of a hundred other methods. Only then, when it is nearly mad from pain, can it be bound safely. Otherwise it will still have too much of its wits to be tricked into being bound.

I watch Te round the cab of the nearest truck, watch her take a long, careful look at its comatose driver.

The Man told me only not to let the Kitsune be caught. Te can't catch him. She doesn't have anything offensive in her repertoire.

So why am I so nervous?

"'Here is the Belladonna, the Lady of the Rocks, the lady of situations.'"

Te rounded the bulging wheel of the truck and slipped into the narrow shadow between it and the one beside. At the opposite end, Yun, now only gold hair, gold shoulders, and shadow, tapped his cane rhythmically against the ground.

" 'Here is the man with three staves,' " he said, " 'and here the Wheel, and here is the one-eyed merchant, and this card, which is blank, is something he carries on his back, which I am forbidden to see.' "

Te edged closer, feeling the nearness of the cold steel on either side. There was a difference in Yun's posture from the previous times she'd seen him. His head was down and his shoulders hunched. Te could not see his face, but she felt that if she could have, he would not have been smiling.

"Let's talk," she said.

Yun gave a primal snort. "For all my sophistication," he said, "for my grand words and my charm, I am still an animal." His head lifted a whisper, and she felt his eyes pierce her. "I am a cornered animal, Miss Evangeline."

Te held a defensive hand in front of her, but did not stop her approach.

"Yun," she said, "I don't want to do this. I really don't. But . . . Bird, and the Maskim and The Haunter in the Dark . . ."

His head tilted inquisitively.

"Yeah, I know what it's called," Te said. "You have to stop letting them all free."

With a sharp jerk that made Te jump, Yun lifted his cane and twirled it into place beneath his arm.

"I do only what I do, Miss Evangeline," he said. "Free choice is something of a human luxury. Our kind gave up much of that when we took our shapes, when we chose to live here instead of in that lost golden land of our birth." Yun straightened up, and the dull light falling from above shifted to reveal a sewer grate at his feet.

"He who lies here is called by mankind the Vanisher," Yun said. " 'Come with me under the shadow of this red rock, and I will show you something different from either your shadow in the morning striding behind you, or your shadow in the evening rising to meet you: I will show you fear in a handful of dust.' "

Te felt it, then: a tremor, a shifting of some huge presence beneath the concrete. She felt an echo of its thoughts in her own, a sluggish, mindless happiness in the anticipation of play. There was nothing in those thoughts of compassion, nothing even of the awareness of other living creatures. All was playground, and what was not, was banquet.

She willed the fire out of her, cracking open her mental door to a reservoir of rage culled from all the ages of human misery. The fire slipped into her nerves, running up and down the flesh chains of her limbs, in and out of her throbbing heart in time with her breath.

"Don't do this, Yun," she said.

Yun jammed his cane between the slots of the grate, angling it back to pry the grate open.

"I must, Miss Evangeline," he said. "I exist only to grant wishes. Some are simple and can be granted by my own power. Others cannot be granted, but only achieved within, and these require the creation of . . . appropriate conditions."

"I can hurt you," Te said. "You know that, don't you?"

Yun's smile came again, resigned and sinister. "I certainly do."

"Then don't let it loose."

"These are your brothers," Yun said. "And your sisters and your cousins. They are your kin." Yun pushed back on the cane and the grate shifted. Te immediately brought her fire out to her fingertips where, invisible to the naked eye, it glimmered and lashed out angrily in the imagination.

"Yun . . ."

"I can act on nothing," he said, "but the manner of my essence. My own sentiment I have long since buried." He looked softly, caringly at the concrete and the creature beneath. "And yet I walk in this place, and I feel the sorrow of my kind, and I, too, cry for them. Things should not be this way."

"Yun . . . don't make me do this."

"And being wrong," he said, "as with all things in their nature perverse, these things must be unmade." Kitsune pressed back on his cane, lifting the grate out of its space with the sound of scraping steel and the cracking of long-set mud. Te let her fire loose.

As before, it rang through her with the laughter of a thousand thousand of the most cruel and vindictive of the human race. She was the general without mercy, the judge pronouncing sentence, bound by reason. She was the dominatrix and the serial killer, the revenging son and the holy warrior. Yun's scream of pain cut the withering day like the howl of a tortured animal. His human facade exploded away from him in strips of flesh and light, and beneath he crouched low on his paws, and whipped his nine tails around him like leaves in a hurricane wind.

Te felt it, too. Like the restless shifting of the Vanisher beneath the ground, Yun's pain resonated in her, a sympathetic dying of the soul. Te knew exactly what it felt like. And she knew that, because of what Yun was, she could inflict it forever and he would not die from it.

It was too late. It was for nothing. The grate, its seal broken, slid slowly and noisily aside. From the hole beneath, a luminous gray tentacle, rubbery and slick with sewer fluid, reached into the clear air.

With a titan thunder the pavement split in spiderweb cracks out from the hole. Te stumbled against the cold side of a truck. Her fire dwindled. The righteous smile of the conqueror grew blurry. The second impact flipped her prone, and was strong enough to rattle the trucks on their suspension.

Her fright drove her fire back to nothing. Yun was already gone, and the thing under the pavement hissed and gurgled its displeasure.

Te ran.

Lester's nerves prickled when he heard the growl. They frayed when the pavement shifted. They broke when Te Evangeline came running at full tilt up from the trucks.

He spun and dug his nails into the pavement, fleeing on four limbs. He'd never run like this when he'd been human, but since, when the terror swelled up and overwhelmed him, it was the most natural thing in the world.

Angrel was a white streak as he flew by, Te's friend a flash of wide eyes.

Another animal joined him the instant he hit the sidewalk. Lester glanced over at it as, for a moment, it paced him, stride for stride. Gray eyes squinted at him. A white-tipped muzzle with fingernail teeth snapped at him. With a quick sidestep, it bounded between his feet and he went down, face-first into the road. He rolled to a stop on all fours, crouched. With horror, he realized he could feel a breeze whispering over his skin.

Wait a minute!

The glove on his left hand had torn open during his fall, leaving a patch of skin vulnerable to sunlight. In a panic, he curled himself around his hand, waiting for the pain and fire to start.

And even when they didn't, he stayed curled. *I'm not on fire. I'm not on fire.*

Carefully, he stood up and stretched his exposed hand out of his own shadow.

The earth jerked. The handful of pedestrians walking by stumbled and fell. The road split sidewalk to sidewalk.

A car blindsided him and he went down.

Tentacles broke up through the ramp, gray and grainy and half seen, colorless like a badly developed photograph, moving in stops and skips like the frames of an old movie. They wriggled, glistening into the dull daylight, blocking Te's escape. One of them lashed up into the air, reaching suddenly six or seven feet from the asphalt, and Te stumbled, her momentum broken.

Thank God Jack made no stupid run in to help her. Angrel stood straight and calm just beyond the reach of the tentacles penetrating the ramp, her face an intense, calculating expression. She did nothing.

Te cast around her. In her mind's eye, she saw the creature move beneath her feet, tentacles without number toppling over each other in great swarms, prodding the underside of the asphalt. The Vanisher's thoughts echoed in her mind—basic, inborn drives to move, to touch, to swallow: simple animal impulses with nothing about them suggestive of conscious direction. It was so unlike the rest of the creatures of the Old Country, even Bird, who could at least speak. But still, she felt a strange kinship with the monster under her feet. Surely as it was there, it was her brother, her sister, her cousin. And just as surely, that wouldn't stop it from devouring her.

As one, the tentacles ringing the loading dock constricted toward each other. The pavement across the whole stretch of the dock shattered like tempered glass. The two trucks slammed inward as the ground crumbled beneath them. It was making a nest—a lair—to suit itself. It was making a pit.

The pavement undulated like water under her feet. In a moment, all her footing would be gone. She looked back at the tentacles whipping around at the base of the ramp. She had to try before the ground disappeared. She went for it: one step, two.

Her third step plunged through the shifting asphalt. The end of the ramp hammered against her forehead. Solid ground slipped out from the tips of her fingers as her vision swam through dark blots of pain.

Her ears filled with the screaming of rebar as it was bent and torn, then a landslide rumble as the Vanisher pulled the dock and all the open area, both trucks, down into itself. Te launched herself forward, still on her belly, reaching one hand out to the intact segment of the ramp, inches away.

She saw a vision of Jack's hand, stretched out to her, real or imagined. Her fingers closed a mile from his as her body was torn backward, riding a wave of concrete and steel.

The fire. She could stop it if she had the fire. She screamed at it, out loud and inwardly; she pried at the mental door with as much force as her real fingers clutched at the shifting ground. There it was, twinkling and dancing just out of reach, useless to her. It needed anger, and in that instant Te was completely afraid.

The tentacles of the Vanisher hit her in a dozen places at once—ribs, hips, skull—powerful, wet strikes. Te couldn't fight, couldn't even scream anymore as the wind was hammered out of her again and again. Spots swam in her perceptions as she fought to rein in her limbs and curl around herself.

Then the rocks hit her. Pieces of concrete and rebar, spinning meteorlike in the Vanisher's motion, scraped at her skin and clothing. Impacts rocked her, each so potent with momentum that they for an instant obliterated everything—even pain, even fear—as Te's body reeled from the forces.

A concrete slab crushed her ribs from the side. A stick of rebar cut through her jacket and her skin. She knew she was going to die.

We can't die. Babu said we can't die.

Another stone struck her so hard across her face that for a long, long moment the world was nothing but vibration. When her vision flashed on again, it was just in time to feel her back slam into a flat surface, then the sickening pull of gravity and the empty smell of wet dirt as she hit the bottom of the hole.

Her world filled with primal, animal fear.

Not hers; the Vanisher's. Something was hurting it. Something more devastating than her fire.

She tried to move and the effort brought blood and vomit to her lips. Most of her body sent her nothing but dulled, numbed sensation. She *could* feel her fingertips, vibrating uncontrollably, stinging as if pierced by a hundred needles.

The Vanisher's roar exploded in her mind. It was breaking—its will, its soul, its essence. She felt it happen, felt the creature thrash one last time against the weapon turned on it, and, with a sob of infinite, desperate sadness, it gave up.

The ground shook as it fell back into the hole from above, from somewhere above. Had it climbed out? It was smaller now, shrunken and burned, meek and afraid, and in the edge of her still-swimming vision, Te saw a little gray ball of shivering worms flop over on itself, hardly able to move.

Its sorrow was Te's sorrow. It wasn't right that it should be so hurt, even being the monster it was. How could it be at fault? It was a creature of impulse and drives, and could never understand that it hurt other living things in following those drives.

Compassion for it welled up into her, spilling into her mind through a mental door—not the fire, but the first door—and a thousand, thousand years of human love and forgiveness manifested in her. The binders, through the ages; how they'd been misunderstood, she thought. How they'd been misused to imprison innocent creatures condemned by the fear of little men. They, and she as one of them, were not on this earth to cleanse it of alien monsters, but simply to understand those monsters—understand them as only they themselves did, and to love them.

Te extended one shaking, unstable hand toward it. Even then it shied away.

Don't be afraid, she said to it. *I will protect you. I*

will keep you safe. I will give you a place of your own where they cannot hurt you anymore. The words passed through its shivering heart without comprehension, but it moved to her anyway, drawn by her sincerity, by the affinity she offered.

I will not hurt you, she said. And she wouldn't—never again, until the end of time.

It came to her, flowing and rolling across the base of the pit. One of its tentacles brushed her twitching fingers, and what passed into her from it was a deep death-without-death that is the sole knowledge of immortal creatures. She knew it well.

The rest flowed into her, practiced mental motions inherited from countless generations before her. By small movements of the will, shifts of the emotions, she guided the Vanisher to a vessel she chose: one of the two trucks, still intact though badly bent. She coaxed it with love and protection into the back of the vehicle, into the waiting, warm, embryonic dark. As it disappeared within, Te bid it pull the doors closed after it, and it obeyed. The doors filled the hole with their metallic clang. Then she laid a seal over the doors, not to keep the Vanisher in, but to shield it from those outside who would harm it further. The seal was but a precise mental image, a figure made of pure thought that would persist in the world in the same way as the memories of binders and tyrants survived, age after age.

The creature was bound.

Chapter 15

The Dying of the Light

"Jesus Christ, Jesus Christ."

Babu knew he was muttering. She couldn't be alive. Not down in that gaping, rubble-choked hole. Not the way it was churning when Babu had pulled the car up and first seen it. Not down in that storm of concrete. She couldn't be alive.

He sucked back on his cigarette until there was nothing left and then jammed another one between his teeth before he could start muttering again. Te's friend Jack was already down there, he being the only one capable of the monkey climb down the protruding rebar—except maybe Lester, who was in no shape to do anything other than stick around by the car, cringing.

Angrel stood up there beside him, softly shuffling her cards, looking at one every once in a while in between directing rubbernecking pedestrians on their way. She'd retreated to the street when Babu had brought his brother down the ramp to do his thing. Ahmadou terrified her. He was the one thing she seemed to fear.

Babu didn't have a clue how Ahmadou knew what he was supposed to do. It just sort of happened when he got close to something from the Old Country. His eyes glassed over, his head fell, and the world went crazy for a few minutes while the target screamed, struggled, and folded into itself in a matter of minutes. Babu didn't understand his brother's form of suppression. King had used a tribal dance; Munin, a ray gun; Father O'Shae had used prayer—and Babu . . . usually just a 9mm and a stubborn enmity for the supernatural. But Ahmadou, he seemed to live and breathe suppression.

Ahmadou was back in the car now, staring at the back of the passenger-side front seat. When it was over, he'd stood in place until someone—Lester?—had walked him back to the car. He hadn't said a word. He hadn't grimaced. He hadn't cried.

"Any luck down there?" Babu called. "Probably got police and fire rescue coming."

"Just hold on," the kid replied. His voice sounded thin and scared.

God, let her be okay, he thought. Red shame washed over him, as he thought for a second he cared more that he'd lost his binder than about Te herself. And then came the flood: *Christ, why her? Why did it have to be her? Is it my fault? Am I just cursed? I mean—Rob and O'Shae and King and Julia, and Nyawela, and now her? What the hell did I do, man?*

And then those thoughts fell away until there was only one left: *God, let her be okay.*

The sky continued to darken, dipping shade by shade into a leaden dusk, at two in the afternoon.

Jack's voice sounded. "Hey!"

Babu sprang out of thought and nearly pitched into the hole in his haste to see where Jack had got to. "Did you find her?"

A pause followed, then, "Yeah." Then another pause, longer. "She's okay, I think."

Relief almost toppled him. "Jesus Christ," he muttered, then turned toward the street. "Lester!" he bellowed. "I got some rope in the trunk. Bring it down here, quick."

In less than a minute, Lester was at his side, a fifty-pound coil of rope under his arm, held as easily as a ball of string.

"Look!" he said, jutting one pale, long-nailed hand into Babu's face. "Look!"

"Gimme the damn rope," Babu snapped, snatching it from him and grunting as his arms took the weight.

"I'm not burning," Lester said. "Something's happened to the sunlight."

He was right. Babu cast a cautious glance upward. Past the tops of the office towers, dark clouds churned in what must have been a turbulent wind. It was darkening, but there was still a hint of the sun coming through up there.

Mystery for another day. He slipped out a few lengths of rope and tossed it over the edge.

"Go back and stay with the car," Babu said. Lester nodded and slunk off. Babu turned back to the hole, wondering that he would place his brother in the care of a man who drank blood and spent his spare time doping up with teenagers.

"I'm putting rope down," he called. "Can you see it?"

"Yeah," came the reply. "Just a minute."

"Is she conscious?" Babu said. "Is she hurt?"

"No, she's . . . um . . . she's . . ."

"I'm all right."

It was Te's voice, and not Te's voice. Babu leaned out

over the edge. Something was wrong in the tone of the voice, or in the pitch. Damn it, there was too much echo off the buildings around them. Babu couldn't see Te or Jack. They were probably right under him, hidden by the lip of broken concrete at the end of the ramp.

"Te? That you?" he called.

"Yeah," the voice came again. It was more normal this time, but not entirely, and there was still too much damn echo. "I'm fine. We'll be up in a second."

"Hurry up," Babu snapped, more comfortable presenting himself as the irritated boss than the relieved friend. "We have to get moving before he gets too far away."

"Just a damn minute, Babu." That was definitely Te's voice.

Babu grunted, trying to fight off his uneasiness with the tenuous reassurance that perhaps the strange voice had been caused by the echo and nothing more. With the rope in hand, he turned to see if he could tie it to the ramp's steel railing.

He found Angrel behind him, with a tension he'd never seen in her before—porcelain skin stretched tight over the bones of her face, tendons in her neck and wrists taut and prominent, eyes sunken with a loss of vitality. She was wandering dazed, staring at a card.

"You all right?" he said. It was unbelievable that he would ever say that to her.

She seemed to start at his words. She blinked and took a few seconds looking at the surroundings before she focused on him.

"Yeah," she said, hastily slipping the card away. "I'm just not used to being this close to things when they happen. I . . . don't usually get to see what they look like."

Babu nodded, not in simple acknowledgment. "Now you know what it's like for the rest of us."

A little of her old smirk returned. "I suppose I should have more sympathy for you now."

Babu grunted back at her, glad to be rid of the clinging urge to be nice to this woman. As he tied his end of the rope to the railing, he wondered about the card she'd been looking at—he'd sneaked a peek before speaking to her. On the back, it had the same pattern as the rest of her cards. On the face, it had been completely blank. What did that mean?

"Rope's ready," Babu called down.

"All right."

Te and Jack clambered up the rope in sequence. Te cursed and swore the whole way up. Near the top, Babu grabbed her under the shoulders and hauled her the last few feet. She actually did look all right—not even a bruise on her face, and besides the dirt sticking to her and the tangled mess left of her hair, there didn't seem to be anything wrong at all. There was a bad tear in her jacket on the right side, where Babu could see a dark red stain on the fluff poking out. He took it for blood at first, but, since Te seemed to be moving without any pain, he decided it must be oil from one of the trucks. Damn lucky.

"Haven't climbed a rope since high school," she said with a smile.

Babu set her down and pulled his hands back, grateful she was wearing a thick coat that prevented him from feeling too much of her. "That was a stupid thing to do," he said.

"It's called taking initiative," she shot back as she bent to help Jack onto the ramp.

"Well, don't," Babu said. "Next time, wait for my brother. He and I go first."

"Whatever you say, boss," was the reply. Despite how often he thought of himself as just her boss, hearing the word stung a little. With a final grunt and strain, she hauled Jack up onto the ramp. She brushed a bit of dirt off his shoulders.

"That was a . . ." Why did he always fumble with this stuff? "That was a good job on the binding, anyway."

"I know it was," said Te. She crossed her arms and stared at him. His insides started to squirm a bit and he felt suddenly as if he had to say something else.

"Uh . . . Your dad would be proud."

"Babu, don't," she said. She dismissed him with a blink and turned to Angrel.

"And you," she said, "next time we get in trouble, a little help would be nice."

Angrel's smile was chocolate. "You seemed like you had everything under control."

The two stared daggers at each other. Babu never claimed to know much about women, but he knew enough to shut up at times like these.

Eventually, Te broke off. "Babu," she began, then paused. "I've been confused a lot recently. I know I've gone around behind your back and I'm sorry. I just had to figure some things out."

"Like what?"

"Stuff," she said. "But I agree with you now. Yun has to be caught. Eventually, he'll free everything in town. He doesn't have a choice. So . . . we don't, either." She pointed into the hole. "This could happen everywhere. And I know eventually he'll get around to freeing the thing under Darktown—The Goat with a Thousand Young."

Babu felt that shock of surprise jolt him again. It was getting distressingly familiar.

"How the hell do you know about those? I didn't tell you about them, did I?"

Te hesitated a long moment before seeming to come to a decision. "I stole your casebook."

"So you *did.*"

"It's in the bottom of my closet. I'll get it back to you." She patted him on the shoulder. "Don't be mad. We've got work to do, right?"

According to the tiny green numbers on the dash, it was two thirty in the afternoon. Even in November, the shadows should barely have started to tilt at that point. But as Te watched from the backseat of Babu's car, St. Ives' streetlamps came on one by one, and its citizens began to turn on lights, lamps, and neon signs, as if everything were normal and it was simply that the sun had set unexpectedly early that day.

The clouds above had that heavy impression that usually prefaced rain, but when Te cracked her window to get some fresh air, the wind that slipped over her face was dry and raw, hard edged, and parching to the tongue.

Distantly, over the rattle and rumble of Babu's car and the thrumming night sounds of downtown, Te heard the cry of a predator bird in flight, echoing down the skyscrapers. She rolled the window shut, sealing herself back into the oppressive atmosphere of the car. Babu drove, slowly following Lester, who wandered back and forth across the streets and sidewalks, sniffing at everything. The traffic should have been murder at this time of the day, but they encountered hardly another car, hardly another human being. When Te looked up, she could see people in the high office buildings still at their desks, slumped forward and dozing or just sitting, like statues, waiting.

Angrel rode shotgun, constantly shuffling her cards but drawing none. She kept looking out the window, letting her gaze linger on the vacant pools of light below the streetlamps as the car cruised by, and then going back to her shuffling.

Te was in the back, behind Babu, with Jack uncomfortably pressed up against her. She couldn't blame him for it: he was just trying to put some distance between himself and Babu's brother.

Ahmadou Cherian, as broad in the shoulders as Babu despite his thinness, took up more than one seat in the back. There wasn't much to see of him underneath the huge, brown, knee-length coat bunched around him, but his face was the same as Babu's. Te was certain they had to be twins. Ahmadou sat hunched, head and chest compressed downward, gnarled hands open on his lap, staring dully at the back of the seat in front of him. He hadn't moved or spoken since the ride had begun. He just sat there, breathing heavily and smelling of disinfectant and sweat.

Te had asked, automatically, if he was all right. Babu had answered, "What do *you* think?" She'd really wanted to ask if Ahmadou had been born like that, or if . . . something had *made* him that way. She felt a powerful impulse to touch him—skin to skin—to see if she might be able to sense what was wrong with him, and maybe sing to him to make it better.

But fear checked her. Down in the hole, when Jack had found her, she'd been unconsciously humming to herself. From that small sound had come a glow, spiritual and literal, and a swarm of fireflies dancing around her body. The music had brought out of her her other self, her self of the Old Country, a luminous creature whom she had never seen, but who had been so beautiful that she'd made Jack cry, right there in that crater. And at that moment, the *other* had healed her, just as it had healed Jack the night before. It was just dumb luck she'd been lying under a lip, hidden from view.

But what if Babu found out? What if he turned his brother against her?

In the yellow glare of the headlights, Lester waved for them to stop. Babu stopped the car in the middle of the road and heaved himself out. Te, Jack, and Angrel followed. They left Ahmadou still and staring.

They were in the suburb called Schrevston, just outside the Darktown bowl, and not far from Babu's safe house. The clay cliffs around Darktown loomed over them from the north, and the mountains ringing the valley behind them were washed of color and devoured by the clouds. Babu had pulled them up in front of a wretched-looking tool shop that couldn't have turned a profit in twenty years. There were bars across the windows and cracks in the stucco facade. To the left and right, stores in similar states of disrepair were repeated over and over until shadow overtook detail. The street glowed in the light of neon signs, flickering OPEN to the empty sidewalks.

Babu lit a cigarette, then tossed it into a puddle, where it sizzled and died. "You're sure?" he asked.

Lester, standing hunched by his side, nodded.

"All right." Babu turned and looked back over his shoulder. His sunken eyes flicked over the rest of his crew. Tē saw sadness pass for a moment there, and she remembered how many of his friends had "deceased" written beside their names in his casebook.

He sucked in a deep breath, then nodded to Jack. "Hey, kid."

Jack jerked in surprise. "Yes, sir?"

"Run around back to the alley," Babu ordered. "There's probably a back door to this place. I want you to find it and watch it. If Kitsune tries to get out the back, start yelling."

Jack, eyes wider than usual, looked to Tē for confirmation.

Tē nodded her agreement. "If he tries to run," she said, "just let him go."

He swallowed. His face was bleach white, but he went—off down the row of shops, walking at first, then changing to a run.

"Be careful," Tē called, then whispered again to herself, "Be careful."

"Plan," Babu said. "When he comes out, he'll start to talk. He always talks. Even so, Lester, I want you, there"—he pointed—"to the left. And I'll be there, to the right. We won't be able to stop him, but he might hesitate long enough for Ahmadou to get a hold of him. Ahmadou will be there, by the car. Tē, Angrel, you'll be back there with him. Tē, wait until you see Kitsune collapse, then bind him."

Everyone nodded.

"Angrel, what's he after here?"

Angrel dutifully shuffled her cards and drew one. She held it up.

"The Worm," she said. The card showed a millipede-like beast, with no head and no tail, just a succession of body segments, each with a single talon. "Do you know it?"

Babu frowned. "No."

"He may be deliberately going after ones you've never dealt with before," Angrel suggested.

"Doesn't matter," said Babu. "Get Ahmadou up. He can sit on the hood of the car. Make sure he has a good view of the door."

Angrel nodded, and retreated to the car.

"Now look," Babu said, casting his glance from Lester to Te, "if he comes at you, let him by. He probably won't kill you, but he can do things to your head, and we don't need that." Hearing those words, Lester shuddered and withdrew into himself. Babu didn't seem to notice and went on. "Te, if the binding fails, just give the thumbs-down."

Te nodded. Babu approached her, looking down on her, brows knit, eyes partially squinted, as if from tears. He looked old and worn.

"I need to know you can do this," he said. "I don't know what you and Yun talked about earlier. I don't know what he's said to you, and maybe it's not my place to pry, but I need you to tell me you'll do this."

Te gazed up at him, hearing something in that deep, scratched voice that she'd never heard before—pleading. He was begging her to be on his side. Wasn't she? God knows, she'd given him enough reasons recently not to trust her, and if she were in his place, every logical instinct in her would be screaming never to place the operation in the hands of someone so suspect. But Babu didn't have a choice. Te was the only binder he had. He had to trust her. But more than that—in the expression in those troubled, raw eyes, Te saw that he *wanted* to trust her. Against all his instincts, he wanted her to be worthy of trust.

Ah, Jesus . . .

"I will," she said. She didn't bother to hide the edge of regret. "It has to be done."

Babu nodded. Alert once more, he gave the order. "Positions."

Lester and Babu sprinted to the sidewalk, standing about three yards on either side of the tool shop door. Te retreated back to the car, where Angrel was maneuvering Ahmadou with cautious taps of her fingertips to a place where he could sit comfortably on the hood of the car. She didn't say a word, and after Ahmadou seemed stable, she stepped back to the rear of the car, behind the still-open back door.

Te took up a position beside Ahmadou. She took a deep, steadying breath. Yun could have taught her so much more, and even from what he did tell her, the hope he'd given, he deserved better than what was about to happen—assuming they could get him, that was.

Babu, pistol in hand, banged against the tool shop glass. "Yun!" he said. "We know you're here."

Then he stepped back from the door another three strides. Opposite him, Lester did the same.

A little bell above the door rang a wobbling, dented note. The door drew aside. A clack of fine shoes on the sidewalk. The "pok" of a cane smartly rapping.

Yun stepped out, in white and gold, onto the street.

"'I think we are in rats' alley,'" he said. "'Where the dead men left their bones.' Mr. Cherian. Lester. Miss Evangeline."

Behind him, filling the entire open doorway, marched the feet of the worm—layer on layer, swarming back and forth across the doorway, stepping on themselves, rolling and twisting but never stopping, never slowing, always in perpetual motion.

"I don't suppose I will run from you now," he said, addressing Babu. "Come what may."

Then he stared directly at Te, and she met those gray eyes not without seeing the sadness in them. She felt it resonate in her, just as had the animal emotions of the Vanisher: sadness for him, trapped by the wishes of others, sadness for Te, for all she had gone through, for what she had to do now, and, she felt, for what she must bring herself to do, in a close future.

"'I am moved by fancies that are curled around these images and cling,'" he said. "'The notion of some infinitely gentle, infinitely suffering thing.'"

He spread his arms as if tasting the rain.

Babu's gun was up. "Ahms!" he shouted.

Ahmadou Cherian moved. Under his own power, he lifted his head. His eyes opened wide, and Te saw those eyes come into focus on Yun. She had never seen such concentration. Some twitter, some flutter, sparked in her heart, and she turned away. She didn't think she could watch.

At first, there was nothing. Then the muted sounds of the street faded. The dry air stilled, became flavorless and neutral to the nose. The silence descended by increments, until Te realized she could not even hear her own breathing, her own heartbeat. In alarm, she glanced back at Ahmadou, and saw him in a flat monochrome.

Color faded from the street. Yun's golden hair, his yellow suit, both flickered and turned gray. Static began to build up in Te's ears—radio static, pointless and random noise. As it swelled into the street, the pain began.

Te felt it ring into her from Yun as he doubled over, grimacing. He stumbled back, his fingers spasming against his sleeves as he crossed his arms to shield himself. His face twisted into a mass of creases, and his teeth ground against each other. Every part of him began to quiver. Te felt it tear through him, wave after wave of savage, acid pain, swelling higher in him as the static grew.

He flickered and his human form winked out. A nine-tailed fox toppled to its side. Its tails whipped around it like panicked snakes while its jaws worked at nothing and its little white paws scratched for purchase on the air. She felt Yun's resolve breaking, felt *him* breaking. *It should never have to be like this.* Seconds now and it would be over—he would be a shattered, childlike nothing, fit only to take up space in whatever vessel Te chose for him.

She wanted to sing to him. With tears prickling her cheeks, she tried to, but nothing came out of her mouth but static and noise.

Something was wrong. Pain—her own. Needles in her fingers. Hands shaking. Muscles constricting. The static was in her skin, in her flesh.

No. She shot her eyes to the man beside her. Ahmadou had turned. His infinitely clear gaze struck through her, full of awareness, and of recognition.

Oh, God, no. The static tore into her, flooding like a storm of cuts from her skin down into her body. Stinging, scraping sound sliced her open. It was worse than she'd ever thought. It tore away everything—thoughts and feelings, awareness and identity. She collapsed downward. The static tore her other self out of her, then dragged it to the surface, where it exploded onto her skin in a burst of fireflies and white light. Second by second, the relentless noise destroyed her, devoured her, peeled her away layer by layer, stripping off the strata of her existence in bloody sheets. The static pierced to the last veil of herself. There, it penetrated her and then all was agony.

An impact. The static exploded into melodies. Another. The melodies burst and ordinary city noises leapt back into startling, vivid life. The pain vanished, and Te watched the world dilate into being once more, illuminated in the crystal blue light of her own skin.

Ahmadou crashed to the pavement, inches from Te's face. Above him stood Angrel, her face twisted with horror and fear, a bloodied tire iron hanging loose in her grip.

"You bitch," Angrel screamed at her. "You stupid bitch!"

Angrel whipped the tire iron away. As Babu, across the street, turned his weapon toward her, she drew a card from her deck and flicked it at him. The instant it touched the ground, a searing line, magnesium white, shot down from the sky and speared through the card. A flash of heat and a pulse of air hammered Te back and rolled her. Then the boom came, followed by a rush of air back in toward the space where the white lightning faded and died. When Te came to herself, hyperventilating, gripping on to the asphalt for dear life, it was to see Babu and Lester tumbling to the ground, and the glass of every window on the block sloughing down.

But Babu wasn't hurt. Te saw him spin on his back, and from a prone position take aim at Angrel and fire.

Te saw the rest in her mind's eye. As Angrel stood

facing the bullet, a shadow rose up behind her—a man's shadow, wearing a long trench coat and a wide-brimmed hat. He reached for her and took her close to him, and they were both gone before the bullet punched a hole in the car's windshield.

For an instant, as the shot echoed up and down the street, everyone sat frozen. Then Babu's eyes fell on Te, full of shock and horror, and hot rage.

He swung the gun at her.

Te leapt for the car, trailing a wave of fireflies. A bullet struck the pavement where she'd been lying. Landing in a crouch, she hauled open the driver's-side door just in time to hear an impact on the opposite side.

Inside, Babu's keys dangled from the ignition. She reached one hand, already fading to normal, onto the steering wheel and hauled herself in low. She heard the cracking and scraping of glass and peeked over the steering wheel, to see Babu struggling to regain his footing.

She slammed her foot onto the brake and cranked the key. The car roared to life. She threw it into reverse and, ducked down so far she hadn't a hope of seeing anything, took off. When she'd put a full block between her and Babu, she switched into drive and peeled away down a cross street.

The city should have been packed with traffic at this time of day, but every turn took her onto an empty stretch of road. She didn't let up on the gas until she was well into downtown, and by then she'd started crying.

Chapter 16

For Thine Is the—

I am in the dark. There is static hissing and I am waiting for Ahmadou Cherian to destroy me.

With my Old Powers, with my Sight, I see, far from this place, a white and golden shape streaking low to the ground, who, by way of alley and rooftop, crosses the edge of the Darktown shadow, heading for the eternally closed door.

He does not want to open it, but he must, because it is the wish of those things entombed there.

The moment of clarity is lost. The Kitsune washes away into other visions, and if I focus on him, my imagination slides away. Tired by the effort, and drained from the sacrifice of my card, I let the visions go and turn to my human eyes.

There is nothing here but flickering white light.

A voice is speaking. "It's all been planned," it says. "Seventy years ago, all planned."

I blink. The static fills my eyes, and all else is darkness.

"I had a vision, you see," the voice says. "The Warden—he came to me in a dream. November 1929.

Everyone in a panic. The whole damn system coming down around us."

I flex my fingers. I feel my rings there. I feel the scratching touch of my dress, the vinyl pillow-ness of my jacket. Then I *am* alive. The Man saved me.

"He said the instability meant they could pick someone new." There's a shift in the dark. A man sits beside me in a separate chair.

"The people might pick a new Warden," the man whispered. "That's what he said. He said people still needed order and stability, and the crash got them all excitable and he had to stop them from making that mistake."

I look aside at him. I squint, and I realize the static is simple noise from untuned radios; the light is that of a half dozen televisions without signal. I realize I am in a room. I recognize the speaking voice. It has spoken to me before.

"I thought he was speaking to me," said the voice. "I thought they'd chosen *me*."

The sprinkling light trickles over his face, cutting wrinkles into depthless slashes. He is an old, old man. His eyes are pale, his head bald, his fingers gnarled and absently working in his lap. The voice falls into despair, into such a depth of loss, it stirs even my thousand-times-dead heart.

"But he didn't come for me," he says. "He came for *him*."

"Who?" I ask. My voice against the static is like smoke against the sunshine, and drifts away as quickly.

"My shadow," he says. His head turns. His hands fall still. Then I know him.

I recognize his voice because I have heard it before. It is the voice I hear in my mind when the Man in the

Empty Chair speaks to me—not a clairaudient projection, but something my imagination makes up to go with his words and thoughts. The manner of the head, the hands resting—it is all the same, as if the lightless hole that is all I ever see of the Man has been filled in, but by a painter long past the prime of his skill.

"He was the part of me that wanted great things," the man says. "Wanted to save the world from itself." He chuckles softly, regretfully. "He wanted to sit in the big chair."

I sit now, still, as attentive to this ancient creature as I would have been to the Man himself.

"The Warden cut us in two," he says. "Pulled him out, all the great things, pulled them out, locked them in here."

The man's breath catches. He runs bloodshot eyes over the television screens in sequence. Whatever he sees there makes his face twitch.

"Saved the system crashing, at least. Saved his own position."

"Where is he?" I ask suddenly.

The man looks at me. I suppose he always knew I was there, but for the first time he seems aware of me.

"Just listen," he says. He settles back and closes his eyes. "Listen. Static, you see—it's the randomness of the universe. It's the ripples in the general radiation. Everything that moves alters that radiation—just a bit, just a bit I know—but it all *means* something. It all ends up as static and with radios . . . I remember in the war, when we had radios and they would hiss at us. That sound," he says, "is everything there is. And he hates it."

He grows very, very still.

"So listen."

And I do. I let the sound into me, imagining waves and patterns in it, but perceive nothing.

I wonder if perhaps this man can use the Old Sight, just as I can, and mistakes it in his feeblemindedness for ghosts in nonsense sound.

"Listen for the holes," the man mutters, as if talking in his sleep. "He leaves holes."

Again, I attempt it, feeling instead the sluggish heat of the electronics, the whispers of chill that brush my exposed skin from the walls. There is the sound of metal scraping against wood, and I search it out in the half dark, until I see the glint of a revolver. The man's fingers are curled around it. It sits in his lap like a stone.

In my pocket I find my deck. It's useless now, having lost one of its number. Years and years of trust between it and me have come to nothing, and so I don't regret getting another ready to throw out.

The man struggles to lift the gun. His hands shake terribly with its weight, and it falls back to his lap. He crumples, exhausted.

"If I were young enough, I'd kill you," he breathes.

I reach over to him and pluck the weapon from him, then wrap my own fingers around its handle and point it at him.

"Why kill me?" I ask him.

He chuckles.

"He needs you. I told you, it's been planned. Why do you think he dumped you off in this place? He has to keep you safe." He sighs. "Doesn't mean much to you, does it? A man who doesn't exist becomes Warden of the world. The Warden is the world. The world is the Warden. Then, poof—a world that doesn't exist."

I smile at that. I've had the same thought myself.

"A world of things that don't exist," escapes my lips, and I finally understand. "A world for us, and not for you."

His jaw and fingers are trembling. His eyes open, staring into the flickering lights, leaking tears.

"God, I'm tired," he whines. "It's all happening just like we always thought it would. And Te. It's too late for her, isn't it? Too late. I waited too long."

At the mention of Rob's daughter's name, I remember what the Man said: that Te Evangeline would come to me, and that I would have to remember who I was.

"He doesn't love you, you know," the man says.

And I answer, "He saved my life."

"Of course he did," the man says. "Of course he did."

And we sit in the hissing dark. And we wait.

The car stalled at the edge of town. At first, Te thought something might have shaken loose with her flight down the potholed, bumpy highway, but it started again easily enough. Then she put her foot to the gas and it guttered to silence.

"Fuck."

Te pulled the hood release and got out. There wasn't a soul to be seen in either direction. Ahead, the lonely two-lane highway twisted its way along the banks of the river, following a gentle slope down through the mountains and out of the St. Ives valley. Behind, it stretched back over the fields to the suburbs of the city, and into the shadow of black clouds that coated the valley from side to side.

There was light here. Though winter rain clouds still choked the sky, at least their gray luminescence gave evidence that the sun was still up there. A sign twenty feet ahead proclaimed the existence of an invisible line at the St. Ives city limit.

Te opened the hood and checked that nothing was loose, nothing was leaking, which exhausted her automotive knowledge. She slammed the hood closed and leaned against it.

What now? She rubbed her cheeks, sticky with dry tears and smarting in the winter air. Go back or go on?

Te hugged herself against the cold, against her own fright. She'd never been outside the valley before. Where would she go? She had no family outside the city. She'd long since lost touch with any of her high school friends who had moved away, not that they were very good friends in the first place. She didn't even know which roads to take. She had no map, no money, no credit cards, no destination.

And now for reasons of mechanical failure and spiteful fate, she didn't even have a car.

Go back or go on?

How could she go back? Babu had known her his entire life, had watched her grow up, had come to dinner at her family's house, employed her and trained her; and he hadn't hesitated for a second—not for one instant—when he saw what she was.

And that hurt so badly, Te couldn't help but start crying again.

She let it come. There was no sense in being strong anymore. There was no one to impress. There was nothing left to hide. Secrets she didn't know she'd had five days ago had robbed her and ruined her.

She sobbed into her hands, into rough, veined, bony-knuckled human hands. Her body felt denser than it used to, coarser, as if every fine line and hair emitted its own sensation that she could no longer ignore. It was her other self that caused it; the other body was smoother, as Jack said. It was less random, less messy, less real than this one, and something in Te was starting to miss being that way.

I'm a monster, she thought. Even admitting it to herself, mentally trying to accept it, gave her no comfort. This wasn't something any psychological trick could erase.

She would run. That was her choice. She wasn't safe in St. Ives as long as Babu was there. What if he hunted her after she left? What if he got Lester on her trail, on her scent?

Well, there were ways to fool smell. And Te could toss her IDs somewhere and start over. New name. New town. Some big place where she could just melt away— vanish as if she'd never existed. A sudden ache came to her at that thought—*as if she'd never existed*—a sudden longing for it.

Well, the car wasn't going to help her.

She started walking.

It was a stinging regret that she couldn't make Babu see she wasn't like the rest, that it wasn't her fault she was how she was. She wasn't conspiring against him, although it probably looked that way now. Well, she hadn't betrayed him, except that she'd stolen a bunch of his stuff and went around talking to the enemy behind his back.

No wonder.

But he wouldn't listen to her now. That look in his eye, hurt and furious, when he'd seen her . . . There was no compromise after that.

And Jack. Te hated to leave Jack, but he, at least, would understand why she had to go away. Maybe she could write to him, when she got . . .

Wait a minute.

She was standing under the CITY LIMIT sign. She realized she'd been standing there for more than a few minutes, thinking.

Not going to get far unless you leave the city, are you, girl?

She snorted at herself and started walking again.

Her legs didn't move.

"What?" she said aloud. Staring down at her foot, she tried to take a step. She was certain the signal reached the foot—the muscles tensed properly—but the foot didn't move.

Anxious now, she tried stepping back. Her legs obeyed her. She stepped sideways, shuffled her feet, flexed her legs and toes. All functional.

She tried to walk forward again. Nothing.

Oh, no.

The CITY LIMIT sign hung above her, dirty and white, rocking a bit in the wind.

An invisible line. A second barrier. The walls of the prison.

Trembling, she reached a hand forward. She gasped and drew back when her fingers spread against something solid.

No, no, no.

She beat against it, kicked it, blasted it with her fire. She screamed at it, first to open, then wordlessly, until she sank, spent, to her knees.

The wind tore through her hair, fleeing the city that

she couldn't escape. On that empty stretch of road, she let her hands fall open, defeated—a monster in a monster's prison.

"What the hell is this?" Babu growled. Lester winced at the tone, but kept a firm grip under Ahmadou Cherian's shoulder, trying to ignore the scent of the bloody wound on the back of Ahmadou's head. His blood smelled thin and sour, but Lester's vampire body thrilled to it anyway. How long had it been now?

Babu pointed and they started moving again, across the emergency room to the long hall heading into the hospital proper. It wasn't that there weren't people in the waiting room—there were two mothers with assorted children, a couple of guys who looked like housepainters, and an old man with a cane, all very much alive by their smell and the faint beating of their hearts. But the people stared with dead eyes, like his Strutters. Like his poor Strutters.

Babu didn't seem to waste any time wondering about it. He led them past the reception desk, where a blank-eyed nurse stared helplessly at a blank form. Lester heard the stumbling whimper of her heart and swallowed back some sticky saliva.

"Why are they like that?" he asked.

"A half dozen reasons," Babu said. "Hello!" he called. "Anyone still awake?" The closest seemed to stir for a second, as if disturbed out of sleep, but then fell limp again.

"Munin," Babu said. "Munin's still in the hospital. Go back and find out which room he's in, all right? I'm gonna find some bandages."

Lester fled back to reception. He maneuvered behind the counter and delicately slid the attending nurse and her chair a few feet to the right. She blinked, and adjusted, and squinted again at the form, and then fell still. And her heart had beat, just a few times, strong like a proper heart. It sent electric chills up and down his spine—sexual shivers, lances of desire.

Cautiously, Lester looked around. No one else was behind the reception counter. No one was in the hall. No one would see him. He could just . . .

He bent down to her neck and smelled her. The beautiful, primal scent of her blasted his nostrils with layers of tangy sweat, acrid perfume, and the slight char of a recent sunburn. No one would know, would they? His mouth ran with thick slaver. He panted like a dog over her, inching his tongue down, and after it, his teeth.

God, oh, God, oh, God.

He pulled away.

He went to the nurses' computer, put in Munin's name, and got a room number. Then he stole a map and ran a fingernail over it until it rested soundly on the words "Blood Storage."

Lester found Munin in a double room with a similarly ancient, vaguely Slavic man lying across from him. Deprived of his glasses, his gadgets, and his invariably plaid wardrobe, Munin looked as old as he probably was. His arm lay out on top of the bedspread, heavily bandaged around the stump. His eyes lay open, ringed in wrinkles. He breathed but didn't move.

Lester decided he should go get Babu.

But first he had to find blood. The room labeled BLOOD STORAGE, it turned out, was locked, and the door was a metal plate too strong for even Lester to break.

He would have to bite someone. God, he hated it. People kept themselves so unclean.

He checked several rooms, dismissing each because they were filled with men. He didn't bite men—there was something too homosexual about it—and he didn't like biting old women. That really left only younger women and girls, and Lester didn't like biting them, either. It felt perverted.

He let his nose guide him, to put off making a decision. It took him into a little double room down the hall from Munin's. There he found a girl, maybe fourteen, fifteen, with purple streaks in black hair. She stared up at the ceiling, comatose.

He breathed to steady his rushing nerves. "Just a little," he said out loud. "Just enough to take the edge off." Shaking, he bent down over her, pressing his nose close to her throat. She smelled like onions and the aftertaste of alcohol. Her pulse rippled under the flesh of her neck like worms breathing.

The orgasm started just as he broke the skin, the melting, buzzing, full-body rush as fresh human blood slipped between his lips. *Oh, heaven.* It slid, rolling slow and thick, down his tongue, around his teeth, its copper tang turned to ambrosia by his twisted senses. The taste blinded him, shooting out to the tip of every finger and toe. He sucked, he swallowed, he drank, until, barely perceived in the periphery of his mind, the girl's already shaky heartbeat sank to silence.

He pulled back in shock. The last of the girl's blood dribbled down his chin and dripped onto the white-gray bedspread.

Oh, no . . .

Get it off, get it off. Lester grabbed the bedsheets

and scrubbed frantically at his lips and chin, then at his cheeks, his neck, the collar of his shirt—Christ, it was everywhere. He scrubbed until his skin felt raw, then fled into the room's tiny bathroom and wetted a towel and wiped until he was sopping down to his stomach with cold water. But he was finally clean.

When he emerged from the bathroom, he imagined it was Jill lying on the bed, Jill with her eyes open and empty, staring upward. He wished that she was dead like the rest. But, no, he'd made sure it didn't happen like that.

He'd just wanted to help. She saw that, didn't she? He'd just wanted to keep her safe, to spare her. He hadn't known the Maskim would keep her alive, would do ... whatever it did to her.

He blinked and it wasn't Jill. The corpse of that innocent girl lay cooling beneath sheets slathered in thinning tracks of blood.

Just a twitch, but Lester's eyes didn't miss it. He staggered up and lurched closer.

While the rest of her kept perfectly still, the girl's head rocked, shook, and tilted back and forth. She was still dead—he was sure of that. A black worm slipped out of her ear, then another, then a third, and something plopped onto the pillow. Lester drew in a breath.

The little creature rubbed itself on the pillow to clean itself of clinging earwax. It looked up at Lester and squeaked, then danced its way down the bed, looping and tumbling in fluid, merry motion until it dropped off the far end and disappeared.

A Night Terror. One of an army of them he'd watched Yun set free while he just stood aside and begged for it to be over.

What should he do? He should tell Babu. He should . . . Was it one of these things that was keeping Munin unconscious? Could he get them out without killing him? *Babu's the one who knows about this stuff. Go find Babu.*

He found Babu trying to revive a young doctor, slumped and staring in a chair. Ahmadou was tucked into bed next to them with his head wrapped in bandages.

"It was the best he could do before he passed out again," said Babu, his eyes focused intently on his brother's face.

"It's little b-black th-things, man," Lester stuttered. "Keeping people unconscious."

Babu nodded. "Munin?"

"Yeah, him, too," said Lester.

Babu nodded again, and fell silent.

Lester waited minute after long minute, fidgeting, while Babu did nothing. Lester took a smell of him, listened to his heartbeat: the man was panicking; maybe he was paralyzed.

"Babu?" Lester said. "Babu, don't freeze up, man. His scent's still in my nose, man, and he can't have got too far since we left him." Babu didn't react, his breath hissing in and out of his big nose.

"Come on, man," Lester said. "I'll track him. We can't just sit here and . . ."

"I know!" Babu's voice exploded into the room. *"Don't you tell me what we need to do!"*

Lester's claws came up reflexively. "Jesus, man."

Babu deflated. He drew out a cigarette.

"Sorry," he muttered. "Just . . . It's not as if he doesn't know how to fool your nose, Les."

Lester nodded and swallowed. Kitsune wouldn't be

misleading him about Jill's scent, would he? Could he do that? Too many doubts, now—they crowded into his brain.

"He can fool me, man, I know," Lester said. "But . . . don't we know where he's gonna go this time?"

Babu looked up for the first time. The horror that came on his face at that moment was much worse than the anger.

"Yeah," he said. "Yeah, we do."

While Lester's body still held itself ready, Babu lumbered past and into the hall. "Maybe we can find your kids," he said. "Ravndark and Dracia, or something?"

"W-what do you know about that?"

"Maybe they won't be dead," Babu said, not listening. "Maybe they're all having a drink somewhere. Jesus Christ. Maybe everything's gonna be ooooooh-kay"

He muttered his way off down the hall.

He couldn't know, could he? I didn't tell him.

Lester chewed his talons with his fangs.

He doesn't know. Only I know.

Jill.

He ran after Babu, and after the girl he'd abandoned, and after the respect he'd sold for a stupid wish made, like, thirty-five years ago.

Chapter 17

A Red Plague and a Blue Plague

One rap. The door opened.

"Mom," said Te, "we need to talk."

Sonore's smile stretched her ruby lipstick too far across her meaty face.

"Yes, m'dear," she replied, "yes we do."

She held the door open and Te stepped inside. A few pointless pleasantries passed between them. They didn't make eye contact again until they were seated across the living room coffee table from each other, a pot of tea on a coaster between them. When they did, Te saw Sonore's eyes twinkling.

"First question," Te said. "Who are you?"

Sonore's laugh was a butterfly trill. "That's a silly question," she said. "And don't humans just die to ask it every time. Do you want to know what I was called? Do you want to know what I did before your father trapped me in this godforsaken place?"

"Let's start with who you were before you came here," Te said evenly.

Sonore rocked back and forth on her generous haunches. "Ooh," she cooed. "Oh, honey. It's soooo good to see you finally amounting to something. And to think Babu had you taking pictures of cheating husbands. God, you could have turned out so dull."

"Mom!"

Her mother's laugh filled the room with color. "Oh, if your father could see you now ..."

There was nothing wistful in that statement, only the wicked pleasure of imagined revenge. The way she settled her teeth together, it was as if nothing could have hurt Te's father more.

"He *did* know," Te said as the realization came to her. "That's why he got Babu to look after me. That's why he wanted me to live a normal life." Her mother's laugh trailed off into thick, piggy breathing. "He was hoping I would never find out."

Sonore leaned across the table, almost touching the teapot with her bosom. "Your father," she said, "was an oppressor. The instant you were born, he geased me and my sisters never to tell you anything. In any other day and age I would have struck him blind for that, and Babs would have eaten his bone marrow."

Then she rocked back onto the couch cushion, cheerfully smiling, tea and saucer in sausage hands. "I was very happy when our prison keeper took care of him for me. It was nice of him, don't you think?"

"Mom!" Te said. "I *loved* him." And she really did. After he walked out, after he died without an explanation, after all the failed times, it was how she really felt.

"Someone had to." Sonore sipped her tea.

"Mom, just stop." Te slumped in the wicker armchair.

Stray pieces of wicker poked at her back through her shirt.

"You want to know the truth, that's the truth," her mother said simply. "He hated both of us. He hated what we were and he bound us both to this uninspiring little town." Her lips seemed to kiss the tea as she sipped it. "He would never have had you in the first place, except that I tricked him into it."

Te flushed. "What?"

"Men's minds are very malleable when they're sleeping. It's the best time to pluck at those little suppressed urges."

Te fought a sudden dizziness. "But you married him. You keep wedding photos."

"Binders have to love something to bind it. I'd imagine you know that by now," Sonore said. "And I've always loved weddings. Even the most pedantic of them gets a little inspired. So why not have one myself, I thought. Took some doing, but I worked him into it." Her face grew dark. "Of course, that was before I realized he intended to keep me in this whitewashed house for twenty years. Do you know," she continued, her nose wrinkling up, "that when we first moved in here, all the walls were white and there wasn't a lick of furniture but two chairs and a table and one mattress upstairs? The yard was a patch of dirt and he said he intended to keep it that way. Do you know why, dear?"

Te shook her head.

Sonore snorted. "To keep me under control. No inspiration. No stimulus. Nothing I could get a hold of. Nothing I could play with. He wanted to numb me down so I couldn't break my chains." She gestured around the room, to the heaps of ferns, short palms, bamboo, and tiger-print cloth everywhere. "But I got the best of him on that, I think." Her scowl returned. "No one has *ever* done that to me. How *dare* he deny me my inspiration, my essence—*me*, of all people!"

"So who were you?" Te asked.

"I had a lot of names, just like we all did," Sonore said, returning to her pig smile and her tea. "Most recently, men called me the Muse."

"*The* Muse?"

"There's no other kind," Sonore said. "No human inspiration could compare to mine. They all loved me for it and I lived like a queen on those dreams." She took a distant look in her eye. "Though, since I've been in here, they've had to run on their own steam, and it isn't pretty. They just repeat the same ideas over and over, thinking they're fresh and new, while their souls shrivel up. It won't be long before they draw the number five in red ink and think it's beautiful."

"That's why you never had a problem with my art," Te said.

"And why your father hated it." Sonore sighed and drained the last of her tea, then poured herself some more. "You should drink something, dear. You have a body and they're an awful lot of work. Pick something you like."

Sonore gestured to Te's untouched teacup, which became, between eyeblinks, orange juice, milk, cola, and a clear fluid.

"That's good," said Sonore. "That's the kind of stuff they made on Olympus and Hanan Pacha, back in the day."

"Um . . . Ambrosia?"

"If you like," said Sonore. "Drink up. You need to stay healthy."

Te reached out and gingerly lifted the teacup, now much heavier, and examined the nectar inside. It slid back and forth like honey, and let up a cooling, moist aroma. Te watched the stuff settle and thought about how few times her mother had ever done something nice for her.

"*Why* do I need to stay healthy, Mom?"

Sonore sipped her own tea before answering. "You know how much pain there is in human labor? It's a stupid, painful, animal way to procreate. Eggs would be better, or mitosis. I could have been happy with mitosis. Did you ever wonder why I went to all that trouble?"

Sonore blinked and her eyes began to spin in a kaleidoscope of primary colors.

Unsettled, Te nudged her chair back.

"No," said Te, honestly.

Sonore sighed. "I know you've been talking to some of the family, dear. What's the word with them?"

Te knew the answer and spoke it hesitantly, not sure where her mother was going. "They all want to get out of here."

Sonore purred. "I'm an artist, Te. I'm *the* artist. And here I am, stuck in a little house with nothing to decorate but walls and a garden. Do you have *any* idea how frustrating that is?" Her fat fingers caressed the tiger-print cloth over the coffee table. "I used to make art with clouds, m'dear. With nature, and with all the stuff of life. Some of my best work is out there being hunted on the savanna right now."

"I'm—I'm just a piece of art, to you?" Te asked.

"Oh, yes," said her mother. "And not a very good one, either. Your father's genes kept getting in my way. Lord knows I tried, but I just couldn't make anything beautiful out of you"—Te's jaw dropped in shock—"so I decided to make something useful."

Te bit her cheek. How many knives could her mother stick in her in just one conversation, anyway?

Sonore raised her teacup as if in a toast. "You're my ticket out, my dear. You're my skeleton key. Custom-made, down to the threads of your soul. Took you damn long enough to grow into it."

Te's head reeled. Custom-made? What was she, an appliance? *A tool. You're just a means to an end. You always have been.*

Then another thought struck her: the barrier at the city limit—was she able to get through it somehow and just hadn't figured it out? She put the question to her mother.

"Oh, not yet, my dear," Sonore said. "You've seen a bit of what you can do by now, I'd imagine—the silly human stuff your father gave you—but there's much more in you, as one of us."

Her other self. The power to heal. What else could it do? Te hadn't had time, or really, any desire, to find out.

"You're sullied, my dear," said Sonore. "You're impure. You've got all that meat in you weighing you down."

"You . . . you mean my *body*?"

"You need to get rid of it."

Te hugged herself, possessively. "That's crazy."

Sonore just shrugged and didn't bat an eye. "It's the way it's done, when you're a half-breed. Not an easy thing, though, as you've found out." She gestured to the holes and tears in Te's shirt where rocks had split her open and broken her bones only a few hours before.

Te clutched her skin, the same skin she'd raged at for giving her blemishes the night before a dance. This skin, these hands, these breasts that were too small and hips that were too narrow, and this neck that was already developing rings before she was twenty-five—these were *hers*; they *were* her. That other creature, the one made of light who could barely be said to have a face, that was something else—*that* was the monster.

Te shuddered and sank into a curl.

"Oh, I don't know why you're so bothered by that," said her mother. "You can't take it with you anyway when you go back to the Old Country."

"Who says I'm going to be doing that?"

Sonore smiled. "It's your home," she said. "Someday, we'll find a way back to it, and you'll come with us. Don't doubt it—it's in your blood."

Te shot to her feet. She'd had enough. "I won't let you out, Mom."

"You were made to. It's your essence. You can't help but do it—and, besides, everyone's counting on you."

Te stormed away, spitting the words back to her. "Well, Babs and Syd are just going to have to live with it."

"And you?" Sonore called after her. "I think you would hate drinking tea in this room for all eternity as much as I would."

Te stopped, her hand on the door frame. Ferns tickled her knuckles.

Her mother's voice danced into her ear as if carried on a breeze: "I've been in your world fourteen million years, m'dear. Do you want to spend that kind of time in this depressing place?"

Te's stomach fell. Her mother was right and they both knew it.

"How?" she asked.

"We are shapeless creatures," said Sonore. "In the Old Country, we're living possibilities—never realized or fixed. But *this* world"—she slapped the couch angrily—"is one of shape. Everything here has to be a shape and you were born into one. If you're going to be one of us, you have to learn to be formless."

"What do you mean?"

"Shapeless. Existing without certainty." Sonore rolled her eyes, perhaps at Te's guarded expression. "What are we, m'dear, if not possibility? And what is possibility, if not the absence of certainty?" She dipped one finger in her tea and swirled it. "Right now you're fixed in a shape, and the rules of your little world are your limits. Rules like . . ." She mused for a moment. "Distance. Gravity. That conservation-of-matter thing you people are always going on about."

Te rubbed her face. Her insides churned. "I don't understand."

"Shapes are just limits manifested," said Sonore. "Free yourself from that and everything becomes malleable."

"How would I do it, then?"

"Death, m'dear," said Sonore. "It's the only way I've found that a human soul can reject its shape."

Te licked her lips before speaking. "I'm not sure I *can* die anymore."

Sonore's eyes sparkled.

"Not the conventional way, of course. But your people have other methods."

Memories and visions whirled together. The history of the binders—the dark doorway, shunned, feared. The nightmares of her childhood. Te's stomach sank.

"The cave."

Sonore nodded. "It always shows up once you start looking for it. In you go, and the rest is up to you."

Te remembered it from her visions, a memory from the binders of ages past—sometimes a cave, sometimes an arch, a mountain pass, a pair of statues or forbidding stones. Some had seen it and turned away. Others had seen it and passed through. Some came back out. Others didn't.

Angrel's words whispered from her memory: *"Binders always die."*

"Has Yun called you the infinitely suffering thing yet?" Sonore asked, with a soft chuckle.

"Yun!" Te exclaimed, suddenly realizing. "Darktown!"

Her mother inhaled sharply, her entire body posture stiffening and her eyes narrowing. "What *is* that young man up to?"

"I have to go," Te said. She bolted into the hall and snatched her coat from the rack, then jammed her feet into her shoes. God, she'd been selfish, running off like that—sulking, moping, despairing. It didn't matter if Babu hated her now. It didn't even matter what she really was inside. What mattered was that Te was the only binder in town, and that she was needed.

Te had drawn images of the things under Darktown after waking from some of her worst nightmares, and then burned the pages in the family fireplace. Nothing had terrified her more, but her father had told her they were just dreams. All the horrors of her young imagination had been reduced to that. Just dreams.

"No such thing," said her mother, standing now at the arch into the living room.

Te looked at her, and saw in her mother's mocking smile for the first time, a hint of apprehension, tension. Had she dreamed of them as well? Could she see them now? Her emotions faded back, and the interrogative strength Babu had taught her, the calculating mind, bent on the task at hand, returned. *Protocol over personal things.*

"Mom," Te asked, "can you help?"

Sonore shook her head and pinched a roll of flesh between two meaty fingers. "Not while I'm weighed down."

Te looked at her mother's fat, wide body, so completely unlike her own, then up into Sonore's expectant eyes.

"You were created to do it, m'dear," she said. "Set me free."

Te stood paralyzed. She could do it—she knew instinctively that she could break whatever seal her father had left behind. It was part of her essence, a deep knowing in her soul. And Sonore was suffering, wasn't she, trapped in here? And Te was certain her mother could help, that she had a wealth of inhuman talents that reached beyond rational thought.

But Te knew her mother. She looked into that face and saw the smirk beneath the fear beneath the expectant smile. She remembered how many times her mother had snapped at her for moving something out of place in a room that was otherwise a perfect work of art. She remembered how often her mother would become bored with even the simplest things, and wander off to fiddle with her furniture or her garden. She couldn't be relied on. She couldn't be trusted.

"I have to go," Te said.

Without another word, she pulled open the front door and strode out. She slammed it behind her and didn't look back.

The stolen car roared over the thin street that separated Darktown from the rest of the world.

"Well?" Babu snapped.

In the passenger seat, his head hanging out the window like a dog's, Lester sucked in the passing air. He nodded. "Recent," he called back into the car.

Babu ground the already-floored pedal with his foot. Why now, damn it? Why didn't Yun go crawling around the rest of town? Plenty to do there, and it would have given Babu time to regroup, time for his brother to heal.

Time to figure out who the hell he'd been training as his partner these last four years.

Was she a plant? he asked himself. *Was she something sent by the Man? To do what? Distract me? Sabotage me?* The thought came with a clenching in his heart: *Tempt me?*

That white and shining, woman-shaped creature burned out at him from his imagination. Every curve of her taunted him, played with him, enraged that frustrated urge that had died with his wife on a lonely rain-soaked stair. In that first glimpse of her, shining and in pain, all he'd felt was desire, but before it had even penetrated from his eyes to his body, he'd wrestled the impulse to such a rage it startled even him. The gun came out—automatic, hammer back, trigger down.

He should have aimed at Angrel. He should have seen that coming.

Jesus Christ, Ahmadou ...

He hammered his fist into the car's dash and felt a welcoming sting bite into his knuckles. Lester almost jumped out of his seat.

This little compact he'd hot-wired had a tiny engine and no guts at all. He pushed it hard, corner by corner, through the shadows and the empty streets and the lifeless air. Lester fell back into his seat. They didn't need to track Yun anymore. They both knew where he was going.

Babu's lungs burned with smoker's phlegm, but he refused to cough. His throat ached as he sucked the dry, dead air back and forth across the damage he'd done to it over the years. He savored the pain, devoured its clarity. He had to focus now. He had to make a plan.

But Ahmadou was lying on a bed in the hospital, bleeding from his nose and ears with no one to treat him.

But Te Evangeline was a creature of the Old Country and he hadn't noticed—years and years and he hadn't even *suspected*.

But Angrel was out there somewhere, and a half dozen other things more dangerous than any mortal human being.

But with no suppressor and no binder, he couldn't stop Yun Kitsune.

But he kept the gas pedal down, kept his eyes on the road as it twisted in and out of the car's headlights, because right then, there was nowhere else to be.

He brought the car skidding to a halt half on the curb in front of Lester's ancient, dilapidated abode. Babu clenched and unclenched his fingers on the steering wheel, staring at the lichen-encrusted stairs up to Lester's door.

After a minute, Lester leaned into his field of vision.

"Babu?" he said. "Come on, man. Don't space out on me."

"Lester," Babu said, the thoughts coming slowly.

"What?"

"You know there's nothing I can do here." His eyes traced the door. "I'm just a man. There's nothing I can do."

"Shit, don't talk like that, man."

Babu swung his head around and looked at Lester right in his bloodshot eyes.

"*I* can't do anything. *I'm* just a man."

Lester's fingers curled up as he realized what Babu was insinuating.

"Wait . . . wait a minute, you can't think that I could . . ."

"Get out of the car."

Babu glared at him until he complied, then shouldered his own way out. The clay cliffs towered all around them, and far above that a mass of black clouds. The little house, clamped between two tenement buildings and hidden even from the sour light of the streetlamps, was a hole in reality. It appeared now as what it was: the gate to hell, the abyss given a suburban mask.

He became aware of Lester's whining.

"Babu, man. I'm a tracker. I can't do all this hero shit. That's for you and Munin. And King and Angrel. I'm just support. You can't think . . ."

Babu reached out deliberately with one hand and dug his fingers securely into the collar of Lester's shirt. Lester yelped as Babu dragged him close. Then Babu clamped a second hand onto his shirt front and lifted Lester's scrawny, hundred-and-twenty-pound ass in the air.

"I'm through tolerating your crap," Babu growled. He pulled Lester in nose to nose, so close every wasted line of drug abuse and a life in darkness was crystal clear. "Munin lost a hand yesterday because you weren't there to back us up. King got fucked up and now he's MIA. I spent half of yesterday looking for *you* instead of hunting down Kitsune. If you'd fucking showed up when I asked, we might have stopped this whole thing *days* ago."

Lester's meat-scented breath came in hyperventilating gasps. Good.

"Instead," Babu spat, "*you* were hiding in *garbage*."

He shoved Lester roughly away. The little man hit the ground on a twisted ankle and staggered back onto the hood of the car. He didn't take his eyes off Babu for an instant. Babu stared down with a grimace of loathing he couldn't contain.

"Time to earn your keep."

When Lester just stared at him, Babu finally lost patience. He grabbed Lester by the arm and practically threw him toward the steps. Lester slunk like a whipped dog up the stairs of his house, Babu right on his heels. It occurred to Babu that if Lester was going to have to fight Kitsune hand-to-hand—suck his blood or whatever—then this probably wasn't the best way to motivate him to a fighting spirit. *Fuck fighting spirit.* He'd seen the look in Lester's eye when he drank from a live human being. He just had to keep Lester afraid long enough for him to get that first taste, then let him do his thing.

Babu drew his weapon and sidled up to the top step, where Lester's long-nailed fingers hesitated on the doorknob.

"Hear anything?" Babu asked, his voice low and quiet.

Flinching at the question, Lester shook his head.

"Smell anything?"

After a moment spent calming his breath, Lester took a few deliberate sniffs of the air. His eyes went wide, and a smile leapt onto his face.

"Jill!" he said. "She's here!"

He sniffed again, seemed to be considering the input.

"She's still alive!" he yelled. "It's not too late!"

Babu held out a palm to quiet him, but there was something wild in his eyes, erasing everything Babu had just said.

"I'm coming!"

Lester cranked the doorknob and ripped the door open, shattering the board that had held it closed. Claws up, he bounded inside.

"Dammit, Lester!"

Babu ran in after him, tripping and fumbling over pieces of shattered timber and other crap he couldn't see. Light from the street didn't seem to penetrate more than one step inside the door. Lester had already vanished into the house's incomprehensible set of rooms and hallways, moving with his supernatural speed. Babu heard a crash and a shuffle to his left. He pulled a flashlight off his belt and thumbed it on.

Guided by the sounds—sounds of footsteps, breath, the whisper of clothing on clothing—Babu navigated the filthy halls. Every step kicked up dust and the smell of mold. The walls were battered and slashed, scratched through their plaster in some places, all at human height.

There was little damage at floor level—not even the rats could stand this place.

The noise led him to the stairs, and he went down, step by wailing step. One story, two—he'd been this way before, when he'd come to see Lester when all this began. The sounds led him to Lester's living room, where he kept his threadbare throne.

The door was open a crack. Beyond, he heard a half dozen footfalls and Lester's voice whimpering.

Something was in there with him. He could only deduce that it was not something that Lester had expected to find in his living room. *Protocol over peril*: Lester was a teammate and he needed help. Babu pushed into the room, swinging gun and flashlight together.

Kids. Dressed in black and gray, the smeared remains of makeup on their faces, they filled the room, steel piercings and spiked collars glinting in the light. They didn't seem to notice him. Babu took a step closer, saw that beneath their makeup their skin was blanched and torn, the edges of bloodless wounds showing the first signs of rot. Their eyes stared. Their breath hissed.

Lester was on the floor five steps from the door, on his knees, hands to his mouth and rocking. The teenagers stood around him in a circle, staring down, whispering to him, touching him with probing fingers.

"Master . . . Master . . ."

"Lester," Babu warned, "just don't move." Frozen in tears and terror, Lester didn't even seem to hear him.

Babu circled into the room, staying along the wall, gun trained on the circle of teenagers. As he approached the other end of the room, another voice penetrated his consciousness.

And in one darkness the specter crouches
With hands calloused, with the whetstone and
    the wheelbarrow,
Eager for the harvest.
And in one darkness stands the vampire,
And he does not sharpen his nails nor
Whisper the secret pleasures of Oblivion in
    close ears.

Lester cried out and began to sob. With two breaths
to fortify his courage, Babu pulled his light off the circle,
and swung it in the direction of the voice.

It is not of the grave that he comes,
And not the grave he bears,
Gift-wrapped
In silk and straw.
His gift is the noise of the specter screaming, of
The Damned unquiet in their rest.

His light fell on a young girl, not older than fourteen.
Up and down, she was dressed in black—boots, sweater,
frilled skirt trimmed in lace, zebra-striped leotards.

For his presence is the Son and the Father,
    but nothing so false sprung from the minds of
      the mad.

She, too, didn't seem to notice the light. Her skin was
still flushed with color beneath her thick, rain-smeared
makeup. Her chest still moved with the beat of regular
breathing. Babu realized he'd seen her before, in this
very room. This one was Jill, the poet.

"Lester!" Babu called, trying to snap the man out of his comatose blubbering. "God damn it!"

Babu swung his light back to the circle of kids surrounding his partner. The kids had leaned in, and now, while he sat there helpless, they dug their nails into Lester's skin, into his scalp and clothing. Their fingers grasped and scratched, coming back wet with black blood, while Lester sobbed and sobbed.

They aren't kids anymore, Babu told himself. He took aim and shot one of them through the temple. The body slumped to the floor in a spray of dust and dry particles of skin and bone.

The pawing hands drew back. Lester collapsed. The kids' whispers of "Master" died away, until the only sound to accompany Babu's rasping breath came from little drops of blood, dripping from their fingers to the floorboards.

Their empty eyes turned on him.

Jill began whispering again:

> The splinters of the pine, the scratching of the
>   homeland soil,
> Quiver the dead in their wakening torpor.

Babu backed up as the circle of children took a step toward him.

> The blessed of that dream of the mortal coil
> Stand outside of memory
> And know the world,
> And the people in it.

Babu put two bullets into the chest of a teenage girl. Her skin cracked like broken pottery and she toppled back.

"Lester!"

The wolf stalks,
The raptor snatches from contentment to fright
    to useful matter . . .

Babu emptied three more rounds into a broad-
shouldered young man, whose shoulder and arm shattered and sagged inside his shirt, but who didn't stop.
Babu felt the wall at his back. In circling to see the girl
Jill, he'd cut himself off from the door. *Stupid.*

The vampire only smiles;
Those animal savages do not call him brother.

Three more shots. One took out the big kid; the others, two smaller boys behind him. The rest stepped over
the bodies. A good half dozen left. Babu dropped out
the clip and pulled another from his belt. Glistening fingers reached for him.
"Lester!"

He hunts beyond the grasses and ferns,
Where the world waits in thrall to be devoured.

Babu brought the gun and his flashlight back up and
let fly two more rounds into a thin, mascaraed face,
inches from the gun's barrel. It shattered and fell inward, and there was nothing behind.
As the body started to fall, as three sets of hands felt
at his clothing, Babu heard a noise like breaking crock-
ery. One set of hands slipped back and disappeared.
Then another. Then the third. Still sobbing, Lester lifted
a Strutter in the air and slammed him to the floor, where
the kid's whole body crumpled like cardboard inside his

clothes. His face torn with a grimace, his eyes leaking bloody tears, Lester stomped on the bodies, all of them, over and over, with his shadow jumping and deformed on the wall behind him. He didn't stop until their heads were powder, and their bodies lumps of debris under cloth. Then he stood, weeping, panting.

The girl spoke again:

> So falls the vampire's black light
> A sun in mourning, for the kisses lost and regretted,
> The majesty of that which cannot be seen.

There was something wrong—crazed—in Lester's eyes as he spun toward her. His tongue hung out of his mouth, and the dust of his victims clung to his open wounds. Babu backed away, suddenly conscious of the supernatural power coiled in Lester's wrecked, emaciated body.

"Jill." Lester went to her on his knees, his hands out. "I'm here. I came back for you."

The girl bent down to him, her mouth open.

Not right, not right . . . Babu leveled his weapon at the girl.

Her mouth kept opening. Her lips stretched back, her jaw dislocated with a pop, then broke in two places. Her throat bulged out.

"Lester!" Babu screamed. "Get . . ."

A red streak shot out of her and severed Lester's arm at the shoulder. Babu spotted red scales, black spines, and reacted. The next few seconds were lost in flashes of gunfire.

The Maskim. It was waiting for them this whole time. Yun probably had it planted here in case they caught up with him. *Holy God Jesus Christ.*

His light caught a flash of it, but it slithered to the side before he could take aim. When he followed it with the flashlight, he found only an empty corner.

Gurgling and wet noises came from the center of the room: Lester's cough, someone gasping for air. Everywhere, particulates in the air, and the smells of sweat and old meat.

"Lester," Babu said, "can you move?"

Nothing sounded but a gagging noise from the darkness outside his flashlight beam.

"Let's go!" Babu said. Lester didn't react. He didn't even try to staunch the bleeding from his arm. As Babu's light passed over him, Lester swung his lowered head back and forth, sniffing. Tracking. Hunting.

Babu had seen it before: how Lester became less than human, a creature of lust and hunger. Babu backed to the door, conscious only that he didn't want that predatory sniffing to catch his scent.

Suddenly, Lester lunged forward and swatted his armchair throne aside, sending it crashing into the walls. The Maskim was on him immediately, a blur of serpentine scales and powerful muscles. It went teeth-first into Lester's chest, penetrating inches into him in a storm of tearing and cracking. Lester's nails came down on its back, his teeth into its eyeless skull, and the two went down into the shattered corpses of Lester's gang.

With nothing to offer, with his stomach clenching from fear and shame, Babu stepped out the door and closed it behind him, abandoning his partner to his fate. He ran for the stairs. Kitsune was the priority. He had to be. *Protocol over personal things.*

Sounds of thrashing and screams of pain followed

him down, until they faded to nothing ten stories underground.

The stairs beneath Lester's house had been there for thousands of years, cut from the dead earth by people lost to history. Babu ran down them two or three at a time, stumbling, wheezing, wheeling left and left and left down the spiral. His lungs and his bad back contested every step, and more than once brought him to a halt, where he coughed up black phlegm. Sticking to his fingers, to his pant legs where he wiped it off, it looked like cancer, like rot.

By the time he hit bottom, he was coughing every step, straining to pull oxygen out of the stale air. He fell through the archway when it appeared, landing square on his shoulder bone on the cut stones of the floor. Spitting up blood, Babu rolled himself to the side and cast his flashlight across the room.

The shadows fell wrongly, in defiance of line and physics, from walls composed of hundreds of stacked geometric shapes. Beyond the flat space at the arch, the floor heaved and tilted with a mad architecture alien to human orientation. Each angle, each plane seemed to lead the eye farther into the room, and without even realizing it, Babu let the flashlight fall on a stone seal, circular, set into the wall opposite and carved with writing Babu couldn't read. To one side of it stood Yun Kitsune, leaning heavily on his cane. To the other, a shadow with nothing to cast it: the Man in the Empty Chair.

"Mr. Cherian," said Yun, not taking his eyes from the Man, "despite what you may think, I'm glad to see you weren't killed by my kindred above."

"Yun!" Babu said between gasps. "You can't . . . You can't let them out . . ."

"If you are speaking in terms of my ability, Mr. Cherian, I can assure you that I am quite capable of doing so," Yun said. "The question my esteemed opponent and I have been discussing is whether it is *time* for me to do so."

The ring of that was too congenial, too premeditated. Babu struggled to a sitting position, still fighting to draw breath from the air. "Wh-what?"

"When I was born," Yun said, "it was on this world, *your* world. There is a difference between the Old Country and this place, Mr. Cherian. In the home of my people, all things possible *are*. Here, they are merely dreams and wishes, and are not." He straightened himself and twirled his cane until it rested under his arm. "When I experienced my genesis, it was this discrepancy that I was most aware of, and so I took as my essence the desire to alter such a state of affairs. It has defined me ever since."

A deafening impact shook the chamber as something battered the opposite side of the stone seal. Babu cried out, covering his ears against the racket. Clouds of dust whirled up from the room's crevices. While Babu scrambled for stability on the shifting floor, Yun and the Man didn't seem to feel anything at all.

"I heard a wish from halfway across the globe," Yun said. "It was the wish of a pure-hearted man, who, holding his daughter for the first time, wished that she would be safe—from us. My esteemed opponent believed it to be his own wish that brought me."

The Man drifted between Yun and the stone seal. If he responded, Babu didn't hear him.

"He wished to be free of the prison of St. Ives," said Yun. "The Warden decreed that he could wander within its confines, but could never leave it. I cannot break the seal on St. Ives. Against the willpower of five billion human beings who do not believe in monsters, I am powerless."

Babu blinked to see Yun as the Kitsune, the nine-tailed fox, glowing with a soft golden light, facing the shadow of a thing that didn't exist. *Because I am not one of them*, he said. *But she was crafted by the oldest and greatest of the Old Country's queens, specifically for the breaking of seals. She need only awaken to herself, and her wish and her mother's, and those of a hundred prisoners and that of my esteemed opponent, will be answered at a stroke.*

Babu saw her in his mind. "Te?"

There are some wishes I cannot grant, Mr. Cherian. Some wishes can only be granted by adversity and trial. If I open this door, she must either awaken to herself or die, along with everything holy and unholy upon this world of yours.

"You . . . bastard piece of . . ." Babu raised his weapon. "You stay away from her!"

The blast, echoing off the misshapen walls, hammered at his ears. The bullet sparked and bounced until it crushed itself under its own momentum somewhere unseen. The Kitsune hadn't flinched, hadn't moved. A cold and empty ache blossomed in Babu's arm, and his gun fell from empty, twitching fingers. The Man in the Empty Chair returned his attention to the Kitsune.

When I came here ten years ago, my opponent decided that I was too early, that Miss Evangeline was not yet ready to accept the responsibilities due her.

In that, we did not see eye to eye. And so we fought.

Together, he and the Man in the Empty Chair flanked the seal.

But time alters opinions on this world, and now we are of one mind about such things. The fox turned its gray eyes on Babu—detached, yet not malevolent.

She must go through fire, Mr. Cherian, said the Kitsune. *And if she lives, so shall her father's wish for her.*

The fox turned away, to contemplate the seal. The Man, too, shifted and appeared to be looking at it. One hand reached up and traced the ancient writing with a single finger.

Babu dragged himself forward, crawling, through the dust.

"Yun! God damn it, don't do this!" he pleaded. "Te's not ready. She can't handle it. For God's sake, she's just a *kid*!"

It was all he had: he begged. He cried out and beat his fists on the stone.

With a quiet crinkling, the stone seal split top to bottom: a single crack.

Babu's Cadillac rumbled through the empty streets of downtown. Te held tight to the steering wheel, fighting to see the road. The old thing had started right up the instant she put it in reverse and headed back into the city.

Visions had started hitting her almost as soon as she left her mother's. She had tried more than once to wipe them away through sheer effort, through distraction, once by using her own fire on herself, but they persisted. They were waking nightmares, reiterations of the most terrifying dreams of her childhood: visions of the black abyss, haunting hints of the dwellers there. She could not see them whole, only stretches of them, vast as the ocean, with their movements as impervious to perception as the spin and revolution of the earth.

These visions, her imagination's representation of something sensed and not understood, flowed together with her binder's memories. She saw—she *was*—a lone man on a hilltop, with the darkness of the night sky his only companion, a darkness alive with alien malevolence. He-she did not speak to it, but, looking into the starless expanse, understood its will, its purpose, and hunger. Then he-she and a hundred others on a hundred hilltops, in grass and snow and dirt, in cold wind and unrelenting rain, had taken pity on it, this limitless, devouring creature from the stars, and sealed it in their own earth in many parts.

St. Ives was one of those places, one of those visions. The rest jumbled together, and she didn't recognize anything in them, except the dark creatures.

She blinked, shook it off. The walls of the Darktown bowl loomed over the buildings now. The streets had been eerily deserted all the way here—occasionally, a shape slumped against a bus stop, or sagging in a store window. All around were closed blinds and drawn curtains. Once, she'd glimpsed a woman in a lit apartment window, shaking a comatose man until he fell from his chair. Those who weren't comatose were staying inside, chilled by the same thing Te felt—a compelling sense of wrongness at the dark sky, the quiet streets, an implacable fear that evaded understanding and had no name. Te *could* name it. That didn't lessen it at all.

She didn't know where to go. In her visions, she saw a repeating image of a round door, but didn't have a clue where to find it.

That might not matter if Babu had managed to get Yun back in reach of his brother. Yun wouldn't stand a chance. But Angrel had come down hard on Ahmadou's skull—Te wondered if he was even still alive. She bit her lip.

God, Yun. Why can't you just listen to reason? He'd said he had no choice, and if he was going to free those terrible creatures ... she had to believe it. And if she could get there in time, and if they had Ahmadou, then maybe ...

Something ran into her headlights.

"Jesus!" She rammed the brakes hard. The old vehicle whined and shook. The tires shrieked against the road, but she managed to rein the car into a jerking halt. It stalled immediately.

She blinked out the windshield at two white palms held up defensively in front of reflective eyes. The hands came down and she recognized him.

"Jack!" Te shouldered the door open and leapt out. He looked awful—black circles rimmed the bottoms of his lenses; his hair pressed against his scalp with sweat; his shoulders bent inward with tension. Te ran up to him and put her hands on his shoulders. She ran her eyes over him, touched him. His eyes wandered over her face, unfocused, full of emptiness and fatigue.

"What happened?" Te asked.

Jack managed a shrug, though the movement made him grimace.

"They forgot about me, I guess," he said. "There was the worm thing, like Mr. Cherian said, coming out the back door, and I yelled, but I guess they didn't hear me." He drew a ragged breath through dry lips. "The worm has a face," he said. "I saw it. It was awful."

"Oh, Jesus," Te said. She drew him into a fierce hug. He didn't hug back.

He shouldn't even be involved, her conscience wailed. God, she'd been selfish even bringing him along that first day. She'd thought she'd needed someone—a partner, a friend—just not to be alone. She hadn't thought of what could have happened to him. She wanted to turn around and drive him home that instant.

But she couldn't. There wasn't time. And she couldn't leave him here, hurt and drained as he was. It was a certainty that crept through her like an urge to choke: she had to take him with her.

She broke the hug and held him at arm's length. "Jack. God, I'm sorry I have to do this, but you'll need . . ."

A boom sounded. The earth shook. Windows and deck railings rattled up and down the street.

"What was . . ."

Another boom: a shifting of the ground, like the twitching of an awakening muscle. Te turned a wide eye toward Darktown.

Oh, no.

Lit only from below by intermittent streetlights, the walls of the Darktown bowl seemed to ripple like seaweed disturbed. High above them, the black clouds gathered together and drew lower, spiraling down like a hook dipping to draw something skyward.

"Get in the car," Te said, but neither of them moved.

The ground rocked again, this time a swell up and down like the inhalation of a buried giant. A second finger, blacker than the absence of light, reached up from between the gray shingles of Darktown, curling and dancing with its counterpart. The two moved as one, linked the ground with the sky, and when the next impact came, the ripple went through both.

Pavement cracked and windows split up and down the street as the first of the angry howls broke free from the Darktown bowl. It was followed by a chorus that seared the air and burned Te's ears. Wolf howls and predator shrieks filled every corner in the city, sweeping out from Darktown in bursts that rippled past with doppler distortion, and the uncoordinated footfalls of thousands of limbs vibrated the pavement in their wake.

Tears leaking from her eyes, pain stinging like needles in her ears, Te grabbed Jack close. In the skies between Darktown and the clouds, a face looked out at the valley. The cards had called it a goat, but in its face were a hundred staring eyes. Dozens of curling horns pierced its hide between strands of ropey hair and the glinting of misshapen scales. There were no teeth in its maw, just a hole so dark as to drain the color from Te's vision, with the shapes of lesser, parasitic things swarming in and out in a whirlwind of screaming and death.

Jack shook uncontrollably beside her. Te buried his head in her shoulder, and told him not to look.

At the first quake, Lester's eyes fell open. He breathed. Blood bubbled in and out of him instead of air.

He rolled. Something snapped in his abdomen. His clothing stuck to the wet floor as he pulled himself forward with a slow motion of the bone stump that was all that remained of his arm.

I'm here, Jill, he said. *I came back.*

Jill lay on her back, bleeding from her nose and ears. Her eyes stared upward, tracking nothing, as she sucked involuntary gasps of air through her torn cheeks and broken jaw.

I'm sorry. I told him not to let you die.

In a far corner, the Maskim spasmed, sending up a spray of sticky, black blood. Severed in half and lying in a puddle of its own skin and scales, it silently healed. Lester knew that the instant it could move again, it would kill him, and he didn't care.

I'll do it for you, Jill. I'll help you. He swiveled his stump again, pulling himself another three inches through lakes of dust and blood.

You called it the Kiss, remember? Or sometimes the Embrace. I always liked that one. The Embrace . . .

His stump brushed her arm. She jerked at the touch, but her eyes did not focus. Her lungs still worked in spasms, jostling her on each inhalation, gurgling on each exhalation.

Will you read me poetry? he asked. *I love your poetry.*

He slid his nose up to her throat, where the blood simmering back and forth through his lips splattered against her pale skin.

I remember you asked me once to bite you, but I was too afraid.

The earth moved. The floorboards cracked. In the corner, the Maskim jerked in spasms of shock and fear.

I'm sorry I was afraid.

Lester stretched his teeth toward her, knowing his jaw would not obey him to bite down. His fangs were still there, however, and the weight of his head would propel them. The walls fell back into darkness and vanished. The floor slipped away in splinters and spinning slats. Jill fell away from him, into an endless space unfurling behind the walls.

Wait. Jill, wait . . .

The dark reached out to her, and with coils insubstantial as smoke, gripped her by the fingers and eyes.

Jill . . .

Suddenly, her eyes blinked, and she stared right into his, petrified with fear. Then the tendrils of the emptiness reached into her choking, struggling throat and tore out a little vibrating point of light, and then they stripped her apart layer by layer until her body dissolved into the black.

Ah . . .

Hands reached into him, through open wounds and cavities, into his mouth, his eyes, his ears, into his stomach, where the Maskim had torn him open. Their pointed fingers sliced and tore; barbs on their skin dragged pieces of him out, to be consumed by the dark.

Ah . . .

The fingers wrapped around his bones and broke them. Unseen teeth gnawed at his muscles, ripped at his skin in spurts like wild dogs. And before they put out his eyes, he saw in the dark before him a face coated in dangling, mangey hair. He felt breath that stank of rot, and heard a bark or bleat that echoed over and over into the distance. A thousand faces—all the same, all looking into him with the will to invade, to infect and violate.

When they had broken him open and found what they were looking for, the claws pulled back and tossed him, empty and worthless, into the void.

Chapter 18

We Are the Hollow Men

Babu shifted in the grip of the teeth. Wind chilled his limbs, buffeting them like clumsy sails, as the beast carried him stair by stair from dark up to dark.

Moist breath slipped back and forth around his body, carrying the scent of grasses and sunflower seeds. With each four-legged gallop, Babu jostled and bounced, flailing like a rag doll. And then he *was* a rag doll, stitched together from brown cloth, filled inside with cotton batting. The beast's teeth closed over him, pressing down into his textile skin and squishing him; but he yielded, unconcerned with holding shape, and so the teeth did not pierce him. His head flopped this way and that, held on by a few stitches of ropey thread. His button eyes caught flashes of something running at the beast's heals—a white paw, wiry, straining muscles under yellow fur.

Then came the clatter of claws scraping wood, bursts of light from holes in walls, mildew and mold, clinging to his fibers, just as quickly drying away in the moisture-famished air. A hole in the wall—the beast slipped through. Then came paws across dirt, onto pavement, onto concrete, winding and dashing through streets without names, through alleys where the bums stared unmoving into the sky, to streets of dead neon and low, low prices.

The beast dropped him, soaked through with saliva, beside a torn garbage bag that leaked rotten bread and jam.

Babu coughed up something black. His limbs shook and his skin prickled with cold sweat.

"I knew it," he said.

Yun crouched beside him.

"The Man in the Empty Chair holds them in now," he said, "waiting for the blindfolded girl to look up and see the swords staked around her. Eventually, he will weaken and they will devour him."

"You *did* come for Te."

"I came for every one of my kind, Mr. Cherian," said Yun. "The Warden is destroying us. For creatures of dream and possibility, imprisonment is the most thorough of horrors. Now, either Te will deliver us to freedom or the whole of the Warden's world will burn to ashes and vacuum. Both are better choices for us."

"She was one of you. This whole time . . ."

Yun smiled in sympathy. "Since the day of her conception."

"I . . ." Babu wiped a tear from his eye, wiped clinging dust from beneath his nostrils. "Yun, do I . . . do I love her?"

"Do you love her or do you love the idea of her? Or do you love yourself when she is near? Humans make things so complicated."

"Does she . . ." Babu choked, coughed. Breath and vitality leaked out of him onto the cold pavement. "Where can I find her?"

"She'll shortly be with Miss Blumenthal, though you will not find her there if you look."

"What do I do?"

Yun's voice faded to a whisper, echoing across his ears. "Rest, Mr. Cherian," he said. "Let me grant a wish for you."

His body like lead, Babu sighed his feelings away. Into his mind and body crept a vibrating whiteness, erasing sensation as it spread. The world vanished. Memories played to him, more real than even when they had been formed. There again, he sat with Rob Evangeline across a café table, swapping stories to the shocked stares of the other patrons. There again, he watched Te at six years old holding a kite, asking if he would take a family picture for them with a disposable camera. There again, the strong face of Nyawela, his wife, dark and beautiful, gazing at him over the top of a glass of wine, smiling—on one slender finger, a ring.

The flickering light plays with my mind. I see visions, though I do not know them as such. I see myself in my thousand incarnations, flickering in face and name and deed past me, one after the other, an unbroken line of sour fate stretching back to prehistory.

"Are you doing this?" I ask.

My ancient companion slumps in his chair and wheezes with each breath. I think for a moment he may be asleep, but he works his lips and croaks an answer.

"He's doing it," he says. "I'm tired. I can't . . . My static won't stop him anymore."

My visions play back three thousand years—and now four thousand. In these earlier incarnations, I can see the hints of what I once was in my bearing, in the powers I had over men and livestock, in the curses that stripped my enemies clean with swarms of ants. As each vision flickers back into the next, I feel stronger, more aware. The confusion of my thousand lives ebbs, leaving my mind clear, my nerves calm.

"He needs you now," my companion whispers. "You're his tool."

The visions end with a shivering child waking in horror to find its immortal self gone, its power lost and its name forgotten. What comes next is my face as I was before the curse.

I look up. The silhouette of a man stands before me. Not a man at all, but a slice of him, a man with all the fat cut free, a man in his purest essence as shadow.

He offers me his hand. I take it. All the televisions wink off. All the radios pop and die, and we are alone, hands together, nowhere.

The safe house was the only place they could go.

When the shadows had grown faces, the spots of the streetlights fangs and spines, the cracks in the earth crawling spider fingers, they'd dove into the car and fled. When a hairy blur had pulled an entire wheel off the car, they'd jumped out and run. When hands human and animal and other had probed the edges of their vision, they'd headed for the only place that was safe: the little building beyond a chain-link fence and a field of priest-blessed trash.

It's my fault, she knew, fingers raking through her hair, pulling at knots, creasing her scalp. *I should have trusted*

Babu. I should have been with him since the beginning. I should have been right there with him.

The air in the safe house was cold: the chill of concrete floors and drafts of winter air. The dry heat of the outside didn't penetrate here, only the mildew damp from too much rain on a rotten ceiling. Errant springs in the old couch poked her thighs. The sigils and fetishes on the walls stirred a fear in her other self, deep and irrational, that gnawed at her insides.

"Are you okay?" Jack asked her. He was beside her, watching her carefully.

Te sucked in a breath, not quite ready to answer. Her gaze passed over a series of equations penned onto the opposite wall with a black marker—like a physicist's chalkboard. Munin was another victim of her screwups. She should have been able to bind Bird.

Asleep. Her mom was right. She had been asleep. She'd been blind to everything going on around her, her whole life. Why hadn't she ever picked up on her dad's secrets? Why hadn't she noticed her mother had never left the property until he died? With all the strange things that happened in St. Ives, why didn't she put the pieces together sooner?

"Te?" Jack prompted. He laid one hand delicately on her shoulder.

She put her palms on her knees to calm the shaking. "I really screwed up, Jack," she said.

"You didn't screw up," Jack said.

"I did," Te said. "I should have told Babu everything. I just . . . I was mad at him for lying to me. For not telling me anything. If I hadn't . . ."

The words choked out. It was too much to say aloud. All the worry of too many days, all the tensions of a lifetime of family strife built up, one on the other, until she shook head to toe. Her palms ground her kneecaps out of place. Her muscles cramped with the shivering. Now it was all too late and there was no one left to apologize to. Not that it would matter if there was.

She cried, not into her hands but onto the cold and unyielding concrete between her shoes. Each drip splattered as it landed, sucked down into cracks and chips and imperfections. Her mind screamed for her to beg a forgiveness for the way things turned out, but then another voice screamed how pointless that was, how much an insult to everyone that she should ask for absolution from the horrors that she could have stopped, if she'd only got her shit together sooner.

She cried hard, trying to eject her guilt. Tears and saliva dribbled onto the floor and she wished she could die, but if Babu had been telling her the truth, even that wasn't an option for her anymore.

Something touched her back, settled around her shoulders: Jack's hands touched her arms and drew her, hesitantly, toward him. Shocked, doubting, she let herself be drawn against the hard bone of his chest. Underneath, his heart thundered and his breathing grew quick and deep. While she lay against him, disbelieving but suddenly very aware, feelings welling up and confusing each other inside her, Jack slipped one hand into her hair and stroked it.

She broke from him, sitting up sharply. His hand lingered on her back as she slipped out of his arms. Her eyes met his, staring unblinking. She saw in his face such fright, and yet such hope and courage; it was enough to touch her, enough to give her comfort.

She kissed him, hard and sudden. She locked her

hands behind his head as he placed his lightly on her back. She kissed him though he was shaking, though he inhaled sharply as she did it. He didn't draw away.

A wordless spike of terror shuddered through her, and Te broke off. She drew her fingers back, saw them shaking. His eyes began to narrow, to droop.

"I'm sorry," he whispered to her. "When you told me about what the Kitsune did, I made a wish."

She realized she had her hands held up defensively between them. She realized she'd moved six inches backward. He wiped his mouth, his face crimson, and turned away to study the floor between his shoes.

Te's mind raced with half-formed thoughts, explanations, justifications: *not your fault ... I've been lonely forever and ... You actually care and I just ... A moment of weakness ... You're just a kid and I shouldn't have ... There was no one and then ... there was ... you ...*

Jack, this wasn't your fault.

There was tension in his whole body. His face was red and his breath came fast and loud. Te forced herself to look into his eyes, eyes that looked away from her, away from everything.

Her mouth opened, closed. What the hell did she say here? Did she tell him it was a stupid, silly thing to do and crush his feelings more? Did she say nothing and let him think she'd done it against her will because of a wish? Did she try to get across how lonely she was, how no one in her life had ever trusted her except for him and how for a moment she'd loved him for that small thing? Wouldn't that lead him on? God, had she been leading him on somehow the whole time?

For God's sake, say something to him.

"I'm ..." Her throat went dry as his eyes flicked the

tiniest bit in her direction. It was as if his whole body vibrated with some emotion, and his eyes were scrunched up as though he might cry.

Talk to him!

At last she swallowed. "I'm ... going to take a look around. See if there's food or something."

You're a fucking coward, girl.

Jack nodded. It was as if he'd released her from a chain: she shot up and walked swiftly toward the back of the little room.

There was a fridge in the back corner. She found some beer and expired colas inside.

Good enough.

He accepted his cola without comment, without even looking up. She sat at the other end of the couch, cracked hers, and guzzled it, almost gagging as the fizz welled up. Then she sat there, wondering what he was thinking, fishing for something to say.

Into the silence between them came cries from outside—screams, animal roars. They were faint, and far away, but they slipped into her mind anyway. Maybe she wanted them to be a distraction.

Her thoughts turned on events, on people, on things that were impossible—on things that shouldn't be real.

Babu; Yun; Sonore; prisoners; monsters and ghosts—they swam together in front of her eyes—things her mother said; things the binders of ages past had seen and knew and faced. It came back to her, over and over—the vision of the cave, the dark doorway, from her dreams. The image flashed into her mind, pushing out memories of monsters and horrors. It pushed out fear, and shame, and confiscated more and more of her thoughts until she

was unaware of her surroundings and could not hear the
calls of creatures in the night, nor feel the turmoil in the
young man sitting beside her. The door grew until it was
her whole world.

I have to go.

For the first time in an hour, she turned to look at
Jack, ready, perhaps, to finally speak to him.

She smiled despite herself, seeing him slumped
against the arm of the couch, mouth open, cola untouched in limp fingers. He'd fallen asleep. She registered somewhere the relief that she didn't have to talk
to him, but the door was calling.

She left her coat over his body, covering his legs with
his own coat. Then, she knelt beside him, watching him
breathe, for long minute after long minute.

She kissed him on the forehead, then rose and stepped
outside.

Faces stared at her from the other side of the chain-
link fence. Dark shapes like fluttering bolts of silk passed
overhead on the wind. From Darktown, only a dozen
blocks away, screams of things human and inhuman
echoed up the cliffs and out over the city. Te walked,
each step a pounding heartbeat, carrying her through
the scrap yard to the broken gate, out into the shadowed
dark, into a corridor of creatures half seen, who reeked
of animal musk.

She walked through them, untouched, the dry winds
biting her cheeks and lips, scraping across her bare arms
like coarse sand. Pupil-less eyes and mucus-lined nostrils passed in and out of her vision. Hooves and claws
scraped the concrete, and breath laden with the scent of
rot and dust washed back and forth over her. The children of the Goat watched her, licking their mandibles

and snouts, and though they did not touch her, Te could feel they were not afraid.

She passed through the city streets, guided by her feet, unconsciously, step after step. Where people had once lain comatose in café widows and offices, only empty chairs remained. Her feet took her to a ramp, a slope of concrete leading down from the street into a parking garage under a shopping mall.

The cave. The binders of history had seen it. Time after time after time, they had sought it. In each memory, it had been different—a familiar doorway, a path between two pillars, a hole, a forest road—but always on the other side: dark, and the unknown.

Down the ramp the world vanished into a void.

The children of the Goat gathered close behind her, their rank odor burning on her tingling skin, ripe with filth. They closed the path behind her, crowding in. To go back was to deliver herself to their lust and their hunger. Te knew that was a choice if she wanted to take it, but the creatures did not step upon the ramp, and the darkness beckoned.

Her father had done this, she knew. From her visions, she knew that every binder had seen the dark place. Some had simply turned away, too small to take the steps, and let their fate devour them sooner or later. Some had gone inside, to be lost to the dark. Only a few came out.

But many went in. She was at least equal to that.

She remembered Jack; she remembered Babu, consciously bringing them to mind and holding them there. She remembered Sonore and Munin, even Angrel and Babu's terrifying brother. And she remembered her father, the sadness in his eyes when she'd told him that she had nothing to say.

As her feet carried her past the threshold of the garage, they met something soft, and the darkness seeped into her. She remembered nothing more, as she crossed into the void.

Chapter 19

Orpheus

A garden. Ferns of shifting rainbow color. Palms, with luminescent bark that shimmered and shifted between ticks of the eye. A wind warm and fragrant, a thousand scents slipping in and out, carried on the breath. Whisper music, the strains of a hidden aoelian harp, played on the ears.

Te's shoes met soft grasses. Without dirt beneath them, they held her up.

Where was she? She had been expecting something . . . darker. Her visions had never led her inside the cave, but the binders before her had been so terrified of it, so very afraid, as if they knew what waited within. So had she, standing on the edge of that ramp. But this, she would never have dreamed.

It was beautiful.

The ferns bent in to touch her as she walked, brushing her face and then pulling back and spreading like open hands. Each touch lingered on her skin in a tingle of changing sensation. Even the grass seemed to convey a warmth through the soles of her shoes. Everything glowed.

Except for her. She was just Te Evangeline here. The light of her other self had vanished.

She made her way forward, ducking the ferns that tried to touch her, squinting her eyes to cut out some of the input. The palms leaned aside from her path, as she came closer to the music, and the musician.

Shimmering like crystal, the last of the trees bent to the side. Beyond was a clearing, a perfectly round section of flickering grasses. In the center was the stump of a tree—not a palm like the rest of the forest, but a thick, brown oak—and the stump was occupied.

It was a being of kaleidoscopic light—a woman—leaning back, her long legs stretched and crossed before her. She held up one arm, suspending from two delicate fingers an aoelian harp the size of a thimble. She pursed her lips and blew into it, and the music spun around the glade, and the trees shivered.

Te took a cautious step forward. The creature blinked demurely and let the harp fall. Te knew this was a creature of the Old Country—what else could it be? But her affinity for it, her empathy for these things she now understood to be her people, was gone. It frightened her, to be without that kinship now, even though she had only experienced it a few days ago. She was afraid to be just a human girl.

The creature turned its whirling, multicolored eyes on Te. It smiled and gave a soft, feline chuckle. Te knew that sound.

"Mom?"

Sonore's smile broadened. Even in that much-thinner face, the smile was the same. "Oh, my ugly little girl," she said, wistfully trailing one finger through the grasses, "I wish I could have shown you this sooner."

Te stepped into the glade. "Is this the Old Country?" Te asked.

Sonore laughed. At the trill of her voice, the leaves shook and the colors of everything flashed around the clearing in rotating sequence.

"No, no, my dear," she said. "This is the world as I like it to be. And it's also your cave. This is the first gate."

Te looked around at the uniform foliage. At the touch of her gaze, two trees leaned apart behind her mother, opening a path off into the forest.

"What gate?" Te said.

Sonore sighed, and spoke in the manner of humoring young children. "The gate to the underworld, my dear. The first of seven."

Te stepped around the dead oak stump, her mother's eyes following her, and looked down this newly opened path. For a while it continued like the first one had, leaves reaching in and out, colors flashing, but farther on, the leaves and grasses flickered and sparked like dying neon lights, the trees' glimmer faded to a dull glow, and beyond that, there was darkness.

Te pulled back, her heart pounding. From the other end of that vanishing road, she heard a silence, like a piercing cry, reach out for her. Suddenly she was aware only of her own breathing, her shaking hands, her queasy stomach—all her messy, inconstant human parts. It seemed her every memory of papercuts, scraped knees, curious fingers on the stove, came back to her: visions of her vulnerability, a remembrance that she was not immortal.

"Mom," she said, "what's going to happen to me?" She looked to her mother—looked to her for reassurance, something she hadn't done in more than a decade.

Sonore looked back at her with a tilt of the head, the feigning of motherly concern.

"What happens to all of you mortal creatures," she said, "death. But this is death as your ancestors knew it to be: death as a choice. You'll either return"—she twiddled her fingers—"or not."

"Aren't you going to wish me luck, even?" Te said. "You're counting on me, too, remember."

Sonore tapped one finger to her lips. "I can always have more children," she said. "But if it will satisfy your insecure sense of your own power, then—*good luck*, my dear. May all those years of bad art carry you through."

Te's first impulse was to snap back, but a thought stopped her. "You really mean that," she said. "My art was practice, wasn't it? Practice for my imagination."

"Imaginary is the most accurate human term for what we are," Sonore said, clearly pleased. "Oh, Te, there may be hope for you yet. But there's one more thing."

"What?"

"Take off your shoes. Socks, too. You don't go tromping into the underworld with armor on your feet, dear," she said. "It's disrespectful."

Te blinked. "All right." She reached down and pulled off one shoe and sock. When she set that bare foot down in the grasses, her skin suddenly exploded in sensation— like tickling, massage, and standing on pointy tacks all at once. It hit her so fast, she gasped in surprise and stumbled against her mother's stump.

Sonore giggled. "That's not a thousandth of what we can make humans feel," said Sonore. "We can play with any part of them. It's a good way to pass the ages."

Gritting her teeth, Te struggled out of her other shoe and sock, and set them all down on the stump. She sat beside them, gingerly running her feet over the grass, hoping they would acclimatize to the feeling.

"Mom," she said, "this underworld ... will Dad be there?"

"Do you want him to be?" Sonore asked.

"I don't know."

"Then neither do I."

Te stared down the tunnel of trees.

"What happens to me if I don't come back?"

"That's up to you."

Te looked into her mother's whirling rainbow-eyes. "You won't even care, will you?"

Sonore shook her head, grinning.

"Screw you, Mom."

Te shot to her feet and marched away, gritting her teeth against the jolts of sensation blasting into her feet through the touch of the grass. A dozen strides in, the leaves ceased to bend, the grass to change color, the tree trunks to shimmer. Fueled by anger, Te passed without hesitation into the dark. Her mother didn't care. She never had. Te didn't doubt it at all.

As she walked deeper into the shadows, the feelings in her feet and skin dulled. Spots on her eyes blinded her at first, then faded. Sound retreated until she heard nothing but the howl of distant wind. Her sight began to distort, to fade between visions of black and gray. Cool damp prickled her skin, moss and soft soil rose up to meet her feet. She emerged from the dark onto a moor, a rolling, misty landscape of stones and lichen, stunted grasses, and twisted, leafless trees.

"Hello?" she called. The mist recoiled from her as she spoke. It wove itself together, swirled upward, and expanded. It grew two tendrils that became arms, two vaporous clouds that became translucent wings, and a face Te knew.

"Auntie Syd?"

Still more smoke than solid, the creature put both wispy hands to her lips and giggled. The mist shook with her laughter.

"Little frog," she said, her voice like an echo without a source, "swimming for the tall reeds. Welcome to me."

"Where are we?"

"Me," Sydney repeated, her eyes hardening to faceted crystal. Her hair, streaming down from her shoulders like running water, glistened with color. Behind her, her wings, pale and transparent distortions in the air, fanned back and forth, moving the mist like the evidence of some giant heartbeat. "Paintings of the *daoine sidhe*. In the mind. And out of it. And where the flesh is breath and death is in the whisper of words."

On a misty form resembling feet, Sydney alighted to the ground. "The second gate," she said, gesturing behind her, to a distant hill where two monstrous standing stones blocked the rising light. "The path."

"Where does it lead?" Te asked.

"Death," Sydney answered, with one of her moments of complete lucidity. "Nothing. Everything. The end of the road."

The path was a thin divot in the grasses that wound between exposed bedrock—an animal trail.

"Were you trying to kill me?" Te asked. "When you were feeding on me, is that what you were trying to do?"

The face in the mist smiled, its features simple and rounded, like a line drawing, like a sketch in charcoal done by an unconscious hand.

"Death is a mirror the next day," said Sydney. "Death is a cloud on a cloudless day. One thing dies. Another thing is there, and it's the same as the dead thing."

Te looked down at her hands, her bony wrists, freckles on her skin. Dead things? Mortal things, at least. And her other self—not mortal?

Sydney hissed air between her teeth, a deeply satisfied sound. "The same," she said, "isn't it?" She drummed her fingers against her lips. "Isn't it?"

Once again, the thin road stole Te's attention. "Guess I'll find out."

Her aunt swept down close to her, trailing smoking bits of herself. Icy, moist fingers snaked across Te's face, and Te found herself staring at her own shattered reflection in Sydney's eyes.

"We love you, little tadpole," she said. "Or little frog? Bonies and wormies, we love you, or plumpy-plumpy." The spectral fingers pinched at the skin of Te's cheek. Frost clung when they drew back. It stung, and Te wiped it away.

Te looked into Sydney's ethereal face and decided there was something there, of love. "Thanks, Auntie."

Syndey's fingers settled on Te's wrist, slithering over it like blades of rotten grass. They came back with Te's watch dangling. "Ticktock woman," she said. "No time. No sun, under there. No need."

The too-smooth, smiling face slipped downward. Faceted wings folded flat into the mist, and Te's aunt was gone, a part of the still air.

The gate called. Something in the tilt of the two monoliths against the morning light, in the inexplicably dark space between, where light should have spilled through, drew her eyes. She set one foot on the path, smarting at the chill and the poke of tiny stones against her bare soles.

The walk was long and cold, over rolling hills empty of any living thing. Hugging herself against the damp, Te scanned the landscape for insects, birds, mice, but there was nothing there. Alone, she passed between the two pitted standing stones, and back into the dark.

Within a few steps, her toes fell on tree roots, then leaves slick with rain and rot. Unhealthy slime oozed between her toes, sending up a putrid stench. Branches swung in from the dark on either side, and within a few more strides, Te was shouldering and elbowing her way through a dense wood. She cursed and swore. Unable to see any kind of path in the dark, she ducked her head and pushed through.

The forest broke into a clearing, the edge of a cliff, where a mammoth rock, bitten by lichen and rounded by wind, hung out over a deep valley lit by the full moon. Cautiously, Te stepped up to the edge. A blast of wind coming up the mountain pushed into her face. It was not the St. Ives valley. There was no river, and no signs of civilization—just the forest stretching to a set of peaks on the far horizon. Except for one thing: a cottage, tiny and alone, so high it seemed level with the treetops. Winking candlelights bled from the windows in sets of two, like eyes.

"Russia," said a voice, "as it was."

Te spun, hands out, forgetting for a moment that she'd lost her fire. A crouched and rounded shadow lurched from the woods into the moonlight.

"Before the czars," it said, "before the Soviets—when your people had reason to fear the wild places." The voice cracked as it spoke, jumping into high registers like the squeal of tight wind: the sound of an ancient feminine throat. The visitor took a step; one spindly leg no thicker than chicken bones stretched into the light. Above the skinny legs, the bloated, gray torso and its sagging, fleshy breasts swayed with each step, and above that, a face with a wolf's luminescent eyes, with witch's teeth and hair like strings of fine ash. In one set of arthritic fingers, it dragged a broom made of a dry, dead birch sapling.

"Auntie Barbara?" Te ventured.

The creature split its lip as it smiled. The wound dribbled black sap.

"Baba," she hissed. "Yaga the Grandmother. So I was called, for age after age, in my forest here."

Te grimaced as her aunt slunk forth on her bony legs. She was hideous, and the smell of rotten vegetation swelled as she came closer. "They all reacted as you do," she said, grinning. "And now their skulls are lamps to light my little house."

Te pressed her hands to her stomach and swallowed as her aunt mounted the rock beside her. "You really do eat people, then," Te said.

"Some eat the spirit, some the mind, some the flesh. It was in meat and bones I found the one appeal in the little race of this world." She had been dragging the broom behind her feet, but now turned it over and leaned on it heavily. She stared out at the still valley. "Your people come to me for advice," she said. "Age after age, they seek me in my chicken-leg house. They think I have wisdom and want to ask me questions." Her face contorted from smile to snarl. "I hate questions."

Te took an involuntary step back from that terrible

face. Her aunt caught the movement in the corner of her eye, and her smile returned.

"But for you, my dear. For you"—she offered an open palm with swollen knuckles, yellow nails, and white, wiry hairs—"I offer what I know."

Te shivered. Her breath hung in front of her. "What's going to happen to me, Auntie?"

"You have been a strong girl, little one," her aunt said. "And yet strength is a rock shattering against a rock. Only if there is no strength left in you can you survive."

"I don't understand."

Baba Yaga stepped forward, curling her hands along Te's ribs. They drew back, scraping nails along Te's belly, snagging on her shirt, ripping little holes. They hooked into her belt, and in two deft twists unbuckled it and ripped it away with such violence Te was thrown to the wet moss.

Coughing, she spun onto her back and stared at this crone that was her aunt. Silhouetted against the valley, Baba Yaga held the belt dangling in her gnarled hands.

"Leather," she said, "a fear of the animal, worn at your hips like a sword, to protect you."

She let the belt slither to the rock.

"There is no protection you can take into the underworld, little one. Only death awaits you there—and surrender."

One finger rose, pointing.

"There," she said. "The third gate." It was an ancient and dead tree, split by a bolt of lightning, burned to its roots, and then collapsed together to form an arch. Beyond, Te saw only the impossible dark just as she'd seen it before.

Te planted her hands in the wet leaves and shoved herself up. Her breath shivered in and out of her lungs in puffs of white. As before, the darkness pulled at her, and her feet moved.

"Good-bye, Auntie," she whispered. Baba Yaga was silent, but as Te stepped through the tree into nothing, she heard a broom behind her, sweeping away her footprints.

The dark came more quickly, more familiar now. As the trees drew apart before her and the smell of the mountainside vanished, Te began to get a crawling feeling on her skin as if someone were watching her. But who could even see in this dark? Someone, something— Te hadn't forgotten that she, too, had seen things without using her eyes.

Paper crinkled underfoot. A hum reached her ears— steady, electric—followed by the distant knocking of a ventilation system. The air grew warm but stale, devoid of any smell but a faintly chemical odor. And then she came upon something she wasn't expecting.

A door. Nothing grand or ancient or mystical, but a plain metal door with a steel handle, painted some shade of white. It looked as if it belonged in a hospital or a school. She looked up. There was an EXIT sign above it, glowing in weak red.

Te took a breath and pulled on the handle.

It was an office. Huge plate windows lined the wall on her left. To the right sat row upon row of cubicles, not even but set at strange angles, some tilting precariously to the side. Papers and empty coffee cups lay strewn on threadbare pastel carpeting. Here and there, phones dangled from their cords, making no sound.

Te stepped in and the door swung closed behind her.

The room was empty, just desks and cubicles stretching off into the dark, seeming to go on forever in the absence of a back wall. Te stepped up to the window, the only source of light, and looked out. She was high up, probably on the fortieth or fiftieth floor. Below her stretched a city—not St. Ives, but a grid of streets and skyscrapers blocking her view of the horizon. She saw no lights. She saw no people. From the darkness, she was certain it was late at night, but she couldn't get a good look at the sky.

"It's how he wants it."

Te spun around, hands out, cursing herself for being caught by surprise again. A woman staggered from the dark, unsteady on her feet, knocking her hips against cubicle walls and desks as she approached.

"Somewhere out there is a system," she said, "running without any kind of goal, without any end product, and without any people. It's perfect and it's pointless."

Te backed against the window as the woman shuffled closer. Her body swayed in frumpy clothing, tottering on legs that angled wrongly, maybe broken. Her shoulder-length hair stuck to her cheeks and forehead, and fell shielding her face. Te realized with horror that one of the woman's arms was missing, and in the faint light she could see an exposed shoulder socket, and ragged, blackened skin.

"Who the hell are you?" Te asked, still backing away as the woman continued to lurch forward.

"My name was Julia Kinnen," she said. "The Maskim bit my arm off. I died in the hospital."

"You were in the casebook. You worked with my dad."

"Your dad, yeah," she said. Her breath came and went in protesting gasps. "You know what this place is?"

Te shook her head.

"The Warden's divine plan," she said. "I got to meet him once, in person. Master of the world—Master of the whole world. Want to know what he looks like?"

Te didn't answer; she just backed away, rounding a dead potted plant.

"Nothing," said the woman. "He looks like something you can't quite remember. But you feel things, when you see him. You feel as if"—the woman staggered and knocked her absent shoulder against the window with a sound that made Te's stomach turn over—"as if you're *made* wrong. As if you want to reach into yourself and rip out all the little imperfect bits. Your heart and your guts, your lungs."

She found her balance again and started walking. As the woman swayed, Te spotted something in her right hand—long, metallic, pointed.

"He makes you want to be a machine," she said, "be a part of a system. And I was. I was part of it. I caught the deviants. I put the monsters in jail. Monsters like you. And I loved it. After meeting him, I had to love it."

Still backing, Te darted her eyes around, looking for a weapon. Coffee mugs? Adjustable chairs? Ballpoint pens?

"The Maskim's dead," the woman said. "That means I'm free of it. I can pass on. But you ... you're the one who's going to stop all this"—she waved her knife at the building—"and I can't let you. I just can't."

Maybe I can knock her down, thought Te. *She'd have a hard time getting up. Maybe if I rush her ...*

"The Warden has a vision," said Julia. "This is it. Don't you see? It's the best thing to happen to civilization. No pain or suffering. No kids starving in Africa."

A kick. No, a shove. Quick, hard. Te breathed in hard against her fear. She set her heels and rushed the woman. Julia coughed as Te hit her, both palms to the upper chest. Skin and flesh squished underneath Julia's soiled sweatshirt. She toppled back and Te pressed down with her toes to stop herself.

Julia's arm came up, swinging her weapon at Te's head. Reflexes kicked in. Te ducked. The arm swung around and locked behind Te's neck. When Julia fell, Te went with her.

Te landed on top of her and immediately started to struggle. She lashed in with her knees and her hands, but Julia held her too close. Julia jerked her grip tighter, pulling Te's face close to her own. Out of the corner of her eye, Te saw lips, cracked and spotted with blue, whisper to her.

"You're a deviant," they said. "You're built wrong."

Julia's arm wrenched at Te's neck as she pulled them both over, into a roll that left Te on the bottom, still wriggling. Julia's weight, far too much for her size, crushed the breath out of her. Te gasped as black emptiness screamed at her from her chest. Dust and cleaner smell from the carpet swirled into her mouth and out.

Then came an awful pain in her side—not the knife, but a fist, a blow. Te felt muscles cramp up, felt her body recoiling from the shock, felt blazing pain fire through adrenaline-primed nerves. A weakness followed, oxygen fading away, spots on her vision, distortions in her ears.

"See?"

Te clawed at the carpet. Hard bone dug into her back as Julia kneeled on her. The knife came around, slipped between Te's throat and the carpet. Freed of the restraining hand, Te craned her head up. Perceptions started to swim. She gasped and gasped, but couldn't breathe in against the woman's weight pressing on her.

"Your shirt," said Julia. "Take it off."

What? Te thought. *Why does she want me to . . . ?*

Her mind started to fuzz and Te felt the touch of metal against her neck. Gagging, she tried to nod.

The metal slipped away, and an instant later, the pressure of Julia's knees left her back. Te gasped in, then coughed, choking on the dust still thick in the air. Her flanks jerked against the point of the knife, pressed now hard into her lower back. The dry whisper of Julia's panting slithered through Te's hair.

Te laid shaking hands on the carpet and, conscious of the knife, pushed herself up. Julia kept the knifepoint near Te's ribs while she reached down and stripped her shirt off. Julia reached past Te's head and yanked the shirt back. The instant the knife withdrew, Te kicked herself forward and rolled away. She came to all fours and threw her head up, expecting to see Julia coming at her. Instead, the woman had cast Te's shirt over the nearest desk. With a grunt, Julia drove her knife down through it and into the desk. Te caught her first clear glimpse of the woman's face—she was younger than Te had thought, barely thirty, but her skin sagged, and splotches of black-purple—bruises that had never healed—marred her.

Julia leaned heavily on the desk, and as Te climbed cautiously back to her bare feet, she thought she heard the woman crying. "Don't ever see him," Julia whispered. "We were invited. Rob didn't come in and I thought he was stupid not to want to meet the ruler of the world." She sniffled, a sound without any wetness. "It was after I met him, something changed in my head. I love him now. I'm his forever."

Te folded her arms across her bare stomach. Wearing only a bra and jeans now, lungs burning, small poke in her back stinging and dribbling blood, Te found she had absolutely no sympathy for the woman.

"Where's the fourth gate?" she snapped.

Julia looked up in surprise, probably at Te's harsh tone. She wiped her eyes, though Te could see no tears there, and silently pointed into the dark. Te followed her fingers and spotted the faint glow of an EXIT sign.

"You said you can pass on," Te said.

Julia nodded.

"Do it," Te said, "or you'll see me again when I get through this."

The woman's eyes and nostrils flared, but she did nothing. Te dismissed her with a shake of the head, and stalked off into the maze of desks. It wasn't until she'd pushed through the exit door, back into the eternal black, that her fear really hit her.

There in the gap between places, Te let herself go and sank to the floor. She clutched her knees and drew them close; they were shaking. She still felt the ghost pressure of that woman's knees between her shoulder blades. The small puncture on her back stung. With a clarity and a certainty she had never felt before, she'd thought she was going to die. Even when her mother and aunts had drained her, when Bird had come at her with her claws and teeth, even when she was down in the Vanisher's hole, she'd never felt so small, never felt so vulnerable. Everything in this strange place, this underworld, was magnified. Here, she found she couldn't construct any illusions of confidence, any assertion of capability that would remotely fool her own shrinking emotions. She knew what she was now, without any distortion: small and weak and very, very human. It terrified her.

This is what they saw, she thought, remembering the binders, generation after generation, facing their own caves, looking into that depthless shadow. *This is what they went through—just facing what they were. What we are, as human beings.*

We're so small.

Her breath came in small, shaking bursts. The quake spread to her shoulders, her hands, her abdomen, her whole body. In the dark, and alone, she pressed her forehead into her knees, and cried.

This is what they did, she told herself. *Thousands did this. Dad did it. I can . . .*

The assertion died in infancy. She couldn't lie to herself, not here. This stupid human striving to believe in a good future, to bolster the ego—it rang hollow to her now. There was nothing in it—no substance, no power, no reality, not even the lingering energy of something possible but unrealized. It was just hollow. False.

Te realized that the binders who didn't make it back, who went into the cave and never returned— she realized then that they hadn't been the victim of some spirit or guardian or crazy woman with a knife. They'd done exactly what she was doing now. Faced with themselves as they were, with the destruction of their illusions, they'd sat down in the emptiness and given up.

Te didn't want to give up. She didn't want to sit here, lost, forever. She didn't want Jack and Babu to be murdered by the Goat's children. She wanted to get out of St. Ives. She even wanted to see the Old Country. And, somewhere in this underworld that was a parking garage and a nightmare and her own imagination, she wanted to find her father.

She had *so much* to say to him.

Outside of her, the nothingness stretched to infinity, but inside, there were these little things, little sparks, little wants and needs and petty concerns—small goals, things undone. This was what she was, this collection of wants, a web of conflicting yearnings anchored to nothing, held together by its own tension. This was her, against the still, inanimate dark.

She *was* small. She *was* vulnerable. There were forces in the world—in the very streets of her town—with clarity in their desires, and sheathed in bodies perfected to their purpose. Nothing as messy and complicated as a human being.

Her fingers brushed against the faint hair of her arms. Her side cramped and ached. Her feet throbbed from the roots and stones and thin carpet. The waist of her jeans bit into her belly, and the air, touching her skin, made her shiver.

I'm a mess. Humans are always a mess. Inside and out. The Old Country's people, they know what they're here to do. Mom's a muse. Yun grants wishes. It's simple, and clear, and perfect.

But I'm a mess.

For the first time in what seemed like ages, she lifted her stiffening neck and looked through the dark ahead of her. Her mind started to run again, turning over like gears without grease, noisy and slow, grinding against themselves.

Three gates left.

Still shaking, every muscle twitching and fighting her, Te stood—and walked.

The dark carried her into a cloud of pungent incense. She coughed and tried to wave it away from her face, but her hand caught on a curtain. Dragging herself past it, Te stepped into a tight and smoky room. Thick, soft carpets coated the floor; strips of fabric patterned the ceiling like stars. There were no walls, but only layer after layer of thin silk in soft and vibrant colors that rippled in an unfelt wind. Firelight behind the silk cast the shadows of women dancing, posing, gyrating, all hips and breasts, with long hair scattering about them as they moved. From somewhere off in that forest of silk curtains, Te heard giggles and purrs and the shuddering gasps of a woman's orgasm.

"You are a pain to me," said a voice. "Go away."

Te followed the sound, brushing through several layers of curtain until she found the source. In a pile of pllows and soft blankets, tables of glistening fruit and wine on either side, lay a thin Indian man, naked and with blood caked to his ears, chin, and beneath his eyes. Te recognized him.

"You're Sanjay Sharma."

The man pressed both palms to his eyes. "I cannot see you," he said. "I am without desire. I am empty."

The phantom women beyond the silks giggled and cooed. Sanjay snatched a pillow and pressed it over his privates.

"I am without desire," he repeated. He sobbed quietly.

Te knelt beside him. "I'm not one of those women," she said.

With one hand stretched across both eyes, Sanjay sighed.

"Yes, I know," he said. "You are real. I have seen you before."

Te swallowed her fright as the memory jumped back. "You remember?"

"Yes, I remember," he said. "I do nothing *but* remember. My life comes to me over and over, and I cannot embrace it!" He hurled his pillow at the nearest female silhouette. The silk curtain twitched at the impact, rippling to reveal the curve of a thigh before stilling again. Sanjay shuddered and sat up. "I am sorry," he said. "I am not a stable man."

Te nodded, keeping herself at arm's length. "It's all right."

"Before the last moment of my life, I had never met you," Sanjay said. His eyes remained closed. "Yet I know about you. I know you are Mr. Evangeline's daughter. I know you are Babu's assistant. I know I am a guardian on this strange path you walk. I know why you are partly . . . naked."

His breathing quickened. He shifted to place his palms on his eyes once more. Te caught a glance between his legs and shuffled back a step.

"Yeah," she said, "I'm beginning to figure it out, too."

"For transcendence, you must leave all things behind," Sanjay said. "You must surrender all your earthly possessions. You do not walk into the afterlife with all the accoutrements of living."

Te nodded—her aunts had said something similar. "Was Yun Kitsune really inside your head?"

"Ah! Yes," Sanjay said. The shadow-women's cries shifted to something sympathetic, but still yearning, still tempting. "I thought it would be a test—a way to harden myself against the desires of the material world. But he whispered to me and told me how he could make anything for me. Any of my desires would be real, if I only let him free."

Sanjay's eyes cracked open to slits, and Te saw red irises around wide, deep pupils. "I resisted, but he wore me down. I wanted things. I asked the Man in the Empty Chair for a house and a car . . . and a television. He gave me whatever I asked."

"He didn't really help you out much, then?" Te said, thinking aloud.

"It was my own weakness," said Sanjay. "I resisted for ten years, until all the resistance I had was my abstinence. But at the end . . ." Sanjay's eyes traveled up and and down Te's body; Te felt a cold shiver in her spine. "I asked him for a woman."

"And he brought you one," Te said.

"Yes, he brought me one."

"Was she about twenty with white skin and dreadlocks?"

"Yes, she was. I knew her, but that didn't matter."

What else had that bitch done? Then it occurred to her—if the Man could send Angrel to seduce this poor guy, maybe he sent her to seduce her father.

The thought passed out of her head and she found Sanjay staring at her breasts.

"I knew I would die," he said. "I took her anyway." He looked away, to the dancing forms that surrounded the room in overlapping layers of shadow. "Because I understood that it was a wish I had made that the Kitsune had granted."

"He said you wanted to start over."

Sanjay's eyes came back to her, dwelling piece by piece on her body. "Yes. This place is to force out of me my desire for enlightenment. I want to become carnal again. It is much . . . easier." Te saw a flush creep up his neck and cheeks. Her skin crawled.

"I'm going to go now," she said. She got up, keeping her arms folded over her chest.

Sanjay stood up as well, exposing himself to her, and gestured with one hand to a part in the curtains. "The fifth gate," he said.

"Thanks." Te hurried to the exit.

"Wait."

Te stopped. *Right.*

Te looked down, swallowed, steeled herself. While Sanjay watched her, she stripped off her jeans and tossed them away. She passed through the curtain folds without another word.

She was thankful for the enveloping darkness when it came. Once she passed beyond the reach of the incense, she took a moment and covulsively wiped the scent off her arms and legs. She felt like she needed a shower. She tried to shake it off. Two more gates. She walked on.

The night air bit her once again, and with her legs exposed now, she started shivering almost immediately. Sharp pebbles jabbed into her feet. It was a desert, not of sand but stones, stretching to far mesas at the edge of the plain. Above, the stars hung like a million glinting needles.

Smarting at the rough ground, Te made her way forward, clambering down the occasional layer of strata and rounding several large cacti. She'd seen pictures of North American deserts and didn't think this was one of them, but where it could be she didn't know. The rocks were a rust red, the scrub brush white and dry, and she didn't hear a single insect.

What she heard was drumming. She followed the

rhythm down into a shallow canyon, and, wending her way past its sharp-edged walls, she realized there was light ahead. The canyon emptied into a rounded bowl. In the center burned a bonfire, a pyramid of dry and twisted trees cast together, roots and all. From the branches of the trees hung hundreds of dead snakes, sizzling and dripping. As she stepped out from the canyon, the drumming surrounded her, reflecting back off the walls, their deep sounds thrumming beneath her skin.

The drummers were arranged in a circle at the top edges of the bowl, nearly invisible, so far from the light. Te caught glimpses of ruddy skin, faces painted white to look like skulls, and the firelight playing on the huge animal-skin drums each player held. They beat in unison, hammering a steady thunder.

Te heard another sound pounding in time with the drums. Rounding the fire, she saw a man standing close to it, head down, stomping with every second beat. The fire played on his red skin, on sweat dribbling down his limbs and torso. He raised one foot and brought it down with a clomp. It was clearly prosthetic, attached to the bones of the shin by metal rods. It was a cloven hoof.

She'd seen him before—the dancing man in her imagination who had fought Bird. He was Cyrus King and according to Babu's casebook, nearly three years dead. He didn't seem to notice her, so she tried to pass by him to see if the canyon continued on the other side of the bowl.

He stomped. She buckled over, gagging. Her abdomen spasmed with the aftermath of an invisible impact. *This is what he did to Bird. But why is he . . . ?*

Another stomp, and this time it was a hard blow

across the cheek. Te's head spun, wrenching her neck. As she struggled to keep her feet steady, another stomp sent a hard hit into her side, driving her to all fours. Then another shoved her to the dirt, as if the cloven hoof had come down slantwise on her shoulder.

I have to get up. I have to run . . .

She rolled over and the next blow came down on her hip. The next stomp came down on her forehead, slamming her skull into a rock.

Stop . . .

The next crushed her hand.

I don't want to . . .

A kick to her side.

Make it stop.

With a final strike, all the drummers fell silent. Te's coughing and the sizzling of the dead snakes were all that were left in the night. Quaking from the pain, she curled her arms and legs up around her. For a moment the only thing she could handle was the fight for breath. Blood dribbled out her open lips into the dust. *Something might be broken*, she thought. She couldn't tell. Everything hurt so much.

Carefully placed steps disturbed the ground near her. Te pried her eyes open to see King standing over her, a burning snake stretched out taut between his arms. With a quick motion he grabbed it along its length and squeezed. The charred skin cracked open, and little drops of sticky, viscous blood splattered over her. She cried out and turned her face into the dirt.

His hands fell on her, twining their fingers in the back strap of her bra. He ripped the clasps free and then tore it off her, and she curled up screaming, arms across her chest.

After that, he walked away. Te lay there, in silence, until the snake blood had cooled, until the cut inside her cheek had stopped oozing. Tenderly, she unwrapped herself, wincing as every movement compressed some fresh bruise. She took an eternity to work her way back to her feet, pausing often to let the pain subside. She was exhausted, coated in dirt and smeared in snake blood. Did he not recognize her? Was it a test, a sacrifice, anointing her with blood?

It took a long time for the dizziness to fade once she got herself upright. Leaning on the bowl's slope, Te worked her way around to the other side.

There was another gap, another canyon, darker than the first. Te knew it for what it was.

"The sixth gate," she muttered.

An age in darkness followed. As she walked, her injuries hardened into purple bruises, generating pounding aches with every heartbeat. All she could think now was that it was almost over. Only one more gate, and then ... whatever was going to happen, would happen. The blood dried into her pores and clung to her skin, crinkling against it as she moved. She wanted to wipe it away, but ... she still felt as if someone were watching her in these gaps between gates. She felt isolated but never completely alone.

When she felt grasses under her feet, she slowed, hesitating. She didn't want to go on. She didn't want to see anything else.

Hasn't it been enough? she asked her unseen watcher. *Why are you doing this to me?*

The dark gave no answer.

Of course it didn't. This wasn't a matter of pleasing someone, of passing someone else's test. *It's about be-*

ing small and human—a deep breath brought fresh pain from her bruises—*and being hurt.*

She stared ahead into the darkness, where vague images played on her mind, distant and not yet formed.

But I can't not be afraid.

I'm so afraid.

I'll always be afraid.

She couldn't conquer whatever fear the gates had put into her. She couldn't fight it. She couldn't ignore it. What was she supposed to do with that?

It swept over Te just how much she'd been afraid of—her mother's smile and her father's worried face, Babu's opinion of her; of not knowing her own future, and of knowing it; of staying the same, of changing. Everything had paralyzed her; her whole life had been lived through reactions against this fear—headstrong or flippant or terrified, her responses had been falsehoods and masks. Nothing in her life had been lived free of that, and nothing ever would.

Afraid of going forward, afraid of staying in the darkness, Te stood, unseen grasses scratching her legs, heartbeat after heartbeat. She clenched her teeth until her jaw hurt, until tears leaked from her eyes. Her fingers dug into her arms; her bare legs pressed together.

When she moved, she moved from her fear: she was afraid of the indecision, and so she made a choice.

As she walked on, the ground became a hillside of dry grass, dry moss between the clumps that pricked the soles of her feet. A sky melted into being above her—stars again—and the flat path through the dark became a rolling hillside, surrounded by round-topped mountains.

The St. Ives valley: Te knew it immediately. A cold, wet

wind blew across the hills, biting at her exposed skin. She shivered and rubbed her arms against the goose bumps, but it didn't help much without any clothes. Teeth chattering, she trudged up the slope in front of her.

At the top she saw the guardian of the last gate. At first she just thought he was silhouetted against the sky, but taking a few steps closer, she saw that he himself was a shadow—the shadow of a man, a hat, a coat, standing on the crest of the rise and lord of the lands around. She'd have known him anywhere:

The Man in the Empty Chair.

Te folded her arms over her chest again, and climbed up beside him.

There on the hill, she stared into him, and he stared back at her. Then, into her mind, like a voice not heard, but poorly remembered, he told her to turn, and to look, and she did.

Below them, the hill curved down into a gully. In its center stood a tree, clearly dead, its dry orange needles littering the ground beneath it. Around the tree, there was a perfect circle of dry, cracked ground without a single shoot of grass, or spot of moss, or any mark at all. To her surprise, Te knew this place—she had seen it in her visions; her father had stood there.

The Man in the Empty Chair gave her its name: the Sacred Grove.

Into the circle from one side stepped a shadow—the same shadow that stood beside her. A duplicate? A vision? From the other side, out of the night, stepped Robert Evangeline.

"Dad!" Te cried out.

He was alive. Haggard and stooped, drained by whatever had happened to him in the last year of his life, Te's father walked quietly over the edge of the circle. The Man's double stepped over as well.

It was a memory, the shadow beside her explained. It was the last hour of his life.

Robert and the Man approached each other, coming face to face under the drooping branches of the tree.

"I know now," said Rob. His voice was so tired, so emptied of vitality. His every movement shouted how weak he was. "Sonore told me."

The Man said nothing as Robert took a moment to swallow and moisten his lips.

"You want to get out of here," he said. "I understand that. And you need someone to free you because you can't do it alone. I understand that, too." He took a long breath. "You needed Kitsune to come here and grant Te's wish, because she can break the seal over the town and you can't."

Robert seemed to choke on his next words.

"But she's my daughter, Kent," he said. "She's my daughter."

"Oh, God," Te whispered. "Dad, don't . . ."

The Man's head bowed, and Robert nodded solemnly. They turned from each other and walked to opposite sides of the grove.

Te's hands came up to her mouth.

"Oh, no . . ."

Her father turned. So did the Man. Robert opened his hands. The man drew the folds of his trench coat close around him.

Te's eyes saw nothing, but in her imagination, over-layed on her perception, she saw the fire erupt out of Rob's palms and eyes, saw it rip across the Sacred Grove like a cresting wave. The Man in the Empty Chair weathered it with a raised arm. Robert faltered. His weakened body spasmed, and his fire guttered and died. In an instant, the Man was standing in front of him, his hand reaching through Rob's rib cage, into his body.

Te screamed.

When the Man drew his hand away, he tore with it spectral white strands, peeling them with jerking, painful slowness from Robert's ribs. Robert reacted, convulsing, until the strands came away with a sickening snap, and he collapsed backward, crashing into the grass.

Te ran to him. Down the hillside, she slipped and fell, got up, ran, slipped again, scraping her knees and feet, cutting her fingers on the grasses' edges. She reached him just as the Man in the Empty Chair did, and threw herself between them.

"Don't," she said—*begged*. But the Man ignored her, stepping through her to stand over Rob's body.

"Please . . ." Te knelt beside her father and reached shaking hands out to touch his shaking arm. His eyes focused clearly from within a face drained of life and twisted by pain. He coughed up white froth.

"I already made my wish, Kent," he said, his words burbling through saliva.

The Man said nothing. Rob choked violently for a minute and Te reached out to him, one hand on his chest, feeling the curdling of fluid inside his lungs. Her father's eyes widened and lost focus, and such doubt and fear crossed his features.

She heard a swish on the grass. Through tear-blurred eyes, Te watched a white figure approach over the hill and kneel by her father's head.

Not her, Te said, pleaded.

Angrel and the Man in the Empty Chair shared a

communication without words: instructions. Start now, he told her, but leave something for his daughter to see.

Angrel nodded, and Te saw tears on her cheeks.

How dare you! Te screamed. *You have no right to cry over him!*

But she did, drop after drop, as she bent over Rob and brought her face to his.

"I'm sorry," Rob muttered. His eyes traced nothingness—the remark wasn't meant for her, for anyone.

Angrel kissed him, with such a tenderness that Te felt her blood boil.

Get the fuck away from him!

When Angrel's lips drew away, gossamer strands clung to them, strands she breathed into herself like cigarette smoke. Te saw that white skin flush, saw her father's eyes spread in panic, his body fall into a shaking fit.

You . . .

Te knelt in the grasses and shook as Angrel lifted her father up—he was so thin—and dragged him away over the hill.

For a long moment she sat, thinking nothing, feeling her loss, her building rage, and reveling in it.

"I want her," Te said, scraping away her tears with the knuckles of a closed fist. "When this is over, she's *mine*."

The Man in the Empty Chair made no response.

"And so are you." Te's breath hissed in and out between clenched teeth. She no longer felt the cold; her skin burned. Her fingers closed in tight fists around the grasses and tore them out, roots and all.

Te rose to her feet, slid her panties down her legs, and stepped out of them. Naked on that hillside, damp wind touching all of her, she looked into the nothingness of the Man in the Empty Chair and snarled.

"Where's the seventh gate?"

The Man bowed his head and spread his arms, and Te understood. He was the only patch of darkness on the hillside. He was the seventh gate.

Her rage drove her through without hesitation. The wind and the stars faded, and the darkness came again. The unseen watcher was closer now, so close that Te reacted to imagined feelings of breath on her shoulders. With nothing to see, her eyes envisioned faces that turned her way and were gone. With nothing to hear, her ears filled the nothingness with the laughter of her own anger, and then the whispers of doubts, losses, and sorrows.

Not yet. She had to hold on to the anger. She clung to it, fixated on it, tried to fuel it with thoughts of revenge, but all around her lurked a powerful, invisible despair.

She fought against tears, against the terror masked only by her heated thoughts. *I can't be afraid now. Not now.*

Her feet slid into a layer of soft dust, which whirled and tumbled away from her with her next step. Beneath, plates of shale shifted, rattling. The dark above became a cavern roof, split by layers of strata that hung apart like guillotine blades. The walls came next, fading into her vision by a faint but emerging light, flickering like fire, but white as magnesium flame.

She came at last into the cave—the underworld, the place of the dead. She knew it immediately. This was no vacant landscape, no imaginary representation of another place, as all the other gates had been. She felt it in the sudden knotting of her stomach, in the bolts of fright that shaped her fear into something hyper-real, intense, and unquenchable.

To Te's left and right, row after row of corpses, burned, rotted, flaked away down to their bones, watched her with empty sockets. Breath hissed from them, a dry and lifeless wind animating the dust.

Te covered her chest with one arm, keeping the other out in front of her. She found herself walking a path through them, a space they had cleared, where no footprints disturbed the thick dust. Wind whipped through the heights of the cavern, echoing in the crevices of the ceiling, singing discordant notes to the dead. Te walked the path, shuddering as those empty eyes followed her, as those skeletal fingers twitched toward her.

Her heart pounded so loud as to fill the cavern. Her rushing blood thundered in her own ears. Her bruises stung and her skin prickled, and each sensation of her living body seemed a blasphemy, and terrified her.

"Past three not properly alive, and three not properly dead, and one that was never one nor the other, comes a sister of mine."

The path ended at a staircase of jagged slate. At the top stood the underworld's throne: a stack of bones and skulls, and its top laid with a rug woven of human fingers. Upon that crouched a woman with skin the color and consistency of desert-worn bones. She reached forward with twelve-inch fingernails and eyes reflective like hematite. Drapings of human skin hung from her shoulders; black ichor bubbled from between her teeth as she smiled. Graceful as a cat, she squatted on her mound of death, and looked down.

"I never thought I'd see my kingdom again," she said.

"I'd given it up for lost. To think, that after all these ages, it would be you bringing me back to it."

Te hugged herself tighter. "Who are you?"

The creature grinned. "You don't recognize me? Of course you don't. What does the goddess have in common with the wastrel? The queen of the dead with a wandering, spite-broken little girl, so weak she cries over the death of a human lover?" She hissed like a snake. "I am Ereshkigal, creature of flesh, as I was called in old Babylon, when I was so feared and loved, that men and women on the cusp of death gave up their oblivion to worship me." She stood upon the mound, raising those long, black nails. Behind her, all around the chamber, the dead rustled, jostled, stepped forward.

"I have their souls hostage against extinction," she said. Then, to the cavern she said, "Do you worship me?"

The dead answered: "Yes, Goddess." Te shrank away from that many-throated, whisperless tone.

The reflective eyes fell onto Te.

"Will I have yours, I wonder?" She laughed, and slid down the pile of bodies to crouch on the topmost of the slate steps. "You still do not know me, Te Evangeline?"

Te shook her head.

"Then look on this." She picked at her cloak of human skin, dragging it off her veined and slashed body, and dangled it from the scalp. A face, stretched and hollow, eyeless, lips dangling free, gaped forward. The face, white as plaster, came to shape as Ereshkigal manipulated it with her talons: Angrel's face. "You swore to kill me, little lamb," those lips, vibrant with the antithesis of life, spat out.

"Oh, God!" Te backed away, involuntarily, shock now

master of her limbs. The filthy hands of the dead caught her shoulders and ribs, back, thighs, and buttocks, and thrust her back to the foot of the throne. Ereshkigal wrapped black talons around Te's throat.

It was Angrel. It was the same thousand faces of twisted hate, life after life after life. It was the old woman and the young seductress, the dying infant and the witch burning at the stake. Te saw it all in the twitching grin as Angrel licked close to her face with a lolling, reptilian tongue.

"We are sisters, you and I," she said. "I, too, was born of a sow's womb. I had a twin, Innana, called Ishtar and Astarte, who came to me just as you have, at each gate relinquishing one of her earthly powers, until she walked naked into my kingdom, unprotected by hope, art, or symbol."

While one set of nails held Te's neck, the other found her belly, and dragged down, scratching and slicing, down to her inner thigh, finishing with a flick off the knee that tore skin. Te gasped.

Oh, God. I have to . . .

"Do you know what I did to her?" said Angrel's condescending voice, magnified.

I have to . . . Te fought down the pain and lashed out, not with fire but with fists and feet and teeth—with the weapons of the human animal.

Her knuckles split when they landed. Her toes cricked back, sprained. Ereshkigal laughed, and with a twist of her thin wrists, hauled Te down by her throat and slammed her hard into the sharp edges of the shale stairs.

Te's vision swam. There was nothing in her head but sparks, and pain everywhere, the goddess' laughter, the muttering dead. She tried to move her arms and couldn't, tried to lift her head but only set off an explosion of light behind her skull. Blood filled her mouth. Her body chilled, deadened, settled.

"I will hang you as a trophy, next to your father."

Ereshkigal pulled Te up and threw her to the waiting dead. There was no scream, no struggle sufficient for when those rotting hands closed on her. They dragged her down into a dark of dust and eager whispers. The hands grabbed her, pulling, grasping, tearing, penetrating. Everywhere the stench of death, the slopping of blood, the hungry fingers of the dead. It was all Te could do to close her eyes.

And when they were done, they lifted her, carried her to a field behind the throne, and there they raised her above a pointed stake of stained, hardened wood. Grasping her limbs, they pulled her down onto it until it broke through. They left her there, transfixed. Only then did oblivion claim her.

Chapter 20

Spirits of the Earth and Air

Jack sat alone on the couch, Te's jacket in his lap.

He didn't wonder where she'd gone, and he didn't wonder why. He just sat. There was an ache in his stomach.

He'd woken up an hour ago, cold and with a watery sensation in his joints, alone.

She might not be coming back.

He heard another scratch at the walls. They'd been doing that for fifteen or twenty minutes: scratching or banging on the walls. Jack knew they were the "children of the goat," of that big thing in the sky over Darktown, and he could guess that they couldn't get in past the writing and the things hanging on the walls, so Jack hadn't been thinking about them much.

He just sat, remembering what it had been like to kiss Te. At the time, he'd been so afraid but so ... compelled—as if he weren't in control of himself anymore. Now, when he remembered, he actually felt a little sick, and then he felt embarrassed about it.

He'd wished for it—was that the only reason Te had kissed him? If it was, was that wrong? If it wasn't really her choice—was that like rape?

His fingers stroked her jacket. It smelled like her.

The things outside started growling and yipping. Then there was a crash, a goat's bleating scream, and a burst of white light that seeped in through the cracks in the walls and the edges of the door. There were a few more crashes, and then silence.

Jack watched the doorknob carefully.

Were they gone? He listened, hearing nothing. Maybe they'd just gone away for a minute, and would come back. He wished there were a window he could look out of. But, even if the goat-children outside the safe house were gone, what about the Goat itself? Just the memory of it terrified him, and it hadn't seemed like it was going anywhere.

Te had tried to protect him when it rose out of the ground. He was a little embarrassed about letting himself be babied like that, but—the thing was so *horrible*. No one had really done that for him before. He looked back at the door. Maybe Te was back. Maybe she'd driven the goats off with her fire. But the fire didn't make light—not real light, anyway.

There was a knock—not a scratch or a blow, but two short, distinct raps.

Jack stared at the door for a long time. It might be the goat-children, trying to trick him. But it might be Te. How could he know?

Another knock. *What do I do?*

Jack sat for another long minute. It might be the goat-children. It might be Te. But it might be the goats. But it might be Te. Quietly, he got up. A third knock sounded as he crept up to the door and put his ear to it. He couldn't hear the goats' breathing anymore, or their footsteps. "H-hello?" he stammered.

"Ah! Well, of course you're alive," said a voice from outside. "I wouldn't have thought they'd be crawling around here for no reason."

Jack's mind scrambled to place the voice. "Uh . . . Mr. Kitsune?"

"I'm glad to see they didn't get into your brain, Mr. Sprat," said Yun. "If you would be so kind as to open the door, seeing as I am as powerless to do so as they . . ."

Jack placed his fingers on the door handle.

"What do you want?" he asked.

"I require your assistance, young man," said Yun.

"With what?"

"Locating Miss Evangeline, of course. She's in need of our help."

"She's in trouble?"

"She's dead, young man," said Yun.

Jack yanked the door open and stared up into Yun Kitsune's face. He looked utterly exhausted. His hair hung around his head in random strands. His usually perfect jacket was dirty, with scratches all over it. And there was a sadness in his eyes, as if he, too, felt like crying.

"She's . . . she's . . ."

Yun smiled sympathetically and stepped into the safe house, drawing the door shut behind him.

"Dead," he said softly, "but not gone. She sits now in the unfelt wind, undecided between eternity in the domain of some creature like myself, and utter extinction in the void. If she chooses one or the other we will lose her, and yet every moment she fails to choose brings her death anew."

"So she's *not* dead?"

Yun had come in carrying a paper bag, which he set

down on the couch. "Not irrevocably so. Death and re-birth are a dance as old as man's time on this world."

Jack followed him over, his heart thumping painfully. "What do you mean?"

Yun pulled a plastic-wrapped loaf of dark bread and a water bottle from the bag. "Your ancestors practiced rituals of death and rebirth to gain wisdom and under-standing," he said. "It was all very symbolic and mean-ingful. They didn't realize that their customs were based on an older tradition of *actual* death and rebirth."

He passed the water bottle to Jack. "The water of life," Yun said. "In earlier times it might have been kept in a chalice of some sort, but plastic works just as well. Get your shoes on, please. We'll go in a minute."

He settled onto the couch—Jack thought he seemed to be in a lot of pain—and closed his eyes while Jack shoved himself into his shoes and scrambled to tie the laces.

"Are you all right?" Jack asked.

Yun smirked. "Despite our ethereality, we are not above fatigue, young man," said Yun. "The Goat and its ilk are unlike my kind, and resisting them is very taxing."

Jack finished tying his shoes and waited. After a few minutes, Yun took a deep breath and got up.

"All right, let's go," he said. "We're not getting any younger, as they say." Yun picked up the bread and walked over to the door.

"What about the things out there?" Jack asked.

Yun smiled. "I will hold them back from us," he said, "if there are not too many. Bring her coat, please. And yours, too. We have a bit of a walk ahead of us."

Yun opened the door, and Jack flinched at a sudden noseful of dust and animal stink. Jack looked out past Yun's arms, seeing the whole city still in darkness, and shadows that squirmed like living things at the edges of the streetlight.

Yun looked back at him. "You are coming, I hope."

Jack slipped into his own coat. He held Te's in a bundle under his arm. Echoes broke between the buildings—screams, growls, bleats. He looked toward Darktown, where the grotesque alien face still hung in the sky. He immediately shut his eyes.

He took a deep breath and stepped out.

Babu came to with a start.

How long have I been out?

He pressed hands to his skull against a sudden headache.

Kitsune had done something to him: Babu remembered a white light and memories, and he'd felt so happy and peaceful, and relaxed. Now he found himself in a cold, thin alley.

What the hell was he going to do? Things had gone to shit so quickly, and all of his efforts to prevent it hadn't been worth anything. His brother was lying on a hospital bed, maybe dying of a brain hemorrhage right that instant.

And Te. Where was she? Was she still alive?

For that matter, why am I?

He thought back through the fog of the good memories. Yun had rescued him. And the shape-shifter had said something about Te: that she would deliver them to freedom. Yun had known all along that she was one of them—Babu had to beat down the hurt that rose at that—and if he thought she could help, then maybe she could.

And she might be in trouble. Of *course* she was in trouble—everyone was.

Coughing, Babu grunted and cursed his way to his feet. He wiped his lips and his hand came away with smears of blood.

Is that because of the air? he wondered. *Maybe it's finally cancer. Christ.*

What was he going to do?

Lie down and die, that's what. Babu tried to ignore himself.

Yun had said Te would be with Angrel. He'd also said he wouldn't find her there, and for some reason Babu wasn't inclined to doubt that, but it was his only lead. He should follow it up. *Protocol over peril.* The world was ending and he was following a lead. Jesus.

Still coughing, he stumbled out of the alley onto a railed sidewalk, and looked around. He was on the south bank of the river, near downtown where the riverside industrial parks began. Wiping his mouth on his sleeve, he took a moment to orient himself.

Above, the cloud cover still hung thick and black, blocking any sunlight. Across the water, Babu saw flashes of movement, heard animal bleats and yips, screams, things breaking. He couldn't make out anything definite. Closer to the mountains, above the Darktown bowl, something huge moved as if it were looking around. Babu felt such a tightening of his chest, he thought for a moment he might have a heart attack right there. The thing terrified him, even from this far away.

Even if they had everyone—O'Shae and Julia and Rob, Munin and Angrel and even Martin, and King when he was alive—even with *everyone*, they didn't have a prayer.

And Lester. Jesus Christ—Lester.

If he'd been caught over there, by that thing . . . Absurdly, Babu just hoped Lester had been killed by the Maskim before Yun and the Man set that monster loose.

Babu glanced left and right. It looked like the river's south shore was still untouched: streetlights still shone and the smoke seemed to stop halfway over the water. Yun had said the Man would hold them back. Maybe he'd only managed to stop them at the river. And for how much longer?

But the situation wasn't totally lost. Most of St. Ives was on the south shore, including the hospital, thank God. So was Angrel's place. All of St. Ives' citizens might still be helped if Babu could break those weird comas and convince everyone to evacuate. For the people trapped on the north shore—Babu stopped himself there. People always died when one of the prisoners broke out. He was used to it by now, wasn't he?

Too much to think about. Exhaustion in his body took up too much brain space. *Find Te. And to do that, first find Angrel.* Good. He had a plan. That it wasn't much of a plan at all—he just tried to ignore that. He'd have to steal another car. He checked his utility belt, ensuring he still had the tools for the job. He reloaded his gun.

As he held the weapon, something occurred to him: if the Man was busy holding the riverbanks, he wouldn't be around to save Angrel. After Babu got the information he needed, he could shoot her in cold blood, and no one would be able to stop him.

She deserved it. She tried to kill Amhs. There was a line there, something that, despite the vision of his brother bleeding on the street that he couldn't banish from his mind, called out that there was no coming back after it was crossed. He'd spent the last fifteen years trying to save lives. The thought of taking one—that bothered him more than all his recent failures.

But she'll probably attack someone else. Probably.

He set his jaw, ground his teeth a bit, and despite the fire still raging in his lungs, he reached into his pocket and drew out a crushed cigarette. One draw, one more willing step toward his own death, and he'd decided.

It was the right thing to do.

But first, he'd make her tell him where Te was—by any means necessary. Whatever happened to his own conscience was nothing a full-blown case of terminal cancer couldn't fix in time.

He turned and headed for the street.

Protocol over personal things.

When I open my eyes, I am in darkness again. The room is silent with the absence of televisions and radios. Only the breathing of my tired, old companion fills the space.

I abhor silence, so I fill it with laughter, gleeful and uninhibited. I am light as an ember on the wind.

I remember who I was, who I *am*. I am a goddess of old Babylon. I am the godmaker. I am the queen of the dead.

I take my nails and scratch lines into my skin and exult—the pain is only human pain, no more hurtful to me than the touch of the air; the skin is only animal skin, as if I were wearing the pelt of something dead and preserved. It's no longer a part of me, but a mask I wear and discard at my choosing. It is as it should be.

I summon from inside me the changing power of my divine heritage, the potency of that unknown Old Country beast that spawned me in a human womb. Through it, I perceive mundane reality as the papier-mâché illusion that it is. My human eyes cannot see my hand as I raise it, but I ignore them, and I look instead through a mental connection to bones and proteins and nerve endings. I shape the flesh there, simple as a thought, and laugh as my human nails blacken and grow into spines, the mirror of my preferred shape.

My companion moans. "It's too late, isn't it?"

The smile that spreads my mortal features is finally my own. "Oh, yes, creature of flesh."

I rise, my body flowing after me like a piece of silk, and place my sharpened nails on his throat.

"He's laughing at me," the man says. "Oh, dear Lord, I'm sorry for wasting this life you gave me."

"Kent Allard." I know his name as surely as I smell the anguish in his soul. "You don't want to die, do you Kent? You certainly don't want to die a failure."

The man's eyes fixate on nothing in the dark. "I did my best, Lord. I tried to make it right."

"I can keep you from your Christian hell, Kent," I say. "Become mine, and I will save you from the true death."

"Hell's more than I deserve," he says. "I just . . . I didn't know what I should do."

"Are you refusing me?"

"I'm tired of being afraid to die."

"Well," I say, "we'll see if you feel differently when you're gazing into the abyss."

The old man coughs. "What about *him*?" he says. "He's my shadow, or he was. What happens to him when I go?"

I drive one nail deep into his throat, and am pleased at the sound he makes. "I no longer care," I whisper. "I don't need him anymore."

I let him take a long time to die. When his last breath hisses away, I wait. I watch as his soul tumbles out into the winds of the afterlife, watch as the black lightning of the void strikes it, savages it, strips it layer by layer of the personality that a long life has wound tight around it, and then drags it to the edge of nothingness.

And at that last moment I hear him cry out for me.

So easy. When I let them see what they're unable to give up, they fly back to me like a child to its mother. It is ever the same.

I scoop him from the edge of the abyss and pitch him screaming into my own realm, where my hordes will strip off his skin and burn him in sacrifice to me, and make him one of their own. I decide that Allard will be the first of many, for there is always someone dying in the human world, and my faithful legions have been without new company for far too long.

I pluck each of the ten locks off his door and haul it open, welcoming the bite of the dry atmosphere. The dark of night pleases me. I step out onto Allard's creaking staircase and raise my nails to the sky and to a world of weak people waiting for the caress of my clawed hands.

For the first time in a long, long time, it is good to be alive.

And I am dimly aware that, halfway across the city, a man who is only half a soul, now deprived of the human connection that gave him existence, sinks onto the mud of the riverbank, and falters.

Chapter 21

What the Thunder Said

There was no water but only rock.

White in the sky and in the earth. Mountains on the plain: carious teeth without slaver.

She gripped the rock and it turned to powder between her fingers.

If there were the sound of water only . . .

Holes tore into the sky, jagged and long, like black lightning. White storm clouds, devoid of moisture, stirred above, impatient. From outside the white: eyes watching, cold and ancient, vast and uncaring. A decision, made, rippled through the universe: a judgment passed.

The black lightning struck down, through her and into the dry earth. The white tore. She split, as a burst sapling, and the lightning carried splinters through the white, to spaces other. She gripped the rock and it turned to powder in her fingers.

Then spoke the thunder:

Damyata.

She could not answer.

Chapter 22

Ninghizzidha No More

Jack stepped over a tuft of grass, around a dry stem of sagebrush, onto another patch of parched soil. "Why's this water so heavy?" he said.

Yun smiled. "It is not the water, but the gravity of your mythos and history," he said. "This has been done only a handful of times, but nevertheless it weighs heavily on your people's collective unconscious."

Yun had led them up into the hills south of town, up the dirt roads and across the hillsides still covered in dead, dry grass from the summer. They'd been walking a long time, but Jack was sure it wasn't long enough to be all the way up here. He turned and looked back at the city. The river was a distinct black line, cutting the valley in two. North of the river were darkness and the flickering of small fires and electric sparks, and in the sky across the valley hung the horrid shape of the Goat, a shadow against the far mountains that moved in terrifying and inhuman ways. The south side of the river looked like cities always do at night: strings of lights crossing and crisscrossing the valley. It was like having stars on the ground to replace what should have been in the sky.

"Mr. Kitsune," he began tentatively, "are my parents okay?"

Yun raised an eyebrow. "That depends on where they live, I suppose."

"Brightontown."

"That's south of the river," said Yun. "So they are likely merely comatose with small, insubstantial creatures feeding on their dreams."

"Oh," said Jack. "Can I *wish* that they'll be okay? I'm worried about them."

Yun looked tired. "Please save your wishes for the ones that need them, young man."

"All right."

They continued to climb. The water bottle got heavier with every step, until Jack was carrying it with both arms, propped against his stomach. They crested a bit of a rise and Yun nodded with satisfaction. Jack followed him up and gasped.

Before them stretched a bowl in the hillside filled with vegetation as lush and green as a country garden. Small poplar trees ringed the bowl in a circle, with bushes and flowers growing from their shade, and well-trimmed green grass stretching between. Past these, in the center of the bowl, there was a perfect circle, in which the ground was just like the hillside—cracked and dry, covered with orange needles and pinecones. In the center of that circle stood an old, dead pine. At the base of that tree, Jack saw a pale body stretched on the ground, motionless. It was Te.

Much as he strained to run straight down, he hesitated. At the edge of the dead circle, between two colorful bushes, crouched a silver creature, picking at a flower with its talons and flexing its great wings.

Bird.

Jack stood frozen. Yun leaned down and whispered in his ear.

"Whom is your wish for now, young man?"

"I . . ."

Despite everything he'd learned about Bird's kind, Jack found he still liked her. Intellectually, he now knew that it was probably a result of the intoxicating scent she put out, but he still found it hard to ignore.

"Can you get her to leave?" he asked Yun Kitsune.

"Our kind do not fight each other as yours do," said Yun. "If she and I came into conflict, you would likely not survive it."

"Then what do I do?"

Yun smiled. "What indeed?"

Jack got a queasy feeling in his stomach. He waited a long time for it to go away. Te was down there. His glasses bent his peripheral vision and gave him double vision sometimes, but still, he was certain it was her—and she needed his help.

He started walking down. He was quiet, and thought for a moment that maybe Bird wouldn't hear him, but by the time he was halfway down, Bird's face came up.

"Hello, child," said the voice that was both heavy and light, airy and substantial. "It pleases me to see you again."

"Hi," said Jack. "You look . . . better."

Bird smiled. Her face, surrounded by feathers, was plain and flawless. "The air is wonderful, and the freedom, too. They are not the terror winds of the Andes, but they have been good for me," she said. Her avian eyes flicked over him up and down. "Let me see you."

Jack set down the water bottle and Te's jacket. He approached. Bird's wonderful scent surrounded him and filled his mind with pink thoughts. Bird slid her talons over his face, his chest and arms, his fingers, gentle as could be.

"Did you miss me?" Bird asked.

"Sure."

"Why didn't you come to see me again? Others came to see me."

Jack shrugged. "You were a bad guy."

Bird smiled and her teeth showed. "Am I?"

Jack fumbled through a haze rising in his mind. He powerfully didn't want to hurt her feelings. "Well, you eat people."

"Only bits," she said. "And only what I'm given."

"Can I get by?" Jack asked.

Bird's eyes narrowed and she glanced over her shoulder at Te's body. Te was lying on her side, naked and covered in dirt and stains, facing away from them.

Bird's head snapped back. "The binder. She is ugly and she is dead."

"She's my friend."

Bird flapped her wings, sending a new wave of pink dust into Jack's face.

"*You* are the beautiful one here, child," she said. "Show me your wonderful eyes."

The mist slipped into Jack's lungs. For a moment, his thoughts went entirely pink and he felt very happy. He couldn't think of anything but the pink—how soft it was, how marvelous. Then he had his glasses in his hand, and Bird was touching his face.

"May I have them?" Bird was saying. "They are so beautiful."

Jack coughed. "I need to get by."

"But I like them so. They shine."

"I just need them right now. Can I get by, please?"

"They are of the most striking blue. Will you give them to me?"

"If I give you *one* of them, will you let me by?" The words had just come out—a pink thought given voice. It took a moment before Jack fully realized what he'd said, but he held his tongue when, through the blur of his imperfect vision, he thought he could see Bird considering.

"Perhaps later," she ventured, "you would give me the other?"

"Maybe," said Jack, and meant it.

"Then I will take the right, my pretty boy," she said, "and it will make me very happy."

He felt the talons of one claw slide up around his eye.

He realized he was shaking. "Will it hurt?"

"No, child," said Bird. "It will be wonderful."

And it was. The talons sank deep into him, sliding past the skin and bones as if his face were made of Silly Putty. The sensation was wonderful. The sharp awareness of the spaces inside his head was wonderful. When the talons pulled back, cradling Jack's eye, the hole left behind was wonderful, like a stuffy room given a change of air.

Hands shaking, Jack put his glasses back on in time to watch Bird put her palms to her mouth and suck back his eye. She swallowed it whole, and spread her wings with a deep and loud sigh of pleasure.

"You are a treasure," she said. "You are worth savoring." She flapped her wings and lifted herself, then settled several paces to the left.

Jack blinked his one remaining eye, looking around, testing it out. It seemed okay, except he couldn't see past his nose to his right side. The pink thoughts started to clear, and other things started to creep in.

A question: did he really just give his eye away?

And then a host of others: would he still be able to walk straight? Would he lose his depth perception? It occurred to him, absurdly, that his eye would never grow back. What had he just done?

Footfalls on the grass brought him around. He turned to see Yun coming down the hill. Yun nodded graciously to Bird.

"I thought it was you," said Bird, already picking at another flower. "You are very cruel."

Yun placed a hand over his heart. "Ah, you wound me deeply, *fair* lady," he said.

"I taste the air again," said Bird, pointing one wing toward the city, "just to die in the mouth of the Void-dweller."

"We'll see what we can do about that," said Yun, with a wink. He approached Jack and stood with him on the edge of the circle. Jack turned back to look at Te.

"It's really her," he said.

"Yes, it is."

"She's really dead."

"Yes, indeed."

Jack blinked and a tear rolled down just one cheek.

"What do we do?"

Yun pointed to the water bottle.

"Sprinkle it on her sixty times. I shall do the same with the food of life." He held up the dark bread. "And then, if she chooses and if she is not already lost, she will come back to us."

Jack nodded.

"In we go, then."

Jack stepped into the circle. He expected to see Yun beside him, but when he turned, there was only a small yellow and white fox, holding the platic bag containing the food of life in its teeth.

"Mr. Kitsune?"

The fox looked up at him, flicked its ears, and trotted forward, dragging the bag and waving a bouquet of many tails behind him. Jack followed. Together, they knelt beside Te's body.

She'd been beaten, he could see. She was covered in bruises and scrapes, and there were places where it looked like her skin had split from being pulled. There was dirt and dried blood all over her, and a black wound around her ribs which he didn't look too closely at. Swallowing hard, Jack touched her shoulder—she was cold—and rolled her over.

Her eyes were empty, open and staring. Her face was a web of bruises and cuts. She had purple welts on her hips and ribs, bruises on her stomach and thighs. Above her right breast, there was a hole to match the one on her back, where something had been driven through her.

More tears ran down his left cheek. He thought he should be angry, or grossed out, or that he should react somehow, but all he felt was sadness, something coming from deep in him, and pushing all the other things aside.

After a minute, a small, wet nose nudged his hand. Jack set down Te's coat and unscrewed the water bottle. "So do I just . . . ?" He poured some water on his hand and splashed it across Te's chest. He looked to the fox for confirmation, but the fox did nothing. It merely watched him, its nine tails waving slowly.

"Am I supposed to cover her with it?" Jack asked. "Or, you know, just, it doesn't matter?"

The fox didn't seem likely to answer, so Jack went on sprinkling in the same fashion. Sixty times—he counted out loud to be sure.

When he was done, Te's skin glistened with the water. It wasn't enough to clean her off.

After that, Kitsune nosed him out of the way, dragged the plastic bag close to Te's body, and tore through it with his teeth. He clawed the loaf of bread apart with his front paws and then flicked crumbs of it onto Te's stomach with quick digging motions. He did it sixty times.

Then the fox led the way outside the circle. The instant he stepped from the dry ground and dead pine needles to the lush grass, he was Yun Kitsune again, his suit and hair much improved.

"Bravo, lad. You did just fine," he said, pulling a cane from the air and leaning on it.

Jack stood beside him, staring in at Te's unmoving form.

"What happens now?"

"Now," said Yun, "she may return to her body if she chooses."

"Can't you make her come back, sir?" Jack felt himself flush at Yun's indulgent expression.

"Some wishes I can fulfill," he said. "With others, I can only create an opportunity. I can give my subjects motivation and means, but I cannot make them *do* anything." He laughed softly to himself, a rough, mirthless laugh. "That was something I certainly wish I'd known when I shaped myself to be as I am."

"So what do we do?"

"Wait," said Yun.

So Jack sat down in the grass and waited.

Bird flapped across the garden, watching.

The Man in the Empty Chair is dying. I know it. I have half of his soul in my kingdom.

The Goat withers him, devouring him as inexorably as the turning of the universe, as inevitably as the eddies of gravity in the void that is its natural home. I almost pity him, the nameless Man, not even half a human being, who had so manipulated and strived to be more, only to miscalculate so drastically.

He thought I was *his*, like that woman Julia who belonged to the Warden. He thought I would remain his after he revived me to my former self. He thought to have a goddess as his lapdog.

I have a sudden urge to look on him and laugh. In an instant, I am at the river, my essence shearing through subterranean rock. Soil and bedrock slide past my skin as I move, no more viscous than thin oil. It is heaven to become myself again, a creature of pure idea, made real through genesis, through my arbitrary self-definition of long ago. I am queen of the underworld; the earth and the dark places beneath it are my realm. I break the surface as I approach the riverbank, splitting through the pipes, wires, and concrete of man's modern world.

And I see it—the goat, the beast from behind the stars. It hangs, magnificent, between the clouds and the earth, its hundred eyes all-seeing, its single, circular maw all-devouring. It is a creature of hideous natural beauty, warped and shaped by whatever forces determine such things in the void. Parasite spirits crawl upon its skin, dying and being born in its mouth, thinking only of their own hunger and ignorant of the majesty of their mother-monster. It is a magnificent sight. I can almost love it, as one loves an abstract concept like truth or faith.

My memories returned to me, I remember that it was I who brought it to Earth. I opened a hole from my underworld into the void. I reached out to it with human powers of calling inherited from my sow mother. I touched it with the bare stuff of my existence, a talent the heritage of my Old Country sire. It had a ferocious strength to it, something other than intellect, other than instinct, other than inspiration. It was, at its core, something I could not understand, something wide as the empty span of the universe. But I called to it and it came, out upon the surface of the human world.

I still remember fondly how the demons of the earth fled from it into their holes, how the creatures of the Old Country fought it and lost, how that great devouring maw had swallowed entire continents, oceans, and ice caps. My underworld swelled with its victims, eager to be mine if I could save them from the hunger of that abyss given form.

And now it is free again, and once more my caverns will fill with the screams of the dead.

I watch the river churn, reacting to the violent, invisible energies crushing one another above it. Unfettered by normal human doubt, the Man in the Empty Chair has become a master of humanity's Old Powers, but those abilities are only powers of struggle and conflict, and the Goat is above such things. It simply breathes, and those who defy it creep closer to their deaths with each exhalation. It does not struggle and thus it cannot be opposed. I cannot see the Man with my human eyes, but I picture him in my mind, an impotent Canute, standing on the beach and commanding the tide not to rise.

When he dies, I will not offer him sanctuary. It is clear to me now that he could have restored me at any time, and chose not to.

I laugh with the cackle of an old crone, with the twitter of a tiny girl, with the bitter grunt of a hard-lived woman. These are the voices of the hundreds of faces I have worn, and I laugh until, one by one, they crack and crumble and vanish from my tone. When my laughter at last fades, it is the mirth of an immortal, which defies description.

The sound has enraged the goat's children. They surge against the resisting river in a wave of horn and hair and malformed limb. They slaver and drool. They soil the waters with their touch and their excretions. Most of them break free of the bank, and stand now one yard into the river shallows. I feel the Man straining—not straining to hold them back, but rather to hold to his very existence, to distract himself from the reality that he is but the shadow of a dead thing—to fool himself into continuing to exist. He is not doing well. When the goats reach the opposite shore, expecting soft flesh to tear, they will instead find nothing where their opponent was standing—not even footprints.

I want to see it happen. I ply my imagination and open the doors to the Old Powers of humankind. The Sight comes to me without resistance, exactly as it used to. I look forward in time, searching the images for confirmation of the Man's destruction, of my reign in hell and the smoking ruin the Goat will leave of the earth.

I find something entirely unexpected, but it makes me smile nonetheless:

Babu Cherian is coming to kill me.

He stood on this very spot, not half an hour ago. He intends to track me to my shop and execute me, thinking himself noble, knowing himself foul. He doesn't suspect what I really am. He has no idea.

I slide my talons against themselves, listening to the whisper-scrapes, and wonder whether Babu will beg for me to save him from the nothingness, after I stab him through the eyes. It would be a wonderful way to start my renewed existence.

He has revenge's fury in his chest, and such a will to the task, I simply cannot disappoint him. The look on his face alone will be worth the trip. I whisper to the stone and the earth opens, and swallows me down.

His is a soul I *want*. I will stake him beside Robert Evangeline in my withered garden, and the sight of him will give me pleasure for many years to come. Tending my kingdom can wait a little longer. I am a goddess of death, and death is nothing, if not patient.

Chapter 23

Greatly Exaggerated

Te Evangeline tumbled in the in-between places.

She had escaped the black lightning. She couldn't remember how. It had shown her the abyss and she had turned away, terrified. Now she swam in a field of images that screamed in her ears and burned her eyes, though she had neither.

She saw the Earth below her, exactly as a hundred space shuttle pictures had burned it into her brain, and the images were a cloud around it. They were the memories of the earth: the unordered, uncensored history of every human mind alive in the world.

It was so *loud*.

And in it, voices. Dozens of unseen personalities spoke directly to her, their words slurring into waves of indistinct noise. They offered her things, speaking to her as friends, as lovers, as confidants, and authority figures. They wanted her. Each and every one offered to save her from the abyss, if she would be theirs.

She didn't know what to do. She didn't remember her name. She was like a house of cards in the process of falling—motion without form.

She was not the same thing or the same person from one instant to the next. The images slipped through her: milliseconds of lives lived, of happiness and misery, of boredom and stress and thrill. As they flew past, projecting into the void, they swallowed her, consuming her totally in the gap between instants, subsuming her into them, then releasing her in the next abstract pulse of time. She was nothing and no one and everything and everyone. She did not exist. She was everywhere.

She did not remember her name.

It's Te. Te Evangeline, she said.

It's Te. Te Evangeline, she said.

She turned—and turned—and was looking at herself.

She saw her body, a pale, thin sculpture of animal matter patterned with freckles and lines and too-prominent veins.

She saw her body, a blazing, shapely being of light, perfectly proportioned, smoothed of detail, translucent against the curve of the Earth.

I'm Te, she said.

So am I, she answered.

She looked at herself and she looked at herself, hanging in the orbit of the world with memories passing through her, and her.

But who am I? she asked. *What am I?*

I'm a binder, she answered. *I lock things away.*

I'm a skeleton key, she answered. *I set things free.*

I'm a woman. I might be dead.

I'm a figment of my own imagination. I know I'm alive.

I've had my genesis. I've found my definition. I can see the borders of the Old Country, and I know that past those borders is my home.

I know my home is the Earth. I have a one-room apartment in a fifty-year-old house in a welfare neighborhood.

I know two things.

I know two things.

I'm a personality, a construct of desires and conceits held together by its own tension.

I'm an idea, a concept with a million differing projections, all the same, like faces in opposing mirrors.

I'm a human woman.

I am Freedom.

She looked at herself, and looked at herself, and saw her faces fall, saw tears fall from her eyes, and starlight fall from her eyes, and she reached out one hand, and one hand, and her fingers touched.

I love you.

I love you, too.

And she was falling.

And falling.

And falling.

She blinked.

Jack snatched Yun's sleeve.

"Look!"

As Yun turned, Jack's gaze flew back to Te. Her eyes hung open as before, staring.

"But . . ." Jack swallowed hard. "I thought I saw . . ."

"You did," said the Kitsune.

Jack knelt down to bring himself closer to Te's level. He was still just outside the circle, and with one eye it was really hard to see properly through his thick lenses. He squinted hard.

She blinked again.

"There!" he cried, and pointed. Jack felt Yun's hand on his shoulder just as he was about to run in.

"Best give it a minute," said Yun.

Trembling, Jack did as he was told. He watched Te closely, watching little twitches of her muscles, jerks of her head. It made him feel sick because she didn't look alive at all. But she was moving. Suddenly, she drew in a huge breath of air, and Jack heard a wet crack from her torso. He tried to run in, but again Yun's hand held him back.

Te blinked again, and this time her eyes came into focus, darting around from direction to direction. Then she clutched her hair and screamed. She fell into a fit, kicking, rolling, scratching at the ground, all the time shrieking. Jack felt his insides tearing up.

"Can't I just . . ."

"Wait," said Yun. His fingers dug hard into Jack's shoulder. Jack wrapped his fingers into the grass, and waited. The fit went on until Te's hands came away with two tufts of her hair, and then she abruptly fell still.

They waited two eternal minutes.

Te burst into light, a light so intense Jack had to avert his stinging eye. When he looked back, it was to see the glowing woman—Te's other self—rising up from the ground as if floating in water, and settling gently upright, balanced on her toes.

The glowing woman let out a long and happy sigh. Her luminous eyes opened, and flashed over Jack, the light splaying as it refracted through his thick lenses. She began to approach, with each step sending up little pin-pricks of light, like fireflies, that circled around her and then passed back into her skin.

"Oh, Jack," she said, and at that instant Jack was suddenly overcome by a peace unlike any he had ever felt. His insides emptied of every worry, tension, and thought, and such warmth filled him that he cried.

She touched him on the cheek—her touch like a kiss, like a promise that everything really *was* worthwhile—and ran her fingers to the edge of his empty eye socket, lingering there. "Oh, what did you do to yourself?"

He shut his eye. He pulled away, wiping furiously at his face. "I love you," he said.

Then she was falling on him—not the glowing woman, but a body of sweat and flesh. He tried to catch her, but she was heavy, and they both ended up sprawled in the flowers.

Te coughed and made several attempts to swallow. She was holding her stomach. Acutely aware of her naked skin, Jack pulled himself out from under her and tried to roll her over so she was comfortable. She was still covered with dirt and blood, but her scratches were gone, and so was the hole in her chest. And there were her breasts, heaving as she gulped in air, and there were her thighs, clenching together as she fought whatever pain was in her stomach. Jack turned away, his face burning. A second later, he remembered he'd brought her jacket and laid it over her.

Her lips smacked open.

"Sorry," she muttered. "Dizzy."

She peeled her eyes open with definite effort.

"It's dark," she said.

Yun knelt down beside her, smiling with something

like pride. "We are still without sun," he said. "Are you cold?"

She nodded, still breathing hard.

"But you're not shivering," said Yun.

Tears slid from her eyes.

"No."

Yun nodded. "That's good."

Te clawed at her arms. "I feel . . . ," she began. "It doesn't mean anything . . . All those things I am . . . and . . ."

Jack folded his hands in his lap and watched her as tears dribbled down her face.

"I'm nothing. In me—Yun—there's no . . . ," she said. "I don't have to . . . Am I real? Am I . . ."

Yun nodded.

Te rolled her head back and pleaded at the sky. "There's nothing left," she sobbed, and closed her eyes. Each breath came deeper until her shoulders relaxed.

Jack let his head fall. She was okay. That was what was important, right? She was just a bit overwhelmed right now. That was why she hadn't looked at him, hadn't talked to him, since she became herself again. That was okay. She'd just been through a lot and—

"Bird!"

Te shoved Jack and Yun aside and bolted up. Jack, caught totally off balance, fell back onto his butt just as his ears filled with the ripple of feathers cutting the air. Bird's black talons sliced into the grasses, turning up the dry, ruined soil beneath.

"Binder," Bird hissed.

With one hand, Te pressed her coat against her chest, covering herself. She held the other forward, palm out.

Yun stood just beside her, arms crossed, one eyebrow raised.

Bird drew back her talons, her raptor's eyes fixed on Te, her whole body coiled over two bent legs. Bird stretched her wings out. They were at least twenty feet across.

Jack threw out his hand. "Bird, wait."

"The beautiful boy begs your life," said Bird. "He knows I will destroy you."

A grimace crossed Te's face. "Oh, Bird. Please don't."

"No human death for you," said Bird. "No more. Your essence is all that is left to you, and that will be my meal here."

Jack struggled to his feet. "I'll give you my other eye! Just don't hurt her."

No one seemed to hear him. Yun quietly shut his eyes and raised one hand to shield his face. Te quivered and looked about to cry.

"Oh, Bird."

Bird drew her wings back, pinning them against her flanks so that the ends trailed in the grass. Her legs tensed.

Jack threw himself into Bird from the side. As his fingers filled with feathers and his nose with pink dust, Bird let out a harrowing owl cry and slammed him in the temple with the bones of one wing. With his head spinning, with his body dropping to the ground, Jack saw a flash in his mind, surging fire tearing through fields of wheat, and heard three separate voices cry out in pain.

When Te cracked open the mental door, the fire exploded out of her. She wasn't ready for it. She wasn't ready for the thousands of human voices that followed it, the voices of those people over the generations who had made pain and subjugation their life's work. The fire was their ocean, the sum of all the moments of horror committed in their lifetimes, just as the binder's power was the sum of all the moments of forgiveness and understanding.

She knew this. She thought she could handle it.

What tore out of her were the hungry ghosts of the earth, alive and aware, maddened by millennia of being called upon to scathe the enemies of mankind. They were the fire, its substance, and its purpose. Visions of the terrifying history of human atrocity tore through her, reaching two meters out across the grass and into the body of Bird, who shrieked and lashed out, and finally toppled, thrashing, to the ground. Te felt Bird's pain carried back along the channel of empathy she shared with all her mother's relatives. She felt Yun as well, gasping and shuddering as the spirits in the fire sought him out and sank their teeth and nails into his soul and substance.

But Te kept the mental door open. She felt Bird weakening, shriveling up, screaming in fright against the reality of the next few seconds. Te felt it, every instant of it, every nuance of Bird's thought and feeling. She felt it so perfectly, it would have been impossible to fool herself as to the magnitude of Bird's pain.

Oh, Bird. For this monster of the Old Country, this predator that ate human beings piece by piece, Te could only feel sorrow.

Bird broke. Deep within her, past her physical form, past the construct of her personality and the stream of animating energy that made her alive, her essence shattered. Her purpose, her definition, were gone.

With her brain stinging, Te hauled back the fire. She shoved it back behind the mental door and closed it out. The memories of rage went not quietly, scraping at her nerves as she banished them.

Cold earth struck her knees as she faded down. In front of her lay Jack, clutching the side of his head and in obvious pain. To her right lay Yun, just a fox now, twitching where he lay in the flowers. Ahead of her, Bird lay smoldering on the grass, the slow breeze peeling layer after layer of feathers from her wings and spinning them off into the hills.

I can't just put her back in a cage.

Her father would have. He'd done it any number of times, and if he were alive, he would do it again. But Rob Evangeline didn't care about creatures like Bird. He couldn't. They were the enemies of his species and of his only daughter. He couldn't understand what it felt like, to have suppression turned on you, to have Ahmadou Cherian's dead eyes burning into you and know that everything you thought of as yourself was about to come apart in ashes. He probably did it to his own wife—savaged her, then married her, to keep her from threatening his world.

I'm sorry, Dad. I just can't.

She felt other voices now, others from the Old Country, calling out from their prisons all over the world, deep under the seas or buried in the deserts, or abandoned in the back alleys of cities. They were faint, quiet, some sad, some frustrated, some apathetic—all defeated, all made less by the actions of a man like her father. They were her kin. They were her family, and this skin she wore was just an old habit.

Bird wimpered, her pink, fleshy skin beneath bubbling and boiling away, her feathers almost gone. Poor bird—not woman or man, not human or animal, not artist, and not barbarian. Caught in a moment of indecision at the instant she stepped through from the Old Country, she had become both and neither of so many things—not a synergy, but a contradiction. Te cried for her, then set her free.

A gust of wind rattled them all on the hillside, and carried away the last of Bird's remains. Instantly, the grass and the flowers began to die.

"Are you okay?"

It was Jack, kneeling in front of her, one hand on the left side of his head, and on the right side, a hole dribbling blood.

"Am *I* okay? Jesus." She reached out with her free arm and hugged him close. "I'm so sorry, Jack."

He hugged her back. "It didn't hurt." They drew apart awkwardly. While Jack averted his eyes—his *eye*—Te took a moment to put her coat on properly and zip it up. It was a longer coat, and it covered her well enough. She badly wanted some clothes, though.

Yun groaned. Te turned, to see him sprawled on the ground, back to his human self.

"Once, in China," he said, "someone caught me, skinned me, and roasted me on a spit."

"Sorry." She reached down and helped him sit upright.

"Not at all, Miss Evangeline." He wiped some dirt from his porcelain cheeks and smiled. "Humility is such a rare treat among my kind. Or *our* kind, I suppose."

"What did you do with Bird?" Jack asked.

"I let her go," said Te. "I bound her into the wind."

Jack looked up. "She'd like that, I think."

"I hope so," Te said. She listened to the whispers inside her, trying to hear Bird through the ties of empathy that linked her with her fellow monsters. She caught a twitter of motion, an unconscious perception of the pressure of wind passing by. That was all. It faded away beneath the others, raging in their cages or mourning their broken souls.

She had broken two of them, now. Why did that leave her with such regret? They really *were* monsters. They killed and ate human beings. And there were others, like her aunts, who got off by sucking the life out of people, and for all Te knew, these might be the *least* dangerous. But she could *hear* them suffering. She could feel what they felt. She was in prison *with* them, denied expression, denied definition, made into something less than real. They were innocents condemned. And they were monsters.

And Te Evangeline was both.

I can't leave them like that.

"Miss Evangeline." Yun's voice sounded, drawing her back. He lifted himself and knelt by her side. "Respectfully," he said, "our work is not done."

Te nodded. She glanced up to where, on the other side of the valley, the Goat's silhouette blocked the far hills. "How long?"

"Hours," said Yun. "It is the Man in the Empty Chair who holds them back. He is no match for them."

"Was it you?" she asked.

"Yes."

"Why?"

"Because without the sight of them in your mind, you would not have chosen your transfiguration," Yun said. "Your mother and her sisters tried for years to force you to the point of death, so that you could choose to be whole."

Te nodded. The memories stung.

"I first saw you when you were twelve years old," Yun said. "I watched you tossing and turning from your windowsill, and I knew there was already too much horror in your life for ordinary death to wake you."

Te's eyes found the boiling clouds. "So you did *this*." She gestured to the valley. "All of this."

"Yes."

"Because you needed me to shut down St. Ives."

"Yes."

"Because you wanted to use me."

Yun smiled. "Yes, indeed."

Te punched him in the jaw. He staggered back, laughing, and Te ignored him.

"Jack." She held her arm out. He helped her to stand. "Do we have a car?"

"We walked here," said Jack.

"Then we'll walk back," she said. She nodded up the hill and Jack helped her to walk. Her arms and legs felt like wood.

Jack looked back. "What about him?"

"He's coming," said Te. "Aren't you?"

"I am your servant, as ever I was," came the reply.

"Good."

"What are we gonna do?" Jack asked. Te met his worried eye. *You're going to run and hide*, she thought. *You're going to stay safe.* She bit her lip. She couldn't ask that of him. She knew he would give anything for her;

that made her feel loved and it made her sick. He was with her to the end.

"Get a team together," Te said finally. "Make a plan. Then we go and lock that thing up."

And then . . . Te turned to the whispers inside her. *Then I set them free.*

Chapter 24

The Straw and the Grasses

Babu lit his fifth cigarette of the hour. The smoke curled around when he blew out his first lungful, adding to the thick atmosphere of the car's interior. Across the street, Angrel's house sat in mute darkness.

Babu was no stranger to stakeouts. He'd spent a lot of good years camped out in cars, waiting for the cheating husband or runaway kid to reveal himself, though usually the car wasn't quite as nice, and usually he made sure to have a box of pasta or Chinese noodles with him. If she wasn't home yet, he would just wait, and either she would show or the world would come to an end. Either way, there was nothing better to do right then.

His pistol sat on the seat beside him, in easy reach. *Interrogation first*, he reminded himself. *Top priority is finding Te.* Or maybe if Angrel could lead him to Yun, that would be just as good.

Except he knew where Yun would be right now, and if he really wanted to find Te that badly, he'd be up at the Sacred Grove talking to the shape-shifter.

Fine. So he would *rather* be here. He'd *rather* get revenge for Ahmadou, and for Rob—he was sure now that she was in on Rob's death—and probably King's as well. He'd never really answered the question of how an otherwise healthy forty-year-old man had suddenly contracted fatal heart disease without showing any preliminary symptoms.

He ground the cigarette out, half finished. He lit another. *I'm never gonna quit these things.*

He needed some clarity now, not doubts. If he was going to do this, he had to be sure. He could doubt after, but in the moment, he couldn't hesitate.

A light came on downstairs, bleeding through the edges of the posters that covered the door. Time. He swept up the gun and tucked it in his belt holster, safety off. He cracked the car door, stubbed out his cigarette, half finished, and got out. Last time he'd been here, there had been puddles three inches deep; now, the street was desert-dry, with dust gathered against the curbs.

He descended Angrel's stairs and quietly tried the knob. Unlocked. Good.

Adrenaline hit him and he went through, shoulder first. The gun came out. He took stock: store normal; big tear in the carpet, and cracks in the floor underneath—he ignored it; lights on in the séance-room; white dreadlocks, through the bead curtain, facing away. Five huge strides took him through, and he pressed the gun's muzzle to the back of her head.

"Te," he said. "Where is she?"

Angrel silently laid a card on the table where she had a spread already half done. Babu leaned into the gun.

"Where is she?"

Angrel slipped a card into her hand. She raised it up so that Babu could read it: the eight of swords.

"Where *is* she?" Angrel echoed. The card caught fire

and burned to cinders in seconds. Babu backed off an inch.

"What does that mean?" he growled.

"I see a girl walking a road," Angrel said. "The road is built by others and others hold the key to its turns; yet she is curious. She wants answers."

There was something off with the voice: it was too loud and full for the small room. Babu backed off a step as Angrel rose.

"Convinced by the voices of her enemies, the girl leaves herself vulnerable," said Angrel. "And so she is murdered."

Babu's chest tightened. He fought back a sudden urge to cough. "What?"

"She's dead, Babu."

Then he did cough. A pain stabbed him from inside his chest and his entire body broke out in a hot sweat. He gritted his teeth to hold the gun steady. "You . . . ?"

Angrel raised one slim white hand. The nails were black needles, fully two feet long. They emitted faint tones as Angrel scraped them against one another. She smiled coyly over her shoulder. "Who else?"

Babu stumbled as the pain leapt from his chest into his left arm. *Breathe, man. Get control.*

"I wanted her to be mine, Babu," said Angrel. "But she got away from me."

She strode into the sweep of his arms. Babu jerked back, trying to hold the gun on her, fighting the fading strength in his arm.

"Rob . . . You . . ." He couldn't finish. As he gasped for breath, his lungs curdled with the familiar rattle of smoker's phlegm, and a coughing fit drove him back against the wall.

"Yes, I did," Angrel said, advancing on him with small, deliberate steps. "And I thought I loved him. Can you believe that? I cried for him."

Babu looked into her smiling, hollow face and saw no regret, no hesitation, only a fire of vitality that lit her skin from beneath.

"Who'll cry for you, Babu?" she said. "Certainly not Rob's little girl. What must she think of you now? Certainly not that retarded brother of yours. He won't . . ."

Babu shot her in the forehead.

The kickback tore the gun from his weakening fingers. His legs shivered and he faded to the floor, where he pitched over and coughed until black fluid and blood dripped from his lips onto the carpet. His heart clenched and quivered. His chest burned and his fingers shook. He pressed hard on his sternum, trying to stop the coughing. If he could just get one full breath . . .

The legs of Angrel's séance table swam in his vision. This wasn't what he'd thought. He was supposed to die of cancer, alone in some hospital—not like this.

Finally, he managed to suck in a breath without coughing it back out. His heart beat once, painfully and hard, then fell into a jerking rhythm.

"Thank God," he muttered. He wiped his lips on the back of his hand, exhaled, and sat back against the wall.

Angrel's nails punctured his stomach.

"A thousand deaths, Babu," she hissed. Face inches from his, she crouched above him, the bullet hole above her eye streaming blood. With each word, blood spattered from her lips and teeth. "Deaths by fire and sword and cold. Deaths by being drowned in a canvas sack. I *am* Death, Babu. Can *you* kill Death?"

Each nail stung where it penetrated his skin. Past

that he felt nothing but a sudden swelling sickness and a bloating feeling as if his insides were pushing out.

"You're mine, Cherian," she said. "When you see the abyss open for you, when the black lightning takes you—remember me. Remember your place in my garden."

Angrel ripped her nails out. Babu gagged on blood filling his throat and tried to press one hand over the bubbling wounds.

"This body is a shell, Babu," she said. "When the Goat breaks loose, I'll be underground, waiting for you." Through a fog of pain, Babu saw her muscles tense up. "You'll be . . . I'll—"

Her eyes glassed over. She fell dead to the floor.

Blood flooded Babu's mouth. He pitched his head forward, vomitting up next to Angrel's corpse. *A phone. Where would her phone be? Need to call for help. Need an ambulance.*

One hand pressed into his stomach, Babu put his foot down and tried to stand. He coughed. His leg failed. His foot slipped out. He fell. He tried again.

Have to call an ambulance.

Darkness was creeping into the edge of his vision when he found Angrel's phone in a small bathroom just off the séance room. He had managed to knock it off its cradle by the time he realized that no one in St. Ives would answer.

The doctor dreamed he had bugs crawling all over him. His skin pricked with the jolts of little hooked feet clambering up and down, moving like ocean currents around his body. Then they weren't insect feet, but slithering, sucking tentacles of an octopus, and then the sluggish and slimy touch of slugs and snails. Then he was burning. The slugs screamed and shriveled, and he woke up.

"Wakey, wakey."

He blinked and found himself staring into a woman's face. She wore jeans and a black shirt and a severe-looking leather jacket, torn on the sleeve.

"I need two things from you," she said. "Are you with me?"

The doctor rubbed his eyes. Had he fallen asleep?

"What?" he said.

The woman kept talking. "Two things. First, take a look at this kid's eye." She drew back and waved at a lanky teenager behind her. "Then, I need you to get Mr. Cherian ready to go."

The doctor blinked. Something like sense switched back on in his brain.

"What? Wait—Ahmadou Cherian? Mr. Cherian can't go anywhere. He has a concussion and it would be . . ."

"Shut up," said the woman. "In ten minutes, he's coming with me. Do everything you can to make him safe to move."

Who was this woman? She talked as though she had authority. Was she a cop? An admin person or something? "Uh . . . Do I know you?" he managed.

She shot him a look of pure, smoldering frustration. She pointed to the bed, to the teenager. "Patients. Get to work."

The woman spun and walked to the door. She whispered something to the teenager, then left.

The doctor rubbed his temples. He felt awful. His ear stung. He rubbed it and his hand came away covered in a sticky black fluid. He got up. The teenager moved to block the door. "I just want to get some aspirin and some wipes."

The kid shrugged. "She says you have to stay here."

"Oh." The doctor shuffled his feet a bit. "She does?"

The kid nodded.

"Um . . . all right." He pulled some gauze out of a drawer and got to work.

Yun and Te stood on either side of Munin Hartford's bed. Wrinkled and sunken, he looked dead already.

She clung to what Babu had said—that Munin would never want to miss out on a case. Well, this would be the last of them, or the start of far too many.

Te put her hand out close to Munin's ear. She glanced up at Yun. "You might want to step back."

Yun cocked one eyebrow. "No rest for the wicked, eh? I thought you'd maybe have a little sympathy for his brittle old bones."

Te glared at him. "We're a little short on available team members, thanks to you."

"Mmm," said Yun. He retreated to the far wall. "I would request that you not give him back his anachronistic weaponry until we've had a chance to explain ourselves."

Te glanced at Munin's ray gun, sitting, toylike, on his bedside table. "Would that hurt you?" she asked.

Yun nodded to the bed. "He imagines it would. He has all the physics of that absurd device worked out in his brain. So, yes, it would hurt."

Te pulled the ray gun off the side table and placed it on Munin's stomach.

"Ah," said Yun. "Well, I did not come here to gain your confidences, after all. Mine is ever a thankless job."

"Cry me a river."

Te let out some fire, cringing at the feedback. She let a small bit drain down her arm, roll along her fingers, and slip into Munin's ear. Seconds later, she felt the little creature inside shivering, squeaking, and then peeling apart. Reduced to viscous oil, it leaked from Munin's ear, dribbling down the pillow and splattering on the floor. Te left it there. Its hundred brethren would reclaim it sooner or later.

Immediately, Munin's breathing became a choked gasp. For several seconds he fought for air, and then his eyes burst open and he rocketed up, screaming.

Te placed a hand lightly on his withered chest. He blinked, fell silent, started to look around. Te watched his eyes closely for signs of recognition. With the bandaged stump on his right arm, Munin tried to smooth out his spray of thin hair. He stopped, brought the arm down to just under his nose, and squinted.

"Oh. Yes," he said.

"How are you feeling?" Te asked.

Munin raised his nose and squinted at her. "Miss Te," he said finally, "I had nightmares. Tell me, where am I?"

"The hospital," said Te.

"Ah, yes." Munin turned to his other hand, flexing and turning it, as if checking whether it still worked. "I have been sleeping a while, then?"

"Three days."

Munin raised one thinning eyebrow. "I sleep exactly four point six four hours per night. Something has happened?"

Te drew in a cautious breath, then pointed to Yun Kitsune.

Munin immediately went for his ray gun. After two

failed attempts to pick it up with his missing right hand, he snatched it in his left and pointed it unsteadily at the shape-shifter. He didn't fire.

"I'm going to take a minute and explain," Te began.

Munin shook his head. "A calculator," he said. "And three clocks. And the temperature, inside and out. Get me those."

"Why?" Te asked.

Yun answered first. "Human soothsaying," he said. "They used to be able to do it directly, you know. It's only the last hundred thousand years or so that they've for some reason found it necessary to devise rules and charts and horoscopes and mathematics for it. It's all just window dressing to help their psyche along."

"I must independently confirm truth," Munin said, appealing to Te. "I cannot trust anything you or he says. He is the Kitsune."

After a moment of consideration, Te decided it wasn't worth arguing and sent Yun to get him what he needed. Munin tracked him with the ray gun until he was well into the hallway. Then he dropped it to the bed and sighed.

"You are such a nice young lady," he said. "Why are you with that creature?"

Te searched for something acceptable. "Things are pretty mixed up."

"There is a case?"

Te nodded.

"Then where are Babu and Angrel? And Lester Brown? We must have a team together."

Te tossed her head, at a loss. "I'll go through it from the top when Yun gets back." She took a deep breath. "I'm sorry. About your hand. I don't know if I said that before."

Munin looked contemplatively at the bandaged stump. "I am old," he said. "Perhaps I will die a piece at a time. Only this: did we catch Bird?"

"Yeah."

"Ah, good."

Yun returned with the stack of implements requested, including two thermometers. Te laid them on Munin's bed. Munin immediately started working on the calculator, as fast with his left hand as he'd been with his right.

"I am preparing equations," he said. "Talk."

Te took a deep breath and outlined the situation, careful to avoid references to her more personal discoveries. She told him all about the chase, the Vanisher, the Worm, and then how Yun and the Man in the Empty Chair had turned loose the Goat with a Thousand Young. Munin hammered away on the calculator, occasionally muttering phrases like "angle of eyes ... voice pitch modulation in frequency range ... elapsed time versus average letter count ..." When she was done, he continued computing in silence for several minutes.

"Well?"

Munin did not look up from the calculator. His fingers did not stop flashing over the keys. "Why is Babu not here?" he asked.

"We had a falling-out," Te said.

"No," said Munin. "More than that. This is clear from the recurrent hesitation in your voice whenever you speak his name. I calculate it to be on a register denoting fear: mortal and fear: familial. The pattern of breaks in the vowels also tells me this. Why did he try to kill you?"

Yun chuckled quietly. " 'O O O O, that Shakespeherian rag. It's so elegant. So intelligent. What shall I do now? What shall I do?' "

Te shot him a look of death. Munin's fingers slowed.

"I ran your numbers," he said, "and they gave me an equation with two answers. It was not a contradiction, but rather a special type of equation that produces two results, equally true. You are a Schrödinger's cat. You are not who you claim to be."

"I'm my father's daughter," Te said.

Munin looked at her over the rims of his spectacles. "What does that mean to me? I noticed that the Kitsune used 'them' when referring to humanity in general, and not 'you' in the plural. What should I conclude from that, Miss Te?"

Te bit her cheek.

"And this business of the Goat with a Thousand Young," Munin went on. "The Kitsune released it, only to now want to seal it up again. While the Kitsune cannot be accurately predicted, he is not random in his actions. What shall I make of that?"

Suspicion, and a challenge. Once again, Te was on the outside.

She leaned back and crossed her arms. "You know what? I don't care. I've told you what's going on. I'm going downstairs to get Babu's brother and we're leaving." She glared at him. "We could use your help, but if you don't trust me, then don't bother. You wouldn't be the first." She stalked out of the room without waiting for a reaction. Yun trailed after her. After the first corner, she stopped and laid her head quietly against the wall.

Well, what did the suspicions of an old man she'd met all of twice mean to her, anyway? Yun was still on her side. And Jack.

Jack. Te ground her teeth. He'd been right there at her side since she'd come back—hovering, stealing glances at her during the long walk back to her apartment, then here.

Oh, God—it had just been a *thing*, just a momentary impulse and she *knew* she shouldn't have done it, but . . . and now there was this kid and who knew what he was thinking, and sooner or later she'd have to try to explain.

She'd almost rather let the world end than have that conversation.

The one person she hadn't isolated yet stepped up smartly beside her. "Were you ever human, Yun?" she asked.

"Not at all," he answered. "I was created as a by-product of your mother's continent-shaping play some four million years past. I experienced my genesis, chose my purpose, and have been ever since as you know me."

"You don't ever doubt?"

"Doubt *myself*?" he said. "Everything I do is done exactly according to my nature. There is no room for doubt in such an existence."

"Sounds nice."

"Mmm," said Yun, crossing his arms. "Remember, however, that doubt is possible only with the existence of multiple courses of action. Lacking that condition, more things than doubt fail to arise."

Te looked at him, at the faint smile, the doll-smooth skin, the suit now back to its previously immaculate state, and at the eyes that, behind the smirk and the chuckle and the omnipresent amusement, held something like compassion.

"Do *you* trust me?" she asked.

"I do not trust, Miss Evangeline," he said. "Nor do

I worry, nor want, nor choose, nor, as I say, doubt. I am an engine, churning forward on the tracks I myself have laid, to fullfill your wish and those of all my kind."

And what that track had got them—Te shut her eyes against it. "Do you ever regret?" she asked. "Any of it?"

Yun hesitated. "That would serve no purpose, as nothing can be changed."

You can't take it back, Te thought. *"Just work the case" is what Babu would say. Protocol. Do what I'm supposed to do.*

What she was supposed to do was bind something so horrible, she couldn't bring herself to even picture it. *Do I have to feel sympathy for it, to bind it?* she wondered. *Do I have to love it?*

"You can't be around from now on," she said.

"You refer to Mr. Cherian's industrious sibling, yes," Yun replied. "And as for your own safety? We are not so different in his eyes, are we?"

Te thought about it. "Yes, we are," she said. "He didn't come after me until I started singing. That's what brings out my glow."

"Sonore's whimsy, no doubt. How shall I engage my time, then?"

Te raised an eyebrow. "I thought you had this all figured out—me versus the Goat."

Yun smiled. "It is ultimately *your* wish."

Te thought for a moment. "You're good at running away from things, right?"

"So your father and Mr. Cherian assessed me."

"Run interference for me, then. There are a lot of *things* on the north shore. See if you can get them to chase you. I don't want Ahmadou tapped out by the time we get to Darktown."

Yun gave a gracious bow. "If my humble existence can serve, I am ever ready," he said. "Miss Evangeline, it has been a pleasure to be your adversary and that of your father. Give my warmest regards to Sonore, if she ever bothers to speak to you again."

"Right. Sure."

Yun turned to go. She stopped him.

"Yun . . ." She fumbled for the right words. "Did you grant a wish for Jack?"

" 'After the torchlight red on sweaty faces,' " he said. " 'After the agony in stony places. Those who are living are now dying.' " He winked. " 'With a little patience.' "

"Oh, fuck you."

And the next instant he was a fox. And the instant after, he vanished down the hall.

Munin appeared at the other end of the hall, properly dressed, with the sleeve of his collared shirt dangling empty over his stump, armed with calculator and red goggles and plastic weaponry.

"The equations tell me that you are on our side and that you are not," he said. "I will sort that out afterward."

Te nodded.

Five minutes later, they left the hospital in a car belonging to a confused doctor who suddenly had a building full of comatose patients to care for.

Te, Jack, Munin, Ahmadou and, already out in the city, Yun Kitsune: five. Munin said it was a good number.

Chapter 25

The Fire Sermon

The bridge over the river—in the center, the shadow of a man. He was no longer an impenetrable void, but a translucent shape making the vision of the north shore only slightly more gray, and obscuring nothing.

Te left her team by the car, walking onto the bridge alone.

The air was so dry, it stung her exposed skin. Below, the river churned with slimy, fleshy objects and stank like rot and unclean animals. Not a single streetlight remained on the north shore, and the shadows there crawled with their own unseen life. Te spotted hunched beasts clinging to the railings and support poles of the bridge, heard them snuffling and panting, the occasional bark or growl. The north shore moved like an ocean, buildings and hills rocking as if moved by restless hands.

Te stopped beside the Man in the Empty Chair. His arms were raised, his featureless face gazing upward at the creature that dominated the sky. Te's nerves quivered and jerked when she felt his energy charging the air. She looked through him.

"Here I am," she said. "This is what you wanted."

Whatever answer he made withered in her mind, an unintelligible gasp for air.

"Remember what I said."

The Man spoke to her, saying that he had no hope of that now. Te tried to feel pity for him and couldn't. He'd killed her dad. That was all he was to her.

"I'm bringing Ahmadou Cherian through in a minute," Te said. "You might want to clear out, if you can."

His answer suggested something.

Wasn't sympathy for you, you bastard, Te thought. *I need you alive for the next half hour.*

"Suit yourself."

She looked back at the car and waved them forward. Munin clambered out shakily. Jack jumped out, then ran to the back door and pulled Ahmadou out by his limp arm. Bandaged, Ahmadou seemed even less alive than he'd been before. A kid, an old man, a mental patient. Would her father have gone in with a team like this? Would Babu?

Yes, they would have. Dad would have been standing right here. Babu would have been with him, but even if he'd had no one at all, he'd have gone it alone.

Yun should already be on the opposite bank, causing trouble, drawing the beasts away from her. The Goat moved in the sky, extending huge, malformed limbs around it, gouging the hills and the fields and the streets of the city. The movement of the air was its breath, the shifting of the shadows its sickly heartbeat. Te felt no empathy for it—no connection. It was not from the Old Country, and not from Earth. It was something alien to her every understanding. How could she bind it, she wondered, if she couldn't find pity for it? If she couldn't bind it with love?

Munin shuffled up on her left, his red goggles on his face, seeing God knows what, and his child's-toy firearm held in front of him. He was wheezing for breath, and his already-wrinkled lips had cracked like plaster.

Jack came up on her right, supporting Ahmadou. The gauze taped over Jack's missing eye was already gray with dust. Babu's brother had collapsed into his own shoulders and stared at nothing with unblinking blood-shot eyes; he probably weighed no more than Jack.

Munin was too old; Jack, too young. Ahmadou was a man who should have died and was left cruelly alive. It might kill them, she knew. Even if everything went right, they might not survive it.

She placed one hand lightly on Jack's shoulder. Te looked into his one eye and realized that despite all she'd put him through in the last few days, he'd never been more afraid than right then.

But he would come with her anyway. He would follow her anywhere.

She squeezed his hand. He didn't stop trembling and neither did she. The moment passed and Te drew back, eaten inside by a nameless regret. "Ready?" she asked.

He nodded.

"Let's go." Te led their advance, palms open to the things that crawled in their way. The Man in the Empty Chair screamed something after her, but its meaning was lost in his own pain.

The shapes at the end of the bridge became real: a half dozen hairy beasts lurching forward in a mockery of human movement. Te hit them with her fire. The children of the Goat bleated and barked, and ran into the streets with fur smoldering. Te let them go. Her nerves ached when she drew the fire back.

She moved forward, the others trailing behind. Jack's role was simply to keep Ahmadou walking. Munin's was to keep the two safe. Te was on her own.

Te stepped down onto the north bank. The street under her shoes had been broken and levered apart. The cracks swam across the asphalt like snakes.

She let the fire loose. She gave it free rein, and eagerly it took to the streets, snatching and devouring the pseudolife that animated the shadows. In the fire's memories, human beings died—butchered and tortured and burned alive.

Te walked. The door in her mind strained open. Her limbs began to shake, her muscles to twitch, as the fire streamed out of her. It was hurting her—too early; she was barely a block onto shore.

The fire gave light in her mind's eye, and she saw the Goat's children gathering at the fire's edge. From alleys and rooftops and broken windows, they howled their rage. They swatted at the fire with claws and nails, pawed at it with hooves, testing its sting.

They're not afraid, Te thought.

Four blocks in. Jack kept the team ten feet behind. Ahmadou hadn't reacted to anything.

Ahead of her, three of the man-beasts blocked the street. Drooling into their own fur, the three began a grotesque dance. They swung their genitals and clawed at mimed women in their power. As the fire licked their hooves, two of them lifted the third and tossed him, squealing like a pig, into the flames.

The surge was immediate—the ghosts of the fire fell

on him with the savagery of barbarian humanity. The fire swarmed in from the edges of the street, screaming for blood, and Te's mental door slammed open. Behind that open pathway, the pressure of millions of angry souls bore down, and Te gasped as timeless rage exploded through her.

The creature in the fire did not lie still. Burning, shrieking, it stretched forward along the street, hauling itself one step forward, even as the fire unraveled its muscles and stripped it bare of fur and skin. It fought for every inch against the tides of evil called to life again by the fire, not hesitating at the pain, not caring to preserve itself. It fought until the fire's attention fell on nothing else.

Others charged in from the sides. Leaping from buildings, crashing through windows, and breaking up through the concrete, they came on the heels of a wall of sound, at the head of a cloud of stench, the product of their own bodies. Te, teeth clenched against the pain in her limbs that had burst into a searing white heat, hauled back on the fire, willing it to pull away, to sweep back to the sides, as the Goat's children closed.

The oscillation of Munin's ray gun cut the racket; Te's peripheral vision lit up in green. She heard something cry out, but it was only one voice, and there were dozens of attackers. Munin's gun cut the night again. There was no static: nothing yet from Ahmadou.

She couldn't pull the fire off the one in front. The fire ate at it until it was ash and grease, and then set to work on those. She needed more.

The space behind the mental door was not infinite, but it was nothing less than a pool of all the terror and horror inflicted by every human being since the rise of consciousness. If Te drew out more fire, there would be more still. Currents of memories, stewing in their own fury for thousands of years, pressed her to let them free. Te heard a scream behind her—Jack—as the Goat's children closed, and she obeyed.

Every injury or hurt conceivable rushed out of her. Given its head, the fire burned through her like paper, heedless and careless in its mindless need to consume. The horrors that had spawned it flashed across the bodies of the Goat's children as they charged headlong into its grasp. They burned and bubbled, flaked and fell apart, sizzled as their fat dripped to the street. They charged forward until the fire stripped them to their bones, and then until the fire reduced them to powder.

When they were gone, the fire searched for more. Snaking up and down the street, into alleys and manholes, shops and homes and car windows, it lusted for something on which to vent its undying anger. There were only three other targets.

Te saw the thousand murderers' eyes turn on Jack, Munin, and Ahmadou, and immediately slammed the mental door. It took a burst of strength that glittered up from her inherited link to the Old Country—borrowed vitality gleaned from the creature inside her—but it was enough.

Her whole body screaming at her, Te pitched to all fours. Muscles spasmed and twitched. Nerves fired random shoots of pain up her limbs and spine. Not an inch of her was free from the fire's aftermath.

She wanted to sing. The impulse was so powerful that Te had to bite her tongue to stop herself. She desperately wanted to bring out her glowing, perfect, other self, to become that creature that didn't know physical pain, and to heal this body she was wearing. But Ahmadou was two steps behind her, and this pain was *nothing* compared to *that*.

Te breathed until the street was cold and the air was dry. "I'm all right," she said to Jack, who had been calling her name for some minutes. She looked up at the hills, at the street ahead, at the street behind.

Six blocks in. She put her feet under herself and stood. Already the shadows were moving.

This isn't going to work.

"Why isn't he doing anything?" she cried.

Munin, panting, had backed against Ahmadou and Jack. "We have used him many times and never has he kept silent so long."

Te staggered to join them as the edges of the street lurched to life. "Ahmadou!"

"He cannot hear you," Munin said.

Te glanced into Ahmadou's eyes. "How do you know that?"

"I ran his numbers," Munin said. "Babu came to me, many years ago, for help. He also went to the rest of us."

"Angrel?"

Munin nodded. "To her for a prediction. To your father for conventional psychiatry. To O'Shae for prayer. To King for black magic. He went also to Lester, to see if Ahmadou could be awakened with Lester's strange blood. He went, even, to the Man, who would not help him."

"What was the problem?"

"He was eaten," said Munin. "It was a creature from the Old Country. Babu saved him from death, but there was little left of him."

"Te," Jack piped up. His voice was shaking terribly. "Is that like what happened to me, with your aunts?"

Watching the shadows pulse and recover, Te nodded.

"Then you could help him," Jack said. "Like you helped me."

Te bit her lip. *But that would bring out my glow, and Ahmadou would take me apart. Shit.*

"Munin, hold them off," she ordered, then turned and grabbed Ahmadou's chin. She pulled his face down until she could look him in his vacant eyes.

Not vacant, she thought. *Hurt. Afraid. He's probably had that same look on his face since it happened—he didn't understand what was going on.* Maybe he lashed out with that noise of his because he was terrified. Maybe he was too afraid to come out even that far, after Angrel had attacked him.

"Ahmadou," she said. "Ahmadou, listen."

"He cannot hear you!" Munin shouted. He let fly with his ray gun at something unseen.

Te tranced the lines in Ahmadou's parchment skin. "I need your help," she said. "And I can help you, too. Please don't be afraid of me."

The eyes said nothing. His neck stayed at the angle she'd placed it. He gave no response.

"I can help you," she said to him, enunciating each word. "*Let* me help you."

Munin's ray gun cut the air again.

He might kill me.

No—he'll break me, ruin me, and then leave me alive.

"Jack, both of you, step away," she said, not that she knew if distance would keep them safe. "Make sure Munin doesn't get trigger-happy."

She took hold of Ahmadou's shoulders, and, closing

her eyes, she started to hum. The light welled up inside
her, warm and welcome, no longer a strange creature
inhabiting her but a missed and mourned piece of herself. Her nerves, beaten by the fire, vanished into the rising light. The web of worries that was her human self
unraveled, and the vibrant, multifaceted child of the
Old Country ascended in her body like the dawn sun.
A sigh escaped her like the first breath of paradise, and
even the silence of the street sang to her in consonant
harmony.

When she opened her eyes, Ahmadou was staring at
her—focused and terrified. With perfect, shining hands,
she caressed his face. With luminous, depthless eyes, she
showed him her compassion. *Let me help you.*

The music began to die. The shrill keening of Munin's
ray gun faded to a distant thrumbing.

Don't do this, Ahmadou.

Color began to fade from the world. Te's shining
hands became dull as plaster.

Let me help.

Then the static rose, a trickle at first, then a roar. Pain
followed it, fraying the corners of her soul.

Fine, then.

She plunged her hand into his chest and found it
there—the shred of him that had been left behind, the
last scrap of the person he'd been. She curled her fingers around it, marveling at the feeling: it was light as
silk, smooth as glass, changeable as water. As the static
ground her away, thought by thought, perception by perception, she whispered to that little scrap of soul, sang to
it, breathed her own life into it.

It came alive in her hands, swirling and dancing.

The static pierced her through and her world was

noise. Her perfect light guttered out, then on, then out, sparking against the wash of randomness that fought to erase it. Her fingers dissolved into embers, her eyes into afterimages. The little soul-scrap fell away from her, carried on an etheric wind.

As she faded, as her identity came apart and she inched closer to the irreparable shattering, Te did not struggle. She had done all she could, and the static had already taken her thoughts, her memories, her will to survive. She merely waited.

A breath, an eyeblink, a decision made.

The static fell away. Te's glow spilled into the open space. Her body flared into existence, her limbs and eyes rebuilding themselves from the warmth and the light.

Ahmadou's soul spun in front of her, glimmering.

She extended her hands and placed it back inside his chest. With her fingers, she stroked it as it shivered in the grip of panic.

You are a tool, Ahmadou, she said. *Just as I am. You are a living weapon, and I am going to use you as one.*

The little soul shivered and shied away, no longer able to hide from its own fear, no longer able to cut off communication from the outside world.

It will be frightening, Te said. *You've survived by turning away from everything, and now I will force you to look. I am going to show you everything you've been afraid of.*

The soul shrieked, and Te opened her eyes to see Ahmadou's wasted features stiff with terror. Suddenly, after years of keeping safe inside his coma, he was once more standing in the world, alive and vulnerable to all the things that could hurt him. His expression begged her to let him go back.

She placed a hand on his cheek. "This will be the last time," she said. Ahmadou screamed inside. Te withdrew from his soul.

"My God, my God," Munin was muttering. His goggles sat on his forehead, and his jaw hung open, quivering. "What is that? What has happened to Robert's daughter?"

Jack stood beside him, hands on Munin's arm, keeping his weapon aimed at the street. "That's her," he said. "That's what she looks like now."

His sadness and his happiness flowed to her, clear and articulate as words. Te let her hand slip from Ahmadou's cheek and offered it to Jack. He took it, squeezing it between both his hands.

"You have to go back," she said.

Jack shook his head. "I have to stay with you."

She let her fingers slide delicately over his face. "You can't help me anymore," said Te. "I was wrong to bring you with me."

Jack bit his lip. "No."

"This time," she said, "you can't come with me." She let her fingers curl away from his cheek. Sparkles remained, twinkling in the wake of his tears. "Good-bye, Jack."

He shut his eye and turned angrily away.

"Keep him safe," Te said. Munin, still wide-eyed, nodded stiffly and retreated toward the bridge. Her firefly lights went with them, keeping the shadows at bay.

She took Ahmadou's arm. "Not much longer now," she said.

To be a binder is to be a martyr—to face the danger alone so that those you love can stay safe. Even Ahmadou couldn't follow her to the end.

They walked. The shadows hissed and broiled at the edge of Te's light, but did not enter. The few of the Goat's children that dared the light were driven back by Ahmadou's noise. Blocks passed in a blur of motion—streets Te had known all her life, now crawling with the truth of what they'd hidden. It was St. Ives as it really was: the evils of men and those other than men were its foundation.

Their steps became a rhythm, a pulse. Each step carried them farther than the last, over and through the detritus of the damaged streets. Her glow became a streak behind her. Ahmadou became a doll, cradled in her arms. They were no longer real, the two of them: Te moved and breathed and flickered with all the consistency of a dream, while Ahmadou existed only as a symbol, a representation, of something that had had life. They crossed the city in the length of a breath, for why did it matter how long it took an imaginary creature to cross any distance? Te was surprised humans did it any other way.

Her feet felt again the ugly touch of concrete. Ahmadou the doll became Ahmadou the man. With Te's exhalation, they landed on the edge of Darktown.

Nothing remained of the two-story buildings in the old French style. Nothing remained of the Victorian streetlamps, of the signposts without signs. What stretched before them was a cast-off piece of the void between stars. Te bent over it and could see forever, to the nothingness at the very edge and center of things.

Above them, the Goat arched into the sky, a body of rank hair, oozing sores, and misshapen limbs, reaching out in all directions like the spines of an enclosing dome, and above that, the Goat's monstrous horned head and its thousand eyes. Looking on it, Te felt the cold touch of the void, down to the light within.

Look at it, she said to Ahmadou, coaxing his eyes upward with movements of her shining fingers. *Let it frighten you.*

As Ahmadou's eyes lifted, as his jaw dropped and his body went stiff, the noise rose around them. The static blasted out in all directions, reducing the world to gray and black, suffocating the music, even the breath of the beast above them. Te heard his soul screaming, felt his heart threatening to seize. Without mind, without memory, Ahmadou's little scrap of soul had nothing to throw between it and the horror of the Goat with a Thousand Young except its mortal body.

Te stepped away from him. She turned, raised her arms, and loosed her fire. She no longer had nerves for it to burn. It flowed out of her as if she, herself, were the door—an empty space offering no resistance. Age upon age of atrocity poured into the waking world, falling upon the Goat's flesh with all the weapons of humanity's bloody history—weapons of the hand, the body, the imagination.

The Goat burned. A bark issued from its mouth loud enough to shatter windows for blocks around. As the fire climbed the Goat's body inch by inch, a rain began to fall—of blood, ash, and oil, and stillborn, malformed creatures ejected from the Goat's flesh.

Its breath quickened, bending nearby buildings, splitting them apart from the strain. The Goat's gigantic limbs hammered randomly into the city, sending cars and debris into the air. Te felt nothing of this, her body insubstantial, but she glanced back and saw Ahmadou lying on the street, blood leaking from his ears and nose. Even with Ahmadou down, the static continued to grow, peaking to a roar that would have scrubbed away the very memory of sound, had not the rush of the fire been louder still.

The living shadows of the streets gathered in hordes like swarms of insects and shredded themselves against the static. Goat-men galloped in with claws and teeth bared, only to have the static strip them to their essence and then have the fire devour them. Hundreds of feet above Te's head, the Goat tore the sky down with its struggles, seeming to open rents in the air and the clouds.

She felt no connection to this creature—she couldn't tell if it was breaking or if it was just angry. If she pulled back the fire too early, it might recover, or escape, or fight back.

To bind it, she had to understand it. With the fire still streaming out of her in numberless waves, she reached across the void pit of Darktown and touched it.

Immediately, unseen hands found her and pulled her into the abyss. Within the Goat, she floated in a space without dimension, a shard of nonexistence wedged into a living thing. Unseen hands closed on her from the darkness, ripping at flesh and bone, at skin and heart, and finding nothing—the skin, the heart, the body were cloth that Te wore. Now, here, perhaps always, she was a light: insubstantial.

Glory. Exhilaration. Te breathed without breath in that lonely space, perfect and whole. A lifetime of her mother's damning words evaporated; a decade of doubt about her father blew away. Every memory and thought that had pinned and fettered her, that had condemned her and crushed her down—all these were just masks to be worn or discarded, roles to be played or ignored. The release of shapeless existence filled her—the purity of being as an idea, as a conceit unmuddied by human doubt, logic, or rationalization. She was a concept with a million, million projections, all the same. She was Freedom.

Up she flew, searing the hands that reached for her, streaming trains of fire through the inner stretches of the Goat's soul. Deeper she drove, smashing through its experience, memory, and the uncounted ages of its existence.

Images flashed into her: images of the fires of Creation, of the vast, burning nebulae at the beginning of time, where, before the universe had cooled into matter and physical rules, the Goat had been birthed. She saw the horrors of loneliness, when the Goat and its brethren had been cast out into the dark by the explosion of energy, how they had lingered there, alone, gazing into the depths of the abyss for eon after maddenning eon, as stars and planets coalesced and the universe manifested with agonizing slowness.

Waiting there for the expansion of the universe to bring their salvation, they peeled back the veil of all that was real, pierced the boundaries that held space and time together, and looked into the heart of that force that had, by will or whim, brought Creation into being.

Te did not see what they saw. The Goat had long ago torn that piece out of its own soul. The sight that it had witnessed there, behind the truth of all things, had driven it to madness, and now it believed only in the Abyss, and craved oblivion for all things.

There it was.

The Goat's body began to fall apart around her, a cascade of charred flesh and splintered bone and horn. Its last bleat split the cloud-sealed sky, and as sunlight, the antithesis of the void of its long life, struck into it, it shuddered and collapsed, and Te knew it had been broken.

Te called to the fire; its task was done. The spirits of humanity raised arms and railed against her, but they were mere memories of mere moments, and Te was a being of the purest imagination, and when she called them back, they had no footing to fight her.

Pieces of the Goat's shattered soul rained onto St. Ives like a snowfall of glass and ashes. With the one mental door carefully closed, Te opened the other, and cradled the Goat in the warm arms of countless ages of human compassion. The men and women of history walked out from her in legions, their palms open, their prayers echoing from murmuring lips. They were the priests, the caretakers, the loving mothers, and the protective fathers. They were the Buddhas, the saviors, the old men and women who shared their wisdom, the bright-eyed children who loved unconditionally. They were the binders, century after century keeping their race safe from horror.

Te walked with them, and was them. Every sandled foot that fell on the desert's back was her foot. Every palm laid upon a bleeding sore was of her hand. Every wish made, in every Sacred Grove, was her dearest wish.

"I wish for Te to be safe," her father said.

And the little fox, waving its tails under the dead pine, said it would be so.

The ghosts of the past knelt in rows extending to the horizon, and bent their heads as one and prayed. Te, taking on shape once more, knelt and prayed with them. They saw the Goat's pain, so long-ago born and never healed. They understood it without judgment, and with their compassion, they gave relief where no salve ever could; where no medicine would fight the infection, they washed it with simple water, and took away the fever.

They bound the Goat in chains of flowers, and it sobbed in gratitude as Te lowered it into Darktown and bid it rest behind a stone seal. And, finally given leave to hide from the insanity that had ruled it, it laid down its head and its hatred, and was bound.

Te exulted. She *was* Freedom. Freedom from memory. Freedom from pain. Freedom from the worst of fears, whether that be confinement, or whether it be freedom itself.

Burning with her purpose, moving with utter certainty, Te blasted into the sky. There was no doubt, no trust, no thought—there was only her essence, her reason for existing, woven into her soul twenty-three years ago by the most perfect of all artists, driving her forward. Hesitation did not occur to her. Rationality did not intrude on her decision. She rose and rose, pressing through The Haunter in the Dark's black clouds and into the sunlight.

Her flight took her to the peak of the St. Ives barrier. She caressed the barrier like someone she had known all her life. She knew the way it was knitted into the physical world—into gravity and magnetism and the molecules of the air—how it drew strength from the scientific laws that brooked no creative change. She knew it was the sum of all those beliefs that denied the existence of the nonexistent. It was another ocean of memory, a pool of all those men and women who, in their heart of hearts, had believed in the false division between the real world and the creatures of the imagination.

She reached into the barrier. Its maker, the Warden, had woven into it the patterns of every charm and chant known to the history of codified magic. He had written them into the orbits of the electrons: everything from the elaborate circles of modern hermetics to the wild dances of ice age shamans—everything rational human thought had to offer.

But Te had been made by a being of inspiration, not of reason. Where any other intruder would have been turned away, she slipped through without thought or effort. She *existed* for this. She was *made* for this.

She found the barrier's mental door hanging there in the currents of the air, and shut it.

Below, the bars rattled. Cages opened all over the city—in subbasements, graves, and cellars; beneath river stones and flower beds; in forgotten mason jars and old attic trunks; in the minds of human beings. From each cage, those creatures that wanted to be free lurched or crawled or walked or oozed out into the streets, laughing and howling, barking and snarling. They shattered the city, toppling buildings and unearthing sewers, burning and devouring. Each carved a line in the earth or air directly away, toward the hills that hemmed the valley. Their every step and movement was swathed in joy, and Te, blazing above them all, filling the city with light, felt their exhilaration and their gratitude as if it were her own, and reveled in it. In instants, they passed over or through the hills and scattered into the world at speeds only unreal things could dream of.

Only then did human doubt come back to her.

What have I just done? she thought. *What have I really done?*

Chapter 26

Walking Truth

The doctor went and sat on the curb outside the hospital once the sky had cleared and all the earthquakes had stopped. The clouds seemed to push off over the south hills all at once, vanishing from view inside of a few minutes. To his surprise, the sun was shining. He'd assumed it was late at night.

That's something, he thought. Of course, he still had a hospital full of comas he didn't know how to treat, and broken windows to worry about—and from the utter silence outside, he figured the contagion must have spread over the rest of the city, too.

He wished he could find that woman in the black jacket. She'd seemed to know what was going on. He was still sitting on the curb when the curious noise began.

At first it was like rain falling on something metallic, then like several dozen snare drums being beaten out of time, then like an office full of typewriters, then like a stampede of thousands of feet.

He got up and turned around.

They were little spider things: black bodies, each with a single eye or a single mouth or a single antenna-feeler extension, riding on clicking spindly legs or slithering tentacles. They poured out of the door in dozens, then hundreds. The doctor, naturally assuming he was hallucinating, watched them go by.

There were more, too—hundreds more—joining those as they took to the street. They formed a line, a little parade, marching haphazardly away toward the south hills. They skipped and rolled and bounced off one another, an uncoordinated dance not exactly beautiful, but not without skill. As they passed from the shadow of the hospital into the sunlight, they seemed to fade away into puffs of smoke, and continued to dance on their way. The doctor watched them for a long time, until, up on the hills, he saw gray stains—which he assumed to be thousands of the creatures—skimming the ground until they flowed away over the hilltops and disappeared.

That was weird, he thought.

Then everyone in the hospital seemed to wake up at once—suddenly there were screams and moans and curses echoing down at him from every window.

And then a car came barreling around the corner, hopped the curb, and almost ran him over on its way to crash into a column just beside the emergency room doors. A very large black man, with what looked like a purple tablecloth wrapped around his abdomen, opened the door and fell out onto the pavement, where he passed out.

He ran over to the man and squatted down next to him, making a quick diagnosis. Stab wounds. Good. They *taught* you how to deal with stab wounds.

He ran inside to get a stretcher.

*   *   *

Te's body felt confining when she put it back on. She was aware of the scrape of every fold of cloth against her skin, every hair tugged by the wind, every joint and tendon and muscle as they braced themselves against gravity. Nevertheless, it eased her a bit, having a body again. Even though it perhaps wasn't the best shape to be anymore, it was familiar, and it was ordinary, and she wanted that.

She relaxed against the pavement under her shoes. She drank up the sunlight that fell stinging onto her raw, dry skin. She lost five minutes staring at her imperfect hands and crying. She'd missed them.

Sunlight played on broken glass and cracked windshields as she walked through the empty streets. The people had not come back. Here and there, a corpse revealed its presence by a faint smell, or the glimpse of an unmoving limb. She'd seen death before. She moved on.

Darktown had come back. Te caught sight of the familiar pseudo–New Orleans tenements as she approached the edge of the Darktown shadow. They were peppered with decay, with peeling paint and hanging doors and rusted railings. They looked two hundred years old. Something the Goat had done? It wasn't important. She moved on.

After another few minutes, she found Ahmadou, lying on the street where she'd left him. Blood had caked under his nose and ears, and he was almost white with dust.

I promised it would be the last time, she said. She placed a hand on his chest, felt the reluctant pulse, the timid breath.

I'm going to set you free now.

She sang to him.

Chapter 27

The Golden Bough

Babu didn't dream. He sat down inside a black space, the invisible cage of his own dying body. He felt like he hadn't slept in days. Fatigue dragged at his eyelids, sapped his limbs of the strength to lift themselves. Even his chest was heavy, and his breathing came shallow and infrequent. Little starts, little pinpricks in his side, kept jolting him awake.

Let me sleep, he told the pinpricks. *I'm so tired.*

But the pricks wouldn't stop.

He opened his eyes once, to see panicked men in bloody surgical gear bending over him. He closed them again.

It's cancer, he thought. *I always knew it would be cancer.* He buried his face against the floor and whined for the doctors to let him sleep. His voice echoed back to him, distorted and distant. It called his name.

Babu, it said, *I want you. I have a place in my garden just for you.*

Just let me sleep.

I killed you, Cherian. I claimed you. You're mine.

I can't sleep. Why can't I sleep? He was still whining

like that when his eyes opened again, suddenly and completely without his consent.

The first thing that struck him was the horrid, fluorescent white light. He recoiled away from it, barking
some obscenity. The second thing that struck him was
how goddamn much his chest hurt, and how hard it was
to breathe.

Eventually, his eyes adjusted. An hour or so later,
a ragged-looking nurse appeared over him, shone another goddamn light into his eyes, then fiddled around
him checking what Babu then found out were hoses
hooked into his veins and chest. He tried to talk to her,
to interrogate her, but nothing came out of his throat
but a gravelly sound. She must have heard him, though,
since she made a shushing gesture just before she ran
off.

Why couldn't he talk? Hell, it hurt too much, anyway.
He thought for a moment about getting up, but found
that his limbs wouldn't work. He was just too tired.

Then he remembered.

Angrel!

She was dead. He'd shot her. He'd seen her die. The
little beeping machine next to him told him how his
heart reacted to the thoughts. He breathed, as deep as
he dared, until his heartbeat settled down.

He was at the hospital. Did he drive there? He didn't
remember anything after the image of Angrel's still,
white face, spattered in red.

They shouldn't have bothered, he thought, looking
around at the IV and blood bags, the tube sucking fluid
out of the left side of his chest, the respirator strapped
over mouth and nose, the noisy white machines churning away at either side—all of it keeping him alive.

Then he felt tired again. This time he did fall asleep, again without dreams, and when he woke, a familiar, wrinkled face was bending over him.

"Some hours ago, my numbers told me you were not alive," said Munin.

Babu wanted to say that he still wasn't. He couldn't get enough air to make more than a faint grumble.

"You have a hose down your throat, my friend," Munin said. "And several in less sanitary places, I am afraid."

Christ.

Babu's expression must have shown on his face, because Munin nodded in sympathy. "Part of your intestine could not be repaired," he said. "The doctors have removed it. They say if you survive, you will be well. We cheat Death again, you and I, though he comes away with little pieces of us."

Babu tried to nod.

"They will start you on chemotherapy in some months," Munin went on, more quietly, "when you are stronger."

Babu shut his eyes. *They shouldn't have bothered.* The emotions came: regret and anger. He knew it was going to happen. He thought he'd been expecting it, but now, it felt as if he'd been cheated. Hadn't he worried over it enough and stressed about it, and acknowledged it enough, that it should leave him alone? Hadn't he done enough good not to deserve this?

He hadn't quit smoking, of course. It was such a stupid thing to acknowledge now, but somehow he hadn't thought it would make much of a difference.

Stop. Push it away. Protocol first.

Babu opened his eyes again and gurgled a question,

hoping Munin would divine what he wanted to know. It took a few tries, a few meaningless hand gestures and spasms, but eventually Munin nodded and gave his report.

"It is well, my friend," he said. "At least, the Goat is put back. The sky is clear. The people are awake again." He fell silent a moment and rubbed the bandages over his stump before continuing. "There is nothing left of the city across the river. No one has survived. There were also many bodies found in the park, and many buildings and roads destroyed, many killed. And the Kitsune is still free."

Babu swore with his eyes. Munin shook his head.

"He assisted us, Babu, in capturing the Goat. As well, he protected me and Miss Te's young man friend, else we would not have escaped back over the bridge."

He was right with you and you let him get away? Babu thought. He tried to convey his indignation with a stare.

"He escorted us here," Munin continued, "saying it was the place I was most needed. He is gone now, left with the young man. They are going to find Miss Te."

At that, Babu almost sat up. He tried, anyway, before the myriad pieces of metal and plastic piercing his abdomen reminded him why it was so important not to.

"Please do not, Babu," Munin said. "The Kitsune told me that we would not see her again. I have run the numbers and it is so."

Babu winced. Tears picked at his eyes and he blinked them back. Of course it was so. Why would she want to see him again? She wouldn't risk it, even if she did want to.

I'm sorry! I just reacted. I didn't mean it. He'd never

get to tell her. He'd never get to explain. She was gone—just like Nyawela, gone in an eyeblink, gone without a good-bye, without a word.

He wanted to see his wife. He wanted to look into her dark eyes and touch that dark, beautiful skin. He wanted to see that ring on her finger, and have her say those three words ...

Protocol. Snap out of it. There's more to do.

No, there wasn't. It was all over. It was done—*he* was done.

Munin must have been watching his expression, must have been trying to cheer him up.

"My numbers say you will survive," he said.

It fell on Babu like a weight. It was the last thing he wanted now—to live. To keep going, with nothing left to him. With Ahmadou comatose, and without Te, without Nyawela—and nothing ahead of him but sickness from the cancer treatment and a messy, run-down, empty house.

He wanted the cancer, damn it! It was supposed to be his out, his escape. He'd actually been looking forward to it. At times it was all that kept him going.

And now he was going to live.

He blinked his eyes open. Munin was looking past him and smiling. "Ah," he said, "he is awake." Then, to someone else in the room he said, "Do you recognize him?"

Babu fought off his despair, fought off the confusion slipping into his head. Who was Munin talking to?

He strained to move his head and his eyes. Munin placed his shriveled fingers on Babu's head and helped him.

Babu got his first look at the hospital room, at the

ugly art on the walls, the puke yellow linoleum floors
that he remembered from his last visit. He was in a double room, with a bed beside him, the partitioning curtain
drawn back.

The patient in the other bed was looking at him. At
first, he wondered who the hell it was. The man was staring at him so intently.

Then—shriveled face, grayish skin, bandaged skull—
it came back to him.

Ahms?

It couldn't be. It was him, Ahmadou, in the adjacent
bed but—the *eyes*! They were focused, aware, filled with
recognition. It *couldn't* be him.

But a smile tugged at the corners of that wrinkled
mouth.

And it was.

"I have no doubt it was Miss Te," Munin said, "though
my numbers will tell me nothing."

Jesus, Ahms.

Tears started to fall from both sets of eyes. Ahmadou
didn't speak or move, but he was there, in the tears that
tumbled down his wasted cheeks. He was back from
wherever he'd gone.

And suddenly escape wasn't an option anymore.
Suddenly, life was all Babu wanted. Suddenly there was
something very, very important for him to do, that would
take up all his time, for the rest of his days.

Maybe it was finally time for personal things.

One dead tree: the truth of all things. Change. Imper-
manence. Isolation.

Late afternoon, and the wind hissed past Te's ears as
she stood on the edge of the Sacred Grove, waiting.

The tree's shadow fell long, stretching up the near hills, over the long grasses and the bare dirt.

"I see you," she said. The shadow split, peeling apart. One half took the shape of a man, and stepped around to face her.

"Why haven't you gone?" she asked.

The Man in the Empty Chair said only that there was no longer any reason for him to go. There was no longer any hope.

"You still should have gone." She crossed the circle. Her human body vanished, and her true self blazed to life. She faced the Man across the length of the grove. He bowed his head.

I have no pity for you, she said.

She crossed to the tree in two strides and grabbed him with her hands. Leaving her fire locked away, she pierced him with her long fingers. Inside his borders she found only loose strands of intent, splintered fragments of memory, and a ragged, bleeding hole. Whatever powers he had possessed, whatever will had driven him to kill her father and commit the horrors he had, were faded and gone. He really was nothing more than the shadow of a thing that didn't exist.

I have no pity.

She gathered his threads in her fingers—gathered up all that was left of him—and broke them. She unraveled everything he was and threw it away, piece by piece by piece, until she stood in the Sacred Grove with empty hands, alone.

Could her father rest now? Could she?

It didn't matter. It was what she'd wanted. It was what she thought was right, and anything else she told herself was a lie.

She left the dead tree and and its single shadow. As she crossed out of the circle, and her human body coalesced around her, she stepped back into the world of sensation, of things to feel and see and hear. This was the true her, too.

She climbed the hills on tired human feet, reveling in every ache and every misstep. Yun and Jack were waiting for her there.

" 'Sweet Thames, run softly, till I end my song,' " said Yun. "And now you're safe. And free."

"My dad's wish."

"His, and yours," said Yun. "I doubt that I've granted a finer wish, and in only a twenty-two-year span, no less."

Te crossed her arms over her chest; the familiar leather jacket felt good as it brushed her hands. It felt like *her*.

"So I should thank you, then?" she said. "For putting me through hell. And for Munin's hand and Jack's eye. And for killing off half the city. I should thank you for that."

Yun turned his eyes down at the grasses.

"Ever a thankless job, I have said."

"Will you do it again?"

Yun folded his delicate fingers together in front of his chest, a semblance of prayer.

"I have told you before, Miss Evangeline," he said, his voice trailing away, "I live only by my essence. I have no choices."

Te took a step away from him. She opened her palms. *A multiple murderer. A mass murderer.* His cocky, amused smiled played over his lips.

But weren't they all? How many had her mother or

her aunts drained to death? How many had Bird eaten, before they sealed her in that shipping crate in Britain? Wouldn't *they* do it again as well? What about Te herself? Was she responsible for all the horror to come, because she let them out?

She stared at Yun's drooping hair, the slim shoulders under his gold blazer. Yet, hadn't he been a friend to her? Hadn't he offered her hope when everyone else had shut her out? But then, he'd killed so many people—but so had they all. So had human beings—generation after generation. The fire was born of those acts. Wasn't he a sort of friend to her?

"I . . ."

Yun's golden eyes locked on to hers.

"You're hesitating, Miss Evangeline," he said. "I might escape if you hesitate."

Jack appeared at her side. "What are you doing?" he asked.

"What indeed," echoed Yun, "are you doing?"

Te struggled to speak. "I don't owe you anything, Yun."

"Indeed not," the shape-shifter answered. "Favors are poor currency among our kind, anyway. We tend to forget."

Te closed up her hands. "You want me to, don't you?"

Yun sighed and lifted his head. "How can I stand here and accept you now, Miss Evangeline?" he asked. "Why does not some irresistible impulse spirit me away to the next worried father or trapped little girl? I am a slave to my purpose, remember."

"You *want* me to bind you," said Te.

Yun shook his head. "Not quite."

"You *wished* for it," said Jack.

"I wished for it," Yun whispered.

Te swallowed, stammered, found words. "I don't want to do this to you."

Yun spread his arms to the hillsides. "I want *choices*, Miss Evangeline," he said. "I want what even the smallest of your father's race has enjoyed since the day they strode proudly off the savanna. Even walking unfettered, I am a captive of myself."

Jack placed hands on her shoulders. "Te?"

Te opened her palms back up, looking at the lines there. "I don't know if I can."

"Of course you can," Yun said, his eye twinkling. "It's your essence. You *are* Freedom."

And Te realized she could. And she knew how. She knew just what to do. "It'll hurt," she said.

Yun nodded. "I am aware."

Te nodded. She motioned Jack away from them, and, his face pinched with worry, he obeyed. She opened the mental door and burned Yun down to nothing—first to a fox, then to a ball of light, then to a single vibration within. She broke it, and he broke with it. Their connection fed the sensation back to her, and tears burst out of her eyes, sobs from her throat. She had shattered him and pulled him apart. When she drew back the fire, only splinters remained.

She gathered these in one hand, reaching out on that windswept hillside, reaching out in imagination. They sat mute in her palm, without a center to sing to, without a soul to breathe to life.

She opened the other door and let the compassion of her father's people act through her. Buddhas and saints knelt with her when she knelt in the grass, as she reached inside her own body. They, who had seen the joys of the world, guided her hand as she gathered strains of genetic material from her lower parts and knitted them together with the splinters of Yun's essence—and they watched with her as a tiny, shining, human soul blew into existence inside of her.

Choices. Worries. Doubts. Humans had them, and now Yun would, too.

She settled her hands on her abdomen, trying to feel the little pulse of life taking root there.

"A stupid, animal way to procreate." Guess I'll find out.

Jack squatted beside her. "Are you okay?" he asked. "You're crying."

Te sniffled and wiped her eyes. "I'm okay," she said. "I'm really okay." Better than that. She was free.

"You're still crying," said Jack.

She smiled at him, loving his awkward hands and his silly, magnified eye. "I'm just happy," she said.

Jack gave a little smile. "Should we go back now? Yun and I didn't bring a car or anything."

Te bit her lip. She knew what she was about to say, knew how much it would hurt him—and so she stalled, touching his cheek, his hair. At last, she shook her head.

"No," she said.

Jack's smile drained away. "What do you mean?"

"I'm not going back," she said.

"Where are we going, then?"

Te swallowed, speaking around a lump in her throat. "I'm leaving," she said.

Jack's forehead knitted.

"I'm going with you," he said.

Te shook her head. "People like Babu are going to be after me. You won't be safe."

"I don't care about that."

"*I* do." Te wiped her eyes. "Jack, you've followed me around since you were thirteen. You can't come with me on this. I have to get away from everything. From all this stuff. From this town."

He drew away from her, hurt and disbelief mixed up on his face. He threw his gaze angrily at the ground.

"You're my friend," he said. "And I thought—you know . . ."

"Jack, you're sixteen."

"Is that why you want to get away from me?" he snapped. "You don't . . ."

His whole body slumped, constricted, closed down. She laid a hand on his shoulder and he jerked away.

"Christ."

They sat in silence for a long time. Jack picked at the grass. Te let everything settle.

"I have to go," she said at last. "So much has happened, I need time to figure it all out." She took a few breaths. "Maybe you won't understand this, but I . . . I just . . . I kept you around because I felt *lonely*."

Jack stared at the ground, brooding. His jaw worked, as if he were biting his cheeks.

"You need to be your own person, same as me," Te said. "You can't do that if we're together. You need time to grow up and so do I."

He still said nothing. When Te spoke again, her voice shook.

"*Do* you understand? I'm different now, Jack. I'm not even *human* anymore. One of us should at least have a normal life." She sighed. "If you can't do it for yourself, then do it for me. I *want* that for you. You can't end up like me. You just can't. You . . ."

Her mouth kept moving, but nothing came out. "Sorry," she said at last.

Jack shrugged. "It's okay," he said.

Without another word, he got up, jammed his hands in his pockets, and walked away.

Te called after him, "Where are you going?"

"Home, I guess," he said, not turning his head.

Te fumbled for something more. "You just gonna walk?"

"I'll hitchhike or something," Jack said. He descended the other side of the rise, and the grass swallowed him up. Te punched one fist ineffectually into the dirt.

"Fuck."

Te didn't move for a long, long time. The cold winds dried her cheeks. Gray clouds blew in from the west as the sun sank closer to the hilltops. Little rain spatters struck her cheeks.

Jack would be better off. He would grow up and become something normal and leave the horrors of this little town behind, just as she would. She felt that certainty resonate deeply in her newfound self. He would get over her and learn to be happy.

She placed her hand on her belly. *Maybe I will, too.*

Everything was different now. The world was different. *I really hate rain.*

She got up and started walking. The rain thickened, in a short time turning the ground to mud under her feet. As she marched down out of the hills toward the highway, her step became lighter, her stride longer, more sure. The rain and the wind bit at her skin, but inside she was warm. Someone would give her a ride—out to the coast or to the interior; south or north or east, it didn't matter.

When she reached the highway, she saw a sign: ST. IVES CITY LIMIT.

Smiling, she passed it by.

About the Author

S. M. Peters is not an ex-spy, ex-lawyer, ex-physicist, ex–Navy SEAL, or ex–Wall Street executive. He lives in Middle-of-Nowhere on Lake Okanagan, British Columbia, from where he commutes into the city to spend all day telling adolescents to fix their comma splices and spell "a lot" as two words. He is happily married and owns more animals than the Calgary Zoo. His previous novel is *Whitechapel Gods*.

From Kat Richardson

UNDERGROUND

A GREYWALKER NOVEL

Harper Blaine was your average small-time P.I. until she died—for two minutes. Now Harper is a Greywalker—walking the thin line between the living world and the paranormal realm. And she's discovering that her new abilities are landing her all sorts of "strange" cases...

Pioneer Square's homeless are turning up dead and mutilated, and zombies have been seen roaming the underground—the city buried beneath modern Seattle. When Harper's friend Quinton believes he may be implicated in the deaths, he persuades her to investigate. But the killer is no mere murderer—it is a creature of ancient legend. And Harper must deal with both the living and the dead to stop the monster and its master...unless they stop her first.

FROM

Faith Hunter

BLOODRING
A Rogue Mage Novel

In a near-future world, seraphs and demons
fight a never-ending battle. But a new
species of mage has arisen. Thorn St. Croix
is no ordinary "neomage." Nearly driven
insane by her powers, she has escaped the
confines of the Enclaves and now lives
among humans. When her ex-husband is
kidnapped, Thorn must risk revealing her
true identity to save him.

Also Available
Seraphs
Host

THE ULTIMATE IN
SCIENCE FICTION AND FANTASY!

From magical tales of distant worlds to stories of
technological advances beyond the grasp of man, Penguin has
everything you need to stretch your imagination to its limits.

penguin.com

ACE

Get the latest information on favorites like
William Gibson, T.A. Barron, Brian Jacques,
Ursula K. Le Guin, Sharon Shinn, Charlaine Harris,
Patricia Briggs, and Marjorie M. Liu,
as well as updates on the best new authors.

ROC

Escape with Jim Butcher, Harry Turtledove, Anne Bishop,
S.M. Stirling, Simon R. Green, E.E. Knight, Kat Richardson,
Rachel Caine, and many others—plus news on the
latest and hottest in science fiction and fantasy.

DAW

Patrick Rothfuss, Mercedes Lackey, Kristen Britain,
Tanya Huff, Tad Williams, C.J. Cherryh, and many more—
DAW has something to satisfy the cravings of any
science fiction and fantasy lover.
Also visit dawbooks.com.

*Get the best of science fiction and fantasy
at your fingertips!*